Outcaste

Also by Sheila James

In the Wake of Loss

Outcaste

SHEILA JAMES

GOOSE LANE

Edited by Bethany Gibson.
Copy edited by Jill Ainsley.
Cover design by Julie Scriver, with images from iStock.com.
Page design by Julie Scriver, typeset in Bembo Book, with titling in TAN-Mon Cheri.
Printed in Canada by Marquis.
10 9 8 7 6 5 4 3 2 1

Library and Archives Canada Cataloguing in Publication
Title: Outcaste / Sheila James.
Names: James, Sheila, author.
Identifiers: Canadiana (print) 2023056898X | Canadiana (ebook) 20230569013 | ISBN 9781773103020 (softcover) | ISBN 9781773103037 (EPUB)
Subjects: LCGFT: Novels.
Classification: LCC PS8619.A655 O98 2024 | DDC C813/.6—dc23

Goose Lane Editions acknowledges the generous support of the Government of Canada, the Canada Council for the Arts, and the Government of New Brunswick.

Goose Lane Editions is located on the unceded territory of the Wəlastəkwiyik whose ancestors along with the Mi'kmaq and Peskotomuhkati Nations signed Peace and Friendship Treaties with the British Crown in the 1700s.

Goose Lane Editions
500 Beaverbrook Court, Suite 330
Fredericton, New Brunswick
CANADA E3B 5X4
gooselane.com

for
Nalin and Jugal

"I am no longer accepting the things I cannot change.
I am changing the things I cannot accept."
—Angela Davis

Prologue, 1952

Mahbub Nagar

Malika aimed her rifle. She lay astride the branch of a banyan tree with her sari hitched high above her knees. Her thighs circled the limb as her belly pressed against its smooth bark. A canopy of leaves hid her from the hundreds of people gathering on the road below. They were waiting to glimpse the new district collector in his motorcade. Malika was also waiting.

It was rumoured that the district collector was travelling with his family. With young children, perhaps the same age as hers. If his children were present, they would certainly witness the death of their father, but they would survive.

The car came into view. The district collector was seated diagonally behind the chauffeur, alone in the back, perfectly positioned to take the shot in his left temple. An easy kill. No unintended casualties.

Malika drew in her breath as tension knotted between her shoulder blades. The stock of her rifle grazed her cheek. Just as her finger pulsed the trigger, the district collector turned his head upwards. Malika recognized Rayappa.

Part One
1997

1. Toronto

Seventy-year-old Irwin Peter presses his forehead against the cool window-pane. From his room in the Queen Street Mental Health Centre, he looks across Toronto's busy thoroughfare to a rundown nineteenth-century brick row house. Now painted white, its first floor converted into a used-clothing store. The third-storey attic is where his daughter Jaya lives. He focuses on the dormer window and imagines her there. Quiet and contained. He recalls how her clear brown eyes would dart back and forth, betraying her otherwise calm countenance. She was the practical one. The reliable one.

Irwin recreates her apartment as he last saw it twelve years ago. The front room choking on light. The steam rising from the chai served in a stainless-steel cup. The distraught face of his other daughter, Anasuya. The widened eyes of his teenaged granddaughter, Anya. Jaya had not been there that day. If she had, perhaps he might not be here. And the others would be alive.

Irwin exhales. He feels the warmth of the sun on his forearm, coaxing him to leave this place. But where will he go? To Jaya, of course, the only one left. He had killed the others.

He wonders if Jaya has forgiven him. Whether she will come to pick him up. His attendant has reassured him that they have contacted her.

Irwin withdraws from the window and sits on the edge of his bed. His feet dangle inches from the floor. His thick, calcified toenails stare up at him. They remind him to put on his socks and then his shoes and take the necessary steps to leave. He has packed his canvas bag with his clothes and wonders how he will fit in his notebooks, neatly stacked on his bed beside him.

From his breast pocket, Irwin pulls out a gold pocket watch. He cradles it in his palm and looks at the time: 5:05. It is always 5:05. Morning or evening, who is to know? The clock on his wall indicates the correct time: 8:45 a.m. His attendant will soon be here to escort him out. Feeling nauseated, Irwin slips the watch back into his pocket. Instead of reaching for his medication, he opens a notebook and reads a reassuring list of his possessions:

1. One gold pocket watch
2. One Timex wristwatch
3. 24 Hilroy notebooks
4. Two Bic ballpoint pens
5. One Colgate toothbrush
6. Seven pairs of Stanfield's boxer shorts
7. Seven Stanfield's undershirts
8. One pair of pyjamas
9. Three Arrow shirts
10. Two pairs of trousers
11. One leather belt
12. Four pairs of socks
13. One pair of Adidas sneakers
14. One overcoat
15. One canvas travel bag
16. The Sunderlal Report dated 1952
17. A yellowed *Toronto Star* newspaper dated June 24, 1985
18.

Irwin cannot progress to the next item on the list. He remembers living in Nova Scotia. His car getting stuck in the snow. Like the spinning tires, he is desperate to gain traction.

He stalls again. If only he hadn't paid a visit to Jaya and Anasuya's Toronto apartment on June 23, 1985. If only he had waited for Jaya to return home. But Anasuya had offered him a cup of chai and repeatedly asked why he had come. Then it all came out. He told her everything he knew about Jaya. After that, Anasuya did not invite him to stay, nor did he want to with all that had gone on. He couldn't stop thinking about the two of them. All these years, it had been happening right under his nose, apparently with his blessing. Isn't that what Anasuya had inferred? One of the last things she had said to him?

"But Papa, you knew."

How could he have known? How could he have not?

After the visit to their apartment in 1985, Irwin returned to his motel, relieved that Anasuya had taken the airline tickets that he bought for her and Anya to go to Hyderabad. He gave thanks to God that Anasuya and Jaya would be separated. He ordered takeout, a meal of steak and fries, and fell asleep listening to the radio. Then came the breaking news around 2 a.m. He woke up. Had he heard right? Was it a hoax? Air India Flight 182 had disappeared off the radar at 7:09:58 Greenwich Mean Time.

In the morning, after a sleepless night, Irwin frantically checked the papers for the passenger list. Three hundred and twenty-nine people had been laid out in alphabetical order. He began reading: mostly Indian names, all that was left of the lives that were lost.

The newsprint had left an inky residue on his fingertips so he slid a ruler down, down, down each rung of names, until he found hers. Evelyn Anasuya Peter. But where was Anya's name? Erased from the record.

Anasuya and Anya, his daughter and granddaughter were gone. Two people whom he loved and whose love was mutually and undoubtedly shared.

Later that day, housekeeping opened the door to find Irwin unconscious on the floor. They called 911, triggering the events that saw Irwin committed to the Toronto Queen Street Mental Health Centre.

Irwin closes the notebook, while somewhere in the Atlantic, at the scene of the tragedy, the last remnants of Anasuya's body meld into the seabed.

*

Jaya stands at her south-facing kitchen window. The October sun pours in. It is unrelenting. Jaya closes the blinds and separates two slats with her thumb and forefinger through which she surveys the street. She observes the familiar rush of traffic: streetcars clanging, cars and bikes vying for space, pedestrians hurrying along the sidewalks. From this spot in 1987, Jaya had watched activists gather on the lawn of the Mental Health Centre, known to locals as 999. They held placards in protest of the use of electroshock treatment. But it is not traffic or the possibility of protests that draw Jaya to her window each morning. Instead she waits for patients to file out of the hospital for their morning walk, looking for a signal from her father that never comes. She watches until 8 a.m. sharp, whether she sees him or not. Then she leaves for Uncle's Spice Bucket, KFC's "ethnic" competition. Jaya spends her days grinding fresh spices and mixing masala for various chicken recipes and returns home by 9 p.m. After eating a simple supper consisting of one chapati and a vegetable curry, she cleans the kitchen and the living room, dusting shelves filled with books she will never read. From between the two bookshelves, Jaya pulls out the four-runged wooden ladder, once part of

Anya's bunkbed set. Jaya climbs up to retrieve Anasuya's urn. She polishes its brass exterior, ensuring the dimpled pattern gleams. Replacing the urn and ladder, Jaya retreats to the window to stare at the lit-up rooms in the hospital. Part of a ritual she has practised for the past twelve years. Years that have disappeared, weightless and colourless.

But today is different. Jaya has taken time off work to help bring Irwin back into her world.

When staff from 999 telephoned to inform her of Irwin's release, Jaya assured them that she would take care of him. She surprised herself. During his internment, she had attempted to see him but he had refused. She bought him new clothes periodically, inquired about his medication, and dropped off freshly prepared meals on special occasions. Jaya put the bank in charge of Irwin's finances and asked former neighbours to help rent the farmhouse in Antigonish. She deposited the income into Irwin's bank account and never touched it. Periodically, she would receive updates about Irwin's progress and was assured that he was well taken care of. She did the minimum. She did the right thing.

Jaya could not help but think that Anya's return was due to her good deed in agreeing to look after Irwin. How could it be otherwise? Only two weeks after Jaya offered to take Irwin in, Anya telephoned. It was the first time she had heard Anya's voice in twelve years.

"Where's Thatha? I went to the farmhouse and strangers opened the door."

"Anya, are you okay? Where are you?"

"I'm in Cape George. How else could I go to the farmhouse."

Anya had found her way back from New York City to Antigonish, Nova Scotia, thinking her grandfather would be there. Jaya explained that Irwin was still a patient at 999 and would soon be discharged, and asked Anya to help move him into the apartment. Jaya needed Anya to do what she could not. Speak with Irwin. Show him kindness. Be his family.

"He will want to see you. He loves you."

Anya refused Jaya's offer of a bus ticket and hitchhiked from Antigonish to Toronto, arriving at the Queen Street apartment only two days ago.

Jaya was still not ready to face Irwin. She asked Anya to write a letter of introduction, indicating that Anya, and not Jaya, would pick Irwin up. Jaya scrawled her signature at the bottom of the page and sent Anya across the street.

Jaya watches from the window, hoping to see Anya returning with Irwin.

After twenty minutes of waiting, she finally gives up and releases the slat of the blind. It springs back into place, shutting out the sun. Jaya turns to the table where an airmail letter from India sits unopened. Beside it is a shoebox full of picture postcards sent by Anya after she left home. Each time a post-card arrived, Jaya would carry it to work and ask a co-worker to read it out loud. She explained how she dreaded the possibility of learning news that she couldn't bear alone. But these postcards had only disclosed the latest city where Anya was living: Boston, New York, Chicago, and some other cities Jaya had never heard of. Sometimes Anya would write that she was play-ing drums for a house band or was on tour with a new group. Anya never included information about whom she was with or when she was coming back. Never a return address.

Jaya picks up the letter from India. Anya had brought it with her from Antigonish along with other mail that the tenants hadn't redirected. The address is in English, but the name is written in the curvy script of Telugu, her mother tongue. Irwin would know how to read this. Jaya carefully places the envelope on a stack of postcards and dusts off her hands, as if the letter were precious or poisoned. Either way, untouchable.

*

Anya sits in the waiting room at 999, re-reading Jaya's letter. Irwin is finally led in by an attendant. Her grandfather looks frail. His clothes are too big for him. His head, walnut brown, is bald except for a short white fringe from ear to ear. His cheeks have lost their friendly fullness, but his amber eyes are still bright as ever.

Anya waves. "Thatha!"

The attendant directs Irwin towards her. But her grandfather is hesitant. He seems afraid. Of course he would be, Anya thinks. She was only eighteen when they last saw each other. That crazy day in the apartment when every-thing changed.

Irwin turns away from Anya.

"It's okay." The attendant places his hand firmly on Irwin's shoulder. "Your daughter Jaya is here."

"No, no. I'm Anya. His granddaughter." Anya hands the letter to the attendant.

She tries to embrace Irwin but he backs away, gripping the attendant's arm.

Anya persists. "Don't worry, Thatha, I'll be taking you. Is that your only bag?"

After reading Jaya's letter, the attendant slowly pries Irwin's fingers off his arm and hands Anya an 8" × 10" envelope.

"His medical records, medications, and instructions are inside. He's fine. Just nervous about the transition." The attendant returns to his work, leaving Irwin in Anya's care.

Irwin is trembling. Anya takes his hand.

"Jaya?"

"No, silly. I'm Anya."

She reverts to her childhood voice and taps out a rhythm on the back of his hand and sings "Dum maro dam," an old Hindi film song from the seventies. "Don't you remember me? Your chinnie sitaphal." Anya uses the nickname he gave her, to jolt his memory.

"You are here."

"Of course I am."

"You are alive."

Anya realizes he is confused.

"Yes. Thatha. I am very much alive. And I am glad to see you are too." She squeezes his hand. "I was scared you were…I mean, I showed up at the farmhouse and a stranger answered the door. I nearly fainted."

Irwin stares at her, confounded.

"I'm sorry I wasn't in touch all these years. I was in the States, playing music. Different gigs, different groups, different genres. Just travelling around."

"Anasuya?" Irwin's voice is weak.

"Anasuya is dead." Anya speaks firmly, and then more gently. "She died."

Irwin's eyes fill with tears. Anya brings him in for a hug, wrapping her arms around his frail body and releasing him. She picks up his small but densely packed canvas bag, throws it heavily over her shoulder, and guides him outside.

*

Jaya opens the door. Although she is expecting Irwin, she is taken aback by his appearance now that he is in close proximity. This old man standing on the landing is clearly disoriented and could be mistaken for a homeless man. He shuffles back and forth outside her apartment. The dignity he exuded all his life has fallen away.

Anya lets Irwin's bag slide off her shoulder to the floor.

"Guess who's here."

"Just bring him in. I will prepare some tea." Jaya retreats to the kitchen.

Anya pulls Irwin's bag inside. "Come in, Thatha. Sit down."

Anya follows Jaya into the kitchen. "Amma, you hardly said a word to him. You could at least pretend to be welcoming."

Jaya fills the teapot with hot water. "It's been a long time since we've spoken."

"How long?"

Jaya spoons tea leaves into a teapot. "Twelve years."

"Are you saying that the entire time I've been away, you've never seen him?"

Jaya juts her chin towards the window. "They walk him around the yard with the others. Exercise. Sometimes I see him."

"You watch him from the window? Why wouldn't you just cross the street and visit him?"

"He refused to see me."

"He probably didn't know who you were. He's so confused. God knows what kind of meds he's on. They gave me an envelope full of the stuff."

"I did try."

"Maybe you should have tried harder."

Jaya pours the tea through the sieve into a cup. She stirs in the milk and sugar. "We all could have tried harder."

"Meaning?"

"Did you ever try to call me?"

"I sent you postcards. I was in a different country. But believe me, if I was here and you were in a mental hospital across the street, I would visit you."

"Please take this to him." Jaya holds out the cup.

"Maybe *you* should have been committed." Anya takes Irwin his tea.

Jaya's wish had been to keep a cool distance from Irwin. An across-the-street, behind-a-pane, I-see-you-you-don't-see-me distance. Now there is no escaping him—or Anya's judgment. They are both her responsibility.

The streetcar clangs below, and Jaya remembers the night Anya left home. It was June 1985, only a week after Anasuya's death. Irwin had just been interned at 999, and Anya refused to go to her high-school graduation. Jaya and Anya argued. Anya packed a bag and slammed the door. Then Jaya watched from the window as Anya got on a streetcar. When Anya didn't return that night, Jaya should have called the police. But Anya called the next day saying she was at the Montréal Jazz Festival. She would be back after the weekend. When she didn't return, Jaya could have called the police. But Anya sent a postcard saying she was travelling with some musician friends to New York and would write soon. And she did. Anya wrote each month like clockwork for eight months. When one month passed with no word from Anya, Jaya finally did call the police. It was February. The streets were lightly powdered with snow, and Anya had recently turned nineteen.

After hearing Jaya's story about the series of postcards, the officer called it one-way traffic.

"She doesn't stay long enough in one place. She wants you to know that she's okay without revealing where she is. She's an adult," the officer said. "You could hire a private investigator, or you can think about why she's keeping away from you."

The remark had been so personal. Jaya should have filed a complaint, at least told the cop to mind his own business. But she knew it was true. There was something that made Anya flee, just like Anasuya fled, and Jaya's own mother, long before. Something about Jaya. She rakes her scalp with her fingers, parting and re-parting her short salt-and-pepper hair. She knows she has to go out there and face Irwin.

Irwin is seated on the couch with Anya. He is sorting through knick-knacks and dividing them into small piles. Jaya recognizes the contents of Anasuya's urn laid out on the coffee table. Anya spreads her hands over the trinkets and photos, displaying them to Irwin like gems. Jaya notes the tension in Irwin as Anya smudges the borders of his neatly organized piles.

"I remember this." Anya holds up a green scrunchy with a ladybug print to Irwin. "Mum gave this to me when I was eight. Our first Christmas in Toronto."

Jaya focuses on Irwin. She watches him pick up a gold snake-head bracelet that Anasuya had received from her mother, Kanta. He examines it and then lays it down. Then Irwin picks up a photograph of Jaya and Anasuya.

"Stop." With this word, Jaya breaks her twelve-year silence.

Irwin looks up. "What happened?"

"Please. Put it down."

Irwin places the photo face-up on the table, like a card that trumps all others.

Jaya picks up the photograph of her and Anasuya, aged five and three. It is damaged. Jaya's right ear and forehead have been snipped off and Anasuya, who was shorter than Jaya, is missing her left ear and chin. Days after Anasuya's death, Jaya caught Anya with a pair of scissors snipping the photograph in a circular pattern starting from the edges and moving towards their faces at the centre. Jaya rescued the photo just in time.

The photo was taken one year after Irwin had adopted Jaya and her younger brother, Pilla. Holding the photograph to the sunlight, Jaya realizes that she had experienced the first years of her life without Anasuya. Years when things happened to Jaya. Things she doesn't remember.

*

That night, Anya sleeps in Jaya's bedroom on one of her bunkbeds, disassembled from the other. Irwin sleeps on the other bunkbed, in Anya's childhood room. Anya wakes up with a jolt of terror. Although the dream is recurring, Anya never gets used to it. As a girl she would periodically wake in a cold sweat, her heart beating rapidly. In her dream she heard the shrill call of a koel, the rumble of wooden wheels on a bumpy road, the moaning of a calf being tortured. Somehow, she senses these images and sounds belong to someone else and come from another place and time. Yet, she is aware that the koel is female, her call a warning. That the wooden wheels move through a plateau, and that the calf would survive his ordeal. Anya places her hands on her abdomen and breathes deeply.

As Anya's eyes adjust to the dark, the shapes of things around her are revealed. The shade of the table lamp and Jaya's bed to her right. As a child, Anya would come to this room seeking comfort from this same nightmare. Anasuya would lovingly smooth out the rough edges of Anya's fear, and gather her close.

Jaya was the opposite of Anasuya, kind but almost robotic, Anya thought. Seeing Jaya with Thatha brings back the loss of Anasuya. Anasuya was the connector. She filled gaps in conversations, smoothed over tensions. She knew how to have fun.

Anya sits up.

Jaya turns to face her. "Are you okay?"

"It was just a dream. The same old one."

"You still get those?"

"Just when I'm here. Around you, I guess."

"So you blame me for your dreams?"

"Never mind. Go back to sleep."

Jaya turns on the light. "Anya, why did you show Anasuya's urn to Irwin?"

"He keeps asking about her. He needs something concrete to prove she is gone."

"Did you tell him her body was never found?"

"Of course."

"The urn was our private ritual."

"Things change, Amma. Anyway, they are only things. Her old things."

"I thought they meant something to you."

"And it might to him."

"He has no right to see it."

"He's her father."

The floorboards creak as Irwin slowly makes his way down the hall to the bathroom.

"Has he told you anything about Anasuya?"

Anya hears the bathroom door close with a thud.

"Like what?" Anya puts on her housecoat.

Jaya hesitates and rubs her forehead. "About why he forced Anasuya to go back to India?"

"No one could force Mummy to do anything. She chose to go."

Anya gets up and listens for Irwin behind the closed door.

"Do you need anything?" Jaya asks softly.

Anya needs everything. A normal mother, perhaps a father, a new childhood, and responsibilities proportional to her age. She has been floating, living hand to mouth, trying to hustle gigs and drifting around with whatever musicians would have her. She feels entitled to a sunny future with a family that isn't fucked up.

"I'm fine."

Anya steps into the hall and sees the light under the closed bathroom door. Irwin's bedroom door is ajar. Curious, she enters. The light is on and she notices the sheets and blanket on his bed are neatly tucked in except where he turned down the covers in order to get up. His bag is on the floor. On the night table, maybe twelve Hilroy notebooks are piled neatly. Anya leafs through a few, reading the dates and titles, in elegant cursive writing, on the covers of each. She is drawn to one titled *Personal Relationships*. On the first page is a list of:

1. those who loved me—my mother, Alisamma, my sisters, Jyoti and Shanti
2. those with whom no love was lost—my wife, Kanta, my mentor, Professor Connelly
3. those whom I loved—my father, Joseph, my supervisor, Srikaram, my son, Pilla, and my first...
4. those with whom love was mutually shared—my daughter Jaya, my daughter Anasuya, and my granddaughter, Anya

Anya wonders what "my first" means. Why Irwin doesn't complete his thought. Shame sweeps over her. What does she even know about her grandfather? Except for that last grouping in his list, most of the people are unknown to her.

Anya hears the toilet flush followed by running water and puts the notebook back into its place.

"Are you okay?" Anya meets Irwin in the hall.

He doesn't say a word but slips back into his room, closing the door.

*

The next morning, Jaya lays the table as if at a restaurant. She sets a tray with eggs and toast, a teapot, three cups, and containers of milk and sugar on the table. Irwin would likely prefer chai, but Jaya will no longer comply with his wishes. He will have to get used to her new self. She hands Irwin the letter.

"Irwin?" For the first time Jaya calls her father by his first name. "This letter was sent to the old farmhouse in Cape George. Do you know who it is for?"

He reads the address and reaches for the butter knife. With a paper napkin he wipes away all trace of food from the blade before slicing through the top of the envelope.

"Read it out loud."

He does what Jaya asks.

Dear Rayappa.

Irwin pauses and clears his throat.

Dear Rayappa Sir,

We write to you from Korampally, India, which we hope you will remember fondly. We are trying to locate a person whom you may remember. A woman named Malika...

Jaya notices a muscle flex in Irwin's cheek.

"Malika?" Jaya gently pulls the letter out of Irwin's palm.

She stares at the page. "It's written in Telugu."

Irwin asks if she understands. "Arthum aiyindha?"

"Show me her name."

Jaya hands the letter back to Irwin. He points out the name Malika in the Dravidian script and continues to seamlessly translate to English, reading from where he left off.

. . . Malika was last seen in Korampally in 1948, perhaps four months after you left in December 1947.

We understand this was many years ago. An elderly family member, Ashamma, is urgently trying to contact her. Please respond immediately if you know anything.

Yours,

Raghunandan Reddy

P.S. Now with this new internet, feel free to email, etc.

Irwin folds the letter and tucks it back into the envelope, setting it on the table.

He is grateful for food. Grateful that Jaya still feeds him. Grateful that Anya sits beside him. She is different now, but she continues to assure him that she is *she*. Still, he watches her, listens to her attentively. He longs to touch Anya, to know she is real. To be certain she did not perish with Anasuya in the plane but is here with him on Earth. He is heartened by this possibility that those who were presumed dead might be alive.

Jaya pours a cup of tea and hands it to Irwin. "This Reddy person. Do you know him?" Irwin stares at his tea. It is black. It will lighten with a splash of milk.

"And Ashamma. Who is she?"

"I do not know."

"What about Malika. Do you know her? Where is she? Is Ashamma Malika's mother?"

Irwin closes his eyes. Then he scoops up a heaping teaspoon of sugar, drops it into his cup, and stirs his tea. He pauses, then taps the spoon on the cup. Once. Twice. Thrice. The rhythm transports him and soon he is hearing "Jana Gana Mana," the Indian national anthem in his head. He begins singing it quietly and then louder as he directs the spoon aggressively against the cup, increasing the tempo. Clank, CLank CLAnk CLANk CLANK. His spoon hits hard against Anya's knuckles as she reaches to save his teacup from shattering.

"Ow. Thatha!"

Anya shakes her fingers before putting her hand on his.

"Thatha? What is it?"

Irwin stands with his cup and saucer and walks to the window.

Anya follows him.

"Jaya asked you a question. Do you know her? Malika?"

Irwin looks across Queen Street to where he once lived. The reassuring confines of his hospital room. There are too many reminders here. Too many questions. Yet he wants to know. How did Reddy find him? Who is Ashamma? And how does she know Malika?

"I am thinking."

Jaya sits forward on her chair like a schoolgirl. And then it comes to him. Irwin speaks slowly as if being fed the lines.

"I do not know Ashamma. Malika's mother was called Fariza."

"You did know her. Malika!" Jaya's voice is pitched well above her usual range.

"Ashamma is a Hindu name. Fariza is Muslim. Malika and her family were Muslim."

"And you are Rayappa?"

Irwin forces himself to look at Jaya. Her face is hard. He feels her reproach, in this onslaught of questions.

Irwin remembers all these names. Their faces, on the other hand, blur in his memory or completely disappear. He wonders why he has not kept any photographs of that year. Korampally, 1947. Why he has no photo of Malika.

For the longest time, Irwin wanted to forget. He had hoped his electroconvulsive therapy treatment would blast his memory and leave him a vegetable. But such an outcome is the stuff of drama. Now he longs to remember. Irwin turns back to the window and stares into the sun. His mind travels across the street, through the hospital windows, south above the great lakes and eastward to India, hoping Malika's face will return to him.

*

Later that night, as Anya and Irwin sleep, Jaya sits at the kitchen table and studies the letter addressed to Rayappa. She searches the script of her mother tongue for something familiar. Finding it, she sounds it out, one character at a time. Ma-Li-Ka. *Malika*. Her mother. *Malika*. She tries to remember her face. *Malika*. The sound of her voice. *Malika*. Her touch. *Malika*. Another loss.

Jaya picks up a pen and, with difficulty, writes her name in Telugu.

*

Forty-nine years earlier, when the baby slipped out onto the mud floor, Malika gazed into her child's eyes and wept. It was a victory that her baby was alive, that any of them were. Malika, fearing for her husband, gave the baby his name, a name that means victory.

Jaya, of course, has no memory of this, having been that infant. But that was what happened. More or less.

2. Korampally

In the pre-dawn light, Ashamma steps outside of her hut and walks down the footpath to the river to pick some calendula flowers. She looks across the river, towards the hills, to her goddess Pochamma, and chants a prayer under the rumbling drone from the bridge. One by one, she picks off the petals from the flowers and throws them into the mud-brown water.

From a distance, Ashamma can see a procession of lorries roll across the arched bridge set above the Vancha River. Ashamma has lived here for most of her long life and witnessed Korampally's transformation from village to town. The bridge was built almost fifty years ago and at one time brought police vehicles and army tanks to the pastoral village. Now it brings mostly lorries full of bricks, metal rods, people and more people: wiry, sun-dried women who carry cement blocks on their heads where clay water pots once balanced, lanky boys and hunched-over men who shoulder steel pipes and pound them into the mud. Together they construct buildings that displace thatched huts.

Ashamma does not let the noise nor the pollution deter her from going to the river's edge. It is her life source, where she draws water, washes clothes, and performs sentimental, useless rituals. Releasing flowers into the current is ineffective but as necessary to her as breath. She sees no need to change, even if the river does, even if she knows the ritual will not bring back her son. Ashamma knows he is gone forever. So be it. The noise and the fumes would have irritated him to no end, with his sensitive ears and love of nature.

"Cursed," villagers had said of him. "Son of a jogini. What was to be expected?" No one ever said, "Son of the landlord." But *she* knew, and the landlord knew. And their son had also known.

Ashamma scoops up some water and splashes her face. Korampally has survived revolution and invasion, princes and presidents, land passed from hand to hand and back again. Ashamma too has survived these changes. What remains the same is that she lives on *this* side of the river and the Reddys on *that* side. And the one constant witness in her life, Raghunandan Reddy, is still alive.

*

Unknown to Ashamma is that along with the stream of lorries crossing the bridge is a white van, which stops at the mansion of Raghunandan Reddy, the wealthiest deshmukh, owner of forty thousand acres of land between the edge of the Nallamala forest to the outskirts of the town of Nalgonda. On arrival, Sivraj, the head servant of the property, drapes a garland of yellow marigolds on the windshield of the vehicle. Onlookers gather around to witness a mechanical ramp emerge from the back of the van, extending onto the road. The driver and two technicians carefully wheel down a large metal oxygen concentrator. Children rush to touch what looks like a robot from a science fiction movie, while mothers pull them away.

Ragaviah, the village priest, guides a handsome sadhu in ochre robes past the gates and through the courtyard into the large residence. The house has been thoroughly cleansed in preparation for the ceremony to bless the machine. A small entourage have been invited to witness Raghunandan Reddy's first intake of breath though the concentrator. Science, not god, will intervene to supply oxygen to his body and deliver him to his next day on Earth.

Ragaviah has been the village priest in Korampally for over fifty years and achieved some fame for performing a two-week fast that finally brought Gandhi to their village in December 1947. Now elderly, he has made way for the younger Swami Antharyami. *India Today* described him as a spiritual entrepreneur with the finest business acumen in the country. In the same article Antharyami was quoted saying, "godliness will thrive in an increasingly market-driven India." A member of the Hindu Nationalist Bharata Janata Party, the BJP, Antharyami has been particularly successful in soliciting the loyalty of the educated and wealthy classes. He is able to pull self-interested businessmen, ambitious politicians, and cynical scientists into his fold. Antharyami recognized that these men have weaknesses. And it is the image of a mother performing puja that comes to mind when the stock market crashes, when the popular vote shifts, or when death visits and science fails. Antharyami uses both theological arguments and his communication skills to convince them that everyone can have a use for god, and god can be useful to anyone.

Reddy, disinclined to limit his options, has acquiesced to science while keeping god on standby. Ninety-seven years old, living with invasive pulmonary fibrosis for a decade, he has outlived his doctor's prognosis by seven years. Even while in palliative care, he is mentally capable of running his estate. His body, however, requires a continuous supply of external oxygen to keep him going. On this auspicious day, the technician plugs in the machine, adjusts the nasal prong into Reddy's long hooked nose, and clamps the oximeter to his middle finger. The doctor takes Reddy's pulse while monitoring the oxygen levels, intermittently directing the technician to adjust the dial of the oxygen concentrator accordingly.

When the presiding doctor nods, Reddy summons Swami Antharyami to begin the puja. Although open flames are not permitted within the house, the doctor allows one deepam to be lit under his watch. Prayers are sung for the continued health of Raghunandan Reddy, whose land sustains thousands of souls.

Afterwards guests, mostly local businessmen and landowners, congregate in the main room for chai while Swami Antharyami remains with Reddy.

"Have you made amends with the woman?"

Reddy nods and smiles.

Nine months ago, when doctors advised Reddy to arrange for palliative care, he called on Swami Antharyami. The swami explained that enduring physical suffering was necessary for one's spiritual growth and a more fortunate rebirth. It was time for Reddy to make peace with God and make amends with enemies.

Reddy responded, "I have no enemies."

"Of course, but as I said before, even one so pious may have caused harm to some. Unintentionally of course."

"Well there are women, naturally."

Swami reassured Reddy that like roses in a gutter, those women were useless, their beauty gone, their value lost. Their suffering was collective and fell like water off their backs. Antharyami had advised Reddy to choose one woman, symbolic of the rest, to whom he must make amends.

Swami stands at Reddy's bedside. "Tell me, what has been done?"

"The day you advised me, I compiled a list of women whom I might have caused discomfort. And from this, I chose a lowly creature with whom I fathered a most unfortunate son, now dead. You see, Swami, I should have no issue with fulfilling dharma. Amends are already well underway."

*

Ashamma smooths her white hair as she rises from the river's edge. Parveen, the translator, has come to visit again. The young woman, likely in her forties, greets Ashamma with a namascaram and pulls out an envelope from her shoulder bag.

"We received a letter with good news." Parveen translates the content from English into Telugu.

> Dear Mr. Reddy,
>   Thank you for your letter sent to my grandfather, Rayappa. He has since changed his name to Irwin Peter. My mother, Jaya, and I live in Toronto but would like to meet Ashamma and help find Malika. Jaya believes this Malika may be her birth mother. We are interested in coming to India if you can arrange a meeting with Ashamma.
>   Sincerely, Anya Peter.

Ashamma looks across the river, wondering what she will say to Jaya and what Jaya must look like as an adult. A mother now, herself. Ashamma met Jaya so many harvests ago. The little girl's clear brown eyes darted this way and that, looking back to Ashamma. But Malika yanked Jaya forward. Ashamma feared for Malika, pulling the little girl by the hand and carrying the baby boy in a sling on her back. The baby's little head bumped against the hidden forestock of Malika's rifle. This is the last image Ashamma has of Malika and her children. Now Jaya has been found.

"TO-RO-NO-TO," Ashamma says aloud.

Raghunandan Reddy's inquiries and the letters Parveen sent overseas had borne fruit. They found Jaya in Canada. Ashamma wishes this had happened without the Reddys being involved.

Ashamma hears the toot of a car horn. Raghunandan Reddy's son, Linga, parks his car on the road that leads to her footpath. He gets out and leans against his car. A cigarette dangles from his lips. His hair is thinning. He has gone fat. Not the shape of someone who radiates happiness and a love of food but full of bloated resentment. His middle swells grotesquely while the rest of his body remains stick thin. Why has *he* come after all these years? Could he not have sent one of his drivers? Why must he accompany Parveen, if not to intimidate?

"Aunty?" Parveen addresses Ashamma respectfully and in English too. She is kind, but Ashamma cynically wonders if Parveen's show of humility is in jest.

"Amma?"

The elderly Ashamma still addresses the younger woman with the honorific mother, madame. Nothing can induce Ashamma to call Parveen by name. It would be perceived as disrespectful, beyond her station. Ashamma will not even mouth her name. Even if it is Parveen's wish.

"May I have some water."

Ashamma moves to her hut to fetch a cup of water for Parveen.

Parveen was hired by Raghunandan Reddy to translate from English to Telugu and back again. She is a go-between or a spy, depending on one's perspective.

The fact that Ashamma has a home in which to receive guests is due to the grace or guilt of Raghunandan Reddy. Years ago, when she still serviced Reddy, he built a cement house for Ashamma that she refuses to occupy. Over the years she made it clear that his gifts were unwelcome. Puzzled and annoyed by Ashamma's rejection, Reddy sought Parveen's help to ask Ashamma what she would accept from him. She would accept nothing less than her family.

Ashamma returns to the river and hands Parveen the cup of water.

"How long ago did Malika live here?" Parveen asks.

"I can no longer count the harvests. Malika lay in the spot where you are now standing."

"On the ground? Was she hurt?

"No. She was strong. It was the morning after the day she was to marry."

"And who was she to marry?"

"My koduku, my son." Ashamma's voice is matter of fact. "Drink your water." Ashamma juts her chin towards Linga. "He wants to return home."

"I will tell him we will be a little longer. You can tell me how you would like to respond to Anya."

Parveen sets the cup down on a tree stump, hands the letter to Ashamma, and moves towards Linga.

"Badkhao, motherfucker." Ashamma directs her hatred at Linga.

Ashamma sees the shock pass over Parveen's face. Ashamma laughs. As Parveen moves toward Linga, Ashamma examines the letter. She has tried, with little success, to read and write Telugu, which is not an easy feat for a woman her age. But this letter is in English. Her efforts are never enough to keep up with the world. She always follows many steps behind. But she is not without pride so takes from others only what she absolutely needs.

What will she accept from Reddy? It is simple. He and his family have been the source of all she has and all she has lost. He must simply return what is hers.

Ashamma notices that the cup of water remains untouched. Is Parveen rejecting it? Humiliated, Ashamma spits into the vessel. There is no reason why she should dislike Parveen. Parveen is helping her. Yet Ashamma resents that she must once again depend on those of a higher caste to restore what is rightfully hers.

Parveen returns, sits on the stump and finishes writing the response to Anya that Ashamma dictates. When complete, Ashamma demands the pen and outlines the slow and awkward scrawl of her signature. She suddenly feels important. Like a banker or a merchant.

Parveen folds the letter and puts it in her purse. "Linga said that if Jaya and Anya come here, Raghunandan Reddy would like to meet them."

Ashamma gathers phlegm from her throat and hurls it onto the rocky path towards Linga.

"Naturally he wants to meet them. He is what he is."

But how will Ashamma explain to Anya and Jaya who Raghunandan Reddy is to her. What she was and had been to him?

A jogini, married to the goddess as a little girl. An inherited destiny, important for Jatara festivities where she would dance, dressed only in neem leaves, celebrated and despised.

Everyone knows of her role, but no one speaks of it. Why should Jaya want to know? What difference could it make? Who you come from? What you do? Will this knowledge reap a harvest? Will it help birth a child?

Parveen finally picks up the stainless-steel cup. Ashamma begins to stop her, but it is too late. Parveen pours the water down her throat, not touching the rim. The usual way, but this time, a futile precaution. Ashamma feels bad, but not too bad. Parveen will be okay. After all, the old woman is not polluted as others think.

3. Hyderabad

The city of Hyderabad extends from the heart-shaped lake, Hussain Sagar, southwest to Golconda Fort and circles around to the northern lake of Jeedimetla Cheruvu. The Musi River, a source for these, and many of the five hundred other lakes in the area, creates a natural divide between the Royal Old City and the expanding new district. A slight fissure, a premonition of division and heartbreak.

A cool December breeze blows in through the window of the taxi as it transports the Peter family from the new Hyderabad airport, north through the Old City. Jaya sits beside Anya in the back. Irwin is in the front with the driver. Nearly two months have passed since Irwin was released from 999. Jaya finds it incredible that they are here. She fidgets with the clasp of her handbag, her eyes moving from her window view to the driver. Like a tour guide, the driver entertains them with historical facts about his city.

"Have you heard of our Nizam, Mir Osman Ali Khan? He was Hyderabad's last sovereign and the richest man in the world, smack in the middle of the Great Depression? Your American *Time* magazine put his photo on the cover. Very beautiful he was, with his handlebar moustache and turban."

Anya lets the American reference slide. "But India is so poor."

"Ah yes. Many Indians are poor, but the country is rich in multiple ways." The driver cranes his neck to speak to Anya. "Our former Nizam had interesting methods of accumulating wealth. It was said that he could enter any house and demand a painting, a car, or a daughter, simply by pointing a finger. Such was his power."

"A rumour." Irwin waves his hand.

The driver is affronted by this foreigner. "Ah, you are a Mulki, native to Hyderabad?"

"No, but my wife is."

Jaya looks at Irwin with concern and then back out the window.

"You know then what the Nizam left us? Ah, your daughters will see, up ahead, four palaces in one." The driver points out the Chowmahalla Palace. "It is rumoured that one floor was used as a large armoire for silk sherwanis and saris, stitched with gold thread. Another floor was heaped with gemstones and pearls. And yet another housed his hareem of seventy-five wives and minor children!"

Anya feels lucky to get this impromptu history lesson. She learns that the Nizam, from 1911 to 1948, had been the centre of power in the princely state of Hyderabad, a source of fear, pride, envy, and amusement. She doesn't yet know that her great-grandfather, Dr. Benjamin, had knelt before the Nizam and, like many, offered a gold sovereign as a show of subservience to the monarch. This was just one of the stories that Dr. Benjamin had shared with his daughter, Kanta, and then his grandchildren, Jaya, Anasuya, and Pilla. But these tales had never been passed down to Anya. No history or culture lessons, no reminiscing about the good old days. When Anya was a child, Irwin had balanced her on his knee, reading her classic children's literature and on occasion Indian folktales, but he withheld his past.

The taxi moves towards the four minarets of the imposing Charminar monument.

Anya leans forward to hear more from the driver.

"Look at that. Our Charminar! Built in 1591 by Muhammad Quli Qutb Shah, to commemorate the founding of our great city. There were many great rulers of the Asaf Jahi dynasty and our last Nizam continued the legacy of his predecessors. He was a great patron of culture."

"Yes. On that point we agree. He was recognized as the Monarch of Learning as well as other noble titles." Irwin's spinning thoughts find anchor in a list he recites:

1. His Excellency
2. Mir Osman Ali Khan Asaf Jah VII
3. Sultan-ul-Uloom
4. Osman Ali Pasha
5. Raj Pramukh

"The Indian Union gave the Nizam this last title when he was made governor of Hyderabad, a concession after he was overthrown during the police action in 1948."

The driver, moving through the bustling Laad Bazaar, is peeved that Irwin has usurped his role. He points through the open window. "Look to the riverbank."

The Mughal architecture rises above the palm trees that line the high banks of the muddy river below. Pink and blue plastic bags float aimlessly until they get trapped between rocks and flap like the tails of fish. Men and boys lower nets and rods into the murky water, which also serves as a receptacle for sewage.

"See there, that rose-coloured building is the High Court, and up ahead, the majestic Osmania General Hospital."

Irwin does not add that this is the same hospital where Anasuya was born and, at age two, diagnosed with polio. The place she almost died.

Irwin continues his commentary. "The Nizam equipped the hospital with state-of-the-art technology for its day. So, while autocratic, it is true, the Nizam is interested in progress and is not immune to considering the common good. To many, the Nizam is a benevolent dictator."

As Irwin gradually finds his voice, Jaya contains hers. She has no desire to engage with a madman. And she has concluded that Irwin is mad. She hears it in his speech, in his inability to distinguish between the past and the present. Irwin, who was always so articulate. How could she have brought him here? How will he manage? Jaya longs to be back in her apartment in Toronto, where she had both proximity to and a safe distance from Irwin.

Now confined in the taxi, Jaya presses her head against the window and remembers a moment in 1966. That was a close-to-happiness moment for Jaya. Irwin was at the wheel of his mint-green Ambassador and beside him was Kanta, stylish in dark glasses and a chiffon scarf. In the back seat, Jaya sat next to Anasuya, Pilla, and then a British boy named Martin. Anasuya had renamed him Nitram by spelling his name backwards. "More Indian sounding." He had come to stay that January, days after Indira Gandhi became prime minister. And one year before Irwin took Jaya and Anasuya to Canada, splitting up their family for good.

The taxi crosses Nayapul Bridge, a straight paved road on sturdy stone arches set deep in the rocky riverbed, and weaves through narrow roads of the Afzal Gunj quarter.

*

Tucked into the pocket of the passenger door in the taxi is an October edition
of *India Today*. It features the novelist Arundhati Roy on the cover. Irwin
opens the magazine and skims through a number of articles.

1. "Award-winning novel *The God of Small Things* challenges
   'untouchability' and exposes India's worst but best-kept
   secret." Irwin has never heard of the novel.
2. "Queen Elizabeth's recent visit results in a diplomatic fiasco."
   The monarch is unable to stay away from the colonies, Irwin
   thinks.
3. "Kalyan Singh of the right-wing Hindu nationalist Bharatiya
   Janata Party (BJP) is elected for the second time as Chief
   Minister in Uttar Pradesh."

Irwin, curious about this third article, reads further and learns that "forty-
nine Hindu politicians and religious leaders were charged with conspiracy
and incitement to riot, allegedly causing the destruction of the Babri Mosque
at Ayodha, Uttar Pradesh, in 1992. Singh, who was serving his first term as
Chief Minister at the time, was implicated for failing to protect the mosque."
Irwin finds it unfathomable that proponents of fundamentalism would be
voted into power repeatedly, given the lessons of Partition.

These thoughts weigh heavy on Irwin as the taxi enters the Afzal Gunj
quarter, the azaan echoing in the streets. The calls to prayer, at one time
amplified with megaphones, now blast from loudspeakers. The sounds over-
lap each other as several mosques compete for the attention of the Hyderabadi
Muslims who remained in the city after so many migrated to Pakistan in 1947.
Irwin observes that despite the growing popularity of the BJP in other parts
of the country, the All India Majlis-e-Ittehadul Muslimeen political party
seems to be thriving in this area. Their green-and-white flags hang from bal-
conies, flutter from poles, and are firmly planted in flowerpots that line the
boulevard running parallel to the Musi River.

Anya has no words for what she sees. It is foreign but strangely familiar. It
is as if her mind is accessing memories she had no way of forming.

Jaya notices there are fewer cows and bullock carts than when she was
growing up. Instead the roads are full of lorries, honking cars, beeping scooters, and auto-rickshaws. It is loud, the air is polluted, the roads congested.

And it is wonderful. Even though Jaya knows these streets, they feel new. Growing up, Jaya hadn't spent much time in the city; she stayed close to home, like a neglected doll, waiting for her owner to return from school and open the world to her.

*

The taxi pulls up to the Benjamin House. The ancestral home of the late Dr. Samuel Benjamin, father of the late Kanta Peter (née Benjamin), mother of the late Anasuya Peter. Jaya gets out of the taxi and opens the gate. Walls wrap around the Benjamin property and enclose the house and courtyard. Bicycles lean against the inner walls. Chickens squawk and stir dust where a perennial garden once bloomed. Jaya recognizes Lakshmi, sitting in the old cane chair on the veranda. Fatter now, grey-haired, and clearly ruling the roost.

Lakshmi sits where Kanta had looked up periodically from her books, from vivid descriptions of nineteenth-century Lancashire or provincial France or pre-revolutionary Russia. Lakshmi had been Kanta's trusted servant and kept her company when Pilla went to university and the rest of the family left for the West. She cared for Kanta when she became ill from the condition that often plagues mothers who outlive their children. Kanta mourned two out of her three children. She had tried to reconnect with Jaya, leaving messages on her answering machine and sending letters. But save a phone call from Jaya that conveyed the terrible news about Anasuya, everything had stopped. She was cut out. A stranger.

Lakshmi watched as Kanta withered away. Her apple cheeks became gaunt. Her once full body was reduced to bones. Lakshmi nursed her mistress, urged her to read. But even Kanta's beloved books provided no comfort. Although they had kept Kanta occupied throughout her life, she came to perceive these stories as her addiction, a poison that had prevented her from being present for her family. Lakshmi, who had been witness to Kanta's misaligned life, found her way into Kanta's heart and her will, inheriting the house. Now Lakshmi happily chews on betel nuts until she becomes aware of who has arrived. She is expecting Jaya but panics at the sight of her older, familiar face. Lakshmi flees inside.

Irwin remains in the taxi finishing the newspaper article. Anya grabs the luggage and quickly becomes the centre of attention for several neighbourhood children. Their wide smiles and sparkling eyes surround her.

"What should I do?" Anya looks to Jaya for guidance.

"Say hello. They are just curious."

Anya starts distributing mints, pulled from her purse.

A man, older than Anya but younger than Jaya, steps out onto the veranda. "You have come."

Jaya recognizes Lakshmi's son. "Hello, Ravi. May I go in and see your mother?"

Jaya's Telugu trips easily off her tongue, now that she is home. Ravi leads her into the house.

The once large sunlit rooms have been divided into small chambers, dark and dank. It seems like many people, strangers to Jaya, now live here. Jaya finds Lakshmi in the kitchen. The old woman falls at Jaya's feet.

"Jayamma, you are home. Wait, I am making food."

Jaya pulls Lakshmi up and asks that she show her the pots and pans, the dry goods and storage bins, the oil canisters and masala tins. Lakshmi complies, chatting nonstop about the noisy neighbours, the horrible state of the sewage, the water tank that leaks, as if Jaya is the landlord come to do repairs. Jaya listens and takes in the decay of the room that was once her refuge. She also observes how much Lakshmi has aged, although she is likely only ten years older than her. Jaya grew up in this kitchen, assisting Lakshmi when Anasuya and Pilla were at school. Lakshmi passed to Jaya her recipes and cooking techniques. Simple survival skills.

Jaya notes the new electric cooker and turns the dial. She feels the heat rise from the frying pan, pours in some oil, and tosses in mustard seeds followed by cumin. She is at home. In her refuge. The stone floor is cool beneath her bare feet. She remembers the smoothness of it, the hardness under her back when some thirty years ago she experienced her first kiss.

Jaya pauses. She sends Lakshmi outside to meet Irwin and Anya. Then she whips up some channa dal, fried eggplant, chicken curry, chapatis, and rice for her family.

*

It is disorienting to Irwin, this step-by-step entry into his past as he lifts the latch of the gate and crosses the threshold into the courtyard, arriving at a place he has been before.

Irwin stands where once there was a garden. The bougainvillea that climbs the trellis is reduced to twisted branches with yellowing leaves. And *she* is not here. Kanta, his wife, once referred to by the Hyderabadi Christian community as the Rose of Afzal Gunj. Instead, Anya stands on the veranda looking at him; his granddaughter who was conceived in this house yet never lived here nor visited.

Irwin's mind wanders to the young British boy who had come to stay. He should have been unimportant, a footnote in their history, as irritating as a pimple. But his beautiful granddaughter came from this boy.

As Lakshmi leads Irwin into the house, the waft of fried onions and garlic tickles his nostrils. Indian cuisine smells better in India. It lifts his spirit, the way comfort food does, especially after a long journey. Jaya's cooking. Lakshmi returns to the kitchen as Irwin washes his hands and settles at the dining room table. He looks at the portraits of Dr. Benjamin and his wife, Evelyn. A portrait of Kanta hangs just below. He notices the frames need dusting. Then a young man enters the room and, without even greeting Irwin, picks up the telephone receiver and places a call. Irwin is startled. Who is this person? What is he doing here?

"Hello. Excuse me. What are..." Irwin begins.

The man turns and puts one finger to his lips. "Shhh."

Irwin listens and ascertains, he is Mulki, speaking in a Telangana dialect. Why is this rogue using *his* telephone? The same black and heavy receiver Kanta would have held against her ear the last time Irwin called her. It was just before he made the ill-fated trip to Toronto in 1985, when he convinced Anasuya to get on that plane.

"I would love Anasuya to come home," Kanta had said. "But why now? What is all this secrecy and urgency? Did you win a lottery?"

"They are just coming to see you. That is all." Irwin had replied.

"That is all. My foot!" Kanta exclaimed. "Your son was killed ten years ago, and you did not even show your face at his funeral. I have begged you and not once did any of you come. While you were abroad getting rich, I have been living with servants for company, managing this huge house alone."

"Getting rich? Half the money goes to you, the rest into paying for the roof over our heads. Getting rich, you say. These tickets for Anasuya and Anya have cost your granddaughter's education. But you never wanted her, did you?"

"I knew you would throw that back in my face. You were the idiot that ran away to the West, as if all your problems would disappear. Send them back to me. All of you come home."

And when Irwin hung up, he knew Kanta was right. Now he wants to set things straight with her. Admit he was wrong. He should never have taken their daughters to Canada. Irwin grabs the telephone receiver from the man.

"Uncle, let go. I am not yet finished."

But Irwin does not let go. He pulls the wire until the young man shoves Irwin away and the receiver clatters to the ground.

"What is your business here?" Irwin stoops to pick up the receiver. "I have to call my wife, an urgent call to Kanta!"

Jaya and Lakshmi bring in bowls of rice and curry.

"Naina!" Jaya calls him father.

"Who is this person?"

"That's Ravi." Jaya sets the dishes on the table. "Don't you recognize him? He is Lakshmi's son. This is *his* house now."

"Him?" Irwin speaks into the receiver. "Stupid woman. You willed your inheritance to someone else! I will talk some sense into you."

"Stop. Listen to me, Naina. Mummy is dead."

Irwin looks blankly at Jaya. "Kanta?"

"Yes. Sit down, please. Lakshmi, bring him some water."

"Madame." Ravi takes the receiver from Irwin and hangs up. "You cannot order my mother around now. She is no longer your servant."

At that, Irwin recognizes the younger man's face. Lakshmi's son Ravi, now grown up. He should have been another inconsequential character, except that now he is the master of this house. Kanta's house. Dr. Benjamin's house. Never Irwin's house.

"How can this be?"

Ravi, exasperated, follows his mother out of the room.

"Mummy died soon after Anasuya's death. You were in hospital."

Lakshmi returns with a glass of water and hands it to Irwin. She and Jaya go back to the kitchen, leaving Irwin seated at the table. He looks up to see Anya standing in the doorway, watching him. Anya's eyes are full of water, her face looks wet. She must have been swimming. It is unbearably warm here.

*

Irwin lost a segment of his life while in hospital. It was as if he had begun a book, left it open, and neglected it for years. Now he returns to it, to find the middle has been ripped out, leaving him guessing as to what has happened. Kanta has died. And Anasuya. Pilla passed before her. The smell of the house evokes his old life, the people in it, his profession, the opportunities he turned down. He wonders about his supervisor in the Indian Civil Service.

The next morning, Irwin approaches Ravi. "Do you know of a D.B. Srikaram?"

Ravi chuckles. "Of course, how can anyone live in Hyderabad and not know Srikaram. He is the longest-standing minister in Andhra."

Ravi is an auto-rickshaw driver and offers to take Irwin to Srikaram's address in Jubilee Hills, the fast-developing wealthy neighbourhood. On the way, Ravi tells Irwin how he works three jobs and that he divided and rented out rooms in the Benjamin House for extra income to pay for his evening classes. Ravi hopes to work in the emerging IT sector. He asks Irwin about opportunities in Canada. Irwin's replies are disinterested. Although grateful to Ravi, the young man is distracting him. Irwin is on a mission to correct an error.

They pull up to Srikaram's mansion. Like the Benjamin House, a wall protects it. But this one is much grander. It has an iron gate with a uniformed guard keeping watch. Ravi waits in the auto-rickshaw. Irwin, clutching a manila envelope, introduces himself to the security guard and is ushered through the gate. Irwin is shown a seat in a large foyer and offered a cup of chai. He smooths the manila envelope. Number sixteen in his list of possessions. The government of India document, known to political insiders as the Sunderlal Report.

Irwin had forged a stellar career working in the Indian civil service. He was indebted to Srikaram, who offered Irwin his first position. Irwin had garnered respect for his contributions to the Khasra Pahani report, which documented land ownership in Hyderabad. He rose through the ranks, and Srikaram singled Irwin out for a senior role in Minority Affairs. With almost twenty years of service, Irwin was deserving of such recognition. But then Anasuya got pregnant and he panicked.

In 1966, Irwin offered his resignation to Srikaram.

"Let me understand. You are leaving your post in the state government of Andhra Pradesh to be a teacher of community development?"

Irwin wanted to correct him — his position was adjunct professor of international development — but did not.

"You understand I am doing this for my children. Soon they will be attending university."

Srikaram sneered. "Really, man. You needn't give up your career or your country. You can send all your children to read at Oxford if it is a first-class education you seek."

Irwin knew Srikaram was correct. The reason for his departure was not to better his children's future but to escape the shame of Anasuya's illegitimate pregnancy. The night before, he and Kanta had agreed they would do what was best for Anasuya. Oddly, this secret, the argument that ensued, and their ultimate decision made him feel closer to Kanta. When Irwin eventually passed the letter of resignation to his superior, he kept his head bowed to hide the tears that revealed how desperately he wanted to stay.

Thirty years had passed since that decision.

Srikaram walks into the foyer.

"It *is* you." Srikaram is at least fifteen years senior to Irwin but looks in good health. "You've returned from Canada."

Irwin rises and holds out the envelope. "I wanted to return this report. It belongs to you."

"What? You have come all the way here to give me some old document? I always knew you to be meticulous but thirty years is a bit overdue, wouldn't you say?" Srikaram chuckles and pats Irwin on the shoulder.

"My apologies, sir."

"None of that. You will of course stay for lunch." Srikaram gestures to Irwin to come into the dining area. "Come, tell me about Canada."

"Open it." Irwin commands.

Startled, Srikaram, retrieves the report. He studies its contents, glances at Irwin then back to the page.

Srikaram's voice is steady. "How did you happen upon this?"

"It came upon my desk."

"It is classified. You have had this copy in your possession? All these years?"

"Yes, sir. I made a note to return it to you." Irwin puts his hands together in a namascaram.

"Return it? It was never intended for you. It was addressed to me. And only me. Do you know the suspicion and interrogation I endured for not having responded to this?"

"I am sorry. I have never stolen anything before ..."

"You deliberately stole this? And what did you do? With whom did you share this report?"

Irwin had anticipated some disappointment from Srikaram but hoped he would receive gratitude and recognition for having done the right thing.

"No one, sir. I kept this confidential."

"Without thinking of the consequences, the impact on me ... the state even?"

Prime Minister Nehru himself had solicited Srikaram's opinion, recognizing the latter's analysis of communal conflicts in the region. Receiving no reply, and having no strategy to manage potential reactions to the report, Nehru blocked its public release. At that time, the newly independent country was reeling from Hindu-Muslim conflict and Nehru couldn't afford to fight the fires that the controversial report might stoke. So Nehru buried it.

Srikaram gestures to his security guards. "Thank you for returning this. Now go back to Canada before I report this theft."

"It was many years ago. Sir. Please accept my good wishes to you and..."

The guards, one on either side of Irwin, grip his arms and push him outside the property. Ravi, still in the rickshaw, his music blaring, pays no attention.

Winded, Irwin leans against the gate and reads the plaque: D.B. Srikaram, Minister, Minority Affairs, Government of Andhra Pradesh. Irwin's supervisor is still in service to his beautiful country. Now thinking less of him.

*

Having left Hyderabad and on the journey to Korampally, Irwin contemplates the meaning of apology. He had tried but could not properly apologize to Kanta nor to Srikaram. He knows that he owes an apology to Jaya. Maybe he can reach her by reverting to the language that bridged their tentative communication when she was a child. But he cannot find the word in Telugu. Just as there is no *thank you* in Telugu, there is no equivalent for *sorry*. Kshaminchaali is closer to a plea for forgiveness. Perhaps he must beg her to pardon him, but he cannot utter the word. While he still counts in Telugu he no longer dreams in it, nor can he express himself. Hearing his mother tongue floods him with emotion. The Italian of the East, some have said of Telugu.

In the taxi, which will take them from the bus terminal on the highway into the village and to their hotel, Irwin glances to Jaya and Anya in the back seat. Anya has been an active observer throughout the train, bus, and taxi rides from Hyderabad to Korampally, clicking her camera.

"Wow, this is a great shot. Did you see that?"

Of course he saw that. This, that, and so much more, now and when he first arrived in 1947. He had been an earnest and naive twenty-year-old and Korampally was even more beautiful then. There were no half-constructed buildings, stretches of roadside stalls, and metal-roofed dwellings that interrupted the expanse of paddy fields. Raised in the unremarkable town of Nellore, young Irwin viewed the landscape of the Telangana countryside as a foreigner, full of questions. Like a child, full of wonder. Like a native, full of pride. The land lay open, abundant, vibrant, and vulnerable. Now, in the same fields, he sees in the distance red flags fluttering in the wind. Perhaps they signal an irrigation project, demarcate the borders of plots, or simply serve as a place holder for work to be done.

The Vancha River moves along with them, a witness to their journey. Perhaps the river is wary of him now, since Irwin abandoned this village. Because of his betrayal, he deserves to be scrutinized. Maybe he can pay a tax, offer some kind of penance. Irwin feels another apology lodge in his throat. This time to his country. Can he still call it his country? Had he the right to claim it?

Jaya's face is unreadable. Throughout the train, bus, and taxi rides, she hasn't spoken a word to him except to grunt yes or no. He wants to point out landmarks, places from his past that still exist. Her confirmation would make these remembrances real. If only she could tell him, "Yes, they were here, you were here." But why does he expect she will remember? She who had not yet been born?

They move towards the crossroads where an ancient peepal tree rises on the northwest corner. In 1947 the peepal tree was lush. Its canopy of leaves shaded villagers who stopped to pray, gossip, or rest. Now the leaves curl as dry vines crisscross the sturdy trunk. The tree's persistence has cost the government too much in road repairs. For this reason, arborists have been imported from the nearby city of Nalgonda to do the work no villager will do: cut down the sacred tree. Workers direct long-poled branch cutters into the canopy of the tree, bringing a leafy shower down to the pavement below. The tree's thick roots are visible, thrusting through cracks in the tarmac, emerging like half-buried arms, rising up as if protesting its destruction. Demolition tape entraps or perhaps protects the tree from the neighbouring local bus station, where pastel-coloured coaches shunt in and out of small lots. The smell of diesel permeates the air as they pass by.

"Jaya?"

She looks at Irwin, as if irritated, then away. He had surmised her to be four when he found her in 1952. It was months before she spoke. Anasuya, the precocious younger of the two, had drawn Jaya out of her shell through play. Anasuya had not given up where the adults had. Perhaps Jaya is retreating back to her silent world.

"There's the hotel." Anya claps her hands.

Bright blue letters rise on a billboard in large looping Telugu script, a smaller English translation underneath: *The Krishna Lodge*, a painting of the blue god playing his flute directly below.

Before Irwin can reach into his wallet, Anya hands the taxi driver two thousand rupees. She is constantly pulling out bills, like candy wrappers, giving them away to every driver, seller, and beggar before Irwin can intervene.

"Think of the big picture, Thathagaru." Anya addresses him respectfully. "It will not make me poor, and it will not make them rich. We will simply get to where we are going faster."

Irwin has no idea how such a young woman can be so confident and organized. Yet Anya planned the whole trip, reassuring him and Jaya that they should and could travel to India together. Anya renewed Irwin's and Jaya's passports, applied for her own visa. Using the untouched money from the rental income of the house in Antigonish, she purchased the tickets and wrote emails to the Reddy family. Anya had presented everything to Irwin one late October day in Toronto, approximately three weeks after his discharge from the hospital. In an almost somnambulist state, Irwin rose from his chair and signed his name on several documents, beginning the process that would usher him back to Korampally in December of 1997, fifty years after he had first arrived.

Part Two
1947

4. The Village

There was something about the light, the way it fell upon the land. It signalled a kind of magic, a hoped-for transformation of this place that was not yet India. This moment, unnoticed by the natives who went about their work, was apparent to twenty-year-old Rayappa Irwin. He was riding from the bus stop to Korampally on the back of a bullock cart. Dirt sprayed from the wheels of the cart and lightly dusted his grey trousers and white short-sleeved shirt. Dr. Derek Connelly, the renowned Oxford scholar, sat in front, more appropriately dressed in a khadi kurta and dhoti, directing a rapid stream of Telugu into the ear of the astonished bullock-cart driver. Rayappa, content to listen, stabilized the scholar's two trunks as well as his own small suitcase, tanned leather with brass buckles. One of three gifts, apart from his name, that he had received from his father, Rayappa Joseph.

A year prior, Dr. Connelly had come to the Lone Star Baptist College in Nellore as a guest lecturer in social anthropology. He also used his classes to engage his students in the great political debates of the day. He addressed the class of boys as "gentlemen," the promised generation who would be the leaders of a new country.

"I challenge you to step out of the shoes of the British and back into your leather chappals." Connelly's invitation was to the whole class, but he looked straight at Rayappa.

Rayappa glanced self-consciously at his own misshapen feet, squeezed into a pair of polished oxfords at least one size too small for him, the second gift from his father. Connelly's words inspired him.

"When Gandhi leads this country to independence, will you mimic the notion of British civilization? Or, will you build a new nation based on the raw potential of her people? It will take someone like you, Rayappa, educated and a thinker, but native in perspective and experience."

Rayappa was thrilled to be singled out but did not fully understand why the professor had such faith in him. While Rayappa's grades were excellent, he was not at the very top of his class. But he hankered after knowledge, sought opportunities to perfect his English, and aspired to exceed the professor's expectations of him. Three months after independence, the great transfer of power that ceded India to Indians, Rayappa packed a suitcase and found himself balancing on a bullock cart in a rural region of the princely state of Hyderabad.

The driver stopped the cart. They had arrived at a crossroads. It divided the village into distinct parts: the river to the east, the terraced hills to the west, the landlords' mansions to the north, and the fields where the gollas herded cattle and sheep to the south. Behind them was the dusty road just travelled, the bus stop where they had disembarked, the highway stretching south to Rayappa's old life in Nellore.

A large peepal tree graced the intersection. Its dense foliage shaded the ground like a great umbrella. Underneath, almost hidden by the curtain of leaves, a wiry young man, a boy really, some years younger than Rayappa, sat cross-legged weaving a basket. He did not look up but continued his work of folding and layering the straw.

"Hey!" The bullock-cart driver waved his stick at the young man. Still the young man did not raise his head. "You? Are you also deaf?"

"I can hear you."

"Come."

Calmly, the young man set aside his task and rose awkwardly. He let his dhoti fall its entire length to cover his strong, lean legs, leaving exposed only his ankles and a deformed left foot.

"My animal needs water."

The young man thrust his chin towards a huddle of thatched huts. "Take them there to the gollas. You know they keep animals. They may allow yours to drink." He opened his eyes slightly, revealing greyish pupils.

The driver snorted, got off the cart, and unhitched the bullocks. As the young man headed back to the tree, Connelly called after him in faultless Andhra Telugu.

"We are travelling from Nellore. I am Dr. Connelly from the University of Oxford. I am spending a year here with the Reddy family."

The young man turned, smiled, and opened his arms wide, mimicking a British accent. "Welcome to my country."

His mockery was lost on Connelly, who smiled back. But the driver understood it, turned, and waved his stick at him. "kunti vadu!"

The young man returned the gesture, waving the shafts of straw he clutched in his hand. Was he not blind, Rayappa wondered? Rayappa realized that such gestures were part of a familiar conversation between the two, an understanding of the inherited contempt one caste had for the other, regardless of the minute differences between their castes.

Connelly raised his palm to calm the driver. "Ah, that poor boy, both blind and lame."

"Do not feel sorry." The driver made his way back from the watering troughs with the bullocks. "He is mad. Picchivaadu!"

Rayappa would have to agree. How could this person, disabled as he was, risk a fight with the sturdy driver? He was likely unaware of the size and strength of his opponent. Or perhaps he had caught the madness that afflicts those with nothing left to lose.

The driver hitched the bullocks to the cart, climbed back on, and struck the beasts forcefully with his stick. As the cart jolted forward, Connelly commanded the driver to stop. He jumped off, trotted back to the tree, and handed the kunti vadu a silver coin. Rayappa watched with curiosity as Connelly hoisted a large rolled-up floor mat onto his shoulder and deposited it in the cart. The kindness of the professor never ceased to amaze Rayappa. Rayappa could have balanced the whole world on his shoulder that very moment, buoyed by the conviction that human empathy, more than intelligence, would advance his homeland. As the cart resumed its pace toward the village centre, Rayappa, with one slim leg straddling the rolled-up mat, turned his head to the terraced hills that outlined the valley of Korampally.

*

From the crest of the hill, one could view the whole village and its surroundings: the dense and verdant forests that spread for miles around them, the glimmering expanse of the Vancha River disappearing beyond the horizon, and the numerous footpaths meandering into and between the various neighbourhoods. One could even see the road stretching far beyond the village, revealing the comings and goings of villagers and visitors. Three peasant girls were watching Rayappa and his entourage on the road below. Malika, the eldest, whose eagle eye never missed a thing, noted the heavy frame of the white man seated next to the driver. The middle sister, Sayeeda, commented on the skinny man at the back. Alia, the youngest of the three, pointed in a different direction, northwest towards the village well. A colour-ful, serpentine line extended from the well onto the main road of the village. Women in mustard, ochre, and lime-coloured saris bent and straightened as they lowered one water pot after the other by a rope into the well and drew them back up. Afterward, they tucked the pots under their arms or hoisted them upon their heads.

"Never mind the fat Angrezi. Look at the size of Aditi!" Alia singled out a large woman standing to the side of the well.

Sayeeda picked up her clay pot from the ground. "That woman must be as wide as the Vancha itself."

"Surendra Babu's wife has all the food she wants." Malika started walking down the hill towards the well. Her sisters followed.

"I wish I was that fat." Alia rubbed her empty gut.

"It will be a long time before you grow fat."

Malika gave her sister a playful shove. They tripped and skidded their way down the hill, the rims of their clay pots clutched securely in their fists. When they arrived, breathless at the bottom, they took shelter in the scanty shade of a neem tree, a metre from where the women lined up at the well. Veena Reddy, the landlord's wife and mother of two adult sons, was a stout woman with close-set eyes. Her hands moved quickly as she doled out instructions.

The girls watched this familiar drama.

"Where is Linga Babu's new Hyderabadi wife?" Sayeeda shaded her eyes with her hand. "Everyone is talking about how fair-skinned and pretty she is."

Malika moved into the sun to allow her sister room to stand in the shade. "Lalita is said to be beautiful, but no one really knows. She is in purdah."

"But she is Hindu."

"Ammi says Lalita is from Hyderabad. And some Hindus in the city practise purdah."

Alia sighed. "I wish we lived in Hyderabad. I would stay in purdah, rest in a cool room, eat sweets, and drink coconut water all day."

"Even if we lived there, you could not be in purdah." Malika wiped sweat from her throat. "We are much too poor to give up work in the fields."

"We are so unlucky."

Sayeeda pinched Alia's arm. "That's true. If only we were rich, Alia could live in seclusion and everyone would be spared from looking at her ugly face."

As the sisters began arguing, Veena Reddy's sharp voice cut in.

"Arrey, what are you lazy girls doing there?"

"Dorasani, we are waiting for one of you to kindly draw water for us."
Malika lowered her gaze.

"Go wait there."

Veena directed Malika and her sisters to stand closer to the well but in
the hot sun. As the queue grew longer, the women became impatient. They
nudged their neighbours forward and quipped at each other. Monsoon rains
had been infrequent this year and the soil was dry. As the sisters waited, flies
encircled them, landing on their feet and arms. Alia danced to keep the flies
at bay. Sayeeda shooed them off. Only Malika stood still, tolerating the vodla
purugu. The copper-coloured paddy insect, known for its terrible sting,
brushed its silky wings against the skin of her forearm. Malika counted the
number of women filling their vessels —eighteen, nineteen, twenty —fearful
that they would have to wait all day before it was their turn.

Malika's mother had taught her to listen to the well. It could tell stories,
predict storms, and protect her if she knew how to trust it. But Malika could
rarely get close enough to hear the voice of the well. Upper-caste women forbade her and her sisters to touch it, lest they contaminate it. Malika respected
and feared the well on which they acutely depended. It was a dark container,
and no one was certain of its depth. Veena, as if privy to Malika's thoughts,
ordered one of her own young servants to fill Malika's pot.

"Where is your rope?" Veena asked Malika gruffly.

"Ammi traded it."

"Your mother has no sense."

Veena turned briskly to her servant, instructing her to fill Malika's pot only
halfway. When the servant gestured at Malika to take the pot, Aditi, Veena's
youngest daughter-in-law, intervened.

"It is not yet full."

Veena Reddy raised her hand towards Aditi. "Never mind, it is all they
need. Why they need well water at all is my question. They can take water
from the river like the other pariahs."

Other untouchables never approached the well. But Malika's family had
converted to Islam and, perhaps naively, expected to step beyond the rigid
boundaries of caste to a better life. Malika's paternal grandfather had been
convinced that they would have protection under the Nizam. But neither her
grandfather nor his family had experienced much relief: their lives remained
harsh, with another set of rules replacing the first. They did not advance a

rung but moved over, to another precarious position in the hierarchy, within
an even smaller community.

Aditi gave Malika a helpless shrug before turning to follow her mother-in-
law home. Malika and her sisters remained at the well and waited until Veena
and her entourage were a safe distance away and the remaining women in line
finally drew water and left. Then Malika stepped aside, revealing a rope on
the ground, previously hidden by the fall of her sari.

Alia stooped and grabbed it. "Where did that come from?"

"It slipped off one of Veena Reddy's pots. And I pulled it under my sari
with my skillful big toe, before anyone noticed." Malika held out her right
foot and wiggled her toes. Alia giggled but Sayeeda gave Malika the look. It
was a look their mother had invented to convey disapproval. But it held no
power over Malika. She took the rope from Alia and tied it to her pot.

"What if you are caught?" Alia gestured towards Veena far from the well,
but still visible on the road. "The dorasani is just over there."

"You will pollute the well." Sayeeda mimicked Veena Reddy's voice.

The girls understood what they should and shouldn't do, but Malika had
never been caught breaking the rules, so she was never punished. She lowered
her pot into the well, drawing up a brimful of water. She did the same with
her sisters' pots. Then Malika untied the rope from the pot and tied it around
her waist, hiding it beneath the palloo of her sari. Hoisting the clay pot onto
her head, Malika turned towards the landlord's house.

"Where are you going? We must take the footpath," Sayeeda cautioned
Malika, who was already heading down the main road.

"Reddy is having a special guest. I heard the dorasani say it is that white
man."

"Ammi says they look like the devil. Maybe he will glance at us and turn us
into ghosts." Alia playfully jabbed Sayeeda in the waist to scare her.

"Don't be foolish. I have seen a white man before." Sayeeda reluctantly
started to follow Malika. "Remember the missionary who turned 'prayers
into rice, created bread from stone.' There is nothing so different about the
Angrezi. Only they are giant-sized, grow red in the sun, and eat cow flesh
three times a day in their homeland."

"Now I really want to see him."

The younger girls quickened their pace to catch up to Malika, who was
already nearing the Reddys' compound.

*

Raghunandan Reddy was the wealthiest dora of the village and owned much
of the surrounding land, including the rice paddy fields and vegetable plots
that were rented to peasants. Malika's father, Gulaam Rasool Hajam, like
other bonded labourers, leased a small terraced lot dug out of the hillside.
Like his father and his father before him, he farmed rocky land that yielded
little. In addition to the rent, a portion of their meagre harvest was turned
over to the landlord as tax. Questioning or refusing these payments would
result in greater penalties or physical punishment. The family's livelihood
depended on the Reddys, and so they were obliged to fear and obey them.
Malika, however, was never a particularly diffident child. At ten, she would
escape her family's small hut in the early morning and scamper down the hill.
She would creep like a thief towards the Reddy compound, her head covered,
the cool pre-dawn air tickling her nostrils as her skin erupted with goose
bumps. Outside the wall, Malika would gather tamarind pods that fell from
the tree that grew there. She would climb onto its uppermost branch and look
beyond the wall, covered with winter jasmine flowers, and observe Sivraj,
the Reddys' pedda metaru, the head farmhand. He would rub his eyes, clear
his phlegm-filled throat, and air his bedding under a lightening sky. Then he
would sweep and sprinkle water on the ground of the inner courtyard and
supervise the lesser servants milking the buffaloes. Sometimes men would
bathe, clad in their dhotis, pouring water quickly over their heads, shaking
off the excess like dogs.

Malika was astounded at the Reddys' wealth. They kept cows, bullocks,
and buffaloes. Two bullocks were used to transport the eldest son, Linga, to
oversee the farmers in the fields. And of course, they had sheep, chickens,
goats, and servants. Some servants slept in the bullock and sheep houses,
others outside on the courtyard ground. Sivraj, she observed, had his own
small room that opened out onto the courtyard. He was afforded some privacy by a thin curtain that hung in the doorway. When the landlord started
shouting commands from the main house, Malika would scramble down the
tree and run home before sunrise, in time to join her mother and sisters for
prayers.

Now, in broad daylight, Malika set down the water pot and helped her
sisters climb the tree so they could peer over the wall. Suthiya, the child-slave,
used rice powder to create an intricate kolam pattern on the veranda floor in

preparation for the visitors. Malika admired Suthiya's work and wondered what it was like for the girl to live amongst the Reddys.

Veena emerged from the main house, and Sivraj picked up a handful of pebbles, throwing them in Malika's direction. Malika and her sisters ducked and heard Veena's distinct voice. "Useless children."

Malika peeked over the wall and watched Sivraj drop the remaining pebbles to the ground, inches away from Veena's feet.

*

Connelly's arrival in Korampally created a spectacle. As the bullock cart wound its way into the village, people peered out of windows, stepped through doorways, or turned from where they were squatting at their stalls and roadside trades to observe Connelly and his entourage. Rake-thin children ran up to the cart, tapping the wheels with sticks and crying out, "Master, choose me." The children, clapping and waving straw, created a festive welcome for the visitors. Rayappa steadied his pen to take notes to describe the children:

1. bare mud-caked feet
2. partially dressed
3. thin though not starving

The village showed signs of decay, crumbling walls and peeling paint, the odd structure approaching collapse. The temple at the centre of the village, however, glistened with a fresh coat of pink paint. A concrete wall just outside it had been whitewashed. Barely visible underneath the paint was the slogan Vetti Nashincali, "End Slavery," and the pinkish outline of a sickle with the letters CPI underneath. Rayappa recognized the acronym for the Communist Party of India. Below it, a labourer crouched, cleaning his paintbrush, having just finished his job.

In the past decade, this area, like others in the Telangana district, had been heavily taxed. The first portion of revenue filled the pockets of local jagirdars, a greater portion propped up the luxurious lifestyle of the Nizam, but the British scooped up the greatest amount to fund their faraway war. Back in college, Rayappa had argued with fellow students about India's contribution to the allied cause.

"We have to support the lesser of two evils, otherwise the whole world will be enslaved by Germany."

"Why should India's peasants contribute to the war effort?" His classmates had a point. "We are taxing the poorest people in order to protect the empire that exploits us."

Rayappa, however, was not convinced. "Don't you understand? Gandhiji is clear that the outcome of this war will dictate the future of England and all her colonies. Do you think we will be better ruled under the Nazis?"

Although he made his point, Rayappa knew it was better not to be ruled by *any* foreign country. It was on the backs of the colonies that Europe had flourished. And history repeated itself. As in World War I, Indians continued to pay the price on the front lines to secure Britain's victory over Germany. Rayappa's father (who had studied languages through his army career) served in Burma in World War II, translating Burmese into English on the frontlines. He survived the war but went to England shortly after, never to return.

The bullock cart came to an abrupt stop at the landlord's house. Two male servants opened the blue double doors in the nine-foot wall that wrapped around the compound. The younger servant took hold of the yoke of the bullocks while the elder waved his broom furiously at three peasant girls standing near the entrance. The two younger girls tried to dodge the broom but the eldest stood tall and still, balancing a clay pot on her head and staring at the visitors. Rayappa returned the girl's gaze. She was calm, her eyes were large and focused, as if accusing him. He was relieved when she led the others away from the house. She walked slowly, stoic, seemingly unperturbed by the broom.

After the cart was led into the courtyard, the gates were locked behind Connelly and Rayappa. He felt relief as the iron rod settled in its latch and the noise and activity of the village was blocked out. Rayappa had entered another world where everything was clean and cool. The sky turned mauve. White jasmine flowers released a sweet fragrance into the evening air, and Rayappa experienced a rare sense of safety, an illusion usually reserved for the rich. As servants gathered around the cart, Rayappa took note of the three buildings that created a U-shape around the inner courtyard. To the right was a large three-walled structure. The front was partly enclosed by a waist-high fence behind which water buffaloes, cows, and bullocks were tied near a watering trough. To the left was a smaller structure housing sheep, goats, and chickens. And in between, looming large and majestic, was the main house.

Linga Reddy's voice preceded him as he emerged from the front door. The young master clasped his hands and paused on the first step of the veranda. He had a prominent forehead, thick eyebrows, and was dressed in a white shirt, black trousers, and black shoes. Rayappa thought this was an unlikely outfit for village life and was probably chosen to make an impression on the scholar. Linga, whom Rayappa placed at his own age or slightly older, put his hands together in a formal namascaram and broke into a broad and charming smile.

"Professor Connelly! My father is anxious to meet you." Linga pointed out Rayappa. "Sivraj will show your servant his quarters."

Rayappa felt a hot flush sweep over his face. Clutching his suitcase, he jumped off the back of the cart and stood at attention.

"Oh no, my good man." Connelly stepped towards Rayappa, clasping his shoulder. "May I introduce to you Rayappa Irwin from Nellore. He will be assisting me in my research."

"Indeed." Linga smirked. "Do we address you as Lord Irwin?"

"No, sir. My father did name me for the former viceroy, but friends and acquaintances address me by my family name, Rayappa."

"Rayappa. A Madiga name, is it?"

Rayappa reached into his breast pocket and put on his round spectacles, which framed his unusual amber eyes. He wanted Linga to see he was educated, that he succeeded despite the oppressive strictures imposed on his community.

Linga instructed Sivraj to take Rayappa's suitcase. As Rayappa handed it over, Sivraj suddenly withdrew his hand, letting the suitcase drop to the ground. One buckle popped open, like an eyelid, as if to witness what had just happened.

"It is okay." Rayappa crouched down to pick up the suitcase. "I can take care of this."

Sivraj made no attempt to help.

Rayappa dusted off the suitcase. He recalled how he had helped his father pack for the war. There was something solemn about folding and putting in order his father's clothes, wondering when his father would return. But he never did. Instead, a year after the war had ended, the suitcase was sent back full of books. The postage suggested it came from England.

Linga again gestured to Sivraj to take the case. But Rayappa held tight. A small tug-of-war ensued.

"We cannot have our special guest carrying such heavy things." Linga clapped his hands.

Rayappa acquiesced and the suitcase bounced out of his hand into Sivraj's and was passed, along with Connelly's trunks, to four boys who carried the luggage and disappeared into a darkened passage. One servant reached for the rolled-up mat still on the cart.

"Something from home?" Linga asked Rayappa. "You will find we have many silk carpets and decorative mats inside."

"No, no," Connelly interrupted. "We picked this up from the basket weaver at the crossroads."

Linga turned to his servant. "Dispose of this in the barn."

Before Connelly could protest, the mat was swiftly deposited in the bullock house. Rayappa glanced at Connelly, who looked crestfallen. Linga invited the visitors to wash at the bathing sinks in the courtyard before leading them across the wide veranda into the main house to meet his father.

*

Raghunandan Reddy reclined on a divan. He was propped up on his elbow, supported by an oblong cushion. He had broad shoulders, thick arms, and a large torso, and his legs seemed small in comparison. His knees were bent and angled to one side and his feet were demurely fitted one over the other, so that no part of his body touched the floor. Reddy peeled away a piece of dead skin from one heel with his third finger and thumb. He examined it then flicked it away slowly, almost ceremoniously.

Two bald men sat on wooden chairs flanking him. Two with hair sat opposite. One of them was a priest wearing an ochre robe. The four men rose as Linga led Connelly and Rayappa into the front room. Raghunandan Reddy remained seated.

"Ah, our visiting scholar. You do us such an honour. You will be placing our little Korampally on the map. Please come, sit. Our home, all of this, is for your pleasure, your comfort."

Rayappa was touched by the warm reception extended by his host. One year ago, Connelly had written to Reddy, stating that Oxford University Press would be publishing a book containing photographs, interviews, and facts about their village. Reddy's reply was enthusiastic, and he offered room and board plus access to community activities. Rayappa had asked Connelly whether this patronage would interfere with academic freedom. To Rayappa's surprise, Connelly shrugged. "Nothing to worry about. He will never read the book."

Connelly and Rayappa took their seats and were introduced to the other landowners, their faces almost as full as Reddy's. Their paunches stressed the weave of their kurtas. Connelly observed Reddy. "I see you are wearing khadi."

"It is the fashion, no? And I am not opposed to supporting our local weavers. In fact, your visit is timely as the chief proponent of khadi, Mohandas K. Gandhi himself, is rumoured to come south."

Connelly smiled. "Is that so? Even while he is trying to calm the communal riots in the North. What would bring him here?"

"Hyderabad, of course. What would India be without its heart?"

"You have a point. Smack in the middle of the subcontinent. Do you think Gandhi will have a chance at luring the people of Hyderabad away from the Nizam?"

"He will certainly try. And these peasants are stupid enough to follow."

"There is much for them to gain under Gandhi's doctrine. You must be interested in his views on the village?"

"For centuries we have known that the village is the centre of Indian life, but Gandhi writes about it and it becomes news."

"To pen an idea is to proclaim its power." Rayappa cleared his throat self-consciously.

Reddy looked curiously at Rayappa, surprised that the young man had interjected his opinion in the conversation of his elders.

"Some ideas don't belong here. Our farmers will be spinning their own cotton and eating all the harvest if we go the way of Gandhi. Who will till the soil if all are sitting under a tree reading a book? Never mind, we need not worry. We enjoy the protection of the Nizam's Razakar Army. They will ensure our people do not get seduced by this independence rhetoric. Hyderabad will continue under the Nizam, and Gandhi can keep his India."

Connelly leaned forward. "Certainly, Mr. Reddy, you can see the benefit of a unified, secular India."

"Unified indeed. Look at the chaos already created, the separation of Pakistan and India, Kashmir in constant rebellion. Here, we Hindus and Muslims have lived peacefully for centuries. What will we gain from Nehru's ambitions and Gandhi's mumbo jumbo? Even Ragaviah, our own village pujari, though a great admirer of Gandhi, does not altogether agree with his radical ideas on caste. Forgive me sir, but Ragaviah declares that even the British are as unclean as the sweeper in the courtyard."

Ragaviah lowered his head.

"I fully agree with that sentiment, being of Irish stock." Connelly grinned.

Reddy remained serious. "An independent India promises neither a Hindu nor a secular state but a confused one. Better the devil you know. Isn't that what they say?"

"Perhaps. It seems the Nizam will not be convinced to join India, so in theory you have nothing to fear."

"Fear? Who has time for such an indulgent emotion? There is a harvest to gather. Politics are a preoccupation for those who do not work for a living."

Rayappa could not believe his good fortune. He would not only be spending a year immersed in the research he loved but there was a real possibility of meeting the great Gandhi.

After finishing a meal of bendakai, chapatis, and gonkura pickle, Rayappa hurriedly wrote down the names of those who lived in the household. He listed them in order of acquaintance, noting their role and other observations.

1. Sivraj — head servant, appears at least fifteen years younger than the senior Reddy, efficient but cunning, not to be trusted.
2. Linga — eldest son and heir, bright, attractive, outgoing, and arrogant.
3. Raghunandan Reddy — landlord, highly respectable, wealthy, powerful, and generous.
4. Surendra — youngest son, handsome, quiet, not as dynamic as his brother.
5. Veena Reddy — Reddy's wife, homely, respectable, shows deference to her husband.
6. Aditi — Surendra's wife, plump and young, smiles a lot.
7. Lalita — Linga's wife, mentioned but not yet seen.

Following a tour of the great house, Connelly and Rayappa were led into a bedroom.

"Ah!" Connelly clasped his hands. "Like the princely chamber in the Nizam's palace itself."

The room was decorated with vases overstuffed with fresh pink dahlias. The bed was made with a bright covering with an image of a prince riding an elephant, and there was a large stainless-steel cup and pitcher of water on the bedside table. A mosquito net hung over the four-poster bed. A pair of

Moghul-styled slippers with gold sequins were placed at the bedside. Reddy pointed out each special touch added in honour of Connelly.

"I am confident that you will be fully satisfied. My wife made sure to have only top quality for you."

"Sir, you are very generous. But your hospitality is misplaced. I must live as close to the ground as possible. To live in palatial comfort would defeat the purpose." Connelly crossed his arms.

A look of consternation spread over Reddy's face.

"It is unthinkable for you to stay elsewhere. All our rooms are similarly outfitted and are currently occupied. Even now Sivraj is vacating his bed to make place for your man."

Rayappa turned to Reddy. "But sir, in our letter we explicitly requested that we live amongst the villagers. That experience is integral to our research."

Reddy narrowed his eyes at Rayappa and laughed. "Who has the time to read letters?"

Rayappa suspected Reddy had plenty of time to read or to have someone read to him.

"All right," Connelly said, "I would be pleased to sleep here for one night, and in the morning shift to a less ostentatious room."

Reddy clasped his hands in delight. "Yes, yes, very ostentatious."

Rayappa could see that Reddy understood this to be a compliment.

*

Sivraj's room could be entered directly from the courtyard. There was no door but a thin curtain provided some privacy. It was furnished with a narrow cot and a table, on which there was a candle. Rayappa wished there was an oil lamp for reading. In the darkened room, Irwin found his suitcase, set it on the cot, and felt the cool brass buckles snap open under his touch. Along with his clothing, the case contained Rayappa's books, notepads, and pens, his tools for study. By candlelight, he unpacked these items and lined them up on the ledge on the back wall. He withdrew a small silk pouch from the breast pocket of his shirt and pulled out a gold pocket watch. He polished its face with his handkerchief and then put it back in the pouch and laid it ceremoniously on the table. He took off his shirt and dhoti and hung them on the only nail in the wall and changed into his clean undershirt and pyjama bottoms. Lastly, he reached for a brown paper bundle and unwrapped his oxfords. Pressing the paper flat on the table, Rayappa placed the shoes on it. He gazed at them for a few moments then looked down at his own bare feet. He didn't deserve such shoes. Someday, when he established himself, he would have surgery to straighten his toes so they could easily slip into such fine leather.

Rayappa lay on the cot, pulled a thin shawl to his waist, and stared up at the peeling plaster on the ceiling. A slight December breeze blew the doorway curtain in and out of his room. Rayappa realized he would have the experience that Connelly had sought. He was privy to the sounds, smells, and stirrings of all things breathing within and surrounding the compound. Four servants unrolled their bedding and lay under the stars, guarding the gate. The dim sound of the villagers beyond the compound gave way to the noises of nocturnal animals. Acutely aware of these transitions, Rayappa anticipated what he would write in his notebook the next morning. Excitement coursed through his veins, tempered by the slight guilt he felt for displacing Sivraj. The servant was forced to sleep on a small cot in the sheep house, in turn displacing Suthiya, the child-slave, who was banished to a mat in the bullock house. Soon, his unease gave way to exhaustion and, pulling the thin wool shawl up to his shoulders, Rayappa surrendered to sleep.

A distant shout woke Rayappa. Thinking he was in his Nellore room, he reached for a lamp that wasn't there. He sat up and noted all he heard:

1. Footsteps, more than two
2. Murmurs in the courtyard
3. Lifting of the iron latch

Leaning over, he parted the curtain to see someone come in through the great blue doors. Wrapping his shawl around his shoulders, Rayappa stepped into the courtyard. He slipped outside the gate and onto the road outside the compound. In the moonlight, he saw Sivraj up ahead speaking in a low voice to three servants who then scurried away in the direction of the hills. An orange glow spread in the darkness, seemingly suspended in the sky. Rayappa was reminded of paintings of nebulae he had seen in astronomy books. He wondered if there had been a celestial eclipse. It was at once breathtaking and terrifying.

Rayappa approached Sivraj. "What is going on?"

"Only farmers burning grass on the hills."

"But why? At this time and so close to harvest?"

"It is a terraced plot. It is difficult to grow any crop."

Sivraj directed Rayappa towards the house. "It makes the soil fertile in the rocky upland area. Are you needing something?"

"No. No, I'm all right."

Sivraj held open the door for Rayappa to pass back into the courtyard. Suthiya, who had also woken and was watching the fire, was also ushered inside and sent back to the bullock house. Rayappa returned to his room.

Unsatisfied with Sivraj's answers, Rayappa went to the bullock house. Mindful not to disturb the animals, he found Suthiya sleeping on the mat that Connelly had bought from the basket weaver. He shook her awake.

"Child. Tell me about that fire. What is really going on? What happened in the hills?"

Suthiya looked at Rayappa wide-eyed and fearful. She put her hands together. "Master, I am your slave."

Rayappa blinked. He was surprised to see a plump and woolly sheep lying near Suthiya. For a moment he thought he had walked into the sheep house rather than the bullock house. But no, the bullocks and cows were also here. She had likely brought the ewe with her.

"Why all the whispering? Where did Sivraj send the other servants?"

"The goddess is angry with Balamma."

"The goddess?"

"Pochamma. That is what landlord master says. The goddess is angry because Balamma did not pay tax."

"I don't understand." Rayappa crouched so he could be at eye level to Suthiya.

"Her husband is dead, and her sons went into the forest." Suthiya yawned.

"Into the forest. What does that mean?"

Suthiya raised her voice. "She did not give her quota! Pochamma is angry and burned the hills red with her blood."

Rayappa stood to leave. Baffled by this odd explanation, he turned back to Suthiya, but she had closed her eyes, and her head dropped against the ewe.

*

Connelly was researching the working conditions and social strata of feudal life. These findings would form the basis of Connelly's proposed book, *Return to the Village*.

The first field survey was underway. Connelly and Rayappa stood on the back of one of Reddy's bullock carts. The peasants had organized themselves in the field, women on one side, men on the other. The household servants stood near the front of the group. Set apart were the Muslims. Some distance behind them were the Malas, and relegated to the very back of the field were the Madigas. During the bullock cart ride, one of the Reddy farmhands explained that in such intentional gatherings even Malas segregated themselves from their close caste neighbours, the Madigas.

Rayappa understood that some social divisions of the village were evident and could be discerned by shade of skin, girth, type of footwear, and clothing. Other types of divisions were more insidious.

As Connelly addressed the peasants, Rayappa sat cross-legged on the bullock cart to take notes.

1. The peasants wear white turbans or ragged headscarves to protect themselves against the sun.
2. Some women wear cotton blouses with their saris, while the majority simply drape the loose fabric diagonally across their bare breasts.
3. Many women wear palloos over their heads, exposing hair. Some mark their foreheads with bindis.
4. Some Muslim women can be distinguished by the way they wear palloos draped over their brows and eyes for modesty and to shield them from the sun.
5. The Muslim men wear taqiyahs on their heads, more commonly referred to as topis.
6. All men wear dhotis hitched between their legs, exposing dry skin on knees, calves, and feet.
7. Teeth, especially those of the elderly, are yellow, missing, or stained with betel nut.

Connelly projected his voice. "You will see us in the fields, on the roads, in the village, and in your homes if you welcome us inside. The questions will be simple, and there will be compensation for your cooperation. My assistant, Rayappa, tells me his ancestors came from such a village, so you may find him more comfortable to approach should you have any questions. I will be taking photographs with this." Connelly pointed to his Rolleiflex camera, set up on the tripod on the ground beside the cart. "I will ask you to gather in the centre of the field for a photograph. Of course, we will provide food for all."

Connelly jumped off the cart and, with one of Reddy's servants, moved the camera and tripod. Other servants on loan from the Reddy household served large vats of dal and rice on the back of the bullock cart. They plopped food onto banana leaves and deposited these into the outstretched hands of the peasants. Rayappa observed that once the vat emptied, the crowd anxiously pressed up against the cart until the food from another vat, and still another, disappeared. Rayappa moved through the crowd asking each person their name, number of family members, religion, caste, occupation, and whether they owned land or leased land or were free or bonded labourers. He perfected his methodology using codes and checks on an elaborate chart to ensure information was quickly captured before advancing to the next question. He recognized the self-assured girl he had seen near the Reddy compound on the day of their arrival. She stood with a woman, maybe fifteen years her senior, equally attractive.

"May I have your name?" Rayappa addressed the older woman.

She looked away. Then the girl cleared her throat. "I am Malika. This is my mother."

"Any menfolk in your household?" Rayappa wanted to look directly at Malika but was conscious of the need to be respectful to her mother.

"I am Fariza. We live with my husband, Gulaam Rasool, and two boys, one a baby, the other just walking. I also have two other daughters like her."

"And your family name?"

"Hajam. My husband's community were haircutters before becoming Muslims. Then his father was granted a plot."

Rayappa learned that the woman's husband had inherited land, but after a series of failed harvests, Gulaam could not afford to pay the tax, and the Reddys wrangled the deed from him. Gulaam and his brothers were forced to rent the same land from the landlord, handing over a quota of the harvest. As the taxes increased, most of the brothers became labourers on other farms and Gulaam was left to cultivate the plot with only his wife and daughters. Gulaam's parents, like Fariza's, had converted to Islam, hoping that the Nizam's riches would drip down like honey from a hive and save them from penury.

Rayappa moved to the next peasant.

"Can we take some food for my father?"

Rayappa turned back to Malika. Her tone sounded more like a command than a request.

"The professor is gathering the people for a group photograph. I will give you something. Come quietly to the cart while the others are occupied. Otherwise many will follow and there will not be enough food."

Malika gave a small bow. Rayappa was compelled by her luminous eyes. "Did I see you . . . ?"

But Malika had turned towards the road. A young man on a mule had arrived, and a group of peasants was gathering around him. Rayappa strained to see what was happening. The villagers posing for the photograph turned their heads also. Rayappa could see Connelly struggling to win back their attention as they started congregating in tight circles. Rayappa moved into the crowd and tried to slip unseen into one gathering, but once he was spotted, the peasants stopped speaking. Then the crowd dispersed. Rayappa returned to the cart where Fariza and Malika were waiting.

"Do you know why everyone is leaving?"

"Back to their fields, their families," Fariza said. "Can we take the food now?"

Rayappa was disappointed to see the peasants scattering. Now he would have to go house to house, hut to hut, over the next few weeks in order to complete the survey. He had known this strategy of Connelly's would not work. Not under the hot sun, with work to be done in the fields. How could they expect the peasants to answer questions?

Rayappa handed Malika and Fariza more rice and dal wrapped in banana leaves. He also passed Fariza his own handkerchief bulging with fried onion bhajis, the lunch prepared for him by the Reddy cooks, a rare treat for peasants. Rayappa looked around, fearful of being caught favouring the women. He saw Connelly disassembling his Rolleiflex.

Beyond Connelly was the young man on the mule. Rayappa recognized him to be the kunti vadu he had seen on his arrival, seated under the peepal tree. Rayappa watched him disappear down a footpath and into the forest as Linga's cart approached.

*

Food can satiate hunger, but little can settle an anxious mind. Although relieved that she and her mother were taking home a meal for the family, Malika was disconcerted about the recent whispers and the gaps between what she had heard and understood. Was it true that Balamma's crop had been intentionally burned? And why? It was known that the widow could not pay

the tax, but usually the landlord would have his men harvest the crops themselves, reaping all the profits. Malika wanted to ask her mother, but Fariza
was hushing her more frequently these days. So Malika remained quiet and
let her mother enjoy the weight of the bhajis in her hand.

Home was a thatched hut similar in size and shape to the fifteen huts clus-
tered on the hillside that housed poor Muslim families. There was a small
burial ground for Muslims and a stone wall with a curved niche that indicated
the direction of Mecca — a sacred place to bow in namaaz. Except for new
Arabic names and a diet that excluded the delectable pig, there was little
that distinguished their status from the neighbours who lived on the rockier
part of the hill near the dump, the Madigas, the untouchable community to
which Malika's maternal relatives had belonged a few decades earlier. Only
the afterlife, it seemed to Malika, would recognize and reward the followers
of different faiths accordingly.

As Malika and her mother walked through the foothills, she could see
farmers gathering in their terraced plots. Though harvest was only weeks
away, the crops were meagre, stunted from lack of rain. The river moved
lazily.

Near the entrance of their hut, Malika and Fariza saw two men trying to
help Malika's father off the ground. Alia came running down the path to meet
her mother and sister.

"Amma, Amma, did you see the white man? Isn't he big and tall and pink?
Did he wear a hat? Did you see his legs, full of hair and . . . ?"

Fariza ignored her, focusing instead on Gulaam who was struggling to
stand. "Are you so drunk that you need to be carried to the field again?"

"Stop talking, woman. We have just heard that the Communist Party has
been banned. There is a Sangham leader here who can tell us how this news
will affect us. He has helped other villagers oppose raised taxes. Today we will
vote on whether to strike. Finally we will stand up for ourselves."

Amir, the two-year-old, ran out of the hut to his mother. Fariza scooped
him up and balanced him on her hip. "Why do you want to involve yourself
with these gatherings? It is trouble and you have work to do."

Gulaam ignored his wife and reached for the shoulders of his two friends.
As they tried to heave him up, Gulaam groaned.

"It is impossible. You go without me."

The men left, their steps sprightly and sure-footed.

Fariza turned to her husband sitting on the ground. "Come, get into the house."

"Let me rest, woman. I am a sick man."

"We are all sick. Now get up. We have bhajis to eat."

"My back..."

"Your back? Nonsense! I too have worked all morning and all afternoon." Fariza, carrying Amir, moved past Gulaam.

Malika angled her shoulder under her father's arm and directed Alia to do the same on the other side. As they half-carried, half-dragged their father into the hut and laid him down on his mat, their mother continued her angry rant.

"Who is tending the crop?"

Alia tried to protect her father against her mother's wrath. "Sayeeda and chascha's daughter and two sons."

Fariza was glad that Gulaam's younger brother had two boys, almost men. It meant the girls were not alone in the field. If the landlord called either son to work, however, the boys would have to go immediately.

Gulaam had confessed to Malika that mornings were especially excruciating as during the night his muscles seized up. His back was a metal sheet. His neck was an iron pipe. His head a steel ball. As Fariza nursed the baby, Gulaam beckoned Malika and Alia to assist him again. Each daughter slipped under one of her father's arms and hoisted him into a sitting position against the wall.

"Abbu, eat a bhaji." Malika had never seen him so listless before. She divided the bhaji into bite-sized portions and fed her father. He chewed slowly, and some of the food dribbled down his chin.

"Can't you eat properly?" Fariza burped the baby.

"But Ammi," Malika implored her mother.

Gulaam doubled over, vomiting blood. Then he lost consciousness.

Fariza thrust the baby into Malika's arms. "Quick, Malika, hold him. Alia get some water and wipe away the mess." In a moment, Fariza was cradling her husband. "How hot he is. Go! Malika, go to the landlord's doctor. Tell him your father is very ill. No, wait. It is not good for the dora to know he is unwell. Fetch Rammulamma, she will have herbs."

Malika passed the baby to Alia. She was relieved to get away from her father's illness and her mother's anxious voice.

On her way to fetch the village healer, Malika saw Linga's cart approach the two farmers who had earlier tried to help her father. Two of the landlord's goondas were sitting on the back of the cart, cracking whips in the air. As she walked in the opposite direction, Malika hoped Linga would steer clear of her family's little plot, especially when her sister and cousins were tending it. But she could not run and warn them. She was on a mission to save her father.

*

The sun had not yet risen when Rayappa stepped into the courtyard to bathe. After one week in the village, he was now attuned to the many sensations of waking in the Reddy household. The birdsong and the rooster's crow at dawn allowed for a natural start to the day. But Rayappa hadn't expected the landlord to rise early each morning and shout commands to the servants to milk the buffaloes and wash the stalls. This initiated a chain of frenetic activity, servants tripping over each other to get their tasks done.

Rayappa enjoyed living among the servants. Connelly had succumbed to the landlord's wishes and remained in the palatial bedroom, so Rayappa found himself not only documenting the night sounds and day duties of the servants but also sharing a kind of understanding and camaraderie with them.

Sivraj and Rayappa each recognized that their social positions had been reversed. This uncomfortable knowing hovered between them, making it difficult to communicate. In its place, they adopted a kind of formality. Each morning, they bowed stiffly to each other like soldiers in front of Buckingham Palace. It was a contrived greeting, one that Rayappa initiated, trying to express his deference to the servant who had slighted him earlier. When Sivraj responded in kind, Rayappa eagerly explained the ritual of the changing of the guards, just as his father had described it through drawings on a rare letter he had sent home. From this simple shared gesture grew an unlikely friendship.

Rayappa was happy to chat and share his knowledge of the world with Sivraj and the boys that slept on the ground in front of the gate. He patiently responded to their questions about his schooling and family. He displayed small, sophisticated items from his suitcase: his gold pocket watch, his notepad, his shoes, his black pressed trousers still creased, folded, and unworn. Rayappa did not mind them holding the gold watch or feeling the fabric of the trousers. Unlike the residents of the house, he was not suspicious that the servants would steal from him. He knew they only coveted what was useful and would not risk being thrown out of the house for something they didn't desperately need.

Rayappa found that Suthiya had already heated water for his bath. Clothed in an undershirt and dhoti, he poured the bucket of warm water over his head. After applying soap to his extremities, he doused himself again, discretely tucking his left hand under the layers of his cotton garments to rinse his private parts. Then, in the dark quiet of his room, Rayappa changed, combed his hair and re-emerged refreshed, wringing the water out of his wet dhoti and hanging it to dry.

Linga was smoking a beedi and waiting with Sivraj near the bullock cart. Connelly and Reddy emerged from the main house onto the veranda. They were arguing.

"How can you say there is no unrest? The peasants scattered upon hearing that the Communist Party was outlawed. The notion that there is no communist faction operating here is simply preposterous."

"Professor Connelly, perhaps that was not the reason. A coincidence. There are no Communist Party members in this area. And if there were, we would have them arrested, as simple as that."

"The reason we chose Korampally was because of its stability. It will be simply impossible to finish the book if there are any . . . political problems. When that kunti vadu interrupted our gathering, our work stopped. The census was not completed. Rayappa must now go from hut to hut."

"You blame that helpless boy for distracting your crowd? You need to show more leadership, Professor. Keep bringing them dal and rice. The peasants are very agreeable, especially approaching harvest. You will see." Then the landlord turned and called out to his son. "Linga, is everything set?"

Linga tossed his beedi to the ground. "We have arranged everything, sir. The village castrator has a calf. I will take the professor and Lord Irwin there myself. My boys and I are going to inspect the fields. Sivraj! Prepare the cart!"

*

As Linga directed the bullock cart through the village to the fields, he pointed out various aspects of rural life to Connelly and Rayappa. Five young men, Linga's boys, also sat on the back of the cart, turning their heads in unison as Linga pointed towards some toddy tappers balancing precariously high on the trunk of a palm.

"Have you tasted our thati kallu yet?"

When Connelly and Rayappa indicated they hadn't, Linga had the driver stop the cart. He commanded one of his boys. "Go then. Fetch some palm toddy for these gentlemen."

"No, no." Connelly waved his hand. "It is too early."

"The earlier, the better. If we wait until midday it will ferment more than needed."

A young man dismounted and ran towards the treeline, which created a natural border between the river and fields. He returned with two gouds, toddy tappers, carrying clay pots and palm leaves. Connelly and Rayappa sipped the alcohol, sharp and pungent. The taste of the kallu, the feel of the palm leaf funnelled in his hands, and the hot blade of sun on the back of Rayappa's neck were all pleasantly intoxicating. He breathed deeply and felt content. There was something freeing about being in the countryside, chatting and joking with Linga and his boys. The sunlight bounced off the green palms and sparkled on the river in the distance. They were a team on an adventure.

When Connelly and Rayappa tossed back the last of their drink, Linga nodded to the driver who snapped his stick and awakened the resting animals. As the cart jolted forward, Rayappa lifted his gaze to the stretch of land before him. Overcome with the glow of intoxication, he admired the expanse of cotton, tobacco, tapioca, and mustard. Some distance down the road, Rayappa recognized two jeetagadus, farmhands he had met while conducting the survey in the field. He had learned that they owned small plots but also helped Reddy collect the tax. They stood beside a peasant who was bent over so that his back was parallel to the ground. At first, Rayappa thought the men were removing stones from a ditch, but as they drew closer, he made out that the jeetagadus were loading stones upon the man's back.

Connelly addressed Rayappa. "My goodness. Look at what they are doing to that poor chap."

Rayappa felt an uncontrollable giggle begin to escape his mouth. Why did he find the scene so ridiculous? A human shelf.

Linga slowed the cart. "What is going on?"

"This is the one I told you about, master. This good-for-nothing stole grain from his neighbour and still could not pay his debts."

"All right. Give him two hours in the sun, then you can check him."

Connelly shot a puzzled look at Linga. "Two hours. In that position? What possible use is that?"

"It is much better than jail, locked away and doing nothing for days, with his wife and children left to fend for themselves. A few hours in the sun should teach him his lesson, and everyone travelling this road will learn it too."

"Village justice. There is a logic to this cruelty. Make note of that, Rayappa."

Rayappa, reclining in the back of the cart, tried to steady his pen as he jotted down some notes. As they passed the peasant, Rayappa found himself eye level with the man's head, his face turned towards the ground. Veins protruded from the peasant's neck, the sweat streamed from his lined forehead, froth formed around his mouth. Rayappa wished the man were not so old. Nothing seemed funny anymore.

Rayappa repressed the urge to jump off the cart, knock the stones off the old man's back, and set him upright. Perhaps Linga was right. A wrong had been committed and was being corrected. If the man had a strong back, he would be okay. The civil court had no jurisdiction in the princely state of Hyderabad. And Gandhi did teach that each village had its own system of holding people accountable for wrongdoing. Could this mode of punishment be acceptable to both those who meted it out and those who endured it? After all, the punisher and the punished were of a similar caste, perhaps even neighbours. Rayappa wondered how Gandhi would respond.

Linga dropped Connelly and Rayappa in the field where the castration would take place and left to inspect the crops. Rayappa perched on a rock beside Connelly, who had donned a white kerchief over his scanty reddish-brown hair to protect his already sunburned scalp from further exposure. Connelly had removed his sandals and was vigorously rubbing a blister that had formed between his first and second toes. It was nearly 10 a.m. The sun was already hot on the dry field.

"Nothing happens when it should in these parts. What did I expect?" Connelly grumbled and laughed in the same breath. "Oh well, enjoy the experience, what, Rayappa?"

Rayappa nodded and smiled, but even he was becoming impatient. The kallu, sweet while drinking, had left a bitter aftertaste in his mouth. There was a slight churning in his stomach.

Rayappa approached Ramulu, the village castrator, who was sitting in the shade holding an axe blade.

"The Angrasi is waiting for the castration. Will it be today or tomorrow, man?"

"Yes. Today only, sir. They are bringing the calf now. Go take some water."

Ramulu directed Rayappa to a shed. The shed was a small room, the dirt floor scattered with hay. A calf was tethered to a wooden stake. Beside that was a small barrel of water. Rayappa picked up a cup hanging on the side of the barrel, scooped up some water, and poured it down his throat. Then he scooped up more to take to Connelly.

Finally, two peasants brought out the calf, forced it to the ground, and held it down. Rayappa set up a tripod and the Rolleiflex camera near the hindquarters of the animal and stabilized it as Connelly positioned himself behind the viewfinder. Then the farmers brought out an axe and what seemed to be a large and low wooden mortar. They set it on the ground near the calf's abdomen. Ramulu gently placed the calf's scrotum on the mortar and with one powerful movement, brought the axe down. Using the blade as a pestle, the farmer ground the soft skin under its weight. The animal moaned and struggled, its nostrils flaring and snorting, its head flailing back and forth. But this was not a job so easily finished. Again, the axe came down. Rayappa turned away from the agonizing sound of the distressed calf, towards Connelly. The professor had a look of intense fascination on his face. Animal husbandry, particularly this method of castration, was an important part of their anthropological research. Connelly ducked behind the camera and clicked the shutter. "Well done!"

Rayappa felt his stomach convulse and vomited inches away from Connelly's feet.

The professor, still focused on the calf, wiped his kerchief across his scalp and handed it to Rayappa. When the castration was complete, the farmer offered a mule on which the two visitors could ride home. Connelly insisted that he would stay behind to witness the calf's recovery.

Rayappa felt as he did in school when he begged off physical activity in order to sit by the wall and rub his funny tummy. He had always been a sickly child, and because of this his classmates, and even on occasion his mother, had called him soft. As he mounted the mule, Rayappa fought off the urge to vomit the remainder of his breakfast. He couldn't shake the image of the professor's expectant face. As Rayappa rode away, he could hear the pathetic moaning of the animal and Connelly's excited voice rising into the warm air.

*

Back at the house Rayappa sat on the veranda, jotting down notes from the morning castration. Suthiya, who had been sweeping the courtyard, inched her way toward him, looking over his shoulder at his notebook.

"Do you want to try?" Rayappa held his fountain pen out to her.

"Voddu, don't want." She settled herself beside him to watch.

"It is easy." He turned to a clean page, took her fingers and wrapped them around the pen. "Now, hold tight and away we go."

First, she drew a line stretching from one side of the page to the other. The stream of ink bleeding from the tip of the fountain pen was magic enough to impress her. Then she drew a circle. Rayappa showed her a face, which she copied, and a flower, which she improved upon.

"You are a very smart girl."

She shrugged her shoulders. Then she drew what looked like a cow with a stick figure behind it.

She was drawing what she knew, Rayappa thought.

"How long have you been here? How many years?"

Again, she shrugged her shoulders.

"How long have you lived with the Reddys, Suthiya?"

Rayappa's family could never afford to have servants when growing up. His two sisters, Jyoti and Shanti, did all the domestic chores while his mother worked as a seamstress, saving funds for his school fees. Rayappa thought of his sisters, how proud they were of him. He used to teach them at home and promised he would find them good husbands. When he left, the girls threw their arms around him. His youngest sister was eleven, perhaps Suthiya's age.

"How many harvests have passed since you came to work for the dorasani?"

Suthiya held up her hand.

"Aidu." Rayappa counted each of her fingers. "Five. You have been here five years, and perhaps you are ten years old, or eleven. Which means you came here when you were six. Aaru."

Rayappa taught Suthiya how to add and subtract, using a hide-and-seek game with fingers, knuckles, and the palm of her hand. In the middle of this game, Suthiya abruptly jumped up and resumed sweeping. Veena followed her and grabbed the girl's ear.

"There you are, you little rascal. Come here. I have heard what you asked Aditi Amma. You will not be leaving this house. Do you understand?"

Rayappa stood up. "What is it?"

Veena glanced at Rayappa. The two often found themselves in each other's company but had never spoken directly to the other. "Are you now interfering in household matters?"

She turned on her heel and went back into the house.

Rayappa had observed Veena to be a modest wife who didn't address men directly, so he was surprised at her retort. Suthiya glanced up at Rayappa and giggled. Humiliated and annoyed at both Veena and now Suthiya, Rayappa slipped into his room and lay down on the bed. He felt slightly feverish and fell asleep without taking lunch.

*

Veena's sharp voice woke Rayappa from his fitful afternoon nap. He leaned across his cot, pulled the curtain aside, and saw Veena speaking to Fariza. Beside her was Malika, holding her mother's arm.

"What do you mean, he cannot work?"

"Madame, my husband's spine is twisted. The doctor said it is lucky he can walk."

"What doctor? Our village healer is not enough?"

Then Fariza burst into tears. "I don't understand. The village healer has been giving us ointment to rub on his back for many moons now. I have been paying so much paisa every month for this medicine." She produced a betel leaf in which the medicinal paste was carefully wrapped. "She promised me he would get well."

"But he is not getting well." Malika's voice was firm. "We had to carry my father to the Doctor Saab who comes from Nalgonda."

The doctor travelled monthly from the nearby town to provide medical treatment to the villagers. Usually peasants would form a long line, but because his condition was so grave, Gulaam had been seen immediately. The doctor explained that while the ointment had helped soften the muscle, it did nothing to improve his condition. It was not muscle pain that he suffered from but trauma to his vertebrae, perhaps caused by a severe blow to his spine. Her husband could struggle to work in his condition, but in a month or less he might lie down and never get up. His only chance of healing would be to pay for an operation. The doctor would appeal on Fariza's behalf to the Nizam's hospital charity to cover the cost of the operation, but she would need to pay for Gulaam's room while he recovered in hospital.

"The doctor is leaving tomorrow and will take my husband. I must pay the money before they leave." Fariza grasped her daughter's shoulders. "Malika is hard-working and will serve your household day and night until we can repay the loan. Look how strong she is. No sticks for arms, like other girls."

"I already have very good servants. And you," Veena wagged a finger at Malika, "are unruly."

Fariza gently moved Malika aside to appeal to Veena. "Amma, it would be only for a time until my husband recovers and goes back to the fields."

"I don't know why you people think you need an operation. I walk about with these corns on my feet and still we cannot afford the operation to have them removed. Go tend to your husband at home."

Malika followed her mother through the gates.

*

Moonlight fell upon the faces of Malika's siblings as they lay fast asleep in a row on the floor of their thatched hut. Malika watched her mother change into her only silk sari. It was red and worn for festivities. Fariza splashed water on her face and unbraided her thick plait, letting her hair fall loosely down to her waist. Gulaam woke and looked up at Fariza from his mat. She was fixing a jasmine flower behind her ear.

"You are going out at this time?"

Without glancing at her husband, Fariza left the hut.

Gulaam turned towards the wall. Then Malika crept from the hut and followed Fariza towards the bazaar. Those who knew how to make money and those with money to spend were still milling about. But many stalls were closing down. Govindu, one of the more notorious moneylenders, was still sitting behind the counter of his jewellery stall smoking a beedi. The counter was cluttered with stacks of glass bangles and other shiny objects. His shirt was open, his hairless chest and fat belly exposed. Malika hid behind an abandoned stall just opposite Govindu's. She noted that the shameless man didn't bother to cover himself when her mother approached. Fariza draped her palloo over her head.

"Hey, sister, you are looking for jewellery or something else to please you? What bangles can I tempt you with?"

He took a flirtatious tone. Fariza had told Malika that when she was a girl, Govindu had wanted to marry Fariza, but she had rejected him. Since then, he had grown richer and fatter and Fariza leaner and poorer.

"Arrey, Govindu, you know I have no desire for your pretty things. I've come on business."

"Wait, wait. Have some fresh lime juice with jaggery." He poured the cloudy liquid into a glass and stirred it vigorously.

Fariza emptied the juice down her throat. "Oh, such pleasure."

Malika resented her mother, thinking of how good the lime juice must be. It was such a rare treat for her and her hungry siblings at home.

Govindu leaned towards Fariza. "Now. That is much better, it will sweeten whatever words you have to say to me."

"I need money." Fariza lowered her voice. "One thousand rupiya at least. Maybe two thousand, if possible."

"Ah, you are tired of waiting for your good-for-nothing husband to buy you a gold nose ring."

"Please, I just need the money."

"But if you can't tell me the reason, why should I lend you the rupiya?" His tone had shifted.

"I see." Fariza lowered her head. "A woman is allowed no secrets? I must tell all and expose myself."

He smiled at this and waited.

"It is for my daughter." Fariza held onto the edge of the counter as if to steady herself. "Gulaam is arranging a match, but none of the other villagers know yet. The boy likes her but feels she is too dark. A dowry will help ease the arrangement."

"If she only resembled her mother."

"You are shameless to say such things. I am mother to five children. I am a musaldi, already so old."

"To me you are but a child, although a little soiled."

He stared at her breasts, grinning. His teeth were stained red with the betel nut. His mouth was grotesque. His fat fingers opened a lock box. "I have only one thousand here. I will get you the rest tomorrow, but you must stay. Come back behind the counter." Govindu gripped Fariza's wrist.

"I have to hurry back to the baby." Her voice was firm.

He closed the lid of the box.

The streets were now empty as Malika watched her mother slip behind the counter. Fariza stood very close to Govindu. Her shoulder and arm started moving slowly and rhythmically, then faster, until Govindu shouted out, burying his head in the bend of her mother's arm. Malika felt sick, disturbed, unable to define what had just happened.

Fariza threw Govindu off her, wiped her hand on his shirt sleeve, and opened the box, taking the money.

Govindu smirked. "You will come tomorrow?"

"I need the money in the morning."

Fariza started to walk away.

"As you said, you are too old. Bring me the black one. She will need to prepare for married life anyway."

Fariza folded the rupiya before tucking it into her blouse.

*

Malika followed her mother from the moneylender's stall through the dark streets of the village. Malika observed her mother's thick flowing hair, a jasmine flower tucked behind her ear, the silk sari hugging the curve of her hips. Malika felt both admiration and disgust. A group of peasants approached carrying torches.

"Stop the tax, stop the terror. Justice for Balamma."

They crowded the road, heading towards her mother. Malika could no longer keep quiet.

"Ammi, Ammi, be careful!"

Fariza turned.

"What are you doing here? Come!" Fariza gripped Malika's wrist, her nails digging into her flesh.

"Ammi, you're hurting me."

Fariza did not loosen her hold but ran with her daughter until they found a small alley and hid in a leather tanner's stall. The smell was pungent, not unpleasant. Malika drew in a deep breath. She saw the crowd gather outside the Reddy house, holding torches and yelling something to the landlord.

Fariza clasped Malika's face with both hands. "Not a word, you stupid, stupid girl."

*

At that same moment, Rayappa awoke with a film of sweat covering his body. His fever had risen and broken. Disoriented, he reached for the oil lamp that was not there and instead clutched one of the oxford shoes he had placed on the table. The other fell to the floor. Where was he? What was going on? He heard noises, voices, and drums beating. Rayappa could make out flashes of light beyond his curtain, seemingly emerging from behind the great blue doors. He put his hand on the wall seeking balance, the cement chalky under his palm. He grabbed his shawl and went into the courtyard. The flames from torches lit the black sky, and he heard a rhythmic chanting from beyond the wall: "Stop the tax, stop the terror."

Sivraj ran to the rain barrels and began filling small vessels with water. Other servants threw pebbles over the wall. Rayappa went to the gate to ensure it was locked. Through the crack between the great doors, he could make out a flash of white turbans. No one person was discernible. He turned and saw Connelly emerging dishevelled from the bullock house.

"Professor Connelly, we need help. I think the crowd will burn down the house."

"Let's gather water from this side and douse the doors."

As Connelly directed the servants to throw pails of water over the doors, they heard another commotion. A new group of men had arrived beyond the walls and shots were fired. Rayappa could make out Linga Reddy's voice.

"We will slaughter these pigs right here."

*

Malika's heart was beating hard and fast. She was sure the men on the street would hear it.

Peering out from behind the hanging animal hides, Malika recognized familiar faces. These were their people, labourers and peasants just like her family. Roughly forty men were scattered on the street. Some were talking, others chanting. They appeared confused as to what to do next. Why should she be frightened of them? Then two bullock carts loaded with other men in uniform, not her people, approached from both ends of the street. These strangers wielded torches, axes, and shotguns. They tore into the crowd and pushed them down.

Men shouted and waved to Linga. "Do not fear. The Razakars are here!"

The Razakars were a volunteer militia who used crude weapons to guard the deshmukhs' lands, protecting the Nizam's interests. Malika clutched her mother tightly, pressing her face into her shoulder.

*

Rayappa heard more shots ring out. The crowd was dispersing and howls of victory erupted from the other side of the wall. Rayappa and Connelly were relieved. Connelly approached the doors to the main house and found them locked. He pounded on them.

"How in bloody hell am I to get back into the house?"

Sivraj approached Connelly. "The landlord never answers when there is trouble. Best to remain here for the evening."

"Outside?"

Rayappa intervened. "You may have my cot if you wish."

Connelly accepted. Rayappa slept upright on the wicker chair on the veranda.

*

Malika and her mother huddled together even after the streets went quiet, frozen in a crouch behind the hides. It had been a long time since Malika had clung to her mother's body. The sky was lightening. They would have to hurry to get home before sunrise for prayer.

"It's okay. There is no one. No bodies." Fariza peered out into the street.

Malika was frightened. Why did her mother say that? Malika wished they could wait until daybreak when people would begin their morning rituals and could provide protection. Then she realized how her mother was dressed. If they were caught, they would certainly be in danger. It had been years since women and girls in the village had worn flowers in their hair or any other adornments. They dressed modestly to dissuade landlords and goondas from claiming them. Malika pulled the jasmine from her mother's hair. Fariza glanced at Malika but said nothing. Instead, she smoothed and quickly plaited her hair, and she and Malika crept as quickly as they could past the artisans' stalls and the well, and up the footpath towards their home.

*

Rayappa wrapped his shawl tightly around him and drew his legs close to his body, curling uncomfortably in the wicker chair. He was jolted out of his sleep by the sound of the great blue doors being flung open. Linga Reddy and his boys entered the courtyard in the cart. The driver dismounted, unhitched the animals and led them to the bullock house while a servant latched the gate behind him. Linga jumped off the cart and strode up the veranda stairs.

"Tea!"

The doors to the main house miraculously opened from within and welcomed the triumphant heir. Rayappa shifted uncomfortably. Linga's white shirt was streaked with dirt and blood.

1997 — The Krishna Lodge

In 1997, the Krishna Lodge looks much the same as it did in the 1970s, though a little worse for wear. The rooms are small, basic, and clean, each with a double cot, table, and sink. A shared bath and squat toilet are down the hall. Jaya will have to teach Anya toilet etiquette. While Jaya unpacks her bag, Anya looks through the desk drawer. "I, Anya Peter, intend to write my memoir of my first trip to India, if only I could find a pen." Anya finds a sheet of paper with house rules, which she reads aloud.

"Check out at two p.m., no entry after ten p.m., no water and electricity from two p.m. to five p.m. and then ten p.m. to five a.m."

"Hmm. That means we can't shower before Parveen picks us up."

"Can you soften the consonants when you say her name? It sounds too much like Darleen."

"What's wrong with Darleen?"

"And you will be pouring a jug of water over your head. There are no showers."

"I don't suppose there's a pool either?" Anya tosses the instructions aside.

"No pool, no hot water, princess."

Anya kicks off her shoes and collapses on the bed. "I'm not complaining, are you?"

"You could leave your shoes near the door."

Without getting up, Anya extends her leg and knocks her shoes across the room.

"I can't believe I raised you." Jaya rolls her eyes at Anya.

"You didn't. Anasuya did." There is no maliciousness in Anya's voice. Jaya was the working parent, the less present, more distant father figure. Or whatever she was. There is no name for her. She needs air.

"You sleep."

Anya has already dozed off, a faint whistle rising on her breath, reminding Jaya of Irwin.

It doesn't take long for Jaya to slip into her old self. She pulls on her thirty-year-old kurta pyjama set, drapes a chunni around her shoulders, and slips her feet into her worn-out chappals, which she continued to wear after leaving India. There is a slight discoloration of the leather at the big toe and at the heel, but her feet fit perfectly. Then she balances her one-armed sunglasses on her nose; the glasses fell from her head onto the carousel at the airport as she bent to retrieve her suitcase. Jaya prefers to fix rather than trash anything.

As Jaya closes the door behind her, she sees Irwin in the corridor. She wants to step out of sight but his eyes catch hers. She cannot really avoid him. They will be spending close to a month together here.

Jaya nods at Irwin.

"Do you need anything?"

"Washroom?"

"Farther down the hall. I am going for a walk." Jaya does not want to invite him and hopes he will not invite himself.

"The sun is bright. Good you are wearing those." He gestures to the glasses.

Jaya sighs, noting his attempt at conversation. She feels guilty for not responding, and takes off her sunglasses. She tilts the one-armed frame, showing Irwin the damage. "I'll see if I can get these fixed."

Stepping onto the road, Jaya is struck by the heat. The wind doesn't cool her but it caresses her skin, reminding her that she is a sensual being. She feels sexy, her feet elegant in the leather sandals, the slight heel elevating her slim figure and elongating her strong calves. It is odd to feel this way on the dusty road, surrounded by the cacophony of traffic and smell of exhaust. Plopping the sunglasses lopsided on her face, she peeks into a fabric emporium, a teashop, the public telephone, and computer cubicles, noting the spaces occupied by men and those that welcome women.

A chauffeured Toyota pulls up in front of Hollywood Shoes, an Indian franchise. An elegant, elderly man wearing a crisp white shirt steps out of the car. People on the street turn, recognizing him. An old woman disfigured by leprosy stands near the door of Hollywood Shoes and thrusts out her hand, fingers truncated. The wealthy man passes directly in front of her and disappears inside the store.

The woman's grey sari is threadbare and barely covers her naked, sagging breasts. As Jaya approaches the steps to the store, the woman catches her eye. Jaya wants to escape into the air-conditioned comfort of Hollywood Shoes, but the one-second hesitation leaves her cornered.

The woman appeals to her. "Amma?" She stretches out the last syllable. Jaya knows that Anya would have handed over whatever she drew from her purse. It would be an uncomplicated gesture. Jaya is irritated with herself. She isn't the shocked and sympathetic Westerner who falls prey to every beggar on the street. She grew up understanding the perversely tipped scales, the normalcy of suffering, and the resignation of India's middle class *to the way things are* or how they convince themselves that *these people's lives are not so bad*.

Kanta and Irwin made generous donations every Sunday to the mission to educate orphans. Irwin sat on the board of directors governing a school for the blind. Later, Kanta trained and organized volunteers to work at a home for the destitute. Despite the charitable donations from its citizens, the efforts of non-governmental organizations, not to mention international aid, the abject poverty had not diminished throughout Jaya's life in India or, it seemed, after she left. Poverty is entrenched in the system. It is romanticized by the middle class. It is politically willed by those in power.

Jaya unzips and rummages through her handbag, withdrawing a wad of Indian rupees. She cannot decide what is appropriate. Various exchange rates flutter through her mind. Her fingers are unable to grasp individual bills, so she ends up handing a bunch of notes to the woman and then turns, bumping into an elderly man, one-legged, with a crutch.

"Amma?"

Jaya hands him some notes and reaches for the door, but it is blocked by yet another beggar, and then another.

Jaya hunches her shoulders and covers her head. Suddenly the door opens and the elegant, elderly gentleman bellows.

"Po, po. Get away, all of you!"

He leads Jaya into the store. He inquires if she is okay.

She catches her breath. "Yes, really I am fine. Thank you."

But she is shaken, and his condescension, which normally would have been unbearable, is welcome.

"Sorry, my English is not the best."

"That's fine. I speak Telugu."

"Oh. America is it?" He continues speaking in English.

"Canada." Jaya takes off her sunglasses. "Excuse me, but do you know where I could get these fixed. I've been looking up and down the street and..."

The man examines the frames. "Not here, I am afraid. Only shoes. It is best to buy a new pair at the airport when you return to..."

"Toronto, Canada."

"Do you mind me asking where you are staying?"

"My family and I are staying at the Krishna Lodge."

"I am afraid Korampally does not have the best accommodations."

The elderly gentleman reaches into his shirt pocket and draws out a pair of sunglasses.

"Take these. They are men's glasses, but who can tell the difference these days? It may suffice for your stay."

"That is too generous."

The man deposits the case into Jaya's hands and heads briskly towards the door with his packages. Then he stops and turns.

"What is your name?"

"Jaya."

"I thought so. Linga Reddy at your service."

Jaya watches him through the window as he heads to his car. The beggars maintain a respectful distance as Linga Reddy passes. The hills beyond seem strangely diminished in his presence.

5. The Landlord's House

Like Rayappa's fever breaking at night, the tension in the village quickly dissipated. Rayappa sat on the veranda sipping tea and eating potato bhajis with Connelly, listening to Reddy explaining the recent protests.

"The peasants have to let off some steam. Our job is to remind them of the order of things. They will be grateful to me for allowing Gandhi to visit."

"What was that?" Connelly sat up in his chair.

"Our local priest Ragaviah declared he would fast until death unless Gandhi paid a visit to Korampally. After a week of Ragaviah consuming nothing but water, Gandhi capitulated to Ragaviah's demands and agreed to visit our humble village. Perhaps Gandhi cannot bear someone else fasting for a cause."

Rayappa cleared his throat. "But sir, how could that be? So many satyagrahis have fasted for causes. It is one of Gandhiji's most effective acts of non-violent resistance against the British."

Connelly beamed. "Well done. Didn't Ragaviah set up the satyagraha ashram in Gandhi's name?"

Reddy slowly clapped his hands three times. "The Gandhi Centre. Yes. Gandhi is no slouch. Quite the businessman. Birla, the industrialist, has financed ashrams all over India to teach Gandhi's philosophy. They even established ashrams in our Muslim-led Hyderabad."

Rayappa asserted himself again. "But Reddy, sir, given the protests here in Korampally, it may be a good thing that the peasants are exposed to Gandhi's teachings, is it not? If they want to protest, better to do so peacefully than to take up arms."

"I have no issue with Gandhi's methods to overthrow the British, as long as he doesn't try to overthrow the Nizam. Our peasants are grumpy because the harvest is not so good, but they are happy with the Nizam's leadership. Mohandas Gandhi has no business in Hyderabad, but his followers will not stop wasting away until they see his face on the Nizam's turf."

"Still you are loyal to the Nizam, even while most of the subcontinent has already united under India." Connelly sat back in his chair and smiled.

"Nehru and his Congress Party are quite deluded to think that Hyderabad or Kashmir will join India. The Nizam has withstood the British and will endure the Indian Union."

Rayappa dared not speak another word, afraid he might somehow jinx Gandhi's visit. But he could no longer manage his anticipation. "Will Gandhiji actually come? Even at such a time? Is he not in Delhi calming the Hindu and Muslim conflict? What about the peace talks, the prayers? India has been independent of the British a mere three months and there is so much conflict."

"You have a point, Rayappa." Connelly heaped more bhajis onto his plate. "But even if Gandhi leaves crowd control to the politicians, you would think he would visit Kashmir over Hyderabad."

Reddy poured some of the steaming tea into a saucer to cool. Then he brought it to his lips to sip. He set it down and grimaced.

"Yes. Well, Gandhi too is a politician. These lands are too rich to be ignored. And there is this business of the United Deccan States, where all the regions of Telangana are under one political umbrella. Gandhi will come south to calm any pro-Pakistani agitation in the area, and then Nehru and his Congress will claim the glorious Kingdom of Hyderabad."

"This may be the moment." Connelly patted his belly. "Perhaps Gandhi's presence will turn the tide, and force Hyderabad to choose India."

Rayappa thought about this. Can one use force and still offer people a choice?

"It will not be given up so easily." Reddy stretched and yawned. "The Nizam knows what his kingdom is worth. Meanwhile, I am in the awkward position of having to play host to Gandhi."

Rayappa was ecstatic. Connelly seemed intrigued. Gandhi the Bania had risen above his merchant caste, turned his Oxford education into a tool to challenge British authority. Gandhi the Mahatma could convince people to use passive resistance to challenge the Nizam, a seemingly benevolent but autocratic ruler. And Gandhi the politician could arrive with a strategic agenda to claim Hyderabad and unite India.

Reddy slurped the last of the tea from his cup and set it upon the table with a clatter. "We will provide a field, invite the villagers to attend, and offer ample food. You watch, the peasants will learn from Gandhi the importance of village customs. And with the mayhem rocking the rest of India, they will

appreciate the relative peace in Korampally. They will return to their work
and cease their pointless demands."

*

As Rayappa worked on his survey of agricultural and household customs,
it was obvious that the villagers had urgent matters on their minds. Each
question Rayappa asked was a jumping-off point to talk about their problems: the excise duty, the upcoming harvest, the unreasonable grain quota,
and the ensuing punishment for noncompliance. Rayappa began to wonder
if Gandhi's visit would placate them or the opposite: would it raise their
consciousness? Would it inspire advocacy and further agitation? Did Reddy
really think the peasants would stop their ears to Gandhi's pledge of a more
equitable society?

A few days earlier he had happened upon Fariza on the hillside. She
explained that her husband was away in hospital and that the Nizam's charity
had donated the funds for his operation. "Only we are left to harvest. It has
been so dry that we need to find water to irrigate the plot every day. Who
can do all this? Now every brother, father, mother, and sister on the hillside
must help me. But they are busy saving their own crops."

What Rayappa observed but did not note in his survey was the change he
saw in Fariza. She appeared distant and unaware that her palloo dropped,
at times revealing her cleavage. Her hair was unkempt, and traces of kohl
shadowed her eyes.

Rayappa witnessed much during his interviews that he did not divulge
in his reports to Reddy. Connelly and Rayappa were invited to take coffee
on the veranda and update Reddy on their research. While Connelly could
not be bothered and did not feel obliged to speak of his research, Rayappa
happily explained the bathing rituals of the Kapu caste versus the hygienic
habits of the Malas, the marriage traditions of the Nakkala caste, and the rites
of passage for boys and burial ceremonies of the Gudi Eluguvallu Muslims.
Reddy took delight in every detail of the customs and habits of his village.
He was equally curious about British rituals and pulled Connelly into the
conversation. Reddy asked about the terrible diet chosen by a nation that had
the world's culinary skills at its command and pondered the infamous class
hierarchies, which somewhat mimicked and lent logic to India's own ancient
caste system. Connelly tried to escape such conversations, claiming his Irish
ancestry left him disinterested in British culture. Rayappa, on the other hand,
was impressed by Reddy's ardent interest.

Connelly called for more coffee. "Reddy, my young protege is no doubt impressing you with his research?"

"Indeed. You have invested well in this lad. An intellectual experiment and charitable act."

Rayappa smiled uncomfortably. He had become used to Reddy's back-handed compliments. Still, they irked him.

Suthiya came running across the courtyard.

Veena Reddy's voice followed, sharp and loud. "Ungrateful girl!" Veena was at Suthiya's heels, her hand raised, gesturing a slap. "Go back to the bullock house and don't ever ask me for leave again."

"Hush, hush," Reddy scolded his wife. "Settle those things elsewhere."

"It is all right." Connelly heaved himself out of the wicker chair to face Veena. "Please don't shift a thing on our behalf. Go about your business as if we were not here."

"We could all go about our business if she cleaned the latrines properly." Veena stood directly in front of her husband, hands on her hips. "And then this girl asks to go to her village for Makar Sankranti. She thinks she can leave for five weeks with nobody left to work in her place."

Reddy grunted.

Veena used the tail of her palloo to wipe her sweaty face. "When we bought Suthiya from her parents with a sack of grain, she became ours. She ceased having a mother or father and has no reason to go back to her village."

"You purchased her, Veena, now she is your burden."

Connelly sat back down and shifted uncomfortably in the chair. "You know this vetti tradition will soon be a thing of the past, why not loosen the grip? Even the Nizam is being pressured to reform. The world is calling for the abolition of all forms of slavery."

Veena turned coolly towards Connelly as Reddy spoke. "He has a point. What do you think, Veena? Should we let the girl go? Or be viewed as criminals?"

Veena did not level her argument at Connelly but at her husband. "Certainly. Cart us all off to prison. But ask that girl where she would rather be, at home in her village eating grass, or here? Two meals a day, a place to sleep. If not for us, her father would have sold her elsewhere, to someone who would have starved her or worse."

Veena looked in Connelly's direction but avoided eye contact. "You do not know how generous we are to her. If she goes, the latrines will be left *unclean*."

"Is there not someone else to do the cleaning?" Connelly wiped his brow with his hand.

"Gandhiji himself cleans his own latrine," Rayappa quietly stated. "There is no reason why we cannot do the same."

Reddy looked up to the sky. "Interesting."

"Indeed." Connelly smiled. "We must take this on. A pilot project! What do you say, Reddy?"

"Five weeks! She wants five weeks." Veena was emphatic.

"Veena, do not argue with these men." Reddy stretched his big arms over his head and yawned. "They are correct. They are always correct."

Rayappa thought Reddy was warming to the teachings of Gandhi. "Do you know that Gandhiji lived with untouchables, or Harijans, as he calls them?"

"Yes, of course."

Rayappa was impressed with Reddy. "He has even published a journal in their name. I have a Harijan issue in my room if you would like to read it."

"I wonder if he eats their food. Now that would be a test. Like cleaning the latrines." Reddy smiled charmingly, glancing from Rayappa to his sour-faced wife.

"Perhaps we start with cleaning the latrines and contemplate a change of diet later. What do you think, Reddy?" Connelly finished his last bit of coffee and firmly set his cup on the table.

"Fine then. Sankranti is but five weeks away. Let the girl go." Reddy waved off his wife.

"Then you will have to clean the latrines yourselves." Veena made her way back into the house.

*

Days later, Rayappa held a handkerchief to his nose and entered the dry latrine, an open-air cement stall with waist-high divisions where one could do one's business. As there were no doors, the latrine was positioned behind the bullock house and opened out to an alley. To clean it, a servant had to scoop up the excrement with whatever implement they had and deposit it into a basket to be left on the roadside. The basket would then be carried by hand or on the head to the village dump some distance away, usually by scavengers, the derogatory name for people who did sanitation work. The latrine had not been cleaned for two days, since Suthiya had left for her village.

Reddy had instructed that each person in the household would clean up after himself, but as piles of feces increased every day, Rayappa suspected that the male residents were not doing their part. Reddy had ordered a servant to leave a shovel in the latrine, but it was clearly unused. Rayappa grabbed it and began the distasteful task. He found it strange that some servants were insulted and opposed to this chore, while they could and did the same for the animals. He was less bothered by the servants' resistance than Connelly's neglect of doing his fair share. It had been Connelly who first supported the idea. Rayappa filled up the basket and left it for someone else to take to the dump. He went straight to the bathing-sinks, spread ash on his hands, and vigorously washed them again and again.

*

The cot was becoming less comfortable and the authentic experience less romantic. Rayappa stretched out his legs and wiggled his toes. He turned onto his side then onto his back and readjusted the shawl below his armpits, over his shoulders, and finally flung it off altogether. He picked up the oxfords and touched them in the darkness. The smell of leather, the smooth tapered toe, and the straight-bar lacing reminded him of his father. How he longed to please him and make him proud of his progress in school. He remembered his school days when he would sit cross-legged on the classroom floor, feel the edge of his slate balanced on his lap. He would join other boys in a rhythmic high-pitched greeting to the headmaster of the Mission School. "Good morning, sir. God bless you, sir."

Even these fond memories could not lull Rayappa to sleep. There was a rumour circulating among the servants that Dr. Connelly was molesting one of their own. Rayappa asked Sivraj about the truth of such a rumour, but the servant said nothing. Rayappa felt compelled to defend his mentor, but remembered Connelly emerging from the bullock house on the night of the protest. Since then, Rayappa had awoken periodically to strange noises and the sight of Connelly passing ghost-like through the courtyard at night.

Was it true? Had Professor Connelly meddled with Suthiya in the bullock house? The little girl that Connelly had championed, supporting her wish to visit her parents? Where was his sense of decency? Was this some bizarre attempt on Connelly's part to emulate the native? Eat their food, wear their dress, fornicate with their women and girls? This was not civilized.

Once again, Rayappa heard odd animal sounds and shuffling from the bullock house. There must be some explanation. Perhaps an animal in heat. He would find out what was happening, dispel the rumours, and then get some sleep.

Cattle and buffalo were just visible in the stall. Rayappa stood transfixed. Thrusting out of the darkness was a pair of white buttocks. A long strand of hair swung beyond the man's hips. Suthiya's plait? Had she come back?

Rayappa whispered, "God help me. God forgive him."

He summoned the courage to confront the professor but knocked against the watering trough and stumbled. Dr. Connelly did not seem to notice but someone else had. There on the floor, lying down on the kunti vadu's mat, was a girl. Suthiya? She propped herself up, her elbow resting against her ewe. She looked towards Connelly and then back to Rayappa, yawned, and lay back down. Rayappa was bewildered. What was she doing here? He turned back to the white hips, the movement of something, swishing. A tail, not a plait. An animal, not a girl. Dr. Connelly was standing on a footstool pressed up against the flank of an animal. And only a few feet away, Suthiya witnessed the defilement of her sacred cow.

*

"How can this be?" Rayappa asked Veena early the next morning. He stood holding Suthiya's hand on the veranda.

"Suthiya, why did you come back?" Veena spoke in an odd singsong voice and gave Suthiya a threatening look, glaring and smiling at the same time.

Rayappa interjected, "She has been here all along. Hidden in the bullock house. And all these servants remained silent, feeding her at night to maintain the illusion. Bringing her food and water like a prisoner."

"What business is it of yours to go into the bullock house?"

Rayappa decided not to share what he had witnessed there. He would confront the professor in private.

Veena dusted off her hands. "You wanted to clean the latrines? You had your wish."

The landlord sat quietly on the wicker chair, waiting for his wife to calm down. Suthiya stood, one hand in Rayappa's firm grip, the other hand rubbing her eyes as she adjusted to the sunlight.

"Sit, Suthiya. Eat your food and then resume your work." Veena waved the child away.

"Veena, you will wake the roosters with such trouble. The professor is still asleep, our sons too."

"Then *you* deal with your house guest." Veena glared at Rayappa. But instead of stomping away, she waited to hear her husband's explanation.

"Well, Mr. Rayappa, we had a little fun at your expense. No harm intended. We certainly could not part with our girl for five weeks. It takes almost as long to travel there and back by foot to her village. So we tested your Gandhian principles. Neither Connelly, my sons, nor I managed a passing grade. You alone, sir, are the winner of this social experiment."

Rayappa blushed and glanced at Suthiya. She seemed indifferent to their conversation, sitting cross-legged at the bottom of the veranda steps, lapping up the last bit of dal and rice. He could not fathom that they would make this child suffer just for the pleasure of seeing him humiliated. Or maybe she didn't suffer. She stayed in the darkness for two days, was given food, and allowed to sleep. Who was he to judge suffering? But this lie, the very effort of it, incensed him.

Rayappa folded his arms across his chest. "I, for one, can continue cleaning my own mess, but I hope others could do the same."

"And they may have to." Reddy's apologetic tone now turned grim. "My wife has already sold the girl to a landlord in Warangal district. They will fetch her tomorrow."

Suthiya cried out. She threw herself on the ground before Veena's feet.

"No, Amma, please do not send me away. I will stay and clean. I will never ask to leave again. Amma, Amma."

Rayappa was horrified. "But that is senseless. You needn't do that. It is my fault for interfering. Reddy, sir, I apologize. Please, let her stay."

Reddy stared past Rayappa to the little girl who wept at the feet of his wife. "She has insulted my wife by asking to leave. Veena, have her bathe and dress up. Then bring her to me."

Then Rayappa witnessed something extraordinary. Sivraj and the two servants who were sweeping the courtyard dropped their brooms with a clatter and turned their backs on Reddy. Apart from a sly smile that spread across his face, Raghunandan Reddy appeared unaffected by this act of defiance. He neither reprimanded the servants nor ordered them back to work. Rayappa imagined that this was not the first time that the servants had expressed their disapproval. Veena, who had been glaring at her husband, turned the same contemptuous look to Rayappa. Then she ordered the child to follow her to the back of the house.

"Reddy, sir, I beseech you. She is a child. There was no intention to disrespect you or your wife."

Reddy watched his wife and the child move out of earshot. "I would have waited another year or two, until she was of age." Reddy twisted a large gold ring on his finger then heaved his body out of his chair. "But what can I do, she will be gone from here tomorrow. And what's more, sold at a loss."

Then the landlord disappeared into the house.

*

After Suthiya's departure, the Reddys hardly spoke to Rayappa. Not that this bothered him, but the quiet camaraderie he had shared with the servants also ceased. They blamed him for Suthiya's expulsion and her degradation at the hands of the landlord. Even Sivraj, who exchanged bows with Rayappa in the morning, avoided him now. To add to his stress, Rayappa felt that Connelly knew that he had discovered his secret. Embarrassment, guilt, and accusation weighed heavily between them. Connelly's nightly visits to the bullock house ended abruptly. But the quiet nights that followed did not restore Rayappa's sleep.

While he should have been in the fields interviewing and observing the peasants, Rayappa found himself spending long hours alone in his room, avoiding work, meals, and conversation. Rayappa wanted his mother, her soothing voice and reassuring hand upon his forehead. He also missed his father, whom he had looked up to and wished better to understand. His father had given him his Christian name after Lord Irwin, the viceroy of India from 1925 to 1934. In 1927, when Rayappa was born, Lord Irwin had been negotiating with Gandhi, trying to quell Indian civil disobedience and promising eventual dominion status for India. Had Rayappa's father, by naming him so, hoped that his son might exude such influence and power? And if this was the case, why had his father abandoned him? Perhaps his father came to regret this name, given Lord Irwin's spineless appeasement of the Nazis. Rayappa felt a familiar churn of anxiety and turned to his notes to ease his distress. But even reflecting on his research into the matrimonial ceremonies of the Kapu caste could not stimulate his interest. Rayappa was deeply depressed.

It was dawn. Rayappa shifted in his cot when he became aware of women's voices in the courtyard.

"Dorasani, I thank you and I will be forever at your service. May you and your children thrive."

Rayappa recognized Fariza's voice. He stretched and pulled the curtain back from his doorway. Veena Reddy stood in the courtyard, her back to him, facing Malika and her mother at the gate.

"You will see she is a hard worker."

"We will keep her here until her father returns and you pay the tax."

Rayappa dressed quickly to greet Malika, but she was listening attentively to Veena's instructions.

"Begin with the men's latrines there, and then the women's in the back of the house. Don't rely on the other scavengers to pick up the baskets. You will have to carry the waste to the dump. I do not need to tell you where that is."

"Yes, Amma."

"You will eat on the steps and sleep in the bullock house. There is a mat inside. And keep to yourself. I don't like idle chatter. The housemaid will tell you what you need to know."

Veena returned to the house, and Malika picked up an empty basket at her feet and walked past him. Rayappa noted her straight back as she disappeared behind the bullock house. Then he bent over the bathing sinks, scooped up a cup of water, and washed his face. He couldn't stop himself from smiling.

*

Malika woke at 4 a.m. She swept the courtyard and filled two large brass vessels with water from the rain barrels and lifted them with difficulty onto the grate over the fire pit. Malika tied her chunni over her nose. She had not gotten used to the putrid smell that crawled up her nostrils and down the back of her throat as she shoveled and scraped the shit from the dry latrines. She left the basket of excrement on the road to take to the dump later. When she returned to the fire pit, the water was heated. Although she was not permitted to use hot water, Malika discretely ladled water from the men's vessel to wash her hands, face, and feet, and to rinse her chunni. She hung her chunni to dry before carrying the second vessel of water to the back of the house for Veena, Aditi, and Lalita. She hoped they would bathe quickly so the water wouldn't cool, requiring her to repeat the whole task.

Malika seldom saw Lalita. She was quiet and kept to herself. If Lalita left the house, it was from the back and always in the company of her mother-in-law. On these rare occasions Lalita wore a long burqua covering her from head to toe. Aditi, on the other hand, loved dressing up and going out. She was not as pretty as Lalita, but she was playful and confident. Malika found this to be an attractive feature and admired Aditi. Surendra's young wife soon befriended and confided in Malika.

"Because Lalita is so fair and beautiful, Veenamma thinks it is best that she be kept away from the landlord's eyes. And other men in general. It is safer for everyone. Lalita comes from a rich family and has never dressed this way in Hyderabad, but Veenamma says that's our secret."

Aditi would often ask Malika to accompany her to the well. She would lag behind the others and allow Malika to walk beside her rather than many paces behind. This way they could talk. On such an outing, Malika looked to the hills and saw her sister stumbling down the path, waving with her free hand, the other clutching a clay pot. Malika waited for Sayeeda as Aditi continued on ahead with other women.

"Sister, the jeetagadu came today. He says that Abbu refused to pay his tax from the past two years."

Malika was astonished. "Our father would never refuse."

"Ammi does not believe the jeetagadu either. She says she keeps the accounts, and she is certain Abbu paid the excise up until this year. The jeetagadu is doing this because Abbu is in hospital and cannot protect her."

Malika watched the line of women at the well grow longer and worried for her sister.

"Poor Ammi." Malika took her sister's free arm as they walked towards the well. "Tell me something. Does she go out at night?"

Sayeeda's face fell. Malika immediately regretted her question.

"Ammi says you will have to work here longer. Three things we must pay, the tax, the debt, and our quota."

"Don't worry. Tell Ammi I will stay here until we pay all our debts. Tell her to sleep."

Later, when the women returned from the well and went into the house for their afternoon naps, Malika found herself alone. She did three things she was not supposed to do. She stepped up onto the veranda, she sat down in the cane chair, and she closed her eyes to rest.

"Good day." Rayappa stood at the bottom of the steps.

Malika jumped up.

"Would you be so kind as to heat some water for my bath?"

Malika was irritated that Rayappa woke her and demanded more from her. Why hadn't he bathed in the morning with the others? He was such an odd person. Yet she was grateful that Rayappa hadn't reprimanded her, or worse, told Veena that she had been sitting in the chair. While she did not dread her own punishment, she understood that the consequences of being thrown out of the house would have a devastating effect on her family.

The stone fire pit still had some dry pats of cow dung and sticks left over from the morning's fire. Malika added some leaves and twigs and started the fire quickly. As the flames rose, she filled the brass pot with water. Rayappa helped her set it on the grate.

"I hope you don't mind me watching you. I have already learned the hard way how to clean the latrine. Now perhaps I can make my own fire. You won't have to do this for me anymore."

"How will you finish your work if you are cleaning the latrine and making the fire?"

"I don't work every hour of the day. And I need a break from reading and writing. These chores will provide a good distraction."

"You would rather clean the latrines than do your reading?"

"Not quite, but one cannot repeat the same task without some boredom."

"I thought people smart enough to read do not like real work."

"Smart enough to read. Anyone can read. Wait here a moment."

Rayappa fetched his notebook and pen from his room and returned to her. He sat on the ledge by the wall and showed Malika the records he had made of their survey.

"Do you see this?"

Rayappa pointed out the cursive writing in his notebook. "The professor's book will be published in English, so I generally write my notes in English."

"They look like swirls of hair."

"Yes. And here is a word in Urdu. I record the names of people I meet in both English and their language. This is your name. Ma—li—ka."

"My name?" Malika studied the Arabic characters. "Our imam named me."

"Really. That is a special honour. Malika means queen in Urdu."

"I know that."

"Would you like to try?"

Rayappa wrote Malika's name slowly from right to left and handed her the pen. Malika silently traced the letters that Rayappa had written.

"I'm impressed. Your writing is quite precise. Especially for a beginner."

Then Rayappa pointed to and sounded out the names of her mother, her father, and her sisters in the notebook.

Over the next few days, Rayappa taught Malika to write letters of the Urdu alphabet. He would ask her to pronounce each one and then extend and blend them to sound out a word. He showed her how to recognize the difference between Urdu, English, and Telugu. Their lessons took place mid-afternoon while Sivraj and the servants went out and the Reddy household napped.

The heat was heavy and the courtyard silent. Malika sat cross-legged in the shaded threshold of Rayappa's room with the curtain pulled open. Rayappa checked her calligraphy.

"Tell me the truth now. You have never been to school?"

"No."

"And your parents do not read or write?"

"How could they? But they tell me stories."

"Tell me one."

"My father told me that the Nizam visited Korampally and was introducing his new baby to the villagers, but he was so greedy for taxes and grain that he took the gunny sacks and forgot the child."

"He left you behind, his princess."

Malika laughed. "Yes. My mother scolded my father for his story. 'A black princess as the Nizam's daughter?' But my clever father said that he was afraid that the Nizam would come back for me, and so he covered me with soot. The soot seeped so deep into my skin that it could not be rubbed off."

Rayappa was enraptured. "You inherited the Nizam's intelligence, your parents inherited you, and you forfeited your fortune."

"Yes. But I inherited fresh air! Who wants to be hidden away in a palace all day?"

Rayappa grew quiet. Although this was just a story, he felt it contained truth. Malika shone with rare potential. He was reminded of a poem by Thomas Gray and recited it to Malika.

> Full many a gem of purest ray serene,
> The dark unfathom'd caves of ocean bear;
> Full many a flow'r is born to blush unseen,
> and waste its sweetness on the desert air . . .

Malika frowned, not understanding.

"Never mind," Rayappa said. "Continue."

But instead of practising her letters, Malika drew a hammer and sickle. "I see this image painted on the walls."

"Ah, it is the symbol found on the flag of the Soviet Union. A country ruled under the ideology of communism."

Rayappa could see that Malika didn't understand. "There are some people in a far-off country that believe everyone should own and work the land together. That there should be no rich or poor, where everyone is equal."

"Really? Such a place?"

"An egalitarian society is good in theory, but someone always craves power and seeks to overthrow the other. Democracy ensures no one person retains power for too long. It promotes reformation not revolution. For instance, in a democracy the people can advocate for laws that would ensure that even servants are treated well. A law that could protect the right of the landlord to be happy in his home, and be fair to you, so that you can be happy in yours."

Malika reflected on this. The landlord was already happy in his house. Was it not her turn? Her father's turn, her mother's?

"The problem is that the Bolsheviks in Russia murdered their former king and queen and all their children. That happened in 1917, right after the revolution. But in the thirty years since, the Russian people have experienced starvation, autocratic rule, and many atrocities. Was it worth that? And is everyone happier? They may enjoy collective benefits, but their freedoms are curtailed."

Rayappa continued talking, but Malika could no longer hear his words. She dreamed of the faraway country where people ploughed the fields, sang songs, and shared meals. There was no main house, no landlord, no debt. Her family could be happy there.

*

Malika hated sleeping in the bullock house. She pulled the mat outside and positioned it close to the veranda so she would hear the unlocking of the doors, well before the landlord stepped outside. Lying on her back, she gazed up at the stars and listened to the sounds in the compound: the snores of the servants, the chirping of crickets, the beat of her own heart. She longed to smell the jasmines but could only smell herself. And she stank. She was angry about having to clean up the Reddy shit, but her anger made her feel alive. Something in her was ticking like a bomb. She thought about the faraway country where everyone was equal and compared this with the life she knew. Two nights ago, as Malika brought water to the back of the house for Veena's evening bath, she saw her mother step into the compound from the alley. She wore a flower behind her ear, and her eyes were smudged with kohl. Malika called out, but her mother turned and fled through the same doorway back into the alley. What business did she have in the Reddy house at night? She thought her own labour had freed her mother from this ugly work.

Malika was filled with both despair and hope. Something inside her was urging her to act. She rolled up her mat quietly and put it back in the bullock house. A network of lianas, woody and intertwined, grew in the narrow space between the bullock house and the wall that surrounded the compound. It spread up the inner side of the wall but was hidden by the more delicate clinging vines of winter jasmine. The yellow flowers were in full bloom and cascaded over the wall. Just beyond the wall was the tamarind tree. Malika inched herself into the narrow space, taking care to not be seen. She hitched her sari up, pulled the fabric from the back between her legs and tucked it into the front of her waistband, dhoti-style. Stretching her arms as far as she could to clutch the thickest vine, she hoisted herself up and crawled onto the top of the wall. Catching hold of a branch, she swung onto the tamarind tree, wrapping her legs around a sturdy limb. She climbed down until it was safe to jump and landed in a squat on the road.

The bare soles of her feet hurt on impact, but still she ran down the road, far from the Reddy compound and their latrines, past the pink mandir, the artisans' stools, and the tanner's stall where she once hid with her mother. She continued down the main road and past the bazaar and Govindu's stand, the crossroads and peepal tree, across the fields, past the castrator's hut to the palm trees, and onto the footpath that led to the river. A film of sweat covered her skin and her eyes streamed tears. She was alive to every emotion and sensation in her body. No longer bothered by the sting of the cuts in the cracked soles of her feet, Malika ran on the pebbled ground. When she reached the river, it surprised her, like meeting a ghost in the dark. The river caught her in its arms and pulled her inside.

The sky was black. A slight breeze rippled the surface of the water as her limbs propelled her forward. When she was a toddler, her parents tied ropes around her and her sisters' waists and dunked them into the river to learn to swim. It had come back to her, the elegance of parting water. She knew she was strong. Fully clothed and fuelled with rage, Malika shed the stink, the shit, the Reddys' cruelty, her crumbling father and degraded mother. She swam across the expanse of the Vancha. It was impossible. But she did it.

Malika reached the other side, exhausted. The landscape was unfamiliar. Grass, soft and long, bent with the wind. The sky was aglow with starlight. The air was quiet and still. She was completely alone. Malika moved toward the faint outline of the forest, unwrapping her soaking sari. She wrung it out and spread it between two branches. She unplaited her long braid and shook out her hair. Then she removed her blouse and her underskirt and wrung out the water, the stench of the latrine, the heat of the day, the last of her shame. She hung these items on another branch. Malika stood amongst the trees, naked. She sloughed off remaining water from her arms and legs. Her feet and knees were calloused and rough, but the fronts of her legs were smooth, her inner thighs incredibly soft. She explored her vulva with her fingers and recognized for the first time her own feminine beauty.

Then she heard it. A rustling in the forest. Malika reached for her underskirt on the branch but it fell onto the ground, away from her. She hid behind a tree and watched a line of people perhaps six yards away walking single file, quietly and cautiously, carrying sacks over their shoulders. There were eight of them. At first she thought they were forest dwellers, but then she noticed some were wearing saris and dhotis and others were wearing trousers. Where were they going so late at night? From behind her came a man's voice.

"Who's there? Tell me your name."

Malika moved around the tree, away from his voice. She held her breath. Could he see her in the dark? She watched as the man walked towards her with a shuffle. No, a limp of some sort.

"Don't come closer." Malika's voice broke.

"Oh." The man sounded surprised. "Who are you?" Then he spoke in a gentler voice. "What are you doing here?"

"What are *you* doing here? Who are *you*?"

The man parted the branches. Malika retreated, moving farther away from him and her sari, which was suspended in the tree.

"Vijay. Vijay Pullaya. Alletodu, the basket weaver."

"Kunti Vadu?"

"Hmm. Some call me that. Others call me Guddi Kuntodu. Call me what you like. I am both blind and lame. I guess even you know me that way."

Malika felt ashamed. "You are truly blind? What is it like to not see anything?"

"I see things. I just see things differently than you."

"What things?"

"Light and darkness."

"But you can't see me?"

"No. But I can sense you. You are alone. A little afraid and very brave.

Like different degrees of light and darkness. Let's see. You are seventy per cent light, twenty per cent darkness and ten per cent something that lives in between."

"What are you talking about?"

Vijay laughed and moved past Malika, using a long stick to guide his way. "There's a spring just behind you. Would you like to drink some water?"

Malika understood that Vijay was unaware that she was naked. He crouched and cupped some water in his hands before bringing it to his mouth.

"Come here." He stood and turned, holding his cupped hands towards her. She quickly fetched her sari and wrapped it around her. Then she approached Vijay and drank from his hands. His wrist brushed against her wet sari.

"Your clothes are wet."

"I swam across the river."

"You swam the Vancha?"

"Yes." She laughed at his reaction. "More please."

Vijay filled his palms again. "Take your fill. This spring feeds the pond."

The pre-dawn light filtered through the forest canopy. Malika crouched and pulled the water towards her face, splashing it on her cheeks and throat. It was pure, clean, invigorating. She reached in again and the sari fell below her breasts. She turned to Vijay. His attention seemed to be drawn elsewhere. She remembered the line of people.

Vijay stood up. "Where do you live? We will not be alone for long."

Malika tightened the sari around her and walked towards the trees. "I have to go."

Vijay followed in her direction. "You cannot swim back across. The sun will rise and the boats will begin. It will be dangerous. I have a mule. You can ride alone and I can walk along with you if you like."

Malika looked to the sky, a rose blush. The sun still hadn't peered over the treeline. But it would be light before she got across the Vancha. She could see Vijay clearly now. He had a calm face.

"I'll take you through the forest, and we can cross the river by the shoal. It is narrow there. Then I can leave you on the other side, and you can walk the footpath to the village."

"Thank you. Can you wait for me by the river?"

Vijay nodded and smiled at her, a bright confident smile that revealed to Malika his beauty. Malika found her underskirt and blouse and hurriedly dressed. Vijay was waiting for her by the river with his mule.

"You brought your animal quickly. Do you live nearby?"

"Right there." Vijay gestured in the direction of a hut near the embankment.

"So close." Malika was alarmed that she had stood naked not far from this spot. She muttered thanks to God that it was Guddi Kuntodu, the blind man, who had discovered her.

"Does your family live there?"

"My mother. She is asleep."

"Only the two of you?"

"Yes."

Malika put her hand on the flank of the mule.

"Let me help you up."

Vijay interlaced his fingers, creating a step where she placed one foot. He hoisted her onto the mule.

"If we meet in the village, will you know me?"

"It depends. Sometimes I know a person by the sound of their voice, their smell, even the rhythm of their breathing. Sometimes, I just know. The question is, will you know me?"

Malika looked at Vijay. Long lashes fell against his smooth brown skin. She nodded yes. She wondered if he sensed this.

*

Malika balanced the basket of excrement on her head. The dump site was a fair distance, outside the village proper, up the hills, past her home. If she walked fast enough, she would have time to visit her family before returning to the Reddys'. As much as she wanted to see her family, she dreaded seeing the shadows beneath her mother's eyes.

As Malika moved from the footpath to the main road, she knew she reeked and that people were looking at her. She and her sisters had stared at others performing this duty, feeling sorry for them and slightly superior at the same time. Her father had told her that their family never had to do such work. Now she was the one who deserved pity.

As she approached the crossroads, she saw him. Alletodu, Kunti Vadu, Guddi Kuntodu, Vijay Pullaya. Before reaching the tree, she removed the basket from her head, setting it some distance away. She watched Vijay, knowing he could not watch her. He sat cross-legged, alone, his fingers threading one layer of straw through another. Slowly and quietly, she inched herself in front of him. Vijay had a straight nose slightly flared at the base, a firm chin, a

full sensual mouth, and long eyelashes. His skin was smooth like hers but not
so dark, his ears perfectly shaped, his neck long. He was beautiful.

"How long will you stand there and watch?" Vijay asked, not lifting his
head.

"I was not...you knew I was here?"

"I knew someone was there."

"Do you know who I am?"

"I know everything but your name."

She had withheld her name out of modesty. It seemed stupid now.

"Everything? There must be something I didn't tell you."

Vijay's face broke into a smile.

"My name is Malika. Malika Hajam. My father is Gulaam Rasool, my
mother is Fariza."

"As Salam u Alaikum."

"You speak Urdu?"

"Only that much. I listen and learn what I can."

"Then we are the same."

Vijay passed her a small oval basket that could fit in her palm. "For you."

"It is tiny. What can I carry in this? It has no use."

"It is not for you to use, it is for you to have."

"Have? What will I do with it?" Malika admired the lovely object in her
hand.

"Many people simply have things. They look at them, hold them, put them
away, and even forget about them."

"I know that. Bangles are not useful, but we wear them."

"You don't wear any."

How did he know her arms were bare, had been bare for many years?
Everything that her family once owned was disappearing, their land, food,
clothing, and small items of pleasure.

"I've been cleaning the latrines. What use are bangles with my work?"
Malika retreated a few steps, suddenly aware that Vijay might smell her and
be disgusted.

Vijay smiled. "I agree. You don't see me wearing bangles. They are unimportant to me."

Malika stared curiously at Vijay and then chuckled. "Then what is important to you?"

"This tree."

Malika looked up to take in the peepal tree, to see what made it so special. Its ordinary, thick, grey-brown trunk stood tall and split into large limbs that extended into branches giving birth to leaves that created the canopy above their heads. The leaves were waxy and broad, tapering to a fine point, with one clear vein in the centre from which smaller asymmetrical lines extended on either side.

"Anything else?" Malika sat cross-legged in front of Vijay.

"Yes. The fact that it is you and me and all the labourers and farmers who create both the useful and useless things that others have and forget."

Vijay put his weaving aside and picked up a stick. He drew lines in the dirt, and soon the lines became a tree, resembling the one they sat beneath.

"You see these leaves? They get the sun and the air and the rain. In addition, the leaves get water from the stems that suck from the branch. The branch is hard and sturdy, connecting both stem and trunk. The trunk, heavy and unmoving, is anchored by roots. And there, feel it." With his left hand, Vijay followed a long root that began midway down the trunk, extended above the ground before burying itself into the earth. "The roots pull water from the earth to feed all the life above. Does it sound familiar?"

Malika didn't know what to make of Vijay's question but was fascinated with how he guided the stick to loosen the dirt and yield an image. How was he able to create such a picture with only his imagination and sense of space?

"These leaves are the British. The stems, the Nizam. The branches, the landlords. The trunk, the workers, everyone that actually does something: selling, cooking, building, sewing. And below, sustaining everything, are the roots, the fundamental part of the organism. Most of the roots are hidden in the darkness, underground, away from light and heat and air and rain. That is us. The labourers, the peasants, the Madigas."

"I am Muslim."

Vijay continued. "We Madigas hold the tree in place, we enable the rest to live. But everyone else cannot see below the ground, nor do they want to see. And they are crushing us with their demands, growing stronger while we wither. Do you understand?"

"Of course. I'm not stupid, but I do not like it."

"And yet we all accept it."

"I mean I do not like your drawing. You are wrong. This peepal tree is lush and every part is precious. How can you compare the British, the Nizam, and the landlords to the precious stems and leaves?"

Vijay laughed, "Yes, you are right."

"The rulers are the ticks and parasites; the bugs, like the red caterpillar, chewing wood. Look, there is one." Malika picked it up and put it on Vijay's hand.

"Ah. I have been misguiding people with this story, drawing and explaining this over and over to teach—"

"Who do you teach?"

"Anyone. Anyone who cares to listen."

Malika stared at the bright red caterpillar crawling up Vijay's brown hand. The colour reminded her of the red silk sari against her mother's skin. "Doesn't it tickle?"

"It feels soft." Vijay gently picked it up and held it out to Malika.

"Hmm. The landlord is not the caterpillar either. It too is precious. Quite lovely. But it does eat our crop."

"Your lesson works better than mine." Vijay returned the caterpillar to the tree.

Malika stood, seeing Rayappa approach.

Rayappa nodded to Vijay and Malika. "Baaggannaaru. I am going to the Madigas' section on the hills to finish my observations."

Malika turned to Vijay. "This is the man who is staying at the Reddy household."

Vijay nodded to Rayappa.

"I am Rayappa Irwin. We met before. I was travelling with Professor Connelly. He bought a mat from you." Rayappa remembered that this mat was in the bullock house, the same mat upon which Malika slept. He felt a strange sense of intimacy with Malika, knowing this.

"The British gentleman who spoke Telugu?"

"Yes." Rayappa was surprised at Vijay's awareness. The young man did not seem mad at all, as others had said. "It is a good spot you have here."

Rayappa turned to Malika. "Shall we walk together?"

"I have that." Malika pointed to the basket of shit.

"I know. That is why I thought we may be walking in the same direction." Rayappa wished he could offer to carry Malika's basket, knowing he would not. "Remember, I too cleaned the latrines."

Malika tucked the little basket Vijay gave her into the waistband of her sari and said goodbye to Vijay. She hoisted the basket of excrement upon her head, leading Rayappa away from the peepal tree, towards the village dump.

*

The village dump, the repository for garbage, rotting fruit, animal carcasses, shit. Rayappa, who had started to question the notion of heaven and hell and any afterlife, imagined the dump to be the place where they would all end up, cremated or not, piled one on top of another, the landlord and the leper side by side.

Rayappa deplored the kind of work needed to maintain the dump, though he knew it was necessary. While he was convinced each should clean up after him or herself, he was relieved when Malika was hired. After her arrival he vowed he would never again interfere with the Reddy household.

Rayappa hoped to observe and record who visited, guarded, and managed the dump. It was a family business passed down father to son, mother to daughter, a monopoly controlled by the lowest rung of untouchables. The scavengers.

When he and Malika arrived, the vultures had gathered. Rayappa walked around the pit, waving off the flies, careful his chappals did not step on something soft. He observed that the pit was not only a repository for household waste but a communal bathroom for the poor. Children squatted in the open, while the adults found privacy in the surrounding shrubs. Rayappa pulled his kerchief to his nose.

Malika watched Rayappa as he watched her. She had no shoes but was sure-footed, knowing where to step, what to avoid. When she came to the edge, she grasped the rim of the basket on opposite sides and lifted it up from her head, swiftly flipping it over, emptying the contents into the pit. Noticing some shit had stuck to the bottom of the basket, she looked around for something with which to scrape it out. A piece of wood or a rock. These things were rarely found at a site where others also hunted for useful items. Malika remembered what Vijay said about useless items, aware of the small basket tucked beneath the folds of her sari. Then she looked at Rayappa, his feet clad in chappals. Hard soled, leather, clean. She simply stared until he removed one with his left hand and handed it to her.

"We will be able to clean it later."

Malika nodded, in gratitude. Without the chappal, Malika would have had to scrape the basket with her bare hand and then clean her hand by wiping it on the ground. She held the chappal by its toe and used the hard heel to scrape the shit from the bottom of the basket. Some caked under the heel and refused to dislodge. She looked at Rayappa with a smile and a shrug.

"It's a stubborn piece."

They both laughed and Rayappa gestured for her to give the chappal back. The two performed a little dance, trying to figure out how to pass the chappal without touching the shitty heel. Finally, Malika placed it on the ground and Rayappa carefully slipped his foot into it.

They walked through the fields where girls were pressing cowpats in their hands and piling them into neat pyramids. The pats would be used for fuel, and to patch leaking roofs or to reinforce walls of huts.

Malika called out to them, "Baaggannaaru! You are doing good work. You will soon be in the factory in Nalgonda."

The children laughed and invited her to join them.

"Maybe next year, when I get promoted."

A girl about Malika's age waved. "I will tell the boss you are a hard worker."

Rayappa noted Malika's sense of humour and her pride as they talked about the village, her family, and her desire to learn. Rayappa never imagined he could converse so easily with such a girl. She was so confident and he felt relaxed in her company. As they approached Malika's hut, she invited him to have tea.

*

Fariza brought some ash and a water vessel to the entry so that Malika and Rayappa could wash their feet and hands before entering their hut. Rayappa was impressed by how clean and well organized they kept the tiny space. The bedding was rolled up and neatly stacked along with separate bundles of clothes. An area was reserved for a board to roll out rotis, a pile of small stones for cooking, and a few vessels. Nearby, a gunny sack of grain sagged, nearly depleted.

Fariza made tea on the open flame, boiling just enough water for Rayappa, saying she had taken hers earlier. She offered him a bit of betel nut, kept for special occasions. Malika could see her mother was honoured by this unofficial visit but at the same time embarrassed that she had little to offer. Her two sisters sat quietly tending the younger boys. The baby would be fed, as he had his mother's milk, but Malika worried about the others.

Rayappa accepted the tea. "Will your husband be returning soon?"

"The doctaaru says it would take a long time because they are operating on his spine. When the landlord started punishing my husband by putting stones on his back, I knew it was no good. Man is not a donkey!"

Rayappa immediately thought of the man bent over like a shelf on the roadside on the day of the castration.

"How old is your husband, may I ask?"

Fariza smiled. "He is like me."

Rayappa felt some relief. The man on the road had been much older.

When Rayappa got up to leave, Fariza stopped him. "We need help. Someone to help reap our harvest."

The request was so simple and at the same time so daunting. How would this mother, alone with five children, survive? Her eldest and best worker was an indentured labourer; the two other daughters were already working in the field or watching the younger children. No father, no older brothers in sight.

"Did you hear of the widow from Warangal?"

"Will you tell us a story, Uncle?" Alia's eyes grew large.

"Yes. I guess there is a story here, perhaps even a lesson to be learned. You see there is a widow, Chityala Ailamma. Her husband was arrested for some petty thing. To save her four acres from being repossessed, she organized volunteers. Some even came from the city to help. They reaped and protected the grain so the landlord could be paid the tax and—"

Fariza cut in. "How can we get these volunteers? Everyone is tending their own land or working on the landlord's crops." She picked up the baby. "If you can help us. Please."

"Ammi, we must go. The dorasani wants me back."

Rayappa could tell Malika was proud and did not want her mother asking him for help, and while Rayappa wanted to help, he did not like being asked. Such obligations came with responsibility, and each responsibility had a cost. He was glad to leave the hut and walk back to the Reddy compound with Malika.

*

"You must keep your chin down, your head tucked between your arms."

Vijay treaded water, his head barely visible in the moonlight. He instructed Malika, who stood on the rock ledge that jutted out over the pond, in the forest where they had first met. She had removed her sari. She wore her blouse and underskirt, hitched up between her legs and tucked in at the waist. On her second attempt at diving, the deceptively still water slapped her stomach sharply. It smarted, as did the front of her thighs. She positioned herself again on the rock, just as Vijay had, and took a deep breath, then hesitated.

"Shall I show you again?"

Vijay swam to the rock ledge, hoisted himself out of the pond, and took position to dive. His body was lean and hard, his upper arms well-defined, his shoulders square and broad. Standing beside him, Malika could detect the asymmetry caused by the shorter left foot. The clubfoot, the slight deformity that drew stares and disgust. Malika thought him beautiful. On impulse, she gave him a shove. Vijay tumbled into the pond.

She laughed. "So that's how it's done."

"Okay, donkey, your turn." Vijay treaded water as Malika positioned herself again, arms straight, knees bent, and pushed off with her toes. She dove into the water, but her underskirt came loose from the waistband and tangled between her legs, resulting in another flop. She climbed back onto the land. "Come find me."

"I know exactly where you are."

Vijay glided through the water in search of her. She envied him. He was able to swim bare-chested and have the water wash beneath his arms and across his back. She imagined that when she wasn't here, he shed the rag between his legs. While Vijay propelled himself away from her, Malika undid the hooks of her blouse, peeled the wet material off her skin, and sat only in her underskirt, partially exposed.

"Do you give up?" Malika called to him.

"No, I'm just resting." He floated on his back.

Then she untied her underskirt and let it fall to her ankles. Malika regretted her action as soon as she had done it. She felt shame at having betrayed her modesty, her faith, even her family. But then he couldn't see her. So what did it matter? No one could gaze upon her and judge her to be immodest. Malika stood on the rock, her flesh bare, the moonlight casting a shimmer on her dark smooth skin, the water glistening on her shoulders and arms. She was grateful Vijay was blind, but another part of her, a new and surprising part, wanted desperately for him to see her. All of her. She stood for another moment hoping he would turn to her. Then she dove. Her body, free of restrictions, cut into the clear water.

As Vijay swam towards her, Malika felt both fear and excitement. And then he was there, embracing her, learning everything about her, her strength, her vulnerability. And she in turn explored his body. Her hands moving naturally to places that were forbidden even to think about. Together they swam to the bank, climbed onto the earth, and made love. It was the first time for both of them. It was urgent, at times awkward. A moment of joy in their otherwise difficult lives.

After sex, they slept. Upon waking, Malika reached for Vijay again, but he stopped her.

"We should get dressed. Tomorrow I am expecting visitors. I will need to help my mother prepare food for everyone. She will be waiting. Also, I want to take you home to meet her."

Malika was honoured. She dressed in her sari, wrapping the palloo around her breasts before flipping it over her shoulder. She wrung out her blouse and underskirt and carried them in one hand, the other held Vijay's arm.

As Vijay led Malika to his hut, he told her his story. How he was raised by his mother, and swept the floor in the village school, picking up after children his age and older. He had listened to every lesson and committed each to memory. While he knew who his father was, Vijay had never spoken to him. His mother sent Vijay to the alletodu, the master basket weaver, to learn to cut straw. All this before he lost his sight.

The land on this side of the river was full of rocks and not suitable for farming. Only stubborn shrubs and ancient trees thrived. One could hide for days in the dense underbrush without risk of discovery. Vijay's hut was hidden in the thicket. Malika could barely make out the definition of the walls of the thatched hut from the mossy bank to which it clung. It was burrowed into the earth, a natural camouflage.

"Come."

Inside, Malika was surprised to find fifteen people, men and women, her age and older, sitting in a circle around an oil lamp. A gun lay across one man's lap, his hand resting casually on the long metal cylinder. This frightened Malika, but the man was warm and friendly as he greeted Vijay.

"Vijay, you have finally graced us with your presence."

"Oh, you have all come so soon. I thought you . . . we have not prepared."

"Don't worry, Vijay. Your Amma has given us everything we need. We came early to tell you some news. Leaders from Warangal have organized student volunteers to help with harvest. They are on their way now. We need to identify families who will not betray us. Is this a new recruit?"

"This is Malika. She has been learning."

The people in the circle made space for Vijay and Malika.

"Malika, these are my friends. They help farmers harvest their crops. Can you tell them what you told me about your family?"

Hesitant at first, Malika told the circle of people about her father's illness and absence. How her mother was in debt both to the landlord and the moneylender. How their crop needed to be reaped so they could pay the tax. How she was working at the landlord's house cleaning the latrines. She could tell some of these people were farmers. They were familiar to her. Others seemed different, maybe from the city. Some of the women wore trousers, while others wore saris as she and other peasants did, hitched up between their legs and tucked in at their waists. Malika was surprised to see one woman who tied her palloo in such a way to secure a rifle on her back.

"Your mother, is she trustworthy?" The man who spoke was clearly the leader here. The rest deferred to him.

"Must Malika make a decision tonight? She may need to speak to her mother," Vijay asked.

"I know my mother would want this. We know the story of Chityala Ailamma."

"No one can truly know that story unless you were there. She courageously defended her four acres of land, rallied the Sangham and many villagers to support her, but she suffered badly. The landlord retaliated. She was badly beaten. She is a real hero. Do you know what you are asking?" The older woman with the rifle on her back shook her head, seemingly distrustful of Malika.

"It's not the same," Vijay said. "Malika's family has no ties to the party, unlike Chityala Ailamma."

"True. Ailamma's relatives had been organizing with the Sangham for months. This is more like charity work." The woman folded her arms.

"The Sangham?" Malika touched Vijay's hand. "My father spoke about the Sangham leader."

"I am Viswanathan. The Sangham leader. I organize workers to challenge the landlords."

Malika was surprised that this leader, except for the rifle across his lap, appeared so humble. Dressed in a dhoti and kurta, he could easily have been a farmer.

"I am leading this group you see here. We organize strikes and help peasants win back their land and their dignity."

Vijay touched Malika's forearm. "We can harvest the grain so that your mother can turn it over to the landlord. This way she can pay her debts, and the landlord won't take her land."

"If we cannot reap it soon, the little crop we have will die, and then we will be further in debt. As it is, my two sisters and my mother are working day and night." Malika lowered her head remembering the type of work her mother did lately.

"Okay. Speak to your mother immediately," Viswanathan instructed Malika. "And take care. Tell her these volunteers are simply peasants. If this help is seen as a collective action against the landlord, it will be perceived as a threat. We will send word to Warangal leaders who will organize the volunteers, both students and labourers in other villages. You must pay your tax as soon as the harvest is reaped."

A woman with brown hair only a shade darker than her light skin spoke in a quiet but firm voice. "Be careful. All of you. These lands have been controlled by the Reddys since before you were born. Do you think a handful of people guarding a gunny sack will stop them?"

Malika looked at the woman. There was a smoky quality about her, more distinctive than beautiful. She seemed vaguely familiar. Had she seen her dance at Jatara festivities?

"Amma, there is nothing else we can do." There was a tone of urgency in Vijay's voice. As if he had had similar conversations before.

This was Vijay's mother? A jogini. Malika felt ashamed for her but Vijay's mother showed no sense of embarrassment.

"Vijay is correct." Viswanathan asserted. "There is nothing more to do. Your mother must say if she wants our help. And if so, we will have a group of workers harvesting your crop in a few days."

"My mother will agree. The landlord burned down Balamma's crop to teach her a lesson about paying the tax. We cannot let them do this to us."

Malika felt Vijay squeeze her arm.

After the meeting, Vijay and Malika rode on his mule back across the shoal. He nuzzled his face in her neck. He was both proud of her and nervous about the decision she had made on behalf of her family.

"Are you certain you want to do this?"

"What choice do we have? Our land will be taken if we do not pay the tax. My mother will continue going out at night. I will keep cleaning the latrines. My sisters will be sent to work as servants, and my brothers will be sold. My father will return home, and no one will be there."

"You have courage, Malika."

Vijay was unsure whether Malika was aware that she had been meeting with Communists. That she had made love to a Communist. He grew erect thinking of this.

"Let us be married. We already are, you know." Vijay kissed Malika's neck.

Malika leaned into him. "We can marry when the volunteers come. We will have so much to celebrate."

Vijay wrapped his arms around her. In this way they crossed the river to the other side.

*

It was late December, unusually hot, and their crops were drying. Their stomachs were empty. But they came in the heat. Hundreds of peasants. Waiting. For Gandhi. For deliverance.

As Reddy had predicted, the field was teeming with villagers. Farmers, labourers, tradesmen, priests, healers, almost every man, woman, and child in Korampally was here. Reddy had promised food, an incentive for the peasants to abandon their livelihoods for one day to see the great Gandhi. Reddy was loyal to the Nizam and was cautious about the influence that Gandhi would have on their village, but he was also a pragmatist. Unsure where the political maps would be drawn, he chose a neutral stance. Welcoming Gandhi to Kormapally had nothing to do with Reddy's beliefs or understanding of the satyagraha philosophy; it was a show of his benevolence. Reddy believed that his grand gestures would evoke loyalty from the peasants, or at least neutralize those who had protested the tax.

Reddy had arranged for Gandhi's visit. He had invited Gandhi to stay at his home and offered the use of his servants. But Gandhi chose to stay at the Ashram. Reddy accepted the slight. He imposed only one condition. No press. No journalists, no cameras, not even Connelly could take a photograph. The visit was for the people of Korampally, not for the rest of Telangana, nor Hyderabad, nor India. And naturally, not for Reddy. Reddy refused to hear the Mahatma speak. When Connelly had pressed him, Reddy replied, "The heat is unbearable, and so too is Gandhi."

Reddy had much to do, and his bathwater was hot. Instead he sent his sons, Linga and Surendra. They, along with ten other young men, were surveilling the crowd from the bullock cart parked to the side of the field.

Rayappa stood with Connelly near the raised platform where the Mahatma was to address the people. Rayappa noticed Vijay standing at the back of the field. He realized that Vijay occupied a precarious position. The young man acted with independence and a sort of defiance, but he was vulnerable and at the mercy of others. Rayappa had learned from Sivraj that while Vijay was born a Madiga, his mother defied many caste restrictions regarding her son. Giving him an upper-caste name, arranging that he learn to weave, even sending him to school when he was very young. It was also rumoured that Vijay had some claim to land, through a secret promise or inheritance.

Gandhi too had defied caste restrictions by living among the untouchables in the city of Hyderabad in 1934. He had renamed them Harijans, children of God. They rejected this name and Gandhi's teachings, but Gandhi persevered, and they finally welcomed him. Rayappa knew that Gandhi had cleaned the latrines, but did he eat the food they served? Some Harijans ate carrion when no other food was available. Rayappa knew Gandhi was vegetarian and would not go so far just to gain respect from and admittance into this tribe.

A murmur of excitement moved through the crowd as it parted to make way for Gandhi, led by Ragaviah. Ragaviah, whose fast had brought the Mahatma here, appeared no slimmer for his efforts, whereas the great teacher appeared fragile. Gandhi's loincloth was too big, like an oversized diaper, and his legs were wizened sticks. The overall impression was that of a baby taking first steps rather than a learned man in late life. Rayappa wanted to protect the Mahatma. He suddenly feared for him. *Sit down, Gandhiji*, Rayappa thought. *Go back to your ancestral home. Abandon your path before it is too late.*

Connelly pushed past Rayappa to get closer to Gandhi. Was Connelly asking something of the Mahatma? Maybe Connelly was inviting Gandhi to speak at Oxford or inviting him for tea? Was Gandhi rebuking Connelly, preferring to stay with the people, or was Gandhi extending his arm to the professor, asking to be ushered away? Perhaps Gandhi had extracted a heavy tax from Connelly for every Indian life that had suffered under the British? Why not? Anything was possible. But it irked Rayappa that Connelly insisted that whatever he had to say had to be said ahead of anyone else.

Gandhi climbed up on the platform and began to speak. He warned about the danger of Hyderabad joining Pakistan. He insisted India could contain all her people. Gandhi then directed his words to the untouchables, addressing his audience like a mother would a child. The importance of not carrying human waste on the head. The importance of not eating carrion. The importance of practising proper hygiene.

As Rayappa gazed upon this scene, he saw what was terribly wrong with Gandhi's perspective. Gandhi's message needed to be reconfigured and redirected to those who did not work in the hot sun, who did not watch their crops wither, who did not worry where to take a shit. Gandhi's words should have been directed to the powerful, who didn't worry about their next meal, who didn't care who sat in the chambers of government — as they themselves controlled the political game. As this revelation came to Rayappa, he turned to Vijay at the back of the field, who tilted his head in Rayappa's direction.

Did Vijay hear the words Rayappa was writing in his head for Gandhiji to say to the powerful? Or were these Vijay's words? Do not ask others to carry your shit. Do not starve the people off their land, leaving them nothing to eat but the carcass of a dead dog. Do not control rivers and wells, preventing people access to clean water. Do not lord over the lower castes and decree by the word of God that they are less than human. Instead of lecturing to the untouchables, Gandhi should have chastised every Brahmin prince, penalized every industrialist and wealthy landowner. He should have scattered their gold, parcelled out their land, and pulled down their gods.

A deep sadness overwhelmed Rayappa. Would the Mahatma's message one day explode in his own face?

Gandhi finished his speech and the crowd parted to clear a path for him and his entourage, fifteen freedom fighters in simple dress, some carrying clay water vessels. Rayappa followed, inching himself closer to Gandhi, as if he needed to impart an urgent message.

Gandhi moved towards the back of the field where the Madigas gathered in the hot sun. He approached the one who stood out, an outcast among outcastes.

Gandhi stooped and poured water on Vijay's feet. Vijay's jaw tightened.

Rayappa wanted to shout out *no!* But it was too late. Gandhi's hands came together in a blessing for Vijay.

"As this child of God stands before us, his feet washed, we understand that what was once deemed polluted is not so. He is innocent, he is pure."

Vijay lowered his head. The crowd looked on, some with admiration and curiosity, others with puzzlement, even resentment. Their crops were still dying, and taxes were due.

Later, Rayappa rode with Connelly and Linga back to the compound, his heart breaking. He wanted to write down in his notebook all he observed, but the ride was too bumpy to steady his pen.

1997—The Thatched Hut

Jaya is uncomfortably wedged between Anya and Parveen, the translator, in the back seat of a chauffeured Ambassador. They are going to meet
Ashamma. There is room for Irwin in the front, but he prefers to remain
at the Krishna Lodge and recover from the long journey from Hyderabad
City. Unaccustomed to the sudden lack of personal space, Jaya is aware that
her thigh keeps touching Parveen's as the car rounds corners. But something
other than the physical discomfort bothers her. She envies Parveen who
already knows Ashamma.

Anya comments on the scenery. She clicks her camera, advances the film
and clicks again. This continuous and rhythmic activity measures the time
and distance from the lodge to their destination. As the car passes through the
streets of Korampally, Parveen reads and translates the slogans on the walls:
Dunnevaanniki Bhoomi. Land to the Tiller. Samrajyavadam Nashinchaali.
Down with Imperialism.

"What are those red flags in the fields?" Anya points her camera towards
them. "I noticed the flags when we were driving in."

"This is Naxalite country. Jaya, you must have heard of them?"

Jaya shifts away from Parveen and looks past Anya out the window. "Well,
somewhat. I think Irwin mentioned them when we lived in India."

Parveen smiles. "I suppose the simple explanation is that over the years
much of the land was reclaimed by farm labourers, aided by the notorious
Naxalites."

Anya takes pictures of the flags. "I've never heard of them. They can't be
that notorious."

"Not in Canada. They are a revolutionary Communist group. Very
organized and not without power. Think of it this way. Most law-abiding
middle-class families, like yours, fear the Naxalites. Many villagers welcome

them. This area is a hotbed of agitation. I spend a lot of time translating for scholars, researching the political developments in the area."

"Is it dangerous?"

"It depends whose side you're on. As long as you're not a landlord trying to remove the flags, you're safe from the Naxalites. And if you're not a Naxalite trying to plant a flag, you are safe from the landlords."

"I'll play Switzerland and remain neutral." Anya turns her camera towards Parveen and Jaya.

Parveen has a wide smile that takes up most of her face. Jaya does not know what to make of her, but Anya seems to trust her immediately.

"Many people avoid taking sides. It's relatively stable now. Please, don't worry."

Jaya reaches into her handbag and takes out the box of truffles she brought for Ashamma. She wonders if the gift is appropriate. Before leaving Canada, she had bought some perfume. At the time, she pictured Ashamma as an elegant, grey-haired woman in a gold sari. She returned the perfume, thinking the gift too personal for someone she didn't know. She also realized the image she had of Ashamma too closely resembled that of Indira Gandhi. She keeps trying to return to a memory of Malika. An image of a dark-skinned face surrounded by a circle of light keeps coming to mind. Jaya would have been around four when she last saw her mother. The features of Malika's face have long faded from her memory.

Parveen points out landmarks along the way. The temple where harvest festivals are held was also the site of a recent agitation. Dalits — the respectful and self-identified term for those once deemed untouchable — finally won the right to enter the temple. Then Parveen points out the oldest toddy shop, recently closed because of a ban on alcohol.

"That's why I couldn't get a drink!" Anya says. "Thatha and I went for lunch. When I ordered a beer, the waiter rudely ignored me."

Parveen explains that she had been working on literacy campaigns in the area. The sessions were mostly attended by women, who spent much of the time complaining that their men were always drunk. It was the government sale of arrack that was ruining their lives. The women organized and blocked the roads, attacked the government trucks, and eventually stopped the sale of palm wine in these parts. As a result, the Andhra government has banned the sale of alcohol, much to the ire of the middle class.

Anya laughs. "Just my luck, I come to one of the hottest countries on Earth and can't get a frosty beer."

"Ah, the priorities of the young." Jaya adjusts her sunglasses.

"I'm joking." Anya rolls her eyes.

"A lot of people feel the same way you do, Anya," Parveen says, "but really, it is a great victory for the women. Incidents of abuse are declining, and the men are back in the fields. Literacy rates are going up."

"Is that your job then? Teaching?"

"Among other things. I am a trained social worker. Most of my income comes from translating. And over there, are the infamous teashops where the Naxalites led—"

Jaya interrupts. "Why are we heading out of town? I thought you said Ashamma lived in Korampally."

The car heads over a bridge where they can view the expansive Vancha River.

"All of this is part of Korampally. This area is probably akin to suburbs in Toronto." Jaya senses Parveen is making fun of her but can't understand why. She hopes that once Parveen introduces Jaya and Anya to Ashamma, they won't need the translator's help.

The car crosses the bridge, moving farther away from the town centre. Then it turns off the road into an obviously poor area. Anya takes photos of stray dogs and goats wandering along the road.

"Are you sure this is the right place?"

Parveen teases Jaya.

"Yes, yes, we know where we are going. Ashamma is an institution unto herself. I have been here several times. I translated your letter and subsequent emails and read them aloud to her."

They pull up to the side of the road. On their left is the river and on the right is a small footpath, leading up to a thatch-roofed hut. Mango trees shade the area from the hot sun. Behind the hut stands a pale peach cement house surrounded by a wall of the same colour.

"Is this it?" Jaya can't disguise her surprise and disappointment.

"Were you expecting something more?" Parveen raises her eyebrows at Jaya.

"Well, to be honest...I imagined a home in a Muslim enclave, with brass tea sets and miniature paintings on the wall."

"What gave you that idea?"

Irwin suggested that Malika's mother, Fariza, was Muslim. Anya had done research and explained to Jaya the spelling of Malika's name. "One *l* in the name is Muslim, two *l*'s Hindu." Still, they are meeting Ashamma not Fariza.

Jaya is confused by her own thinking. Anya saves her from complete embarrassment. "We were trying to find out more about Malika. So Amma and I leafed through pictures of Moghul art in one of Anasuya's books."

"Who's Anasuya?" Jaya and Anya glance at each other then to Parveen.

"My other mother. She died."

Anya bounces out of the car, grabs her backpack, and heads towards the peach-coloured house in the back. But Parveen stops her.

"Wait."

An old woman comes out of the hut and starts moving towards them. She is lean, with skin hanging off her forearms and torso, small flaps that shiver when she moves. Unusually fair-skinned for the region, her features are striking despite the criss-cross of lines on her face. Jaya wonders if this is Ashamma's servant, come to greet them. The old woman is moving towards them so quickly that Jaya worries she may go right past them and into the river. Jaya turns to Parveen. "Is Ashamma in the house?"

Parveen looks at her with a warm and knowing smile. "*This* is she."

*

Ashamma wears her good sari and has combed her hair. An old woman must stink, she thinks. So this morning she bathed and dropped jasmines in her chembu before rinsing off. Today, her skin feels soft and seems to her suddenly youthful. Still, it hangs loose on her bones and she hopes Jaya and Anya will not be repelled. When she sees them, she feels a deep warmth within and knows there is nothing ugly about her.

Anya is a big girl, Ashamma thinks. And bold. No long kurta covering her bottom. Strong like an ox. Her face has a reassuring familiarity, a triangular nose flaring beautifully at the base. Her skin is fair but darker than Ashamma's. Her heritage cannot be denied.

Ashamma knows about her own father, the plantation dora, the British man who like so many in his day paid wages to untouchable workers, lifting them inch by inch out of slavery while keeping women bonded for sex. He took advantage of her mother, and except for a few annum that tumbled from his pockets, he left nothing but his seed. Baby Asha, born the colour of wheat, grew strong under her mother's protection. When she came of age, her fate was fixed by the gaze of Raghunandan Reddy, the only son of the wealthiest landowner in Korampally. Ashamma was only eleven years old when she was yanked away from her mother by the ambitious twenty-three-year-old Reddy. He told her she was special, different, a very desirable jogini. Ashamma was subjected to the same treatment that her mother experienced with the British dora. Surely it is this lineage that is responsible for the fair skin of her great-granddaughter. Ashamma's descendent. Whether to reveal this history or not is the question Ashamma can not yet answer.

The second woman, Jaya, is sharp-featured and lean. Wiry. Ashamma knows this face and body. She is like her mother, Malika, in every way except for her light brown eyes. Uncommon on a face so dark. She searches Jaya's face for traces of her son but cannot find any. Nonetheless, both children are more beautiful than she could have ever imagined.

Now she understands why Parveen is in her life. Parveen who came from the Women's Centre and works for the Reddys. Who often sits cross-legged on the ground, posing like a peasant. Ashamma regrets spitting into Parveen's cup of water on the last visit. But look, Parveen is here and has survived it. Ashamma had long ago disabused herself of the idea that she is polluted. She hurries towards Jaya and Anya, touches their faces with her hands, and cracks her knuckles on both sides of her head. She inhales their essence. They, like this sudden happiness, are hers.

*

Walking slowly behind Ashamma, Jaya notices it right away. The similarities and differences between Ashamma and the beggar she saw outside Hollywood Shoes. The two women resemble each other, not by any one feature but by their type. Years of drudgery and abuse have left scars on their bodies. The deep lines, the gummy smiles, and the bony fingers, no fat in reserve for "just in case." The woman on the steps at Hollywood Shoes is destitute, whereas Ashamma seems to have carved out a place for herself. Someone is helping her.

Parveen assesses Jaya's Telugu to be good enough and leaves with the driver at Ashamma's insistence. She promises to return in two hours to take the women back to the Krishna Lodge for supper.

Anya must bend to enter the hut while Jaya easily follows Ashamma inside. Ashamma sits cross-legged on the floor. Anya and Jaya sit on two small stools, stainless-steel cups of tea in their hands. Fruit is arranged ceremoniously on a plate placed on a small mat in front of them.

Ashamma stares at the two Canadians. She cannot locate Canada on a map, imagine its landscape, or possibly know its complex and violent history towards its own original people. She stares at Jaya and Anya as if by looking she will learn. She leans in to touch their faces. Anya, feeling awkward but moved by this affectionate gesture, kneels on the ground near Ashamma. Then Ashamma begins to speak rapidly in Telugu. Anya looks to Jaya, who begins to translate.

Jaya stiffens and remains seated on her stool. When she attempts to reply to Ashamma in Telugu, ghosts invade her mouth, allowing the rising rhythms and melodic tones of the language to pour out fluidly. The ghosts speak of things Jaya doesn't know she knows.

Listening to her mother, Anya realizes how rarely Telugu was spoken at home. When at twelve years old Anya asked why she didn't speak it, Anasuya explained. "We had to teach you and Jaya to speak English fluently. As soon as we settled in Antigonish, Telugu flew out the window, off the East Coast and across the ocean, never to return."

The few occasions when Irwin, Anasuya, and Jaya spoke Telugu, Anya thought it sounded like a clarinet played with a dry reed. Without the right amount of moisture, the reed produces croaks and squeaks. The Telugu Ashamma and Jaya now speak sounds lyrical, like a beautiful folk ballad. This stranger, Ashamma, in her well-worn skin and well-worn sari, is beaming. Anya has never met anyone like her before. It is as if gold liquid runs through Ashamma's veins so that she radiates light.

Anya observes the room as it darkens around them. There is no electricity, only an oil lamp. There are the two stools, the mat upon which Ashamma sits and sleeps, a bundle of clothes wrapped and tied with a rope, and a small area reserved for cooking. Towards the back of the hut, looking out of place, is an old leather suitcase with brass buckles. It sits horizontally on the ground. A cloth has been draped over it, and an unlit deepam, a saucer of grain, and an orange sit on top. Behind these, a faded photograph leans against the wall. It depicts farmers gathered in a field. Anya moves towards the suitcase and squints at the photograph. Anya carefully removes the sacred objects from the surface of the suitcase and then the cloth. She snaps open the brass buckles and glances over to Jaya and Ashamma, deep in conversation. While she should ask permission to peek inside, Anya has the uncanny feeling of being at home with *her* things. She is like a bored child left alone who opens boxes and rummages through drawers, not looking for anything in particular but hoping to find something. Anya feels as if she has been here before. As if this suitcase was meant to be passed on to her. As if the koel in her dreams has led her back to this very spot and dropped in her hands the shiny key to unlock her family's secrets.

When Anya lifts the worn lid of the suitcase, she does not see the things that were once collected and stored inside: clothes, shoes, chili powder, nuts and fruit, maps and firearms. All these things have been traded over the past fifty years, leaving behind the one thing that was of no use to those who had opened the suitcase before her. Tucked into the lining pocket is a hardcover notebook dated 1947, bearing the name Rayappa. Anya lifts the fragile spine of the notebook and parts the yellowed pages, delicate like dried leaves. Anya feels as if the notebook is imploring her to read what her grandfather wrote but could not, and still cannot, tell.

6. The Harvest

The front room of the main house was full of people, conversation, and food. A grand meal was prepared in celebration of Gandhi's visit, and even a photographer was present to document Reddy's historic moment. The Mahatma, however, chose to eat with the peasants. The men in the Reddy household, their friends, and Ragaviah, Connelly, and Rayappa would partake in the meal without Gandhi. While Rayappa would have preferred to eat with Gandhi, he was reminded by Veena Reddy that they were making a concession, allowing him to dine with them, and that such an invitation would likely not be repeated. Rayappa felt he had no choice. Veena Reddy would sit with the men on this rare occasion, but would have her meal later.

China plates were distributed to three different tables. Reddy motioned the house servants to serve the food.

"There is a place for everyone, and everyone has a place. If Gandhi wishes to eat with scavengers and the like, he can do so. But he mustn't force others to follow suit."

Rayappa pondered this, as Reddy did not invite but commanded people to dine with him. Rayappa knew even Connelly would have preferred to be in the Mahatma's company.

Ragaviah, deemed the honoured guest in place of Gandhi, was served first, a simple meal of rice and yogurt, as he had only broken fast a few days earlier. Out of respect for the priest, vegetarian food was served to everyone. The aroma of cardamom, cloves, and saffron from the biriyani filled the room. "The very essence of caste is unmovable. Once born on this Earth, your caste is for life. Whether you observe your caste obligations or not is a matter of conscience and determines whether or not you will be elevated in the next life."

Connelly furrowed his brow. "Ragaviah, are you saying Gandhi won't fulfill dharma if he dines with the Harijans?"

"Well, there is always this matter of pollution." Ragaviah looked over at

Rayappa who was seated at a separate table with Connelly; Reddy's youngest son, Surendra; and some non-Brahmin land owners.

Rayappa cleared his throat. "If my memory serves me well, Gandhiji is not altogether against caste, only untouchability."

Reddy gestured at the servant to heap more biriyani onto his plate. "Ah, but that is the contradiction. How can you have purity without impurity, man without woman, day without night? Everything has its opposite. Good and evil. The twice-born and the once-born. The forward castes and the backward castes. That is our world. Connelly, would you deny that your king is upper caste? Does he sit down on the street or eat rubbish? Does he invite the rubbish man to dine with him?"

"You have a point. But just because you are born into disadvantage does not mean you cannot achieve a degree of civilized behaviour, education, and recognition. Take for example Ambedkar. He came from humble beginnings. Let's hear from the young people. What do you think, Surendra?"

"Naina?" Surendra, Reddy's younger son, was pleased to be invited to join in the conversation but still deferred to his father. Reddy nodded his approval. "Ambedkar was born untouchable and studied to become an economist, a lawyer, and much more."

Connelly patted Surendra's back. "Well said. He is a serious politician. Today's paper reports that he is advocating for separate electoral polls for lower castes in the new India, much to Gandhi's chagrin."

Reddy shook his head at Connelly. "Ambedkar can wear a suit and produce any number of degrees, but these successes still cannot change the fact that he was born a Mahar, an untouchable."

"Reddy, I dare say, you are declaring that no material, intellectual, or spiritual pursuit can dislodge what has been embedded for thousands of years in the Hindu psyche." Connelly pushed his chair back and gestured towards Reddy. "And perhaps that is India's real battle. Spiritual conviction versus political power. It is not just Hindus who will take to the polls in a democratic India but Muslims, Christians, Buddhists, backward and scheduled castes. I am convinced that Gandhi's, Nehru's, and even Ambedkar's dreams of a secular India will come to be. And people will have the freedom to do as they please without needless religious restrictions and confines."

"We already practise secularism here. Hyderabad's Muslim minority governs the administration and the Hindu majority controls the land. That is secularism in action."

Reddy devoured the last morsel of food and beckoned the housemaid. After she heaped another scoop of biriyani on his plate, Reddy gestured that she do the same for the others. Rayappa declined politely, and his wishes were likewise politely ignored. Connelly welcomed another heaping spoonful of the Hyderabadi eggplant specialty, baghara baingan, on his already twice-emptied plate.

While the newspapers had announced this year's poor yield of rice and declared a crisis in food distribution, this had little impact on food consumption in the Reddy household. Rayappa understood that those who could eat would, and usually more than their fair share.

"I do hope Gandhi is enjoying eating from a banana leaf." Linga Reddy spoke softly but all eyes turned to him.

Surendra, given his father's encouragement, became more talkative and engaged. Newly married, he had been spending more time with his wife and less with his brother. He was thrilled at the opportunity to have gone with Linga to see Gandhi. "Honestly, Naina, it was such a circus. Gandhi washing Kunti Vadu's feet."

"What is this? Linga, can you make any sense of what your brother is saying?"

"It is true. Gandhi stooped down and washed that idiot's feet. And all the others, even his precious Harijans, looked on with disgust. I am glad Gandhi chose not to come here. I wouldn't have been able to look at his fingers."

Reddy looked up at his son. "Really. He washed that child's feet?"

"Maybe we should have invited Kunti Vadu here." Surendra laughed.

Connelly tried to save the conversation from becoming ridiculous. "Boys, boys. Gandhi's gesture itself was unnecessary, but it proves he is sincere. Gandhi has shown himself to be at peace with the real India. In a way, he and I are both social anthropologists. We understand the intricacies of the Hindu social structure and work gently to disrupt it and evolve it. I study and analyze the codes, and he sets out to fracture them using a similar approach. We do not preach or teach from a distance. We get our hands dirty and walk among the natives."

Reddy tsked, annoyed by Connelly's meaning. Was the professor suggesting Reddy was one of the natives? Rayappa, observing this exchange, glanced at Connelly. For the first time since discovering Connelly in the barn, their eyes met. Connelly looked down at the heap of rice on his plate and resumed eating.

Linga had hardly touched his food. "And to make matters worse, rumour has it that Kunti Vadu is converting to Islam, trying to escape his station, and that you, Naina, have blessed his upcoming marriage."

Veena gave her husband a disapproving look. "That is true. Your father will also be sending a meal tomorrow to the wedding."

"And why not? I have blessed all the marriages of our children—"

"You are not suggesting..." Linga abandoned his plate.

"—including our servants."

Rayappa focused on his meal. Mixing and remixing the biriyani and baghara baingan with his fingers.

"But our shit carrier?"

"Surendra!" Veena gave Surendra a stern look. "Let us speak about something else."

Reddy waved away his wife. "And why not? Even beasts must mate. Rayappa, you will be happy to learn that my wife has been kind to the girl and allowed her to return to her home and marry according to her choice. Now that is progress."

"You will see, once the mother pays her debt, we will lose another girl. First Suthiya, poor child, then Malika."

"Nonsense. Because of your generosity Malika will remain loyal and clean the latrine for years to come, debt or no debt. Now go tell her she can leave for the wedding and return the next morning to resume her duties. And if she doesn't come back, she can always send her mother to replace her. Or a younger sister." Reddy grinned.

A look of defeat passed over Veena's face. Rayappa understood that nothing escaped her.

"Naina, how can you support such a union?" Linga rose to his feet. "It's a mockery of marriage. He is acting too big for his station. First, he gets Gandhi's blessing, and now a wedding?"

"You act like you know something about marriage. If you did, we would have an heir by now." Reddy turned back to Connelly. "And then there is this Nehru Jinnah business."

Linga stood for a moment, watching his father. Then he turned and headed for the door.

"You haven't finished your meal," Veena called after him. "Babu."

Rayappa rose and appealed to Veena. "Excuse me. I will fetch Linga Babu." Veena nodded, but Reddy did not even glance in his direction.

"I wonder which one of those fools will win the jewel of Kashmir." Reddy licked his fingers, leaving no trace of food. He signalled to the maid to fetch a finger bowl.

Rayappa picked up his and Linga's plate and went outside. Sivraj and two younger men were standing by the blue doors hitching the bullocks to the cart. Linga was sitting on a wicker chair brooding. Rayappa extended the plate in his direction. "Please, your mother wants you to finish."

Linga looked up. "You think I will touch that now?"

Rayappa put Linga's plate on the table. "I also took issue with Gandhi, but perhaps for a different reason." Rayappa felt empathy for Linga. He had been put down by his father in front of everyone.

"Then why didn't you say so?"

"It is not my place."

"You too believe in the right order of things. You're not so modern after all."

"Why do you resent him so? The basket weaver?" Rayappa hesitated to utter Vijay's name aloud.

"First of all, he is not a basket weaver. Even that lowly role is above him. It is only through my father's generosity that he has any trade at all."

"Your father?"

Linga went to the rain barrels to wash his hands.

"Sivraj, get the cart. It is time for the party."

Rayappa scooped up the last of his rice. "The party?"

"For the bridegroom. It has all been arranged."

The cart was hitched to the bullocks, and the driver helped Linga mount. He summoned the blue double doors to open. The driver snapped the stick on the bullock's flank; the large wheels bucked and rolled forward. Linga turned to Rayappa with his wide and charming smile.

"Coming for a ride?"

Stunned by this sudden invitation, Rayappa was compelled to join Linga. He abandoned his plate next to Linga's and clambered onto the moving bullock cart, shaking the rice off his sticky hand.

*

As Linga's cart rolled through the village, ten of Linga's friends, aged sixteen to twenty-five, were summoned aboard. All were heirs to property, power, and prosperity. Linga ordered the driver to take them to the river's edge. On the way, Linga spotted travellers walking towards them on the road. Most were young adults, wearing dhotis and saris and carrying farm implements. Linga ordered the driver to pull over. Rayappa inched his way from the back of the cart to the front to hear the conversation between Linga and the man leading the group.

"You are not from here?"

"We are from Dosarajpalli. We came to see Gandhiji."

"Ah. Korampally's star attraction. You are heading home then? A long distance to travel."

"We are used to it." The man shielded his eyes from the glare of the setting sun but looked directly at Linga.

By standing, Rayappa could observe each member of the group, ten or twelve strong.

1. Clean faces and chappal-clad
2. Most were wiry, but some had thick waists
3. Fit and strong

Rayappa wiped his hand on the edge of the cart, the bits of sticky rice dry on the tips of his fingers. His unclean hand irritated him. The fingernails of the visitors were clean. Not the fingernails of peasants. The tone of the leader was confident and defiant. This somehow bothered Rayappa. Obviously from a higher caste, educated but dressed like a peasant, with a paunch, uncommon amongst the working poor. Rayappa felt a kind of empathy for the travellers, a need to protect them, from what he was unsure.

Rayappa willed the cart to roll onwards before Linga could observe what he had. He wondered if his thoughts were being transmitted to Linga, as he believed they had been to Vijay earlier that day in the field with Gandhi. Anxiety rose inside Rayappa. He forced himself to think of something else. He thought first of his mother, his two sisters at home, but thoughts of the kitchen, rice, then fields, circled back to *this* land, *this* road, *these* travellers. Then he thought of women, something Rayappa never allowed himself to do. A beautiful woman, dark, without bangles. Malika, her luminous eyes, her straight back, the basket on her head near the peepal tree, saying good-bye to Vijay. But these thoughts were dangerous too. Rayappa's voice was pitched high.

"Could we not find some water? My hand is unclean. Still sticky from the meal."

Linga was irritated by the interruption and looked down at Rayappa's fingers. "You didn't wash?"

As the cart resumed its motion, Linga turned back to look at the travellers. "Obviously, they are liars. They are headed into Korampally, not out."

"Perhaps they are staying for the wedding." Rayappa immediately regretted his words.

"Of course," Linga said in a faraway voice. "The wedding."

They approached the peepal tree. On the day before his wedding, Vijay sat in his usual place. No special bathing or sandalwood paste, no rituals or celebratory feast for Kunti Vadu. He wove the straw cut from the field outside his hut into a mat. If it did not sell, he would keep it for his new wife. For his new life. Cheers and yelps interrupted him.

Linga called out to Vijay from the bullock cart. "Come along and have some toddy with us!"

"No, master. Why would you want an idiot to join your party?" Vijay did not stop weaving. He did not stand up.

"Come, man. It is your wedding tomorrow. We are doing like the British. What, Rayappa? A party for the bridegroom. What is it called?"

"I believe they call it a stag. Like the animal, the deer. It was originally a feast..."

"I cannot. I have to finish my work."

Linga jumped off the cart and waved to the others to follow. They pulled and lifted Vijay onto the back of the cart. The mat he was clutching fell onto the dirt.

"Every bridegroom deserves a drink," said Linga. And two men held the funnelled palm leaf up to Vijay's mouth, forcing kallu down his throat, the rest dribbling off his chin. "Good stuff, what?"

"I think I must return to the professor." Rayappa moved to the back of the cart to jump off.

Linga still standing behind the cart, blocked Rayappa. "The professor is with my father. He is well taken care of." This marked the beginning of what Rayappa would later file away as his descent into hell.

The cart approached the river. Palm trees, thirty metres tall, arched their trunks to create long shadows over the fields leading to the river's edge. It was a far distance from where the women washed vessels and the dhobis laid their laundry flat on the rocks to dry in the sun. The river's current and seasonal swells deposited pebbles onto the shore. The water sparkled. The only sign of human intrusion was the castrator's shed. The cart turned off the main road and headed towards it.

On his first visit to this spot, Rayappa had been hot and nauseated. Today there was a breeze, and the setting sun cast a pink sheen across the sky. The toddy passed to him was cool and refreshing. The recent meal had formed a cushion in his belly so that the drink created just the faintest buzz, calming his rising anxiety. Rayappa glanced over at Vijay, who sat upright, his legs hanging off the back of the cart. The celebration was in Vijay's honour, though Linga held court. He expounded on various subjects, Gandhi and memories of other village weddings. Suddenly Vijay jumped off the cart and fell to the ground, followed by Linga's friends who landed on their feet. They grabbed Vijay's arms. The cart stopped.

Rayappa disembarked. "Let him go, man. Please. We must be on our way. The professor . . ."

"Fuck the professor." Linga moved towards Rayappa and put his arm around his shoulder. "Are you going to ruin this man's stag party?" He shouted to three men at the river's edge. "Has the boat arrived?"

A man waved his arms. "It's here. Everyone is waiting inside the shed." And the men on the cart responded with cheers. The sport could begin. Rayappa followed the others as they moved towards the castrator's shed.

Two men at the entrance welcomed those arriving with pats on the back, some flung their arms around another's neck, an affectionate gesture between young men. Linga now gripped Vijay's arm and led him, stumbling, into the shed, followed by Rayappa. The shed was lit by an oil lamp. Rayappa could make out something in the centre of the room. Six additional men, already inside, formed a circle around it. When Rayappa squeezed between the men, he saw a woman. Four men held her down, gripping her wrists and her ankles. Her mouth had been muzzled with a rag, and her eyes were huge with fear. With one decisive action, Linga hoisted her sari above her waist, exposing her.

"What are you doing?" Rayappa cried out. Someone clamped his hand over Rayappa's mouth and with the other, pinned his arms behind his back. Rayappa had never seen this woman before. She was poor, to be sure, maybe fifteen years his senior, but unlike Malika's mother, she wore no traces of kohl. Her lips were not painted; there were no flowers in her hair or chains around her neck to indicate she was a prostitute.

"Vijay!" It was the first time Rayappa had heard Linga refer to Vijay by name. "May I introduce you to the most beautiful whore from the east side of the Vancha. She will guarantee a good time. Our wedding gift to you."

"No! This is not for me..." Vijay pulled out of Linga's grasp. Another man caught hold of Vijay's arm and another yanked off his dhoti so that he stood naked except for his kurta. "Let me go!"

Vijay tried to resist, grabbing helplessly in the air for his dhoti with his free hand. Then two men pushed him between the legs of the woman. She struggled, her torso writhing, while the four men continued to hold her legs and arms. "She's a wild one." The two men who had pushed him down, now stomped on Vijay's back and buttocks with their chappal-clad feet. The woman freed one of her arms. Instead of pushing Vijay off, as Rayappa would have expected, she reached around and patted his back gently. She began to hum a gentle melody through the rag. A deep groan erupted from Vijay, and he threw the men off. He was wild, an enraged animal. The goondas let him go; Vijay stumbled and grappled to find his way out of the shed. All the while Linga and his boys continued laughing and clapping. The men released the woman, who grabbed her sari and covered herself. Rayappa was also set free. He reached out to help the woman up, but she swatted at him and broke through the men.

"Rayappa!" Linga clapped his hands together slowly. "You are her hero!"

No one stopped the woman. Rayappa grabbed Vijay's dhoti from the floor and moved to the hut's entrance. It was dark outside. He looked in all directions wondering where Vijay and the woman had gone. He could only see the outline of the palm trees by the river on this cloudy evening.

Rayappa searched the riverside and forest for hours, calling Vijay's name. There was no trace of him. By the time Rayappa gave up and got back to the landlord's house, it was daybreak. He knocked on the gate, and Sivraj opened it with a disapproving look. The bullock cart was stowed away. The animals were visible over the gate of the bullock house. Malika was asleep on Vijay's mat, just beyond the veranda steps. Rayappa looked down at his hands. Vijay's dhoti was still tight in his grip.

*

Veena Reddy kept a clean house. With strict command over the servants, she was not averse to working hard herself. Her respect for tradition and decorum kept her busy and lent order to the household. Rayappa saw this and respected her authority in this area. Ever since the incident with Suthiya, he knew to defer to Veena. If she asked him to take more food, even if his stomach was full, he would aim to please her. Rayappa understood that she, like Reddy's sons and servants, were under the patriarch's command.

It was the day of Malika's wedding. Veena Reddy had just finished supervising food preparation. She planned to give Malika a large tiffin of mutton biriyani and send her home in good time to bathe and get dressed for the wedding. Veena was explaining this to her husband and Connelly, who were taking tea on the veranda. Rayappa was standing in the courtyard in the sun. It was late afternoon, the heat was intense, but Rayappa could not shake a feeling of coldness inside him. He kept wrapping and rewrapping the woolen shawl around his shoulders.

Veena shouted to him from the veranda. "Are you not taking tea?"

In deference to Veena Reddy, Rayappa agreed to join Raghunandan Reddy, Connelly, and Veena. To Rayappa's relief, Linga was not there. Veena was pouring more tea into her husband's cup when her youngest daughter-in-law, Aditi, called out from the doorway. "Amma, Naina, I have something very special to show you." They all looked in her direction. "Come on, don't be shy." Aditi pulled Malika out of the house and onto the veranda.

Bathed and perfumed and wearing a red sari, flowers in her hair, Malika had been transformed by the maids, at Aditi's command.

The men went silent. Their eyes were fixed on Malika. Then Connelly let out a delighted laugh. "Oh, the girl is stunning. Shined and polished and ready to be wed."

But Veena Reddy did not share in Connelly's delight. From the look in her eyes, Rayappa thought Veena would snap Malika in two. "Get her out of here."

Aditi crossed her arms and stomped her foot, as if used to getting her way.

"But Amma, I thought . . . we had such fun."

"Veena. Not so fast. Let us take a good look." Reddy gestured to Aditi to bring Malika forward.

Rayappa now understood why Linga's wife, Lalita, maintained purdah. It was not the tradition of this region, nothing that practical Veena Reddy would normally impose. Veena Reddy had ordered her beautiful daughter-in-law to remain under cover or in her room to keep her away from the lecherous attention of Raghunandan Reddy, who was now focused on Malika. And Malika was beautiful. Had always been beautiful. It was as if in this very moment Rayappa realized that she was going to be married. Married to Vijay who had . . . What had happened to Vijay?

"Go wait by the gate!" Veena commanded Aditi and Malika, contradicting her husband's wishes. Then Veena ordered the men to leave.

On his way inside, Reddy grunted at his wife. "The latrines will need cleaning tomorrow. Best bring the girl back tonight." Veena's shoulders shuddered as if she had been struck.

Rayappa tried to piece together what Raghunandan Reddy was implying. He recalled the tradition in the region where the village priest or landlord would command a bride from a lower caste to sleep with him the night before she was to be wed. Was Reddy actually suggesting that he deflower Malika before the marriage was consummated? How could Rayappa be surprised, given Reddy's abuse of Suthiya?

Rayappa sought the isolation of his room, but he could find no peace. Outside, Veena Reddy's voice was harsh with reproach. Rayappa peered into the courtyard. Veena stood before Aditi and Malika, who was removing the jewellery Aditi had given her. Veena collected these in her left hand. And then she raised her right hand and slapped Malika across the face. "Do not show yourself when you return tonight, and dress in your rags." Then she opened the double doors and sent Malika away. Veena Reddy had forgotten, or not, to give the bride the tiffin of food.

Veena then turned to Aditi. "Never again do such a thing to any girl, or you will be turned out on the streets."

Aditi burst into tears, and ran up the steps into the house.

*

Malika climbed the terraced hillside, on which her ancestors had tilled the soil and sown their own grain. No leafy tobacco or glorious golden mustard. They were forced to choose a stubborn crop. Rice. The only seed that forced itself open in the worst conditions. The monopoly crop that had replaced the more nutritious millet, sucking water from the earth, filling stomachs with starch. Still, it was sellable.

Farmers on the hillside, looking up from their plots that day, may have thought they saw the goddess Pochamma, fiery and bold, bedecked in red silk, jasmines arranged like a tiara encircling her head. Her back straight. Her stride quick with purpose. But it was only Malika, one of their daughters. Of their community and kin.

When Malika reached her plot, she saw the volunteers had arrived and were working. Healthy, strong bodies joining her family to bring in the harvest.

Malika broke into a run when she saw her mother finishing the rangoli decoration at the entrance of their hut.

"You look so beautiful, my daughter. You are here so soon."

"Veenamma sent me out of the house." Malika laughed, the smarting of the slap now forgotten. "Oh Ammi, this is wonderful." Malika pointed to the volunteers. "The Communists said they would come."

Fariza brought her index finger to her lips. "Don't ever say that word. They are volunteers from Dosarajpalli. They are farmers like us. Tonight, your wedding, and tomorrow our taxes will be paid."

"Perhaps we should wait for Abbu to come back home."

"No. It is not possible. And you cannot remain unmarried another day. Especially with the way you look."

"As if a husband can give protection." Malika dropped her head, thinking about her mother's work at night.

"We take what we can."

Malika was unsure whether her mother meant to slight Vijay or was simply making an observation about her own life. She chose to believe her mother was being philosophical rather than cruel, even though she knew Fariza did not understand Malika's choice of husband.

"Come inside. Your sister can decorate your hands and feet. Then the feast will begin. The workers are almost finished."

But they were finished, even before they started.

*

The grain was collected, packed, and stored.

The paddy was husked and the chilies picked and powdered.

The goat was slain, seasoned, and roasted.

The bride was dressed and waiting.

The entranceway was decorated with rangoli.

The music was playing and neighbours gathered.

The imam called all to prayer.

But the bridegroom did not appear.

Men went to Vijay's hut and asked his mother about his whereabouts. She had no answer. Then they searched for Vijay. Unsuccessful, they returned to Malika, suggesting explanations for Vijay's disappearance, offering some comfort. The sun had set, and prayers were completed.

Finally, Fariza invited people to sit. "I will serve the food. No point in this going to waste."

Banana leaves of rice and goat curry were distributed outside the hut. Malika remained inside, sitting against the wall where her father once rested. She ate in silence with her two sisters, who sat on either side of her. When they had finished eating, Malika went outside and looked at the sacks of grain, collected by the volunteers, filled to the brim, lined up against the hut, and ready to be sold.

They thanked the volunteers and other wedding guests who then dispersed. Fariza passed Malika a bright green sari.

"Malika, take this. My wedding gift to you."

"But I didn't marry."

"Your sorrow is my sorrow, your joy, my joy. You will wed one day, my daughter."

Fariza helped Malika undress, and then wrapped the green sari, the colour of the forest, around her firstborn. They folded the red sari and Malika tucked it under her arm to return to Aditi.

Malika embraced her mother, her little brothers, and her two sisters. "Come to the well tomorrow. I will meet you."

Alia handed Malika the rope that she had taken from the well the day the white man arrived. "Here. You can return the Dorasani's rope. We will be able to buy our own rope now." Malika bundled Aditi's red sari and tied the rope around it to carry home. Alia followed Malika to the crest of the hill and then waved to her as she descended, before rejoining her mother in the hut.

Even though there was no wedding, Malika had shared a meal with her family, neighbours, and a community of strangers. They had reaped a small harvest and felt a sense of accomplishment and joy. Malika recalled her mother's words. *If the belly is full, one can tackle a nawab.* She would find and confront Vijay.

Malika did not take the road that serpentined down the hill but took her usual path, direct and steep. She was sure-footed but stumbled on something soft and rubbery on the hillside. An arm. Severed from its body. She turned and found a limbless torso and beside it, a head. She recognized the face. It was one of the volunteers who had helped with the harvest. Hearing the rumble of wheels, Malika clambered to the edge of the road and waited for a cart to come down the hill. She waved her arms and then saw that it was Linga Reddy and his friends.

"Did we miss the wedding?" Linga smiled broadly.

"Where is the bridegroom?" another man called, waving a machete.

"Maybe in the forest? Check the riverbed. Try the rubbish heap." Linga blew her a kiss.

Still carrying Aditi's red sari, Malika ran back up the hill away from the cart.

As she reached the crest, she could see the flames. Her family's hut and neighbouring huts occupied by Muslims were on fire. Turning back to the road she saw Linga Reddy's cart continuing into the village at its leisurely pace, carrying gunny sacks full of their harvest.

*

The noises began again in the bullock house. Rayappa closed the textbook he was studying by candlelight. He bookmarked the page with his index finger and carried it outside. The gate to the bullock house was open. Inside, Connelly was standing on the footstool behind the cow. Rayappa threw the textbook against the wall behind the professor.

"What . . . hold on, man."

"What are you doing to that poor beast?"

"Nothing. It's of no consequence." Connelly moved away from the animal.

"And you call yourself civilized."

"And you are?" Connelly made for the gate. "At least what I do does not harm anyone. Unlike you."

"What have *I* done?"

Connelly turned to Rayappa with a look of disbelief. "Did you think Linga could keep quiet about *your* pranks in the castrator's shed. He told me everything you did." Connelly slammed the gate shut, leaving Rayappa inside.

Rayappa was stunned. Linga had assigned him a role, a responsibility in that horrific event. And Connelly believed him. Rayappa allowed this information to slowly seep into his brain. How could he explain his presence in the castrator's shed? What could he have done in such a moment? What could he do now? Rayappa opened the gate, left the buffaloes and cows shifting and snorting inside, and returned to his room. He needed to make sense of it all.

Rayappa wondered what had happened to the woman in the shed. To stop his brain from reimagining it, he wrote it down, as he had borne witness. Not in graphic detail, the kind of descriptions that are featured ad nauseum in pornography, but the meaning of it. This crime. This cruelty. Rayappa understood that women were often the victims. It mattered not that they were from different classes and castes, dark or fair, rich or poor. They were pushed into these roles. And the men would blame their crimes on ignorance, hate, jealousy, lust, and even love, offending again and again, enabled by one tool. Power.

Linga Reddy had held the power that night and Rayappa hadn't had the power to stop him.

*

"Burn down the house!"

Flames from torches once again illuminated the sky from the other side of the wall. Rayappa rushed outside his room to find Sivraj and the servants leaning their weight against the two blue doors. Shots rang out, heralding the arrival of the Razakars. Rayappa understood this was a battle between the village people and their landlords, and he felt trapped on the wrong side of the wall.

An authoritative voice boomed through a megaphone. "Strict action will be taken against rifle-wielding goondas and rabble-rousers alike!" It was not the Razakars but the local reserve police.

As the crowd quieted, the servants moved away from their positions and gathered in huddles to talk. A policeman rapped on the door, demanding to see Reddy.

Reddy invited the policeman inside and agreed to answer some questions. "What burnings are you speaking about? Why do you assume I have ordered any such burnings? Why should I? It is the home of our servant girl. We provided her food and a new sari for her wedding. What would we have to gain by this? I implore you to arrest those responsible for this crime. Let my family have peace."

"All right, sir, but we may be back tomorrow."

Reddy ordered Sivraj to see the policeman out and bolt the doors.

"If my son should return, bring him to me."

*

Rayappa lay restless in his cot. He heard the cart roll quietly into the courtyard and the driver call out.

"The young master is hurt."

Rayappa rose and hurried out of his room. Sivraj and the driver were helping Linga off the cart. Linga had a deep knife wound in his upper arm. Rayappa tore the hem of his dhoti and wrapped the material around Linga's arm to stop the bleeding.

"Ah, Lord Irwin, you are also a nurse." Linga looked at Rayappa with mockery and affection. "Very much like your namesake, I see, playing both sides. I heard Lord Irwin was a Nazi lover."

Irwin tied the cloth tightly. "Perhaps at one time he was conciliatory towards them, but later, as Britain's ambassador to the United States, he influenced Roosevelt to enter the war. Lord Irwin completely changed his own views on Germany."

"My point exactly. Your loyalty shifts like the wind."

Rayappa wasn't sure why he was engaging with Linga or what propelled him to help such a man. Maybe it was his odd sense of loyalty or simple decency. Decency that was so lacking in Linga.

Rayappa wiped the blood off his hands onto his dhoti. "Your wound may need sutures."

"And now Lord Irwin is a doctor." Linga swayed and grabbed Rayappa's shoulder to balance himself.

Rayappa and Sivraj helped Linga up the stairs and across the veranda to the house. Before Rayappa could enter, the doors shut in his face. Then the sky exploded with thunder and it started to rain. Heading back to his room, he heard someone call out from behind the bullock house.

"Master Rayappa."

He moved towards the voice. "What are you doing here?"

Malika stood flush with the wall, gripping a woody vine as if preparing to climb it and escape. "I need to leave this place. Please give me money."

"What happened to you?"

"I need money. Please."

"I have none. I will get paid only after I finish here. Come with me."

Malika's brilliant green sari was plastered to her skin. Rayappa reached for Malika's hand but she was gripping some red material. "You can't stay out here. I will think of something." He led her into his room and pulled the curtain closed.

She was breathless but couldn't stop talking.

"They murdered my family, they burned down our huts. Please help me." Her voice was hoarse, her body trembling.

"Best sit up here." Rayappa patted the cot and fetched her a cloth to dry herself. "That way no one will see your feet and discover you."

"I cannot stay." Her pupils were dilated, her eyes darted from one side of the room to the other.

"But where will you go? Perhaps your father? Where is he, which hospital?"

Malika sobbed. "I don't know. I can't remember. My mother made the arrangements."

"But certainly someone knows. The landlord?"

"No, no. I will try to find Vijay. He didn't come. No one knows where he is."

Rayappa felt sick remembering Vijay.

"Malika. Vijay is . . . he ran into the forest yesterday. I searched for him."

"What are you saying? How do you know this?" Rayappa said nothing. Tears filled Malika's eyes. "What more, what more am I supposed to endure?" Malika sobbed. Rayappa thought about the wailing of old village women. It was a sound of inconsolable grief.

"What can I do? You must help me!" She grasped Rayappa's arm.

"I will try. Tomorrow I will ask the professor for an advance. I will protect you."

Rayappa knew what he must do. And what he wanted to do. A fierce and passionate realization hit him.

"I will marry you. I love you. We can leave this place."

A shot rang out from the streets outside the compound. Malika looked up at Rayappa. He wrapped his arms around the trembling girl.

*

Vijay stood in the river as a sliver of light lingered on the horizon. He sensed the light, a flicker that signalled a portal to somewhere else. Like a delicate hand reaching out for his. In a split second it could disappear. And then it did. The light was gone. Vijay felt a chill as his chin submerged in the Vancha. His feet, the whole one and the clubbed, sank deeper into the soft riverbed, enveloping the part of his body that had emerged first in his breech birth. The part of his body that made him a target of ridicule and pity. The part of his body that didn't allow him to run. The part of his body that helped bring him here.

He was sinking in soft mud. It reminded him of the clay his mother shaped into bowls. He thought of his mother's hands, kneading dough, mussing his hair, pinching his cheeks, patting his back, preparing him for sleep. A familiar lullaby played over and over in his head as he descended deeper into the riverbed. He would have a new mother. She would be cold and dark. She would enfold him and allow him to forget.

*

Dawn revealed three gunny sacks of grain in the cart, streaks of blood on the wheels, and a gash in the bullock's flank. Later Rayappa would come to know that Malika's family were killed along with thirty others, including the volunteer leader from Warangal. Nineteen peasant protesters from the night before were arrested and forty goondas, a mix of Razakars and Linga's friends, had been dragged to the station.

There was a loud pounding on the blue double doors, before the rooster's crow. Before Reddy could call out his morning commands. Rayappa was alone. He dressed quickly and went into the courtyard. Sivraj opened the doors.

"Police to see the master of the house."

The landlord appeared on the porch, bathed and dressed, expecting this early morning visit. He nodded at Sivraj to allow the officer in charge to enter.

The officer approached the veranda where Reddy stood. "Sir. We need a witness. We are holding some men outside who are accused of rioting and burning down the homes of villagers in the hills. They say they were in your company last night. If you confirm it, they will be released."

"Let me bring my sons. They will recognize these young people."

Linga and Surendra emerged from the house looking fresh-faced and earnest. The officer asked whether they would come to the truck outside to identify the men and confirm the alibis.

"Bring them inside," commanded Reddy. "They are not criminals after all."

Forty men were brought into the courtyard by several officers. They looked restless and bored. Rayappa recognized a few of the young men from the night at the castrator's shed. He wasn't sure if there was a word to describe what had happened to Vijay. An abduction, an assault, a prank? *Cruelty* was all he could come up with. He knew some of these men were guilty of more than one crime. The men lined up, rubbing their necks and adjusting their clothes, as the three Reddy men stepped off the veranda in order to size them up.

Rayappa hoped the police might question Linga Reddy along with the others and haul him away. He moved closer to better hear what they were saying.

Reddy released a hearty laugh. "Come on now. These men were our guests last night."

"We found them on the streets." The officer pursed his lips.

"Of course you did." Reddy clapped the shoulder of one man in the line-up. "They were leaving our house. Our celebration. You see, my son had the pleasure of announcing that his wife is expecting a child. Jai Ram!"

Surendra stepped forward into his father's embrace as one by one the police officers offered their congratulations and blessings. They apologized for the disruption at such a time.

"Thank you. The women, as well as our distinguished visitor, are sleeping. I needn't tell you that this has been an intrusion." Reddy's pleasant smile disappeared from his face. "We will assist you in any way. We do not want hoodlums running rampant around the village. My son, in fact, said there were some strangers last night in Korampally. Perhaps members of the CPI, which I thought was illegal in every village. Except ours, I suppose. Your officers should look for *them*."

Linga glanced in Rayappa's direction. "Father, might I suggest that our house guest may be able to give the police a description. He too saw these visitors."

Rayappa wished he had stayed inside his room.

Linga put his left arm around Rayappa's shoulder and walked him towards the policemen. "Rayappa, tell the chief officer about the visitors we saw when we were on the bullock cart the other day inspecting the fields. They said they came to see Gandhi, when in fact they were attending a wedding. Is that not correct?"

Rayappa wondered why they were even talking about these visitors. But instead of questioning this, he simply nodded. He looked shamefaced at Linga, who smiled broadly, smug in his knowledge that Rayappa would not contradict him in his own home.

"All right then." Reddy reached into his waistcoat and pulled out a bundle of notes. "Please, give this to the poor family who lost their home."

The chief officer bowed his head. "I am sorry, sir."

"What, you will not allow me to take care of my village? I am the head of the village and I may help whomever I choose. Especially in such times."

"But sir, the family was in the hut when the fire started. Sadly, there are no survivors."

"Ah." Reddy shook his head slowly. "Then keep this and distribute it to your men for the good work done. I am sure you will find the agitators."

The chief officer pocketed the bills, did namascaram to Reddy and left with the rest of the officers and the goondas. Rayappa knew they would be released like rats into the streets. Rayappa remembered Connelly's phrase: *such is village justice*.

The Reddys returned to the great house and Rayappa retreated to the sanctuary of his room. He sat on his bed and wondered what it meant to be human. Last night, he felt he had reached the summit of his life, having found a greater purpose. The possibility to save someone he desired and yes, loved.

After holding Malika, burying himself in her sandalwood-scented hair, and collapsing beside her, Rayappa had made the mistake of falling asleep. When he awoke, she was gone. He ached with a profound loneliness, knowing he had experienced a joy he might never know again. If only he could stay with it. Trust it. His life might amount to something. He tried to conjure up the memory of her dark skin, her strong body and sudden softness. But he could only sit in anguish. She had fled from him. He felt sick. What had he done? He knew it was futile to search for her. The world outside had changed, and he too had changed. The red sari, in which Aditi Reddy had foolishly dressed Malika, was left damp and folded on his bed, and on top of that, a decorative basket, small enough to cradle in one's palm. A frivolous item. He would return the sari to Aditi quietly. But the basket? Was that meant for him?

Rayappa finally emerged from his room and found Sivraj and the other servants sprinkling water from clay pots tucked under their arms onto the dusty courtyard. Inside the house, Veena Reddy was shouting commands for the evening meal. Only Connelly sat on the veranda sipping tea.

"Rayappa, I think my work is over here."

"Sir?"

Connelly cleared his throat and extended an envelope to Rayappa.

"Here is your final payment. It is yours in exchange for your latest notes."

"But sir. No review, no discussion? There is more research to do. We have only spent a month. I can still be of service. What about the book?"

"I think it is best that we part ways, Rayappa."

Rayappa had lost faith in his father, in Gandhi, and now in Connelly. And Connelly in turn had rejected him. Despite his unnatural habits, the professor was all he had.

"I need to explain. I was a bystander to Linga's pranks. I did try to help that woman."

"Just bring me your notes."

The envelope of cash seemed suspended in mid-air. If Rayappa refused it, perhaps he could convince the professor to continue the project that would prolong Rayappa's work here. He could possibly find Malika. He had nothing if his career ended. If he took the money, he could make his way back to Nellore. His old life, from which he had once longed to escape. Suddenly the memory of that life filled him with comfort. Maybe this was the moment when the idealist turned pragmatist. The hopeful turned cynical.

Rayappa shuffled back to his room to retrieve his notebook. Then he noticed what was no longer there. His shoes. His watch. His suitcase. Not a trace of his father. Not a trace of Malika aside from the tiny basket. He now realized she had left him this gift in exchange for everything he had cherished, including his notes. He could not accept Connelly's payment now. Rayappa would leave Korampally poorer than when he first arrived.

1997 — The Crossroads

At the Krishna Lodge, Irwin sits on a wooden chair dressed in his undershirt and pyjama bottoms. He is looking out the window onto the crossroads of Korampally. There stands the peepal tree where they had stopped to water the bullocks fifty years ago. Some workers are measuring its trunk, some have taped off the perimeter around the tree to forbid entry. Others have started drilling into the tarmac where the roots of the tree burst through. Irwin can feel the vibration in his buttocks and thighs. Like the ringing of an alarm clock, it rattles his still mind. Looking down, he sees that his feet are swollen. They seem to reflect the throbbing in his head, his hands, his heart. Irwin has not withstood the travel well, having carried along the familiar churn of anxiety. It is boxed inside him, bundled tight.

Irwin reaches for his pills. Swallows two dry. As an afterthought he rises to fetch a glass of water. The soles of his feet are tender. Still, he manages to walk to the washroom where he finds a bucket of water in which to soak them. Forgetting about the glass, he makes his way back to his room, dry-mouthed and lopsided with the weight of water in the bucket.

It is the first day that Irwin has to himself since they left Canada. In a way, he is glad his feet are swollen. It is a good excuse not to accompany Jaya and Anya. He does not want to meet this Ashamma, whoever she is. Posing as a grandmother. Probably wanting to extort money or secure immigration papers. A charlatan who has infected Jaya and Anya with some sympathetic narrative, like an airborne virus. He will have to wait until the disease runs its course, moves through their bloodstreams and passes out of their systems. They will all return to Canada with a few stories to tell, and more importantly, be inoculated against the curiosity that plagues first-generation Canadians to find their roots.

Irwin sits back in the wooden chair and puts his feet into the bucket. What a relief. He contemplates how his misshapen feet have borne his weight across the world and back to this place. Outside, crowds gather around the peepal tree.

*

After their first visit with Ashamma, Jaya and Anya say thank you and good-bye to Parveen, who, with the driver, has dropped them off at the crossroads. It is a chaotic intersection with the arborists closing in on the peepal tree, visitors disembarking from buses, and traffic flowing in and out from all directions. People like to honk their horns, Jaya thinks. She also wonders if Irwin has gotten any rest, whether any of them will. Anya decides to go for a walk while Jaya returns to the Krishna Lodge. The clerk hands her an envelope. Her full name is neatly handwritten. It is something Irwin would do. Still formal and polite, she surmises, despite the havoc he can cause. Jaya hands the letter back to the clerk. "Would you mind reading this aloud? I have forgotten my glasses." The clerk opens the letter.

> *Dear Madame,*
>
> *I am sorry I did not have the pleasure of presenting this letter to you personally and I apologize that our village does not have sophisticated accommodation for your comfort. Will you consider accepting my offer to stay in a newly built home, currently vacant, and situated on the east side of the river. It is quiet, modest but modern, and you are welcome to be my guest and partake of our services (a cook, a washer man, and maid) as you wish.*
>
> *Please do me the pleasure of accepting my gift. Do not hesitate to contact me at your convenience.*
>
> *At your service,*
> *K. Linga Reddy*
>
> *P.S. How are you making out with the new sunglasses?*

Part Three
1948-1955

7. Respectability

Sometimes there is an opening in a life that heralds the big chance to step off a path, which may have seemed destined. For Rayappa that opportunity had been Connelly's research in Korampally — a project for which he had been hand-picked, chosen from hundreds of potential candidates. He could have been credited in Connelly's book, *Return to the Village*; he could have networked into circles as prestigious as Oxford and from there launched into a brilliant career, living a life devoted to the science of social anthropology. He could have lifted the quotidian preoccupations of Indian social groups into intellectual inquiry, prepared an analysis, to finally understand his own people. He could have shared his discoveries with the world. In this way, Rayappa could have played a pivotal role in emancipating Indians, gaining empathy and respect from the global community. Hopes of a scholarly career vanished when Rayappa was pushed off the project and forced to leave the village after only one month of Connelly's one-year sabbatical. Convinced that his one chance to succeed in his chosen vocation was over, he arrived back in Nellore, disillusioned.

His mother, Alisamma, renamed Alice by the Texas Lone Star Baptist Church, was forty years old and deeply disappointed. Her daughters, Jyoti and Shanti, nicknamed Light and Peace, were illiterate and unmarried, working as maids. Alisamma's own work as a seamstress was precarious, her eyesight dimming behind thick glasses. And the three cherished belongings — reminders that she had had a husband — were now gone: a pair of size-eight oxfords, a tan leather suitcase, and a gold pocket watch.

The day Rayappa graduated from the Lone Star Christian College, Alisamma carefully placed the gold pocket watch into her son's open palm as if to say, "It is up to you now." Rayappa had studied the watch, wondering if it would reveal some hidden insight into his father. He noted the high polish, the thick weave of the chain, the ornate numbers circling the clock's face. He also saw it had stopped. What use was the watch to his mother, if not to keep time? Perhaps she held on to it to evoke a memory or collect a promise. Maybe it served as a small mirror to examine the lines on her face, an indicator of time passed. The face of the clock did not change. It revealed a fixed time of 5:05, a.m. or p.m., who was to know? It had stopped on the day that Irwin's father was scheduled to return from his deployment in Burma. Instead, he had vanished from their lives. And Alisamma became old.

Soon after earning his Master of Arts in social anthropology, Rayappa slipped the watch into a pink pouch, packed the oxfords in the tan leather suitcase, and left Nellore for Korampally. A mere month later, in January 1948, he found himself home and empty-handed. He couldn't help but wonder how his father had acquired these items. Were these gifts from his army friends? Awards bestowed by a hopeful teacher? Objects won in a bet? Rayappa's mother never said, as if ordinary explanations would render them commonplace. The three items had reminded Alisamma of Joseph. Entrusted to Rayappa, they had reminded Rayappa of Joseph. Now, the absence of those items reminded Rayappa of Malika.

Rayappa wondered whether Malika cherished them or had sold them for sustenance, whether she playfully tried on the shoes or gave them to a new lover. What did she carry in the suitcase? Did she turn the knob on the pocket watch and hope to hear it tick? Did she remember the lessons that he had taught her on that sunbaked veranda? Had she turned back with regret after setting off that night? Was she even alive?

Rayappa lifted his head from the desk. He was in his office in Nellore, in his new job, in his new life. A round clock hung on the opposite wall. The minute hand ticked forward to twelve. It was 4 p.m., the end of his break and the end of his remembering. Rayappa stood and stretched. Pulling open the metal drawer of the file cabinet, he imagined his memories from Korampally slipping from his mind into a crisp white folder.

If one happened upon the folder and opened it, what would they find?

1. A cow-fucking, red-faced, Indophile anthropologist.
2. A sheep-loving, bullock-minding, landlord-servicing eleven-year-old slave.
3. A bullock-cart-riding, rape-orchestrating heir to forty thousand acres of land.

4. A tree-climbing, wall-scaling, shit-cleaning, world-wondering girl turned woman.
5. A tree-drawing, grass-weaving, caste-disrupting, Mahatma-washed "Harijan."

The shit-cleaning month, the horror-witnessing month, the innocence-losing month of his life. The folder was full. Rayappa mentally filed it away under December, 1947, marking it confidential.

Moving forward, Rayappa would not waste time reflecting on what he had experienced or with whom. History had been made, and he had work to do. He had joined the Madras Presidency Civil Service and committed to the mission of nation building. This was no easy task. India and Pakistan had been born of Partition, from the broken dreams of freedom fighters. As the great migration of some fifteen million people drew to a close, the scale of the tragedy was becoming apparent. No one could have predicted the extent of the atrocities resulting from Britain's deadline to quit India and their decision to split the subcontinent. Had the national leaders ceded too easily to the political demands of religious fundamentalists? Had they failed to recognize the fervour with which groups would turn on each other? Or had they been cruelly indifferent to the cost of their own political ambitions?

Although Rayappa read about the impacts of violence in the wake of Partition, he felt oddly removed. Physically he was safe, far from the sites of migration, living in the city of Nellore, in the Madras Presidency, in southeast India.

Irwin began the rest of his life, filling time with the countless tasks of administrating an old region in a new country. And for all the hours devoted to detailed reports, the deference paid to his boss, the responsibilities dutifully assumed, it amounted to nothing but his growing capacity to forget.

*

When Rayappa stepped off the bus from Korampally empty-handed, Alisamma demanded that he apply to work in government service. She would not allow him to wallow in self-pity, having invested heavily in her only son.

Rayappa found himself standing in queues, writing letters of inquiry, and filling out job applications. Teacher, teacher's assistant, administrative assistant, clerk—any available position. He even crept back to his alma mater and approached the dean of the Lone Star Christian College. Rayappa was handed his exemplary academic record and a supportive letter of reference.

More importantly, he was given the name of an administrator in the Madras civil service who could be "very helpful indeed."

D.B. Srikaram was a good and learned man. He was seated at a large desk. He had a high shiny forehead and a significant gap between his teeth. Features of intelligence, according to superstition. Srikaram also proved to be empathetic. Born a Brahmin, he confided to Rayappa that when he was Rayappa's age, he had fallen in love with an Anglo-Indian classmate, whom he later married. She joined the mandir, performed puja, and knelt to touch the feet of his father. His family and circle of friends were polite to her in company, but some maintained a sense of superiority in private. Srikaram's personal experience of intermarriage had helped open his mind to the plight of minorities in the state. Srikaram felt empathy towards Rayappa and was duly impressed with the young man's application to the District Collector's Office in Nellore. Rayappa was taken on immediately as a petty clerk. His meticulous attention to detail and obvious intellect secured him a:

1. title
2. door
3. desk
4. pen
5. page
6. purpose
7. promotion

He became a records supervisor and Srikaram's favourite. Rayappa had arrived at an opportune moment, when India was preparing to become a republic. There was much to accomplish. He made a point of being the first to arrive at the office and the last to leave. Eager to please, he met every deadline, wrote substantial reports, and leapt from his seat to volunteer for additional duties.

His superiors took notice. The peons who distributed the mail, however, would not place letters neatly in his tray like they did for others but tossed them carelessly towards his desk. White envelopes, like paper planes, glided onto the floor. There was no kind gesture to help retrieve these items, no one offered an apology, not even a backward glance of acknowledgement. When Rayappa complained, Srikaram admonished him.

"If you had a stain upon your face, would you not wipe it away?"

Rayappa did not comprehend.

Srikaram tapped his pen on his desk repeatedly. "Not only do they see it, they hear it, every day when you are addressed. They are caste Hindus and resent your position. You can tolerate this behaviour and get nowhere in *this* life, or change your name, command respect, and succeed. Unfortunate as it may be, this is the reality."

Rayappa suddenly understood that his untouchable roots kept him tethered. There were those who rose above the burden of caste to great heights such as Dr. Bhimrao Ambedkar, who was currently chairing the Constitute Assembly, charged by the Congress Party to write the constitution of India. But not everyone could be Ambedkar, Rayappa thought. There were lesser-known examples as well—one of his teachers at school and the minister of a Baptist church in Nellore. Rayappa, like these men, was determined to rise above the discrimination and contempt levelled at his Madiga community. He decided to change his name and design his life around three commitments:

1. work—be disciplined and diligent
2. religion—be devout and steady
3. marriage—be faithful and dependable

He would prove that he was every bit as capable as caste Hindus.

Rayappa completed an application for a name change and was preparing to leave the office to submit it when he was diverted by a flurry of activity in the corridor. All India Radio seemed to be broadcasting a special program of bhajans, devotional songs. Clerks who should have been finished for the day were gathering around the tea trolley. Rayappa walked over and turned off their radio. The peon pushing the trolley on which a radio was placed fell to his knees. "Gandhiji is dead..."

Srikaram came out of his office.

"Try to stay calm everyone. I have been informed that Gandhi was killed by a member of the Rashtriya Swayamsevak Sangh. A very tragic day indeed. You are all invited to the main hall. Prayers will be said for Gandhiji."

Rayappa felt a firm hand on his shoulder. "The prayers are for the Hindus. Your time is better spent back at your desk. You understand this means our work will become even more critical."

Rayappa sat at his desk, staring at the name change application he had completed. Gandhi had been shot by a Hindu nationalist at a multi-faith prayer meeting, of all places. Rayappa foresaw the whole country erupting in violence, the stunned leaders entreating the aid of the British, and the reversal of their political progress. His country needed him, and he would not fail her.

*

Hyderabad was the cosmopolitan capital city of the kingdom of the Nizam, Mir Osman Ali Khan, Asaf Jah VII. No area better reflected her grandeur than Afzal Gunj. Named after the fifth Nizam, it was a predominantly Muslim enclave recognized by Hyderabadis as the courtyard of culture. Here, massive domes of the High Court, the Salar Jung Museum, and the magnificent Osmania General Hospital rose from the banks of the Musi River. Beyond these architectural wonders were busy thoroughfares and alleys, where cramped dwellings were pressed between grand houses guarded by high walls.

The Benjamin family owned such an estate. Surrounded by a nine-foot stone wall, the grand house had three stories with large airy, cool rooms. On the main floor, shuttered windows opened onto a large stone veranda that wrapped around three sides of the house. It welcomed the morning light on one side, and on the other side cleverly planted tamarind and sitaphal — custard apple — trees filtered the glare from the setting sun. The home was suited to a large family and felt massive to its occupants, Dr. Samuel Benjamin and his daughter, Kanta.

Dr. Benjamin descended from a well-educated Christian Telugu family. He had made his name through exemplary service in the Nizam's army as the public health medical officer. Charged with heading up the malaria control program for the district, a young Dr. Benjamin went village to village identifying malaria clusters. Villagers had been turning to mantras and animal sacrifices to cure the illness. Unsuccessful, they would circle Dr. Benjamin during his visits, begging for treatment. He was, however, more interested in potable water, chlorination of wells, and sanitation issues. To quell the crowd, Dr. Benjamin took to injecting saline into the muscles of villagers when they would not heed the fact that he had no medicine to provide. Dr. Benjamin's reputation grew. Whether he was viewed as empathetic to the villagers for providing them some psychological relief or unethical for deceiving them with a placebo was never quite determined. He did, however, manage to successfully map the malaria belt in Telangana and was invited to the Nizam's court. With the success of the anti-malaria campaign, his confidence in science and modern medicine deepened. He hoped that his pregnant wife, Evelyn, would give birth to a prodigy who would one day follow in his footsteps and surpass all his accomplishments. He was away on an inspection tour when Evelyn went into premature labour. By the time Dr. Benjamin arrived his wife lay lifeless in her bed.

"Heart attack," the attending doctor said. A beat later, he offered some good news. "The baby is thriving. A lovely baby girl. Her mother named her Kanta."

Dr. Benjamin hardly glanced at the baby cradled in the arms of Evelyn's mother. He began to perform cardiopulmonary resuscitation on his wife, breathing into her mouth and performing chest compressions. Mad with grief and against the protest of Evelyn's anguished parents, he wrapped his wife in a blanket, lifted her body from the bed, and laid her on the back seat of his newly purchased Wolseley car. Dr. Benjamin climbed into the front seat and sped away. His purpose was not to take her to the hospital, but to hit every bump, pothole, and gutter, hoping to jolt his beloved Evelyn back to life. He raced through the gulley at a speed that burned up the 2.6 litre engine of his car and frightened the residents. His attempts to revive her failed. An autopsy later revealed that while Evelyn's heart had indeed stopped, the cause of death was internal bleeding. There was nothing he could have done to save her. Dr. Benjamin finally accepted his wife's death and vowed to make his daughter's life one devoid of suffering.

Eighteen years later, Kanta was still the focus of Dr. Benjamin's affection. He was a proud and protective father and kept potential suitors far away from his daughter. Kanta had her own trick to fend off unwanted attention. She had a wandering eye that made it appear as if she were searching in two different directions at the same time. If a man stared at her, she returned his gaze. He would not know if Kanta were looking at or past him. She enjoyed confusing and then putting off these would-be suitors.

A week after Gandhi died, Kanta sat poised on a cane chair, the large stone slabs of the veranda cool under her slender feet, her sky-blue and gold gossamer sari pulled tightly across her breasts. Her face was a perfect heart shape, her neck long and elegant. Her small hands were crossed demurely over her lap as she waited for the driver to hitch the horse to the tonga. She was dressed for the palace, although she was headed to the central library. Sarojini Naidu, the governor of the United Provinces, had returned to her hometown soon after Gandhi's death.

A protege of the Mahatma, she was also known as the poet of the Quit India Movement and named the Nightingale of India by Gandhi himself. She was giving a poetry reading at his memorial. Kanta, who preferred Keats to revolutionary Indian poets, had been persuaded to attend the event by her fourteen- and fifteen-year-old cousins, Ruth and Rebecca. The two girls, already seated in the tonga, had taken an active interest in the Quit India Movement and needed and wanted their older cousin to accompany them to the memorial. Kanta slipped her toes into her gold-painted chappals before descending the wide stone steps to join her charges.

Kanta was used to a varied and vibrant social life. Muslims, Hindus, Parsis, and Christians enjoyed each other's company, respected each other's traditions, frequented each other's homes, and attended each other's weddings. As Mulkis, the affectionate term for Hyderabadi natives, the Benjamin family was immersed in Persian culture. Biriyani was their food, ghazals their poetry, and Urdu tumbled from their mouths as easily as Telugu, their native tongue. Under the Nizam, art and music flourished. Education was valued and promoted, and religious tolerance was expected. With permission granted from the Nizam, the Christian community built its first church in 1844, where Dr. Benjamin proudly conducted the choir and Kanta developed into a clear lyric soprano, singing Fauré and Debussy to a congregation that did not comprehend a single word. Assured that his daughter was well-heeled, well-dressed, and well-spoken, Dr. Benjamin brought Kanta to the formal functions at the Nizam's palace. She also accompanied him to Osmania General Hospital, where she had the privilege of observing surgeries in operating theatres well equipped with modern medical apparatus. She asked more questions than he could answer, so Dr. Benjamin provided his daughter with medical journals. It was assumed that Kanta would follow in the footsteps of her father, but she was not so single-minded.

Her father indulged Kanta and responded happily to her whims. Her love of literature meant her private library was well stocked. She was naturally athletic, so he set up cricket wickets in the driveway in front of the carriage houses. He opened the gates to neighbourhood children, welcoming boys and girls to play together. When Kanta came of age, her father unlocked her late mother's armoire, overflowing with English gowns and saris from various regions. She popped open her mother's many jewellery cases, containing uncultured pearl chains, uncut diamond earrings, thick gold snake-head bangles, and chokers with semi-precious stones. Kanta, with no close female mentor to emulate, developed her own unique style. At eighteen, she stood out.

Dr. Benjamin had complete confidence in his daughter's judgment as she joined her cousins to attend the memorial. He blessed Kanta, tracing the cross of Jesus on her forehead, just before the tonga driver set the horse in motion. He stood waving goodbye as the tonga disappeared beyond the gate.

Sarojini Naidu never failed to move a crowd. Her inspiring poetry and persuasive rhetoric had been resounding in the ears and hearts of Indians for over four decades. But here she was in the flesh, her moon face and subtle Mona Lisa smile, looking out to a grief-stricken crowd. This dignified states-woman, an advocate of female emancipation and a role model in India's fight for freedom, did not read poetry. Instead she reiterated a speech she had given on All India Radio memorializing Gandhi just two days after his death. And yet these words felt new, as if they were created in the moment, to inspire people to action. Sarojini Naidu's words inspired Gandhians, Congress sup-porters, academics, and students—everyone except Kanta. Not that Naidu's words were lost on her—she understood their power—but she refused to be moved by this nationalist poet and politician out of loyalty to the Nizam.

After the memorial, Kanta and her cousins lingered outside the library, arguing about whether Hyderabad would be better or worse off if it were to join the Indian Union. Kanta held her anti-India stance: "Hyderabad is cultured and protected."

Rebecca contradicted her older cousin. "It is archaic and enslaved."

They volleyed arguments back and forth, each girl steadfast in her con-viction. The tonga driver finally urged Kanta and her cousins to come away. Kanta glanced down to check the time, but instead of her watch she was wearing two snake-head bangles, one on each wrist.

As the evening darkened, the horse clomped slowly through narrow alleys. Kanta and her cousins continued their chatter, barely noticing that the bust-ling neighbourhood had gone quiet.

"Where is everyone?" Ruth looked around at the empty streets.

The tonga halted abruptly. Three teenaged boys stood in front of the horse. The tallest boy grabbed the bridle, the others moved to either side of the cart. Kanta bowed her head.

One boy stood so close to her that she could feel his breath on her forehead. "Why are you ladies out past curfew?"

Rebecca and Ruth started whimpering, drawing their chunnis up and over their faces to hide from the boy who lurched over to them on the other side of the cart.

Kanta dared not look up to see the boy's face but recognized the intricate Persian termeh pattern of the lungi that he was wearing. These were not street thugs but well-dressed Muslim boys.

"You have no answer? Never mind." The boy grabbed Kanta's wrist. "I will take this."

Kanta pulled back and took off her snake-head bangle, handing it over.

"I do not want *that* but I want *this*." He pulled Kanta towards him.

The driver entreated them to stop, saying his master would punish them. The tall boy, who had remained standing near the horse, his back to the girls, forced the crop from the driver's hand. The driver let out a cry.

"Keep quiet."

The voice was familiar. Kanta looked up as the tall boy turned towards her.

"Yasin! It is you?"

"Kan... Miss Benjamin?"

"What would your father say?" Kanta chastised him.

Yasin's father was Dr. Hussain, descendant of the great architect after whom the heart-shaped lake, Hussain Sagar, was named. He was a good friend and colleague of Dr. Benjamin. Kanta and Yasin had spent their elementary school years playing cricket in the courtyard or conspiring under her father's dining table.

Yasin looked from one boy to the other. "Friends, this is Uncle Benjamin's daughter. He is a doctor in the Nizam's army. Leave them. Let them be."

The boy released Kanta's wrist, and her bangle was returned. Yasin gave the crop to the driver. After gently patting the horse, Yasin approached Kanta.

"As Salam u Alaikum." He bowed his head and gestured with his right hand. Kanta knew his soft voice, his tapered fingers, his beautiful signet ring. She was fond of him. Her childhood friend.

Kanta nodded. "Wa Alaikumus Salaam."

The shock of what had just happened dissipated with this sacred and simple gesture. As the horse and buggy moved forward, Ruth and Rebecca burst into tears. Kanta was pensive as she turned to look at Yasin and the other boys standing in the middle of the road, their bravado deflated.

*

"Do you not know the time?" Dr. Benjamin did not embrace his daughter when she stepped down from the tonga. "Do you not know there is curfew?" Dr. Benjamin did not wait for an answer but followed Kanta as she headed toward the house. "The country is going berserk. Communal violence is erupting everywhere. Right here in Hyderabad. How can I protect you if you are gallivanting around town? Do you not read the papers? Don't you know what is going on?"

Kanta hurried across the veranda and upstairs to her room. Her eyes were smarting as she lifted the mosquito net and collapsed on her bed. How could her father speak to her so harshly? She was determined not to cry. She found her book underneath her pillow. *Persuasion* by Jane Austen. She pulled it out and stubbornly focused on its small print, trying to blot out her father's words. He was wrong. She did read the papers. She read that India was imploding and Hyderabad, with its porous borders, was not immune. All over the Telangana countryside, Communists were overthrowing village landlords, and Gandhians had staged sit-ins and marched from town to town demanding a united India. The trade unionists went on strike, bringing production to a halt, and Hindu extremists were raiding government departments, banks, and post offices. Did he think she was an idiot?

For decades, Hyderabad had seemed exempt from the revolutions sweeping other parts of the subcontinent. Kanta was not the only person who felt Hyderabad was a safe haven, and Dr. Benjamin did not contradict her belief. Rather, he explained that under British rule, the Nizam had maintained an understanding with the Crown. The Nizam had declared he would not join the Indian Union, and this was confirmed by the Standstill Agreement, signed by both parties. This ensured that a republic could form around the Kingdom of Hyderabad, securing its financial, cultural, and political independence.

Kanta leafed through her book until she found the passage in *Persuasion* that calmed her mind and drew her into the story.

"You pierce my soul. I am half agony, half hope. Tell me not that I am too late, that such precious feelings are gone forever. I offer myself to you again with a heart even more your own.... I have loved none but you. Unjust I may have been, weak and resentful I have been, but never inconstant."

Kanta imagined herself to be Anne Elliot and Yasin, Captain Wentworth. The setting was the upper level of Charminar, their silhouettes were framed by two minarets, her gaze was aimed towards Golconda Fort and a purple-sunset sky. Yasin turned to her, apologizing profusely for what had happened in the tonga, for he was weak, unjust, and resentful. Then he dropped to his knees, taking her hand...

"Kanta!" Dr. Benjamin knocked loudly.

Kanta scrambled out from behind the mosquito net and opened the door.

"Things are not good, daughter." He walked past her and went to her dresser and began fiddling with her perfume bottles. "The newspapers have not reported accurately on the grim state of things." Dr. Benjamin sat down in an armchair. "The Nizam counted on the British to protect him, but now that they have gone, the Nizam has no allies. Hyderabad is up for grabs. Any faction with enough might can claim her."

"But what about Jinnah? Several of my friends think Pakistan will protect Hyderabad."

Dr. Benjamin squeezed the wooden armrest, stood, and faced her.

"That is absurd. Pakistan is almost 2000 kilometers from Hyderabad. Do you think India will allow such an allyship? And what do your schoolmates know of Jinnah! The Nizam opened his palace to him in 1941. And the arrogant Jinnah blew cigar smoke in His Excellency's face."

Dr. Benjamin, though agitated, tried to explain how the Nizam, blind to his own receding power, could neither cede to India nor bring himself to join forces with Jinnah in Pakistan. "Sadly, the Nizam has backed himself into a corner. He has aligned himself with Qasim Razvi. We all know Razvi's notorious tactics. It's just a matter of time before Nehru and his deputy Patel will use Razvi's violent rampages as an excuse to overthrow the Nizam, and pull Hyderabad into the Union."

"But Papa, my friend is convinced that the Union will destroy our rich culture, our way of life."

"Who is this friend? And what else does she say?"

Kanta felt nervous. Suddenly her father no longer felt like her father, but a powerful opponent. "That Qasim Razvi may be the Nizam's only chance, that he will keep India out, preserve our Hyderabad..."

"Qasim Razvi is out of control. He is using his Razakar Army to terrorize Hindus, Christians, and Muslims alike."

"Papa, what are you talking about? Razvi is the president of the Majlis-e-Ittehadul Muslimeen, and part of the legislative assembly. He is the Nizam's most loyal supporter."

"And that is what makes him more powerful and dangerous. He has used his close relationship with the Nizam to recruit the poorest of the poor into his Razakar Army. Muslims, lower caste Hindus, Mahars, Malas, Madigas, feeding them rhetoric and turning them into thugs. They are nothing but street fighters who wield swords against anyone in their way."

"Papa, let's speak about something else. I don't want to be involved. I wish things didn't have to change."

"But they are changing and you must be involved. I didn't educate you to keep your head in the sand, buried in a storybook!"

"But Yasin says…"

"Hussain's son? What about him? What nonsense has he put in your head?"

Kanta felt cornered. Her father's voice was so loud. She turned to the wall. Staring at the blank space, she saw all of Yasin's contradictions. How he used to play cricket with girls then lately had decreed that girls should not play sports. How he had once recited *Meer Taqi Meer* and *Makhdoom Mohiuddin* but then traded these beautiful rhythmic couplets for clunky rhetoric. How when she had found a dead sunbird, it was Yasin who gently picked it up and laid it in a grave. Now he used his tapered fingers to crack whips, frightening old men and young women. She realized that Yasin, who was the kindest of all boys, had turned himself inside out. He once told her that when a minority rules a majority, there are natural checks and balances of power. But it was impossible for a majority Hindu government to ever protect a Muslim minority. That the idea of minority rights had charitable intent. That charity is only bestowed on those who are humiliated and pitied. That promises of secularism were like love promises: quickly made and easily broken.

When Kanta finally drew the courage to face her father, she could only tell him the facts about what had happened that night. That her childhood confidante, the son of her father's best friend, had held up the tonga. That in the middle of this hateful act, he had stopped, and she had returned home undefiled. She explained that they should both be grateful to Yasin for intervening. Her life and dignity had been spared.

Dr. Benjamin did not say a word. In the silence that followed, he calculated the risks of not being able to protect his daughter. They were too great. He would need to curtail her freedom. No longer would she be able to wander about with her friends, speak her mind openly, and choose her own course. Dr. Benjamin decided to seek a good match for his daughter. A wealthy, intelligent Christian boy, a wedding date, and ideally a move abroad.

*

Dr. Benjamin had two close friends, Dr. Hussain and Dr. Rao. One Muslim and one Hindu. They regarded each other as brothers. All three were physicians in the service of the Nizam; they had all matriculated at the same university at fifteen and graduated at twenty. They each spoke different native languages but could converse in each other's fluently. They had all married by the age of twenty-one and had lost their wives by twenty-five. Dr. Hussain's wife died when her ovary ruptured from an ectopic pregnancy while three-year-old Yasin watched his mother writhe with pain. Dr. Rao's wife committed suicide, leaving behind some suspicion about her husband's infidelities.

Dr. Rao, rich and robust, was by far the most eligible widower as he had no children. He taught in the classrooms of Osmania Medical College and attested he had always been faithful to his wife, before and after her death. He was wary of and avoided the company of women. Dr. Hussain dove into his work as chief medical surgeon at Osmania General Hospital, rose through the ranks within the Nizam's court, and buried himself in his work. He never found anyone who could quite match the beauty of his late wife. Dr. Benjamin saw his witty and intelligent Evelyn in the character of his daughter. He was by far the least scarred of the three.

Throughout Kanta's childhood, her father and his friends were affectionately known in the medical community as the three bachelors. While acquaintances understood them to be widowers, no one saw them as such. For how could men who had endured such loss still have such bright eyes and cheerful dispositions? They donned fez hats and wore sherwanis on formal occasions, looking terribly attractive and hopelessly unavailable at the same time.

Following the deaths of their wives, the three bachelors would console each other by spending hours together discussing medical advances, infectious diseases, current politics, or the latest gossip about the Nizam. Young Kanta and Yasin would hide under the table and listen attentively.

"Let me tell you, yaar," Hussain began. "I had to perform an appendectomy on His Excellency's nephew. And what do you think he did, our Nizam? He walked directly into the operating theatre with no mask, no gloves, and presided over the whole thing!"

"Of course, what do you expect? He owns the place." Rao, a large man, slapped his thigh.

"Naturally, he of royal breath..." Benjamin mocked a sigh.

The three friends doubled over with laughter and could not hear the parallel conversation between Kanta and Yasin underneath the table.

"I love the Nizam."

"I love him more."

"I will marry him." Kanta challenged Yasin, knowing he could never marry the Nizam.

"I will die for him." Yasin smiled, trumping her. Kanta kicked Yasin in the shins.

Unbeknownst to them in that moment, their contest would continue into adulthood, and the stakes would get higher. Yasin would ultimately win. Or lose. Depending on whether one valued winning the game at any cost.

*

St. George's was a whitewashed church situated in a large plot full of trees, set back from Abids Road, the busy and fashionable thoroughfare in Hyderabad. Dr. Benjamin and Kanta attended every Sunday, sang in the choir, and socialized after the service with other pious and prestigious Christian families.

Dr. Benjamin solicited the help of his female cousins, who drew up a list of potential husbands for Kanta. Meetings were arranged without delay. Kanta sat obediently across from the family of a Paul, a Peter, then a David, enduring stilted conversations and long tea-sipping afternoons. Today Dr. Benjamin entertained Mr. and Mrs. Rajan Thomas and their son, Alexander, nicknamed Sunny. He was a skinny, awkward chemistry major. Unable to carry a tune, Sunny had no inhibitions about singing loudly in the choir. Dr. Benjamin and Kanta had enjoyed mocking the boy's voice in private.

Dr. Benjamin saw the lad as respectable enough and highlighted the boy's academic record and family background to Kanta. Sunny would be the last of a dozen suitors whom Kanta had rejected over the past eight months.

As Dr. Benjamin led the family into the drawing room, he could feel the sweat coat his forehead. They sat for tea. The heat was stifling. He felt an itch on his upper lip. His hand kept moving up to his moustache. He felt like peeling it off. Dr. Benjamin's broad frame felt too small for the room. In contrast, Kanta appeared perfectly poised and aloof, answering yes or no when she was asked about her career plans. The conversation moved in fits and starts. Only when Mrs. Thomas spoke of the volunteer work she did at the hospital was Kanta's interest piqued.

"You are not a nurse, but you provide care for injured patients, madame?" Kanta leaned forward.

"Every day since the riots began. The nurses train volunteers and some have learned to train others. It is the least we can do."

Dr. Benjamin was pleased with their rapport, certain that Kanta had found a sympathetic mother-in-law. Mrs. Thomas invited Kanta to a volunteer training session. Kanta agreed. Later, Dr. Benjamin asked Kanta about the boy.

"Sunny? Oh Papa, you don't expect me to marry just anyone?"

"The boy is not just anyone. There are only so many Christian families with boys your age. If you continue to reject these proposals, you will end up with an old man."

"I would prefer an old man with character than a boy as dull as a doorknob."

"Then I am afraid that's what you will get. By the time you have settled on a husband, you yourself will be an old maid and even the old men will not look at you."

"And if I remain as I am?" Kanta knew full well there were many happy husband-free aunties in her family, living in comfortable houses, pursuing higher education, acquiring letters after their names.

"Then you will find yourself even more alone when you venture out in the tonga."

Kanta thought about this. How she still loved Yasin, despite what he had done. Kanta knew, now that her father was aware of the tonga incident and Yasin's political leanings, that marriage to Yasin was out of the question. And she knew she could not broach this subject with her father. Unable to quiet her mind with reading, she commenced her volunteer training with Mrs. Thomas and declined a second visit with Sunny.

*

It was September 16, 1948. Kanta had finished a shift as nurse's aide at the temporary medics' tent set up near the Nampally train station. It was early evening when Mrs. Thomas brought Kanta home in her car. The driver made his way through dense and chaotic traffic. People were rushing home to meet the curfew. Seated in the back seat with Kanta, Mrs. Thomas anxiously spoke about Indian troops said to be on the outskirts of the city. Kanta was silent. Even the dogs who ran across the courtyard to greet her upon arrival could not break her trance. She moved slowly into the house, avoiding the servants who called out to her to take food. Ignoring them, she went straight to her room.

Kanta sat on her bed, trying to make sense of what had happened. Violence had erupted in the city. An overflow of wounded patients from the hospital were sent to the medics' tent. First a cartload of soldiers from the Indian Army arrived, followed by a cartload of soldiers from the Hyderabadi Army, their bodies riddled with bullets. Kanta alternately hated the Nizam and then Nehru. She tried to push away what she had witnessed. A truth she didn't want to accept.

Dr. Benjamin, Dr. Rao, and Dr. Hussain, who had been summoned to tend to a surge of wounded at Osmania General Hospital, finished their shifts and came to the Benjamin House for supper. Although hungry, they could not eat. They were seated at the dining table, gathered around the radio. Months earlier, Dr. Benjamin had spoken discreetly to Dr. Hussain about the tonga incident. Dr. Hussain was shocked to learn that his son associated with such hooligans but assured Dr. Benjamin that Yasin would be set on the right path. Both friends were convinced that their bond would outlast the rebellious and misguided pranks of youth.

Each of Dr. Benjamin's friends held different desires for Hyderabad's future, and were careful about expressing their opinions to each other. Theirs was a disciplined, respectful, and dignified friendship that did not allow religious or political differences to come between them. Whatever the outcome of this conflict, nothing would strain their longstanding friendship.

Kanta had to speak to her father. She made her way downstairs and followed his voice into the dining room. Above the table, a single lightbulb hung from the ceiling, a moth hovering around it. Its wings fluttered, circling as if looking for a spot to land. Kanta stood in the entrance of the dining room unseen, searching for an opening in their conversation, to tell them what she knew. She could not find her breath. Her chest was tight and she felt she would faint. Then, the moth landed on the hot bulb. The radio announcer declared: "India invades the state to no effect! Hyderabad loyal forces beat back the enemy! The Nizam's brave soldiers massacre the Indian Army!"

Several voices overtook the announcer's and burst from the radio. "We were independent. We are independent. We will remain independent."

"Could it be true?" Dr. Rao said, in disbelief, "The Nizam has defeated the Indian Army?"

The radio fell silent. Dead air. The seconds ticked forward. This was Kanta's moment to speak. "Papa." Her voice cracked. No one heard her or saw her. Then the moth dropped from the bulb onto Dr. Hussain's lap. A sad ghazal played from the radio and filled the room, Saqib Lakhnavi's familiar words: "*Zamana bade shauq se sun raha tha*— All were listening with eyes so bright—*Hameen so gaye dastasan kehte-kehte*—Only I fell asleep while narrating my plight."

Most Hyderabadis had spent the evening barricaded in their homes. Their gates had been locked, the windows shuttered, and dogs left hungry. Their howling would hopefully dissuade mobs wreaking havoc on Hyderabad's streets from trespassing. If residents dared peek outside, they might witness a truckload of Razakars or an Indian army tank roll by. But the only way to receive news of what was really happening was through the airwaves. Those who tuned into the Deccan Radio station had learned that there had been a victory for the Nizam.

Hearing the news, people rushed out to welcome busloads of Razakar soldiers back to Afzal Gunj, chanting, "Shah Osman Zindabad." But these soldiers, who had been stationed at various areas to guard the city, had abandoned their posts. Some wandered ghostlike through darkened streets with vacant eyes and slumped shoulders.

The three bachelors listened to the melancholy strains of the ghazal. The dream of a united India was broken, and the Nizam's continued rule upheld.

Dr. Hussain spoke first. "Well, we've all had a good life under the Nizam. And I am certain that he will make reforms. My Yasin at least will be pleased..."

"Chascha, Uncle?" Kanta raised her voice, trembling.

"Good evening, Kanta." Dr. Hussain turned to Kanta where she stood in the entrance.

"Yasin. His body was brought into the medical tent..."

"What are you saying, child?" Dr. Benjamin approached his daughter and held her shoulders firmly.

"Yasin bhai, his face was unrecognizable." Kanta began sobbing. "He's dead."

"Nonsense! They would have informed us. Kanta?" Dr. Benjamin shook her and tightened his hold on her arms.

"It was him. It was him." Her body became limp in her father's grip.

"Benjamin!" Dr. Rao stood up. "Let her go now."

Kanta collapsed into a chair and buried her face in her palloo. Dr. Benjamin turned to Dr. Hussain. "Kanta is fatigued, volunteering in the clinic all these evenings. She must have mistaken someone for Yasin."

Dr. Hussain reached his hand across the table to Kanta. "Beti, are you sure?"

Kanta looked down to Dr. Hussain's fingers, entwined with hers. "Yasin was wearing his signet ring." Kanta looked up at Dr. Hussain. Sorrow looked so strange on his distinguished and usually serene face. She realized his was an older and wearier version of Yasin's.

A new announcer abruptly interrupted the ghazal. "All India Radio reporting from Aurangabad! The Union has succeeded!" Dr. Benjamin and Dr. Rao looked to the other, realizing the outcome they wanted for Hyderabad had been achieved. Then they both looked down, aware of their friend and his immense loss.

Kanta too realized what had happened. India had invaded India. A body consuming itself. To what end.

Kanta watched Dr. Hussain rise, reach for his fez, and walk out the door into Hindustan. His lake-shaped heart, she imagined, overflowing with grief.

*

Soon after, General Chaudhari of the Indian Armed Forces stood face to face with Major General El Edroos of the Hyderabadi Army, and the transfer of power from the Nizam to the Indian Union was complete.

In the months following, city offices were purged of administrators loyal to the Nizam. To fill these vacancies, the Indian Union looked to the rising talent from the old Madras Presidency. Srikaram was recruited into the Hyderabad civil service and offered Rayappa a role. Rayappa Irwin left his mother's home for a second time and found himself behind a desk in a large office. A nameplate on his door introduced him as Irwin Peter, Records Manager, Hyderabad Civil Service. With his new name, in a new city, Rayappa Irwin was unidentifiable, untraceable, and could not be reviled.

After moving to Hyderabad, Irwin became a stalwart member of St. George's Church. The moment he saw Kanta Benjamin, he made her his goal. His many promotions in the civil service as well as his steady paycheque ensured that he was a qualified suitor. With a better diet and physical activity, his figure developed from spindly to muscular. This bolstered his confidence. He had heard from other young men in the church that Dr. Benjamin was seeking a match for his daughter. Under the watch of the Father, the Son, and the Holy Ghost, Irwin began to woo Kanta. Even with no formal musical training, he had a good ear and won a place among the tenors in the choir. Every Sunday for a month, his clear brown eyes searched across the sanctuary to the opposite pew for Kanta among the sopranos. Unable to court her in the presence of Dr. Benjamin, Irwin quietly appealed to Kanta's love of English prose and poetry. He parked himself at the library and sought the aid of the best poets.

"My love is like a red, red rose," he whispered to Kanta as he fell in line behind her during their Wednesday-night choir rehearsal. Kanta smiled at him, confused but curious. When Kanta opened her hymnal, she found a note quoting Shelley.

> *Art thou pale for weariness*
> *Of climbing heaven and gazing on the earth,*
> *Wandering companionless*
> *Among the stars that have a different birth,*
> *And ever changing, like a joyless eye*
> *That finds no object worth its constancy?*

Kanta read the note, looked up, and blushed. During the Christmas service, she found a Shakespeare sonnet written in elegant handwriting on her chorale programme.

> *Shall I compare thee to a summer's day?*
> *Thou art more lovely and more temperate*

When he finally proposed, Kanta nodded yes, forte!

*

It was January 26, 1949. One year later, the country would celebrate Republic Day, when India's constitution came into effect. Irwin of course did not predict this when he and Kanta settled on a date for their wedding. The coincidence would come in handy, helping Irwin remember his anniversary in the years that followed, especially when he grew frustrated and bored in his relationship with Kanta. Their wedding day provided the Christian community an opportunity for celebration. The months following the invasion of Hyderabad by the Indian Army had been stressful, and the community anticipated the joy a grand wedding would bring. The day was unusually warm, resembling the summer temperatures of April. The ceiling fans in St. George's Church were spinning frantically, making an irritating clicking sound while barely creating a breeze. Irwin walked down the aisle, fixing his gaze on the large gleaming brass cross that drew him towards the altar. His neck was hot under the crisp white collar of his starched shirt, and he sweated in his grey wool suit. He was all too aware of the calluses on his toes catching on his black silk socks, rubbing against the fine inner lining of his new shoes. Anticipating his wedding night, he worried that his bride would look disparagingly at his feet and know who he really was. Irwin was reminded that his body would always bear the scar of poverty. And this reminded him of his mother.

Alisamma had been anxious about her son going to school in proper shoes. But she could not afford replacements as he outgrew them.

"You must suffer to gain an education," she would say to him as he squeezed his feet into last year's shoes. He heeded her wisdom and learned the importance of appearance and the appearance of respectability. At seven, he upheld his unspoken promise to his family, ignoring the grinding pain as he stood statue-still reciting his lessons. Duty stunted the growth of his big toe; the smaller toes curled and were crushed under the weight of an English-language education.

When Irwin reached the altar, he saw he was surrounded by strangers and recent acquaintances. There was an older, large, and muscular man in the front row, someone close to the Benjamin family whose name he could not remember. Panic stirred. He felt nauseated. Irwin longed for his mother's reassuring and steady gaze. Irwin had omitted Alisamma and his sisters from the guest list, using illness as the public excuse for their absence. Now, he regretted his decision. He fondly remembered how his mother had walked with him to school every day, her feet comfortable in her chappals. His hand secure in hers, Irwin would nag her to step up the pace, bent on arriving early. How different he would have felt had it been *her* face looking at him from the front pew.

Oh, why hadn't he considered her? Alisamma who had ensured that he excelled at school. He committed to his subjects as if they were his own children. Careful not to favour one over the other, he spent the same time on arithmetic, science, history, and language. He practised writing the Devanagari script used for Hindi as faithfully as the letters of Telugu, his Dravidian mother tongue. Later he mastered the elegant Arabic script used for Urdu. But it was English that stole his heart, as it had his father's. The language was like a gregarious and self-centered child. It was possessive and demanding, though far less attractive or dignified than its siblings. It suc-ceeded because it was domineering and practical. Irwin had tried to explain his obsession with writing cursive to his mother.

"The ink needn't lift from the page at all, except between words and to stop with a spot."

He wrote a phrase to demonstrate his point.

"A spot, a blot, a dot. A period. To designate a thought. A pause."

Alisamma, bored with his explanation, turned to her thimbles and threads. Irwin sought the company of his English literature professors and became more acquainted with the writings of the masters. He believed the language superior and the culture as well. It valued reason more than ritual. Science rather than superstition. He was drawn to social anthropology as a way to understand the roots of his own culture. It provided a method to contextualize his Telugu traditions to the British and to be released from what he perceived as the unrefined native mind. Irwin's knowledge and command of the English language drew Connelly's attention as it had Kanta's admiration.

Kanta was suddenly standing before him. Elegant and cross-eyed? Was she? He hadn't noticed this before. He momentarily averted his eyes. A white-and-gold silk sari hugged her slim hips. Her small hands were placed on her father's supporting arm. Dr. Samuel Benjamin, the distinguished chief public health officer, dressed in a teal-blue sherwani, had not traded the formal wear of the Nizam for an English suit and tie.

As Kanta stepped closer she seemed to look past him. Irwin turned to see what she was searching for. A ghost?

The fan died and the heat intensified. The priest mouthed incomprehensible words. Kanta placed her hand in Irwin's, and he fainted.

Eight hundred wedding guests gasped their concern. Dr. Hussain and Dr. Rao, both seated in the front row, and the bridesmaids, Rebecca and Ruth, rushed to Irwin's aid. Irwin was unconscious and appeared to have stopped breathing. Dr. Benjamin began chest compressions, ordering Kanta to administer mouth-to-mouth resuscitation. Their first intimacy displayed before hundreds of people. Irwin came to and was supported upright by Dr. Benjamin, who counselled him to take deep breaths. One bridesmaid, Rebecca, held a glass of water to Irwin's lips while the other, Ruth, fanned him with the wedding programme. Dr. Rao, the name of the guest Irwin had forgotten and the largest of the three bachelors, pulled him onto his feet. Dr. Hussain, still mourning his own son, took Irwin's pulse before nodding to Kanta.

The organist had played throughout, like a marionette, hands and feet pulled in different directions. Accompaniment for an unfolding comedy of errors, ending with vows, for better or worse.

*

Irwin opened the gates of the Benjamin House. He found Kanta where he had left her that morning, on the veranda, full-bellied, a book in hand, the pages dog-eared, the corners chewed. It was a habit Kanta had when she worried about something, either related to the plot in the fiction or her own life.

"What are you doing? The doctor said you should walk." Irwin stood over her, his hands on his hips.

"I have been walking. Only now have I sat down."

One year into marriage, Irwin had already grown distrustful of his wife. Kanta lied to him easily about inconsequential matters. She never looked him in the eye. He was convinced that this lack of eye contact did not reflect the modesty of a dutiful wife but rather the indifference of a distracted one. It was as if someone else stood behind him, waiting and winking at Kanta, tempting her to a better place. But he didn't challenge her. Avoidance and silence kept them together. If they started speaking, Kanta would have reproached Irwin for his sins of omission. He had failed to tell her that he had no wealth or social standing. He had a family but refused to introduce them to her. He had showed her his degree but provided no explanation as to why he had changed his career path. Dr. Benjamin disapproved of Kanta's choice. And the more he disapproved, the more she insisted that Irwin was better than Sunny, David, Peter, and Paul. She staged her rebellion, and Dr. Benjamin finally agreed to the marriage. Irwin moved into their house. But Dr. Benjamin refused to support the family. Kanta's education would be Irwin's responsibility, as would any children she would bear him. Kanta remained proud, accepted the terms set by her father, and threw her confidence behind Irwin. After one year of marriage she realized that any aspirations for a higher education and career were over. She went into labour, with little hope for herself and her unborn child.

Irwin entered the maternity ward at Osmania General Hospital, where ten beds, side by side, displayed women in various postnatal positions. Some lay flat from exhaustion, surrounded by female family members fanning and doting on them; others sat cooing over their precious infants; still others remained alone and fearful, their newborns nowhere to be seen.

Kanta was in her own category. She neither had circles under her eyes nor a hair out of place. She was well groomed and glowing, one hour after giving birth. The weight gained during the gestation period seemed to have fallen off her body. Face and form were back to normal. But a discontent lay behind her eyes.

Irwin cradled the newborn. "She is simply a wonder. Have you thought of a name?"

"Evelyn, after my mother." Kanta seemed distant. Her eyes, did that thing, looking past Irwin into another world.

"Very appropriate. She is beautiful, our daughter. Just like her mother." Irwin held the infant up, close to Kanta's face.

"Not now. Please."

"Of course." Irwin was surprised by the irritation in Kanta's voice and her seeming lack of affection for the child. "What do you think of your daughter?"

"What's there to think? She will need to be protected, sheltered, educated, then reined in . . ."

Once Kanta started, she couldn't stop talking. She was disappointed with married life, realized that motherhood would pin her down, and believed that her daughter's life would be equally constrained. Irwin thought Kanta was disgruntled because she bore a girl. And what should have been a pure, proud, and joyous moment was instead pessimistic and hostile. "With a boy you just feed him, and he grows, runs, learns, fulfills his desires."

"What are you talking about? God has given you a healthy daughter."

What Kanta expressed was not lack of love for her daughter but a sense of defeat in the face of her daughter's limited options. Kanta saw her daughter's life as full of obstacles, and like a mother cat who rejects the runt of the litter, she instinctively distanced herself. Had she given birth decades later, a kind-hearted doctor would have sat her down, perhaps with her loving husband close by, to discuss a diagnosis of postpartum depression. At that time, however, Kanta only had Irwin. He considered her attitude symptomatic of lazy, privileged, pre-Independence thinking: misguided gender preference and the backwards belief that boys were naturally superior to girls. He had seen some women in the villages turn on each other to gain male attention. But more often than not, the peasant women were strong and resilient and taught their daughters to be the same. It was repellent to Irwin to witness a wealthy, educated woman, his wife no less, relegating their first-born to a category of lesser, simply because of her sex. Irwin thought he understood Kanta's feelings for what they were. She was jealous. This belief confirmed Irwin's own sense of moral superiority.

Irwin gazed into his daughter's eyes, while addressing her mother.

"Our daughter is perfect. She will fulfill the role of daughter and son, our sun and moon. She will be learned, cultured, caring, and kind. She will be valued for her individuality and potential. She is a daughter of this new nation and will be entitled to anything she wants. I will name her Anasuya, *learned one, who is free from jealousy*. She will envy no one."

Irwin finished his speech, looked from daughter to mother. Kanta had fallen asleep, while the infant had perked up. He passed the child into the arms of the nurse to take back to the nursery while he headed towards the surgery. Irwin was convinced that Kanta was an unloving mother, and that their daughter was the only child they needed. He took control of the situation. Irwin booked himself an appointment for a vasectomy.

*

Six months later, when Kanta was fully recovered from giving birth, Irwin told her about his vasectomy. Kanta was livid. Not because she necessarily craved more children but because she understood Irwin's vasectomy to be a weapon against her. So she wielded *her* weapon. She denied her family the two things that a woman is expected to provide: a mother's love, and a wife's duty. By day she refused to show affection to a daughter whom her husband had deemed better than any other child. By night she refused to make love to a man who deemed himself better than her.

Irwin gave Kanta two weeks to get over her anger after they had argued over his vasectomy. He thought this was plenty of time for her to calm down and come to appreciate the logic of his decision. Then he went to Kanta's bed, like he had done every Saturday evening prior to Kanta's pregnancy. He slipped under her sheet and curved his slim body behind her voluptuous one. Her height, the slope of her hips, and the curve of her knee seemed to accommodate his angles and bends. Their shapes complemented each other. They were perceived as a loving couple by the church community, but people were unaware that Kanta and Irwin lacked the special bond to hold their marriage together: mutual affection. They didn't always dislike each other. In fact, a distinct attraction based on loss brought them together. They recognized that each of them had settled, having lost their first loves. While they never spoke about it, they sensed it. Irwin and Kanta learned how to be practical. They compromised and came to understand their marriage for what it was: an opportunity for Kanta to escape her father's control and for Irwin to gain membership into respectable society.

As Kanta lay with Irwin at her back and the baby sleeping in the cot beside her, Kanta imagined herself looking down on their little trio, wondering how she had arrived at this place. She knew Irwin desired her. His body pressed against hers. His fingers trailed down the curve of her leg. And despite her anger towards him, she could not help feeling aroused. It was a contradiction, her mind's resolve versus her body's instinct. Kanta not only withheld herself from Irwin but was unfaithful in her thoughts. She lowered her own hand between her legs and thought about Yasin. He was bent over her. She saw his eyes, his face, his shoulders. She ran her hands down the length of his back, cupped his buttocks, and pulled him towards her.

Kanta realized she had never touched Yasin as a man. Except that one time in September 1948, in the medic's tent when a cartload of bodies arrived.

"What happened to them?" Kanta passed the alcohol-soaked cloth to the doctor.

"They are martyrs." Dr. Ahmed wrapped dressing around the severed arm of one badly mutilated victim, hoping to stop the bleeding. "These boys tried to stop a train filled with General Chaudhuri's soldiers."

Dr. Ahmed applied pressure but finally released the limb he had been holding. It fell limply from his grasp. Kanta recognized the tapered fingers, intact and clean, and upon the fourth finger, the unmistakable signet ring.

"But there is more to be done." Kanta picked up Yasin's hand.

"He has already expired." Dr. Ahmed moved on to the next patient.

Kanta brought Yasin's hand to her lips. She kissed each finger, his palm, his wrist. The only part of him that was recognizable.

The wheels of the train had rolled over Yasin as he lay on the tracks with his two friends. These were not men practising some well-strategized act of resistance but boys playing a daredevil's game in the name of defending the Nizam. He was so young. Oh Yasin!

Kanta's cheeks were wet with tears. Fantasies that began with Yasin's handsome face, chiselled features, and smooth skin ended with the image of his mutilated body and his lifeless perfect hands. It drove out the last bit of desire she might have felt. Kanta abruptly got up, denying both her own and her husband's longed-for relief. Irwin never returned to her bed, and she, turning to the pages of yet another nineteenth-century novel, did not miss him.

1997 — The Well

Jaya and Parveen are riding together in the back of Linga Reddy's Toyota, having just visited the masjid in Korampally. Linga and his driver are in front. Linga has been showing them various points of interest in the village, but Jaya is only interested in sites that connect her — even tangentially — with Malika.

"Of course, your mother wouldn't have gone there. It was built ten years ago by some fanatics."

"Fanatics?"

"Don't get me wrong. Not all Muslims are fanatics, but we've had our share. Trust me, I know Korampally better than anyone."

Jaya senses this to be true. Linga can explain its history and the past and current tensions between different communities. Jaya wants to ask more questions of Linga, but she finds it hard to jump in. He speaks, and she listens. Parveen is uncharacteristically quiet on this journey, so Jaya turns her head towards the open window. A hot wind blows in, brushing Jaya's face and tickling her neck. It is a priceless pleasure, neither purchased nor held, which brings her close to joy. This heat. This Indian heat makes her aware of herself.

"And this is the old well." Linga points out the window.

"Stop!"

"Oh. Of course. If you like. Our family home is just up ahead. You will come inside, have tea?"

But Jaya is fixated on the well. It is familiar and not. She is curious to look inside, touch the stone, and breathe in its damp air. Listen to it.

Jaya swings open the car door.

Parveen follows Jaya to the well. "This well is an anomaly. Most of these old wells have been covered up."

"They dried up?"

"Some did. Some had concrete slabs fitted on them to prevent suicides."

"Suicides?" Jaya leans over the stone ledge.

"There is a legend about a young woman who had been molested by her father-in-law. It seemed everyone in the household knew. She was the first to jump. A spate of others followed. No one knew the exact reasons."

Jaya moves away from the ledge. She sees Linga approaching. The women stop talking.

Linga resumes his role as tour guide. "It is still in operation, although running water is now available to most households. We have prospered some-what, our little Korampally. Shall we lower the rope? I can show you how it was done in the old days."

"No. No, it's okay. I just want to . . ."

But Jaya isn't sure what she wants. She looks to the hills and the peepal tree farther down the road in the opposite direction. She wipes her forehead with her chunni, slightly disoriented.

"It is beautiful here."

"Yes. I have been living in Hyderabad these past fifteen years, but I grew up here. And no matter where I travel, no place compares to Korampally."

It is hard to know when Jaya's friendship with Linga Reddy began, but Jaya reckons it was the day he gave her the sunglasses. That gift was the first gesture of kindness, and since then he has made himself indispensable to the family. He offered Jaya and Anya the use of his car and driver. He opened the peach house so that they could relocate there. His generosity is simply "the Indian way," he assures her.

Irwin refuses to move from the Krishna Lodge. He resents the Reddys for convincing Jaya and Anya to come to India in the first place and for winning them over with gifts. Irwin refuses to even look at the peach house. And while Anya is not comfortable leaving Irwin, she is tempted by the lovely setting of the house and its proximity to Ashamma. Ashamma is warm and wants to engage. Irwin keeps to himself. There is no contest.

Anya had tried to convince herself and Irwin that she is not abandoning him. "I'll stay for a few days since it is so close to Ashamma's."

Jaya doesn't bother justifying her choice.

The house has its own cook, sweeper, and dhobi. Anya remarked how funny it was that the cook won't sweep, the sweeper won't wash, and the dhobi won't cook. Jaya grew up understanding that labour was determined and divided according to caste and never questioned it. It is their way, she hears herself say. These platitudes, though unfamiliar, seem to flow easily from her. It is as if she were consulting a phrase book on how to communicate in a foreign land.

When Linga handed Jaya the key to the peach house, another line tumbled out. "If you insist."

She doesn't spend time figuring out why Linga is doing the insisting. Jaya simply assumes a role and delivers her lines to perfection. She doesn't realize that she is letting her guard down and is in no mood to resist.

Anya, on the other hand, does question Linga's generosity. He is far too old to think that Jaya or she might be interested in him. And if he shows any sign of *that* kind of interest, Anya tells Jaya, then she is out of there. Jaya decides to accept Linga's offer and enjoys the comforts in the peach house; for the first time in her adult life, she does not have to cook.

*

Swami Antharyami sits at Raghunandan Reddy's bedside, advising him on his path to dharma. Just as Reddy is shrewd about property and power, the swami is equally wise about the ways of the spirit. Swami Antharyami has built an empire selling god. Both men are similarly practical, selfish, and cunning.

A month ago, when Linga Reddy returned home to his ailing father after his Hyderabadi business ventures failed, he was surprised to see the patriarch had surrounded himself with Swami Antharyami and household servants. Each day, the swami injected a dose of "do goodism" into Raghunandan Reddy's mind, encouraging him to be more benevolent to the servants and to put god at the centre of his consciousness. "After all," Antharyami explained to Reddy, "would you rather your land be claimed by the Naxalites or by god?" Bit by bit Reddy's land is being parcelled off to support the swami's work.

Linga immediately contacted his younger brother Surendra in Chicago, who explained that he had received a letter from their father. Raghunandan Reddy made it clear that unless Surendra returned home to manage the land and tenants, he and his whole family would be erased from Reddy's will. Surendra and his wife, Aditi, had long ago cut ties with Raghunandan Reddy and had no expectations. Linga, conversely, expected his birthright as eldest son to be intact. After all, it was he who was entrusted to perform the last rites for his father's eventual death. The loyal son, who will manage the land even if he has failed to produce an heir to the estate.

After their visit to the well, Linga takes the women to the Reddy house to meet his father. Jaya follows Linga and Parveen into Raghunandan Reddy's room to pay her respects. He lies in his bed, his head propped up by pillows. Jaya notes Reddy's vulnerability and feels she is intruding. He is hooked up to a liquid oxygen tank that delivers the life-sustaining gas to his lungs through a tube attached to a prong fitted to his nose. A male nurse takes up residence in one corner of the room while women move in and out, bringing food and water, pressing his legs, plumping his pillows. Jaya assumes these are family members, but Parveen quietly corrects her. "They are housemaids, dressed like princesses."

The whole scene looks like a pageant.

"Kunti Vadu's daughter." Linga grins as he announces Jaya.

What did he call her? Then Raghunandan Reddy gestures for Jaya to step forward, as if she were a schoolgirl coming to the front of the class.

"You resemble more the shit cleaner. But not as attractive."

Jaya is taken aback.

"Please forgive him. My father's English is quite awkward, and his mind is not so well."

"Linga, I am not senile." Reddy now changes to Telugu. "Our shit cleaner was very beautiful, as was her mother. Each person has a station in life, spiritually inscribed, and nothing to be ashamed of." He turns to Jaya, reverting to English. "How long will you stay in Korampally?"

"I am not sure." Jaya pieces together the bits of information that Reddy reveals about Malika. Facts that she does not know. She wants to leave his room, but how? A flock of women roll in a tea tray, blocking the entrance. Parveen makes room for them, leaning against a wall, her arms folded across her chest, her lips pursed.

Raghunandan Reddy gestures for Jaya to take some tea. "You have a daughter."

"Yes."

"Good. Tell her to come to me. She too will receive some land."

"We don't expect anything from you, sir."

"Your first mistake. Never deny your birthright. Your second is not bringing the girl here to meet me. Do you have a photograph of her?" He sputters, waving his hand in front of his face. He gestures for the nurse to turn up the oxygen.

Jaya reaches into her purse and passes Raghunandan Reddy a photo of Anya. "I apologize. Anya wanted to spend time with Ashamma."

"Yes. The girl looks like Asha somewhat. How she looked in her youth."

"I must thank you, sir, for connecting us. It is good to finally meet my grandmother."

"And your grandfather."

Reddy declares rather than speaks. He has an authoritative tone that allows no denial of his demands, no questioning of his pronouncements. Reddy gestures to Linga to retrieve a gold box from the cupboard. Linga passes it to his father who unlocks it with a small key, which is fastened to a chain worn around his neck. He withdraws a thick envelope from the box and holds it out to Jaya.

"Theesko! Take it. Give this to your daughter."

Jaya accepts the envelope from Reddy and watches Linga's inscrutable face as he puts the gold box back into the cupboard.

"Thank you, sir." When Jaya turns back to Raghunandan Reddy, he is asleep. So many questions hang in the air. Was he indeed her grandfather? How can this be? Who is he?

Parveen says she prefers to walk back to her home while Linga drives Jaya to the peach house.

"Your father is very generous."

"His generosity exceeds his wealth. The government confiscated much of our land as part of the Land Reform Act of '51. My father filed and endured a lengthy court challenge citing discrimination against landowners. He has recovered some but not all of his property. Legal costs were quite hefty."

"I am sorry to hear that." Another stock phrase escapes Jaya's mouth.

"But he continues to spend as if none of that happened."

"I really cannot accept this." Jaya taps the envelope in her hand.

"You heard my father. It is for your daughter. If she doesn't accept it, she must return it to him. He has asked to see her after all."

Jaya is suddenly aware of how easily Anya is drawn into the affairs of Raghunandan Reddy. Someone whose connection to her is not at all clear. She wonders why someone like Linga has taken a strange and persistent interest in her and her daughter.

*

Two weeks have passed since Irwin, Jaya, and Anya arrived in Korampally. Jaya is unsettled by her visit with Raghunandan Reddy and wanders around the peach house seeking something to ground her. She goes to the kitchen and starts washing the dishes. She is met with the kitchen maid's indignation in sharp-tongued Telugu. "Go back to your village and clean your own pots."

Jaya goes out to the porch. Like a drug, Linga's attention creates the feeling that she *is* someone. That she matters. But who is *she* to Linga Reddy? A stranger with some connection to an old woman that Jaya doesn't understand. She has niggling questions. Why me? What could he want? But before she can come up with any answers, heat, inertia, and the sense of being taken care of dull her curiosity. Even her purpose in India has lost its urgency. Her quest to know more about her mother is like a walk in the wilderness, her guide continually eluding her. Jaya is hopeful that Ashamma will eventually tell her about Malika. But Jaya realizes that she is doing all the talking. She tells Ashamma about how Irwin adopted her and her little brother Pilla. How they lived with Irwin and their new mother Kanta and sister Anasuya. And she tells Ashamma too about the tragic deaths of both Anasuya and Pilla. Jaya can almost see the workings of Ashamma's mind. In the furrow of the old woman's brow, the tightening of her cheek muscles, her sighs. Although Jaya probes Ashamma to speak, the old woman remains oddly aloof towards Jaya. Instead, Ashamma, like Raghunandan Reddy, is fascinated with Anya. This bothers Jaya, and it bothers Jaya more that she feels bothered in the first place.

*

In the evening, Jaya sits in Anya's room, on the edge of her bed. Anya is lying on her side. The envelope from Raghunandan Reddy also sits on the bed between them. A gift from a stranger, like the many gifts that Linga Reddy has already given them. But money is different. Money changes everything.

"Are you going to open it?"

Anya holds the yellowed notebook in her hands. "I just want to finish this."

"You can, soon enough. Anyway, what is so interesting about it?"

"Hmm. It's about the hygiene and dietary habits of almost everyone in Korampally in 1947. You should give it a try. It's fascinating."

The notebook is mostly dry reading, but occasionally the data is accompanied by vivid and disturbing narrative descriptions. Anya loses herself.

Jaya picks up the envelope and offers it to Anya.

"Why me, anyway?"

"Does it matter why? Raghunandan Reddy is a sick man and he helped Ashamma find us. He is trying to do the right thing. Now *you* should do the right thing as well. Either accept the gift or return it."

"Can't I just write a note?"

"Linga said it would appear rude not to thank Mr. Reddy in person."

"Linga said, Linga said. Who is he anyway?"

"He is a kind gentleman."

"Wealthy?"

"I guess so."

"Is that why you like him so much?"

"I don't like him *so* much. But I do like him. What is wrong with that?"

"You have a father! He is sitting in his room by himself while you are out with some old man."

"What are you getting at, Anya?"

"Nothing. Just trying to figure you out."

Jaya is shocked by Anya's inference that something is going on between her and Linga. Jaya has been celibate for twelve years. And lonely. Now she wonders if she has been indiscreet, keeping company with Linga Reddy. And it is true: Jaya has neglected Irwin in favour of Linga. Jaya hates that Anya is right. She hates that Ashamma loves Anya more. That Irwin loves Anya more. That Anasuya loved Anya more. She hates that she is jealous of her own daughter.

Jaya picks up the envelope and thrusts it towards Anya. "Open it."

"Why?"

"You are a grown woman. At least know what you are rejecting."

"Okay, this is about money?"

"Why not? You could use it."

"I am not going to take money from some old man I don't know. You take it."

Jaya looks down at the envelope, as if Anya is rejecting a gift from her. Why does she care so much? It is as if Raghunandan Reddy is commanding her from afar, telling her how to act with her own daughter. Jaya lets the envelope drop on the bed. Anya turns back to the pages in which Malika's name appears again and again.

8. Revolution

On what should have been Malika's wedding night, the rain came too late to save her family. But it stopped in time to save her. When it cleared, Malika crept out of Irwin's room. All the servants were fast asleep after the previous night's commotion. Clutching Irwin's suitcase, Malika unlatched the great blue doors and walked out of the Reddy compound. She escaped across the swollen river to the forest, where a rebellion was brewing.

Had she been struck by lightning, perhaps the rebels who found Malika's limp body on the riverbank would have realized the severity of what she had endured. But it took time, gentle coaxing, and piecing together her broken phrases to understand what had happened to her and their comrades. The first sign that something had gone wrong came to the rebels when the volunteers failed to attend a meeting following the harvest. The second was the sight of smoke on the hillside. The third was Malika, washed ashore.

Near Malika's sodden body was an impossibly dry suitcase balanced on two rocks, as if intentionally positioned upright to act as a beacon. Malika had collapsed and seemed to blend into the mud. Some men in the squad lifted her up and brought her inside a hut. Others brought in the suitcase. Women wiped Malika dry and laid her on a straw mat. One gentle hand after another was placed on her brow, awakening her senses until she recovered her breath enough to tell her fragmented story.

In the days that followed, Malika found it difficult to feel. Despair numbed her senses and created a barrier between her and the others. It was as if she experienced everything from behind a screen through which she observed the outer world. If only she could refuse food and water, she might drift into death and join her mother, her sisters, and her beloved. But she remained here. And had been here before. Right here on this mat, where she had sat in a circle with Communists. A mat woven by a son for his mother. Then she identified the birdlike woman with the smoky quality. It was Vijay's mother, and Malika was in their hut.

What is it that enables some to cheat death at every turn? That nurtures in some the tiniest grain of hope, even in the harshest conditions, and allows them to rise phoenix-like from the ashes? Perhaps it is not so much the qualities within a person that makes them persist, but the inspiration of others that urges them on. Malika found herself turning to Vijay's mother. Small and alert, she had emerged from her corner of grief, opening her home to Vijay's friends and comrades. Malika watched Ashamma haul water up from the river, separate grain and boil it, invite others to eat first. This woman pulled Malika out of hopelessness not with the grip of a firm hand but simply by her example of living.

*

It was easy for Malika to trust Ashamma and other women who looked like herself, peasants, wrapped in cotton saris hitched between the legs and tucked into the waist. Women who wore the same attire for planting, cleaning, and cooking. But the new Sangham leader who arrived in trousers, commanding everyone with her gruff voice, was off-putting and not so easy to trust. Sujana, who had brought twenty new recruits with her, entered the hut, thrust out her chin, and complained about how cramped it was. She ordered everyone to squeeze into a circle and scrutinized each face while Malika scrutinized hers. Sujana had a formidable presence and attractive features, including small, slanting eyes with long eyelashes and a thick unibrow above the bridge of her long, straight nose. She wore no earrings, bangles, or chains, no jewellery at all except for a blood-red stone in her left nostril. Malika stared at Sujana's high cheekbones, smooth complexion, cropped short hair, and large, white teeth. She was beautiful by any standard, but her tough demeanour masked it. Malika watched Sujana and listened, leaning against the cool clay wall until she was called out.

"You can swim across the river, I hear." Sujana pulled her rifle off her back and thumped it vertically on the ground. Malika nodded, unable to utter a word. Sujana handed her the rifle. "Come outside. I will teach you to shoot."

Malika followed Sujana out of the hut and deep into the forest, the forest where she had met Vijay and lain with him. Sujana expertly loaded the rifle and hit her targets: a branch, a wild pig, a bat in flight.

Sujana helped Malika find her "steady" position, aligning the rifle to her dominant eye, holding the hand grip in the V between her thumb and fore-finger. She helped her tuck the rifle butt against her firing shoulder, grip the forestock, and keep her elbows tight to her chest.

"That's it."

"Shall I fire?"

"Not yet. Never fire a gun until you can manage your breath. You need to breathe from here." Sujana made a fist and pressed it between Malika's lower ribs against her diaphragm. "Now push my hand away with your breath."

Without the luxury of time to mourn her loved ones, Malika began her tutelage under Sujana. She spent the same amount of time in target practice as she did with her new friends. People who gathered in a circle, shared food and stories, cared for and defended each other, planned and strategized to claim land and regain dignity for all. This circle in which she now belonged, was a dalam, a squad, her new family.

Malika listened as they read Marx, Engels, Dange, Sundarayya, and Ranadive. Sujana spoke about Lenin and explained the conditions and tac-tics that made the Russian Revolution successful. She informed them that the United Soviet Socialist Republic was their ally, supporting them with arms, funds, and intelligence. Some in the circle still referred to the USSR as Russia. Recalling these names, Malika remembered the image of the hammer and sickle, the story Rayappa told her about the country where people shared and toiled the land for the good of the collective. The Communist country. Sujana unfolded a map of Telangana and pointed to villages that had ceded to the Communists. Areas where village Sanghams had displaced greedy land-lords. Where vetti and all forms of slavery were relics of the past. Where land was shared. Malika tried to absorb this but felt disbelief. Everyone reassured her.

"Your village is not the world! Your village is not even Telangana. Expand your perspective. There is so much to learn and gain."

Sujana insisted that all comrades pledge allegiance to the movement, that they remember the reasons why they took up arms, the goals for which they would fight or die. If their commitment was not deep-rooted, any one of them could betray the party. Everyone learned about and admired their Communist leaders: Makhdoom Mohiuddin, Baddam Yella Reddy and, the most beloved, Ravi Narayan Reddy.

"Reddys? Our leaders are landowners?" Malika trudged through the forest following Sujana.

"Indeed. Narayan Reddy is wealthy and educated. In 1934 he joined Gandhi and worked to liberate Malas and Madigas, and since then he renounced his upper caste status. Many of us do, you know."

Malika then understood Sujana, herself, was from a high caste.

Sujana told her that Narayan Reddy, affectionately known as Naraya Dora, had defied his caste and left his family for the Andhra Mahasabha movement. He advocated for Telugu language rights, the reduction of land revenue rates, and the abolition of forced labour. Sujana did not tell Malika that his extended family supported him, maintaining a secure home base and a possible escape route if he quit the movement. She did not mention that he had enrolled his children in boarding school, that his daughter would bunk beside the daughter of the district collector of Mahbub Nagar, arguing who would win, "my side or yours," who would be killed, "my father or yours?" Betting on the fates of their fathers as easily as trading dolls, so closely intertwined was one side with the other.

Though she never saw a photograph or read his words herself, Malika formed an image of Naraya Dora in her mind. She felt she could hear his voice in the words of her comrades as they spoke about the shared struggle against the Reddy deshmukhs of Jangaon, the Brahmin priests of Khammam, the Muslim jagirdars of Pulgilla, and all the other oppressors. She pictured her comrades seated in Narayan's circle, rifles on their backs and chili powder in their sacks: men and women, Hindus and Muslims, upper castes and outcastes. She was there too. Malika was eager to understand. She listened and learned until what came out of her mouth were the words not of a simple village girl but a confident revolutionary. She even began to question Sujana.

"Why does someone like you do this?"

"Someone like me?"

"Yes. You have a family. You have a house. You can read and write."

"Yes, I have everything. But how can I enjoy wealth and education when everyone around me is denied? Shouldn't they have these advantages too?"

Over three months Malika grew to trust Sujana. She even helped her recruit more villagers into the squad. Altogether, including the existing members, many of whom had survived the harvest massacre, they were over two hundred strong.

Sujana decided it was time to act. She asked each new recruit to state their skills and talents. She compared the relative strengths of each comrade, assigning everyone a role. There were many like Malika, who knew the geography of the village. But it was Sujana who helped them understand tactically how they could use the land and their knowledge of it to their advantage, from the hills on one side of Korampally to the river on the other. The hills were occupied by peasants, the poorest labourers in the region, the people that would most likely sympathize with Communists and who would benefit from ousting the landlords. Greater awareness, righteous anger, and a thirst for justice were the ingredients they all needed to overtake the Reddy compound and convert it into headquarters for the Communist Party. Korampally was a sitting duck.

Sujana explained how half the dalam would infiltrate the communities on the hills while the others would stay with the fishers near the river. Those on the hills could barricade the roads moving northwest from Korampally while those near the river could block escape by creating an impenetrable border of burning haystacks. The only route into or out of the village would be the road leading south from the peepal tree. Sujana and her troops would be there to either shoot the retaliating Razakars or receive supplies and weapons from squads in nearby villages.

Malika felt the adrenaline in her body, a rising excitement and fear. She asked herself if this was truly possible.

Malika stood out among her strong and loyal comrades, even the men, many of whom she could outrun and outclimb. This was not lost on Sujana, who assigned Malika to lead a squad to attack the landlord's house at night. Malika was familiar with both the hills and the Reddy property. The river squad would target the police station. They would strike the night after the Ugadi festival, Telugu New Year. The landlords would be full of food and self-congratulations for allowing the peasants their celebrations. Korampally would certainly fall.

Malika grew strong. A healthy glow spread across her skin. Her energy and courage inspired admiration from younger members and drew protection from older ones. This support from the dalam was crucial. For around the same time that Malika found her purpose, she discovered that she was pregnant.

*

If Rayappa, the social anthropologist and keeper of records, could have seen Malika then, he would have noted that with each day her skills doubled and her knowledge tripled. He would have beamed with pride knowing he had taught Malika to write her name and had encouraged her learning. He would have grouped her newly acquired abilities into the following categories:

Physical Education
- Handle traditional and modern weapons
- Hit-and-run tactics
- Summer camp guerilla training

Home Economics
- Conserve food grains in earthenware pots
- Divert supplies of milk and food from enemy headquarters to transport them to the villages
- Dry corn, fruit, and ground nuts
- Pick grains from cowpats and boil before eating

Medicine
- Apply turmeric to wounds
- Peel bark for nutrition
- Brush teeth with neem

Drama Class
- Surround village offices and make bonfires from their records
- Don the ochre robes of priests, sleep on train platforms, wait until police are drunk with toddy before occupying trains
- Deposit hay around police headquarters, light on fire, smoke out officers, force them to lay down their arms
- Refuse to pay levy grain
- Hoist the red flag

He might even have added ancillary details about her education:

School Supplies
- Sten guns
- British .303 rifles
- Indian-made 12-bore rifles
- Ramabanam or the arrow of Rama, otherwise known as an American rifle
- bamboo long bows
- broad swords
- javelins
- Sticks and stones to break bones
- Organic offensive, otherwise known as chili powder

School Motto
  • Never Give Up

School Anthem
  • "Solidarity Forever"

Malika had chosen an alternative school, and it was more demanding than most. Even then, she excelled at her studies, mastering the only vocation she would ever know.

*

The victory in Korampally was sweet. Malika could not believe she had ever been afraid of the Reddys. Surrounding and infiltrating the house was easy. Comrades climbed the walls as she taught them, tiptoed through the courtyard, and gagged and tied up the servants in the bullock house in a perfectly choreographed sequence. Others broke in through the women's latrine at the back of the house. Soon Malika had all the Reddys lined up and on their knees in the courtyard. They did not execute the landowners but made them turn over their keys, their riches, and deeds to the land. They were forced out of Korampally with only the clothes on their backs. The servants were given a choice of joining the Communists or leaving with the Reddys. Many chose to follow Malika, but she noticed that Sivraj, the pedda metaru, followed his master. Such was his loyalty or stupidity, she thought.

Malika became an integral part of Sujana's squad, travelling from village to village, educating and drumming up support for the movement. She traded sleep for an adrenaline-powered wakefulness. The endorphins released during her pregnancy made her feel optimistic and strong. She was filled with a sense of purpose and belonging.

Malika dreamed of victory, where peasants rose from their squatting positions on arid land, marched across green pastures, and turned the landlords from their palaces. They sliced open gunny sacks full of grain and poured cups of rice and millet into the outstretched hands of labourers. They liberated the dry plots and watery terrains, shared the wild game and domestic herds, and empowered those who had laboured and those who had been displaced for so many years.

And her dream came true — to a point. The lines that mapped the Telangana region of Hyderabad smudged, transforming landlords' houses into party headquarters. The whole southern curve, from Mahbub Nagar to Korampally, was liberated and parcelled out to the peasants. A new governing structure was put in place, where guerrilla squads became the village administrators. Those who once starved ate. Those who once trembled now stood firm.

*

Four months after the Communist victory in Kormapally, Sujana's squad liberated the village of Mamidala. They were seated in the courtyard of what had once been the landlord's home and was now their headquarters. Sujana unrolled a map of Telangana and with a pencil outlined the borders between the districts they controlled and those yet to be liberated. They awaited a new squad who would remain in the village, working with the peasants to redistribute the land. Sujana's squad would move on to the next mission.

"Here they are now." A comrade pointed down the road to the long line of travellers approaching. Malika could make out individuals by their height, gait, and the colour of their clothes. And then she saw one. Someone she had known before. He followed closely behind the leader, his walk familiar. Malika recognized his full head of hair, longer now, the proud jaw and broad asymmetrical shoulders. She tugged at Sujana's sleeve.

"That man, with the walking stick . . ."

"Don't judge appearances, he does more than his share."

Malika winced at the indiscreet volume of Sujana's voice.

"What does he do?"

"I am surprised you don't know him. He was a useful informant in Korampally, forced to flee his home. Some incident with the Reddy clan. Now he travels under the protection of Viswanathan's squad."

Sujana walked towards the leader. "Viswanathan. You are here."

"Sujana, your victories are legendary!"

Viswanathan was the Sangham leader whom Malika had met in Vijay's hut. She saw that he was wearing Rayappa's shoes. Dusty now, but undeniably his. The shoes she had taken. Malika watched him suspiciously, her eyes darting from Viswanathan to the familiar man who stood by his side. It was Vijay.

The dalam was invited to sit down for a meal.

Children from the village who had gone house to house collecting food, now distributed banana leaves and spooned out millet, rice, dal, and pickle. The two squads sat together in a large circle. Malika and Sujana sat across from Viswanathan, seated beside Vijay. While they ate, Sujana set out next steps.

"The new ceiling for land ownership is two hundred acres, so you need to exert control. All cattle and tools are to be distributed equally. All debts are to be destroyed and toddy tappers must be given one palmyra tree each."

"Sister, you waste no time. Take a moment to be proud. Eat. You have won yet another battle with Mamidala."

"We have no time to be proud. While we sit around patting our bellies, the Razakars will slither right under us and bite our asses."

Viswanathan laughed and patted his round belly. Malika focused on Vijay seated directly across from her. He looked different. Creases framed his full mouth. His jaw was set. For the first time in six months, Malika could not concentrate on Sujana's words. She wondered if he could sense her, like he did the day under the peepal tree.

"In three days, I will lead my squad to Aminapally. Viswanathan, choose two from your group to join me. Malika cannot come in her current condition. She will be better off here with you."

Vijay lifted his head from the banana leaf. He stopped eating.

"That new recruit? By the look of her, she will soon be burdened with a child." Viswanathan folded his arms across his chest. "I must give up two comrades for a woman? At least have her give the child away."

"She works harder than two men." Sujana looked away from Viswanathan. It was her way of telling him the conversation was finished.

"But I really must contest..."

"Viswanathan, sir, neither I nor my child will be a burden to you." Malika spoke louder than necessary.

Vijay extended his banana leaf in the direction of Malika's voice. "Take my portion."

"I have plenty of food. Thank you."

"You will need strength."

Vijay and Malika went back and forth, insisting and refusing, until Malika finally accepted his offer.

That night, under a sky dusted with starlight, the men in the dalam slept in the courtyard, exhausted. Vijay usually slept in half-wakefulness, attentive to sounds that might signal danger, poised to jump up any minute. But he was in the protection of two squads, in a liberated village, and he had found Malika. He slept soundly on his stomach, like he had as a child.

A hand clamped over his mouth and another gripped his throat. He woke and struggled to rise, but someone had their knee on his back. An angry voice filled his ear.

"How could you have done that to me? On our wedding night! I could kill you right here with a quick turn of your head." Vijay breathed relief even as Malika pressed harder into him. "Answer me."

Malika eased her grip. Vijay stifled a laugh. "How can I speak when you're holding me in a death grip?" Mailka released Vijay and moved aside, allowing him to sit up.

"Now speak."

Vijay reached his hand out to touch Malika's cheek. She swatted it away.

"I would never betray you. Something happened the night before our wedding. I would be dead but for Viswanathan."

Malika looked at Vijay's eyelids, his long lashes curving up to the moon. She wished she could trust him again. She wanted to trust him. He was here, miraculously reappearing in her life.

"Something happened to you? Linga and his goons killed my family."

"Oh, Malika. Everyone?"

"My mother, my sisters, everyone but my father. He was still in hospital. But I don't know where he is. We liberated Nalgonda and we searched for him, but... where were you? I was so alone. Am so alone." The baby started kicking, as if to contradict her. Vijay reached for Malika's hand.

"I am sorry."

They sat in silence and stillness but for the baby's persistent kicking. Malika guided Vijay's hand to her belly. Vijay felt the pulse of the little life beneath his palm.

Finally, Malika crept back to her place with the women. Vijay lay awake. He felt sadness and joy — and also fear, that one day he would have to explain the something that had happened to him.

The next morning, Malika approached Sujana and learned that the party had a policy for almost everything, including marriage. A few couples had joined the movement and fought together side by side. Others had come together secretly, while on a mission. A few had multiple partners. Marriage was discouraged, as it was not conducive to achieving revolutionary goals, but Sujana dealt with all requests with fairness and practicality. When Malika told her of the tragedy of their planned wedding, Sujana introduced the two as husband and wife. The questions about Malika's pregnancy were put to rest. Malika and Vijay would remain with Viswanathan's squad in the liberated village of Mamidala.

*

Each member of Viswanathan's squad was assigned responsibilities according to their strengths. Those who could read, like Viswanathan, took up administration of the village property, counting assets and redistributing animals, land, tools, and fruit trees. Those who spoke well, like Vijay, taught villagers history and ideology. Those who demonstrated leadership, like Malika, instructed the villagers in digging canals and irrigating the newly divided plots. It was hard work. Good work. Necessary work.

Over the past nine months, Malika's hope had ebbed and flowed in cycles. It died and was rebirthed like the leaves of deciduous trees. The more she learned of suffering, the more she believed in communism as a cure. Her losses were balanced by concrete gains. Her experience of settling in Mamidala gave her more than hope. It filled her with confidence. They had liberated the village and now peasants participated in governing it. Land was redistributed to a wide range of castes, and the squad worked side by side with labourers in the fields. Malika finally tasted contentment. The months spent in Mamidala made her feel at home. As close to normal as was possible in the throes of a revolution.

It was mid-September and Malika, in her ninth month of pregnancy, was peeling garlic cloves with Vijay outside their hut when Viswanathan drove up in his jeep. He had received a note from Sujana through a messenger, indicating that they were urgently needed. Viswanathan asked Malika to join him to drive ten comrades to Aminapally to be redeployed.

"Can you not take someone else?" Vijay asked.

"Malika is the most reliable shot. I need her to spot and defend the jeep while in motion. She can return with me directly, once we know what is happening and receive instructions from Sujana."

Malika fetched her rifle. "I will be fine, Vijay. The journey is two hours. I should be back before sunset."

Malika set off with Viswanathan and ten others. They drove through forests, which gave way to meadows and footpaths through the rice paddies of Aminapally. Malika turned to Viswanathan as they approached the village. "Smoke."

The smell lifted on the wind. Viswanathan pulled the jeep over. Malika got out.

"Slowly, Malika."

"Something is wrong." Billows of smoke rose from the fields. She moved along a footpath, Viswanathan and the comrades followed her lead. Several huts were smoldering, but others had been burned to the ground.

"Let's get out of here." Viswanathan pulled Malika's arm.

"We have to help."

"We are only a few, we need to go back and get reinforcements."

The memory of her family's hut in flames overtook her. Despite Malika's fear, she needed to see if anyone was alive and if not, she needed to bear witness. To tell their story. She kept walking. Viswanathan commanded her to return to the jeep.

Malika clutched her rifle with one hand, the other supporting her belly as she moved fluidly across the rice fields, her legs pumping, sweat soaking the thin cotton of her sari blouse, the plait of her long hair bouncing off the small of her back. While six of the squad acceded to Viswanathan's command and returned to the jeep, four comrades followed Malika. They spread out to different huts looking for survivors.

Malika approached a hut that was partially burned but still intact. A blackened coconut rolled in the entrance. Malika kicked it out of the way and stooped to move inside. A putrid stench enveloped her. Hanging her rifle over her shoulder, she covered her mouth and nose with her palloo. The small space was empty and eerily silent. A basket hung from the ceiling, rocking back and forth, as if someone had given it a push just before fleeing. She reached out her hand to stop its rhythm, then recoiled.

"Allah." She withdrew her hand in fright.

She found a clay vessel with water, and poured some onto the edge of her palloo, then returned to the basket. Inside, a baby boy was still writhing in pain. She tried to cool him down, feeling the heat of his skin rise through the cloth. The baby's skin peeled off with her touch. His slight movements ceased. Malika covered her mouth. Had she killed him? Where was his mother? The others?

Clutching her wet palloo to her nose, Malika moved cautiously to the next hut, searching for help, for life. She entered a hut where seven women lay face down and lifeless on the ground. They were naked except for chunnis tied decoratively about their heads. A mockery of modesty. Had they been made to dance naked, humiliated before their deaths?

Malika turned over each body, listening for a breath. One body was difficult to turn, already stiff. Sujana? Her beautiful nose had been cut. The red stone was gone. Malika knelt beside Sujana, remembering her strength, her intelligence, her character. How at first Malika had disliked her, distrusted her, then finally came to love her.

Malika took Sujana's chunni off her head and draped it over her body. She tucked the cloth beneath Sujana's chin and smoothed the material over her torso and legs. Then she proceeded to do the same for the others.

After Malika covered the last woman, she emerged from the hut. In the mud, she saw tracks made by bullock carts and trucks used by the Razakars. And something else she could not at first identify. These must be the tracks of tanks, she thought. The horrific war machines that Viswanathan had spoken of.

She reunited with her comrades. Not finding any survivors, they made their way back to the jeep, where Viswanathan and the others were waiting.

*

The weeks that followed were full of anxiety as the squad tried to understand the new threats to the village and the movement. They learned that Aminapally had been crushed by a double offensive. First the Razakars, and then the unbeatable army of the Indian Union. It was September 1948, and General Chaudhuri's troops had crossed into Telangana, launching an offensive for the declared purpose of liberating Hyderabad from the Nizam and the peasants from the Communists. The Indian Union had named this mission Operation Polo, after the ancient Persian sport made famous by Babur, the Mughal emperor. Perhaps the new Indian Army felt it could master it better than anyone, beating the Persians at their own game. Malika didn't know this, for she had never heard of polo, a small and silly word, a code name for conquest.

Narayan and the Communist leadership promised ammunition and reinforcements to protect Mamidala, but the morale of the squad was low, and they were no longer certain that they would be able to defend their peaceful village. In the midst of this uncertainty, Malika's baby decided to be born.

It was just after sunset, and Vijay and Malika were at the prayer wall. Malika was fatigued and wanted to return to the hut. As they were making their way back, a member of the squad rode by on a bicycle.

"All back to your homes. Shut your doors and stay inside. We are under attack."

"Let's find Viswanathan," Vijay said.

Malika tightened her grip on Vijay's arm. "The midwife's hut is close by."

"What is it?"

Malika started laughing. "Bismillah. My water broke. The baby's coming."

As others cleared off the streets, Malika and Vijay arrived at Deviyani's hut. Deviyani hurried Malika and Vijay inside.

"What the fates have brought us!"

Malika lay down on the mat as Deviyani examined her. "The baby is not too early, is it?"

"No, no. No concerns about the baby. It is the others." Deviyani began laying out mudpacks and ginger compresses for the birth. "Strangers have arrived in the village, going door to door asking, Krishna or Allah? They are hunting down Muslims. How can we protect Malika now?"

"Perhaps the Indian Army has finally come." Vijay scooped a cup of water from a large clay pot and held it out for Malika to drink.

Deviyani laid out a nest of rags and directed Malika to squat above them. "They are just ordinary men, peasants like us. Some on foot, some in bullock carts. My two sons told me all this. And they have just now gone to help our neighbours, the Hafizes, who have been dragged from their home. If they come to know Malika is Muslim . . ."

"Ah. I will stand guard outside." Vijay did not know who his opponent was or how he would resist them.

Deviyani lit an oil lamp and then found the sharp blade used to cut the umbilical cord. "Take this, and use it if you must."

*

Malika's contractions quickened. The cool clay walls of the hut shrank around her as the commotion outside grew louder. She tried to suppress her need to cry out as she heard people outside the hut pleading for mercy, the thud of clubs being brought down on their bodies. Malika wished she could control her own body, delay the birth, until all was safe. She heard a gunshot outside as the baby crowned. She bore down and delivered her child into chaos.

Vijay listened to the approaching crowd. Screams were followed by laughter and shouts of victory, as if each atrocity were an act of bravery, an athletic feat. Fearfully aware of his own limitations, Vijay gripped the tiny blade hidden in his palm. Vijay felt as small and useless as the blade. He tried to quiet his own breathing, as if being inaudible might render him invisible. Footsteps thundered in his eardrums, and then he felt the pressure of a rifle butt on his forehead. It forced him to his knees.

"Just a blind man," Vijay heard a voice say. "Who is inside?"

"My wife." The simple truth suddenly calmed Vijay. "She is birthing a child."

"*You* have a wife? That's a joke. She must be old or ugly."

Another man punched Vijay in the shoulder. "Or Muslim."

"Same thing."

"She is old, and I am told ugly," Vijay said. "But I am blind, so it doesn't matter. We were travelling to visit the Sri Venkateshwara Swami Temple near Mahbub Nagar when the baby started coming."

"What a hero." Strong hands grabbed Vijay's arm, pulling him up. "Who are you?"

"Nobody," Vijay responded in a voice borrowed from a role he could slip into whenever danger necessitated it. "A blind cripple." He could feel the man's breath on his face.

"What is your name? Your wife's name?"

"I am Vijay, my wife, Mala."

"Remove your dhoti."

Vijay put his hands together in a plea.

A hand tugged his dhoti off. In the silence Vijay braced for more humiliation. He stood as still as possible, hiding the sharp blade in his fist.

"Jai Ram! Haan. He is one of us. Brother, give him back his cloth."

The dhoti hit Vijay on his chest, and he heard another voice.

"Come with us. We're cleaning up the Razakar scum."

"My son will soon be born."

"All right. The old woman has you in her grip."

Vijay felt a slap on his shoulder. The men strode off, driven by mad purpose.

As quickly as it had begun, it was finished. Vijay loosened his clenched fist and only then felt the sharp pain from where the blade had sliced his palm, a reminder that he was still among the living.

*

As the night quieted, Malika gazed upon her daughter and felt unafraid. She had carried so much fear up to this point. Fear that had arrived the day her mother looked down on her father's broken body and ordered Malika to get help. Fear that grasped at her ankles as she ran from the fire that killed her family. Fear that she kept at bay by keeping one step ahead of it, struggling to find a refuge and then another. No place was safe for long. But here was her daughter, born on the mud floor. Vulnerable like the man who had fathered her, the man who was standing outside, protecting her from yet another danger. Kunti Vadu, Guddi Kuntodu, Alletodu, Vijay Pullaya.

What name would she give her daughter? She counted the infant's digits as she had seen her mother do at the birth of her younger siblings. One, two, three, four, five on the left and five on the right, five toes on each foot. With her cupped hand, she smoothed her daughter's black, slick hair and saw her own reflection in the slope of her child's head, in the dark skin and shape of the face. The little fingers clutched hers. She looked into her daughter's eyes. Open and curious. Eyes that seemed strangely familiar. These were not her eyes, and she had never seen Vijay's eyes, how they might have been. And in this vacuum, she saw someone from whom she had sought help. Her fear returned and she could not outrun it. She knew her daughter would inherit the unusual amber eyes of another man. She had tried to erase the memory of that night. That night in the Reddy compound as she lay inert, in a state of shock, unable to speak or move. She didn't question that her daughter might not be Vijay's. She was certain she had conceived her with Vijay on the bank of the freshwater pond. Could Rayappa have interrupted a biological process that had begun weeks earlier?

"I will marry you," Rayappa had repeatedly whispered, as if these words would soothe her. She lay cold and still, wishing herself dead.

Her infant wriggled in her arms, demanding to be loved. Malika forced herself to gaze into her daughter's eyes — and found the proof of what she already knew.

Malika the practical, Malika the survivor, Malika the mother, seized her power to choose. She decided to love her daughter completely and forgive Rayappa, just a little.

*

While Malika had embraced godless communism, her commitment to the cause could not keep her from prayer. Six months after the purges that had targeted Muslims, Malika carried baby Jaya in a sling to the prayer wall. She arrived well before sunrise, and she would leave before the others arrived. Unrolling her prayer mat, Malika set Jaya down beside her and kneeled. Most of the blood had been washed from the wall, from the place where people, including entire families, had been lined up and executed.

The murdering mobs were not strangers. They were Hindu villagers driven out of Telangana by the Razakars, well before the Communist take-over. Now that the Indian Army had conquered the region, they returned to reclaim their plots. Bolstered by the rhetoric of the right-wing organization Rashtriya Swayamsevak Sangh and also by that of the Hindu-dominated ruling Congress, the mobs took out their fury at the Razakars on their Muslim neighbours. Surviving Muslim peasants and landlords fled the region.

Gazing at Jaya, Malika remembered how her mother, Fariza, had brought her and her sisters to the wall, to pray together. Sunrise and sunset. Malika kneeled and bowed her head to the ground, thinking of her family, sensing that connection with them, with God, with nature. She had fallen in line with atheist ideology, aligned with a pledge to the party, but she could no longer ignore this longing for something bigger. Allah. As her palms felt the coolness of the ground, and her forehead touched the earth, she prayed that her people would be protected.

"Subhana Rabbi al A'la." Glory be to my sustainer most high.

There was a contradiction between what her faith had taught her, a duty to make peace with enemies, and what she knew she must do, seek justice for those who could not do so themselves.

Malika rose from the prayer wall and strapped Jaya to her breast before fixing her rifle over one shoulder. She was ready to join the squad.

*

The convoy of cars curved slowly down the road. Important cars with important people inside. One such important person was the district collector of Aminapally, assigned to govern the village in the wake of the recent Communist defeat by the Indian Army. The collector was reputed to be ruthless. The Indian Union was confident that this new district collector could stamp out whatever was left of the resistance and impose the authority of the Congress Party. Crowds of villagers swelled from both sides of the road, curious to see this notorious collector.

As the entourage moved toward the village, a beggar, limping and leaning on his walking stick, stepped in front of the slow-moving vehicle leading the convoy. The car braked as the beggar scrambled to safety at the side of the road.

Then there was a shot.

The back door of the car popped open.

There was a second shot.

A body, half seated, slumped out of the car.

The crowd dispersed in a panic.

*

With Hyderabad annexed by the Indian Army, the Communist leaders were divided as to whether to build alliances with the Indian Union or continue to regard them as a threat. In September 1948, General Chaudhuri's troops had seized control of the city of Hyderabad and most regions in Telangana, defeating the Nizam's army and the Razakars in five days. Of course they had. Volunteers of the Razakar militia wielded swords and rifles against the steel bulk of Indian Army tanks. The papers deceptively reported a peaceful takeover.

Many Communists hoped to maintain governance of villages still in their authority and to recover regions that had once been in their control. The beleaguered leaders of the CPI argued about strategy, sought Stalin's advice, and kept their squads waiting for instructions. Without clear direction, dalam commanders took matters into their own hands, creating rogue squads. One such leader was Viswanathan.

After the attack that killed Sujana, Viswanathan had meticulously planned to regain Aminapally from the Indian Union. It would start with the assassination of the district collector. He instructed the squad to dig a trench by the road at night and cover it with straw. The next day, when the collector's entourage approached, Vijay, in rags, would create a diversion by walking in front of the vehicles, forcing the cars to swerve off the road. Viswanathan, positioned in the ditch, would shoot the collector himself. Everything had gone according to plan, except Viswanathan forgot to shoot.

Malika stood up from the ditch in which she had been crouching, so that she was eye level with the car on the road above. She fired her third shot, and the collector fell onto the dirt road, lifeless. Still she was worried that he would get up, start waving his hands and shouting orders to execute them all. But he did not. Malika had to remind herself of what her enemies had done. She concentrated on their cruelty so she could finish the task at hand. But as the collector lay there, she had doubts.

She shouldn't have fired at all. But she had. How could she have not? The collector's car was perfectly positioned for Viswanathan's bullet. But Viswanathan, standing inches from her in the ditch, did not shoot. Sujana would not have hesitated. But *he* had. Perhaps he had a problem with the rifle. Or perhaps the problem was the person with the rifle.

Without her, their mission would have failed, she was sure of it.

The squad followed Malika's shot with a rain of bullets. Three police officers who had rushed to the collector's body fell to the ground. Malika held cover while her comrades fleeced the police officers' bodies for identification and ammunition. Some comrades opened the other doors of the car as the bodies of two security officers slid heavily, like bags of grain, into the trench. Three police officers who came out of their stopped vehicles were brought down by bullets or fled on foot. Drivers were allowed to escape with a command: "Run for your lives!"

The squad had succeeded, and it had all begun with her bullet.

Malika's comrades congratulated her. But not Viswanathan. He kept his distance from the others. Malika approached him. "Why didn't you fire?"

"*You* did." Viswanathan seemed to be controlling his anger. "You would have jeopardized the whole squad, had there been more police."

"But there weren't. I waited for you. If I hadn't fired, no one else would have. We would have failed our mission."

Why wasn't Viswanathan explaining that his rifle was jammed, or his positioning wrong, or his leg cramped? Why was he arguing with her? Why was he walking away from her?

Malika found Vijay standing nearby. "Did you hear what he said?"

"Everything."

"But how could he not explain himself?"

"Malika, we must be loyal and defer to him."

"I saved the mission!"

"Yes, you did. But we have a child now."

"And?"

"Things have changed."

"Things are always changing."

Malika moved towards the other squad members. They cheered her and strategized, like a cricket team preparing for their next game.

*

"That which does not kill us, makes us stronger." While the Communists were not proponents of the German philosopher Friedrich Nietzsche, Viswanathan had quoted him to encourage his squad to face harder challenges. Vijay could not help but think, *That which doesn't kill us, warns us of what can.*

When Vijay was six years old, the man he knew to be his father entered his mother's hut. Her voice was gentle. "Ayya, sir, did you bring our boy something?"

"When I have not?"

Vijay's mother brought Raghunandan Reddy a cup of river water. Unlike other men of his status, he had routinely drunk from her vessels, eaten her food, and even kissed her sex. Now, he put his lips to her earthenware pot and emptied the water into his mouth.

"I found a pup, separated from its mother, running amongst the cattle. I brought it for the boy. He can go outside and play with it while we have our time."

Vijay was sent out of the hut and told to stay there until his mother fetched him. He was proud to have his own little pup to run with, to play with, to lie down with in the soft grass beside the river.

Months later, Vijay was plunged into a polarized world of darkness and light. He could not discern colours, identify shapes, or recognize faces.

A fly carrying the Thelazia callipaeda parasite had laid its eggs in his eyes. They became itchy, turned red, streamed fluid, and then became painful. When Vijay's mother noticed the puppy growing listless, pus leaking from his eyes, she made the connection and sought help. But there was no examination, diagnosis, or medicinal eye drops. The village healers had no effective treatment for a corneal ulceration, caused by a curable infection.

When the puppy died, Vijay's mother realized her son had been spared. He was blessed in comparison.

After Vijay lost his sight, he developed an acute sense of smell. Whenever he smelled coal and beeswax, he knew a blacksmith had entered the hut. The sharp stench of fermented fruit lingered long after a toddy tapper came and left. The scent of sandalwood paste signaled that a priest had arrived. He took pity on little Vijay. "Poor wretched child. What he must have done in his past to be born blind."

"He was not born this way. Pochamma is sparing him. This way he doesn't witness my shame or see these ugly shapes that visit me day and night." The Brahmin was unsure if Asha referred to him as one of the ugly shapes. "It is just as well."

While his blindness spared Vijay from having to see these ugly shapes, he came to think of them as earthly ghosts who were invisible but made their presence known. They had heavy footsteps and laboured breathing. Vulgar laughs, dry coughs, throaty grunts, and guttural moans. One ghost kept coming back, sometimes to pat his head or pry his fingers open to insert coins into his fist. This ghost inquired about "the boy" every time he came. The same ghost who brought him his pup.

After the ghosts left, his mother would take Vijay to the river. They would gather calendula flowers and decorate the black stone leaning against the neem tree. They would perform puja for Kari Pochamma, the black goddess who protected them from evil and struck revenge on those who betrayed her. Then she would lead Vijay back to the hut, enfold him into her arms, her sari-clad body faintly smelling of sweat. She would sing a song. He would sleep deeply, in the comfort of her arms, lulled by her rhythmic patting and repetitive verse. In the morning he would wake on a straw mat and wonder how he got there. It seemed like magic.

Vijay never understood the full extent of the degradation his mother endured until the night in the castrator's shed. He wanted to rid himself of this understanding. Rid himself of the shame he felt for his mother. Rid himself of his own shame. So he walked into the Vancha River, the night before his wedding day. This horrific experience and the shame did not kill him, but he was not convinced that it made him stronger.

*

The dalam was called to a self-criticism session to identify what had gone wrong with the mission. It was an opportunity for members to reflect on their behaviour, admit errors, and recommit to the party line. For Viswanathan, it served as an opportunity to humiliate insubordinates and deter others from defying orders. Vijay listened to Viswanathan interrogate Malika. Vijay wished he could protect her. He wished she would seek his protection. He wished she would not defy the leader and accept her punishment gracefully.

"You see the trouble is, as leader of this dalam, *I* must evaluate the situation." Viswanathan paced the floor. "If I judge there to be too many policemen..."

"There were six," Malika said. "Five were killed and one fled."

Vijay winced.

"We cannot have people making their own decisions, without my order."

As if Malika sensed Vijay's concern, she nodded. "Aunandi. Yes, sir." But Vijay knew she really meant, "I understand; you were scared and can't lose face."

Viswanathan declared that Malika would be banned from taking part in raids until further notice.

Filled with relief, Vijay thanked the leader profusely. He thanked him for sparing his beloved from a harsher punishment. He thanked him as he should have that night, when Viswanathan pulled Vijay out of the river. A weary, waterlogged almost-ghost.

*

The night their two squads came together in Mamidala in 1948, Malika guided Vijay's hand over her swollen belly. She knew exactly what she desired, but did not ask for it. For she sensed a change in him, as if a film clung to his soul sealing him off from her. His gentle touch was there, his kind words, but he remained distant. Did he suspect a betrayal on her part? As the sun lifted over the horizon and ushered the birdsong in the morning, Malika went back to where the women slept, unsure if Vijay was the same man she had known.

It was not easy to live as husband and wife during the revolution. The party had imposed rules of conduct, which dictated that men and women live apart. Malika and Vijay met most often in the company of other squad members or peasants with whom they were working. When Malika tried to communicate with him, brushing against his arm, whispering an invitation to meet in the forest, Vijay would decline.

"Remember our work," he would say, but not unkindly.

She grew resentful. At first, she suspected he was jealous of her. Her sudden rise through the ranks, her essential role in the squad. The things she had accomplished that he never would. This explanation easily crumbled, however, for even when they disagreed about strategy, he was her constant support.

When Jaya was born, Malika and Vijay were given their own hut. Every night, the baby slept with Malika on a cot. Vijay slept on the ground. When she pulled his hand towards her, he pried her fingers off, patting her hand as if she were a child. When she smoothed his wild, thick locks, he would lean towards her in near surrender and then suddenly pull back, as if repelled by the simple gesture. Had he taken the party rules too seriously? Had he been indoctrinated into thinking that these natural impulses, these pleasures, were disloyal and unacceptable? What good was it to be married if they could not draw comfort from one another?

Malika suggested they return to Korampally. It was a Communist-ruled region and they could join a different Sangham. The Reddys had been dis-possessed, and his mother was there. They could go live with her. She was the only family left. Perhaps her father had returned.

Vijay's face hardened and he spoke in a tone that Malika did not recognize. "I will never go back there." She asked him for a reason. Vijay took her hands gently. "I do not ask you for explanations, so please do not ask me."

Malika wondered if he suspected he was not Jaya's father. She scanned his face, she searched for an opening, but found none.

They lived in this cool distance for a year after Jaya's birth until Viswanathan gathered the dwindling dalam into his house, which also served as the village administration office. He announced that Malika should lead the next raid in a nearby village.

Malika was surprised. "I thought I was banned from combat?"

"Come, Malika. Enough time has passed. You've proven yourself capable and a good shot. So many others have fallen."

"You also are reputed to be a good shot. But few have had the opportunity to witness this." Malika was defiant.

"Have you forgotten with whom you are speaking?"

Malika looked between Viswanathan and Vijay. "I am pregnant."

Viswanathan kicked over a chair. "What is your role here? To fire a gun or produce children?"

Vijay exhaled and clasped his hands. "If it is a party order, I am sure we will find a solution."

Malika stared at Vijay, ashamed at what he was becoming.

*

That night Vijay left Jaya with Deviyani and asked Malika to walk with him to the forest.

"We need him. Even if you don't care about yourself, we have a child. Without Viswanathan's protection, Jaya will be vulnerable. We cannot be turned out of the party."

"The party is falling apart. You hear what others are saying. Comrades are disappearing. Where is Viswanathan getting his orders? How do we know he is telling the truth?"

"We don't."

They stood in silence under a shivering canopy of leaves. In the distance, they could see a glow from a bonfire where villagers gathered to sing and drink toddy. The echo of drums and voices rose on the wind, sparks floated into the clear starlit sky. Closer still, cicadas buzzed their mating calls.

Vijay spoke so quietly he was barely audible. "Is there really another baby?"

Malika let out a small laugh. And then was serious. "You know there is not."

Vijay knelt on the ground, picked at the grass, needing to hold onto something. Malika took his face in both her hands and tilted it towards her. A tear travelled down his cheek.

"What is it?"

Vijay knew that what had happened in the shed blocked him from reaching for Malika. At the same time, he could no longer hold the shame he had carried.

Malika bent and kissed his mouth. "We two are the same. You and me. We have all we need between us."

Vijay drew Malika down. He caressed her coarse hands, encircled her emaciated limbs, and gently cradled her chafed feet. They were not beautiful youth escaping to the forest to make love but two rebels tired of fighting, pushing away shame, despair, and the inevitable failure of their revolution. Vijay knew they were on the verge of giving up. Almost, but not quite there. When Malika opened herself to him, he was ready.

*

With their commitment to protect Jaya and their renewed trust in each other, Malika and Vijay convinced Viswanathan that their squad should lie low, that further raids would compromise them and Mamidala. They were lucky that the Indian Army had not traced the assassination of the district collector of Aminapally back to them. Mamidala was a small inconsequential village, and they would need to keep it that way for their own survival. Many other Communist villages had fallen to the Indian Army.

Viswanathan finally agreed, and settled into his administrative role, abandoning dreams of liberation or revenge. The dalam would employ their arms only if attacked or if commanded by the Central Committee. Viswanathan waited for news from the Communist leaders.

*

For four years, Mamidala remained self-sufficient, off the radar of the Indian Army. During this relative peace, villagers found pride in collectively working the land. Malika was expecting her second child. In her third trimester of pregnancy, she was instructing a small group of villagers to dig a canal that would supply water to the rice fields. Hearing the cheering of a crowd marching down the footpath towards them, they lifted their heads. Four-year-old

Chinnie Jaya was on Vijay's shoulders. She tweaked Vijay's ear, and he turned towards the sound.

Jaya laughed, delighted. She had learned to lead Vijay from her perch by describing what was happening in the fields, who was approaching, even signalling to him the mood of the person about to speak.

Vijay tickled her feet. "What's going on?"

"Naina, it's a parade."

Malika shaded her eyes with her hand. "It looks like a new dalam has arrived. Comrades are waving red flags."

A young man in a bright yellow shirt approached them. "I am Satyam from CPI headquarters. I have a message for Viswanathan."

Vijay passed Jaya to one of the villagers to mind, and he and Malika led Satyam and his group to the Communist headquarters where Viswanathan also lived. Ten dalam leaders from surrounding villages happened to be gathering for their monthly meeting. Satyam greeted Viswanathan and gave him a gift of cigarettes and whiskey. Malika and Vijay, along with other squad members, pulled up chairs or sat on the ground in a circle. Satyam had such an air of joviality that dalam leaders urged him to speak.

"Our great leader Ravi Narayan Reddy has been released from Chanchalguda Central Jail. Naraya Dora is free!"

Everyone clapped hands and cheered. Some lit cigarettes and passed around the bottle, contrary to party rules. Viswanathan helped himself. "Please tell us more."

"All Communists must lay down their arms."

"And you call this a victory?"

"The armed struggle is over. Naraya Dora has ordered a ceasefire."

"Of course he has. He had to deal his way out of prison. And what about the Central Committee? What are they doing after this ceasefire?"

"They are negotiating concessions. Demands from the government, wages and land reforms."

"With what leverage? Next thing, they will ask us to report to the Agrarian Enquiry Committee. How the hell do they think they will achieve land reform?"

"But the leaders have spoken. We are to disarm, otherwise no concessions, no gains."

"We were the ones that brought down the Razakars. We booted the landlords off and redistributed their land, village by village. Only two years ago six thousand villages in Telangana were liberated by the CPI. Every peasant was given a plot, a cow. Everything they needed to live in dignity. Now the bloody Indian Union wants to take the credit? We are not politicians, we are militants!" Viswanathan was yelling now.

Satyam was calm. "No one is arguing with you. But we have no choice. Ask your group to cease and desist, or you'll be dead in a week."

"And now you are telling the future." Viswanathan took a long swig of whiskey.

"No. But I recognize a real threat. General Chaudhuri's exact words were, 'Communists must surrender, give up their arms within a week, failing which they will be exterminated.'"

Deviyani was seated near Malika and let out a long sigh. "But we pose no threat. We have other support, do we not?"

"Not anymore. Stalin has advised the Central Committee against continuing the revolution. Given the political situation, the geography of the region..."

Viswanathan waved the bottle of whiskey in the air. "Has he ever stepped foot in Telangana? Imagine Lenin, seeking advice from those outside his country. 'It's winter; shall we lay down our arms?' Rubbish! The Russian Revolution would never have happened. We will not make the same mistake as the British. Entrusting Radcliffe, some lawyer and committee chairman, who never set foot in Asia, let alone the sub-continent, to determine the border between India and Pakistan. We know what a disaster that was. No. We will not heed the advice of anyone outside of Telangana. Stalin cannot tell us what to do. He is no longer our ally."

Vijay rubbed the back of his neck. "Stalin is distracted by Korea now. Perhaps he's seeking a future partnership with the Indian government. Protecting his own interests."

"You see, even a blind man can see into the motives of Stalin."

Viswanathan, who had once championed Vijay, had turned bitter towards him of late. Vijay had a wife who defied Viswanathan. Vijay had a child and another one on the way. Viswanathan had devoted himself to the movement and had no wife, no child. He didn't even have a dog to kick.

Viswanathan looked down at his shoes. The oxfords had been passed around at a dalam meeting in Korampally until someone with small enough feet could claim them. These English shoes. Now old and dirty.

"Vijay is correct," Satyam said, "We have no support."

"Everyone is forgetting why we started fighting." Deviyani took the bottle of whiskey from Viswanathan and drank. She passed it to Satyam, who declined.

"It is a matter of whether we can sustain what we have. And that is not possible."

Viswanathan's voice grew urgent. "No, it is a matter of what happens to the peasants. To that man and woman over there. What will happen to their child?" Viswanathan locked eyes with Malika. Now everyone stared at her.

Malika smoothed her sari over her belly. During the past four years she had gotten used to domestic normalcy, living with Vijay and Jaya in their small hut, cultivating her plot, tilling the soil, laying down seed. But things had shifted when Narayan and other leaders were imprisoned by the Indian Army. Everyone had been anxious and hungry for news of Narayan Reddy and the Central Committee members. But this news? Deals had been brokered and careers carved out. Somewhere else, someone else was deciding their fate.

Viswanathan crossed the room to Malika. "Shall we ask them? This young couple.

"Malika? Are you willing to give up Mahbub Nagar and Mamidala to the Indian Union? The same army that crushed Aminapally, where Comrade Sujana was murdered? Are you prepared to give Korampally, your home village, which you helped liberate, back to the Reddys?"

Satyam folded his arms across his chest. "The Reddys will not get their land back. There is already an act in place to outlaw the eviction of tenants, and there are fixed rates on rents. All part of the promised land reform. There will be an election in which we can take part! Narayan himself will run."

"And you think the people will oust the Congress Party? Each area that the Indian Army controls has invited the landlords back." Viswanathan stretched his arms above his head. "You've delivered your message, now get out!"

Satyam's group rose and left, but Satyam remained. Malika glanced at Vijay. He was rubbing his forehead. Was he thinking what she was thinking?

How could Naraya Dora trust the Republic to protect workers' rights and land distribution? The same force that was rounding up comrades and torturing them in concentration camps. The same force that had jailed Narayan Reddy himself. Now it was confirmed that the Central Committee wanted the party to count their successes and move on. How could they? How could she give up? And if she did, where would she go? Malika thought about how Viswanathan ran from the fires in Aminapally, how he failed to shoot the collector, how he drank and smoked and belched and swore. How he continued to wear those ridiculous shoes. Then she said what she thought she would never say aloud.

"I think Viswanathan is right. We cannot give up so easily."

Vijay lifted his head. "But why did the Central Committee give up? Our defeat must be closer than we think. They must know the numbers. How many comrades have been killed. All we have known these last years is that our Mamidala has been spared. But for how long?"

Viswanathan started pacing around the circle. "That's right. We don't know the facts, so we must find out. Vijay, you will come with me to Hyderabad. We will confirm what the Russians have said and find out what our leaders are really planning. We must be prepared for anything on the ground. Our opponent is more challenging now. We still have the advantage of geography and support of the people. We will go further underground. Win over the tribals. Become forest dwellers."

Satyam stood up. "Viswanathan, you are defying the command of Narayan himself?"

"No. I am defying you. What proof do we have that this is Narayan's wish? I will not give up Mamidala so easily."

"This village is not your private kingdom." Satyam headed to the door.

"You heard the girl. If she is willing to fight, why not you?"

Satyam casually put his hands up in the air. "I am just the messenger."

"Just as I thought. A bourgeoisie!" Viswanathan calmly picked up his rifle, which leaned against the wall. "Malika, you'll be needed on the front lines."

"But the baby."

"Once the baby is born you must hand your children over to the villagers. I need you to train tribals, lead a squad, and take reinforcements to Korampally, and then we will move on to Mahbub Nagar. We must protect our strongholds. Deviyani, as a midwife you are a respected native of Mamidala. You will take charge here until Vijay and I return from Hyderabad." Viswanathan caressed the length of his rifle before aiming it around the circle. He paused when he came to Satyam. "If you want to betray this movement, then do it now."

"I take my orders from the Central Committee, not some pompous village despot."

Viswanathan pulled the trigger, and the messenger fell dead.

*

The baby released a wretched cry. Malika closed her eyes. She forgot to count the fingers and toes or check the sex. If she had had the strength to see, she would have discovered that she had given birth to a boy.

It was a bittersweet moment. Malika and Vijay had been ordered to give up their children and separate. The next day, Vijay would leave for Hyderabad with Viswanathan, and in two weeks, after leaving their children with a sympathetic family, Malika would go to Korampally and then on to Mahbub Nagar. The separation of their family was to be expected. Some comrades lost hope of having children. Others had given their children to family members, or left them in "safe" villages, hoping for the best. Most male comrades, whose wives were not in the movement, simply left them and their children behind. And then there were women who fought to keep their children close, while working within the dalam. Malika considered herself lucky. She gazed at her two children, the newborn at her breast and Jaya lying on the mat covered by a thin blanket. She felt lucky to have mothered Jaya for four years. They would leave the children with a family here and in time come back to collect them.

But Vijay, seated cross-legged beside sleeping Jaya, had another plan. "You must take the children to Korampally. To my mother."

"You told me you would never go back."

"It is not my first choice. But we can no longer follow Viswanathan. You have seen what he is capable of."

Viswanathan had conquered his fear of firing a rifle when he killed Satyam. He began turning it on anyone who defied him.

"But the baby is so fragile. We have not even named him."

"We can name him in Korampally, with my mother. You will be travelling with the group in a truck. The squad will move through Korampally in two weeks' time to get to Mahbub Nagar."

Malika felt despondent. "And you?"

"Viswanathan would kill me rather than let me go. I must disappear. Tell him I abandoned you. I will go through the forest and meet you in Korampally."

"But how will you go, without a guide?"

"I have her." Vijay laid his hand on Jaya's head as she slept. "It will take us two weeks to walk. After that, I will go to the village well at midnight until we are reunited."

So they devised a plan. Vijay would immediately leave Mamidala with Chinnie Jaya. The child would be Vijay's eyes as they cut through the forest and made their way to Korampally. They would seek refuge with sympathetic villagers. Malika would tell Viswanathan that she could leave the baby with relations in Korampally, recruit Adivasis in the forests on the way, and lead the new squad to Mahbub Nagar for their next mission. They would need a vehicle, some ammunition, whatever he could spare. She wouldn't reveal that upon arriving in Korampally, she would abandon the mission, meet Vijay, and they would cross the river together to find his mother.

Malika crouched over sleeping Jaya and pulled out a pink pouch tucked into the waist of the child's skirt. She drew out a gold pocket watch that Jaya liked to play with. "If you need money, sell this."

Vijay felt the weight of the metal disc in his hand. "Where did you get it?"

"Rayappa. Remember the strange student with the English man? I stole it." She felt relieved to say his name, as if it told Vijay all that he needed to know.

Vijay roused Jaya, fed her chapatis and fish curry and wrapped her in a shawl. Malika tucked the pouch back into the waistband of Jaya's skirt and packed a tiffin of tamarind rice and fruit and nuts for the journey. Malika stood outside the hut with her unnamed baby and watched Vijay, clutching the hand of their spirited daughter, disappear into the woods.

*

The full moon filtered through the trees in the forest surrounding Korampally. A cool breeze lifted boughs, shaking the silvery green leaves above the heads of Malika and her comrades. Their numbers had grown as Banjara herders and Chenchu tribal people, desperate to protect their lives in the Nallamala forest, joined the Communists. Forty members of the squad emerged from the forest into the rice fields, as the moon hid behind the clouds.

Their truck had broken down outside Korampally so Malika led the group by foot through familiar territory. Her instincts were powerful, and the anticipation of seeing Vijay and Jaya propelled her forward in the dark. Her baby strapped to her chest, she guided the squad down the footpath, past the castrator's shed along the river.

They arrived in the village under cloud cover and could not make out the enormous stone abutments of the new arched bridge that now spanned the Vancha River. Solid, able to bear the weight of thousands of trucks. Built for tanks.

They moved across the fields to the crossroads, where the peepal tree stood, and they continued down the main road to the Reddy compound.

If they had arrived by day, the newly formed squad might have been greeted by peasants beating drums or merchants calling out from behind their stalls. But by night, the streets were quiet and their arrival at the Reddy compound was uneventful. Through the open gate, they could see the red flag waving from a pole on the veranda. The veranda that Malika had once swept. While many squad members moved into the house, eager to meet up with fellow comrades, Malika told them she would be meeting a comrade from Korampally at the well. Four comrades joined her, not wanting to leave her alone.

According to village lore, if you listened carefully, a well would tell you what it held. Tonight, Malika did not need to listen carefully. The well was crying. Malika recognized the sound. It was Jaya's voice. Handing her baby to a comrade, Malika crawled up onto the ledge. In that moment, the moon emerged from behind the clouds. For anyone looking up at her, they might have seen a circle of light, a halo around her head. But Malika, peering down, saw nothing.

Squad members pointed the flames of their torches into the mouth of the well. Malika fixed her gaze on the one thing that moved. Jaya's tiny arms were flailing about on either side of a body collapsed upon her. It was Vijay. His back was riddled with bullets. And underneath his corpse, Jaya was struggling to free herself. Chinnie Jaya, Little Victory.

A comrade moved Malika aside. He had already tied a rope around his waist. Others worked the pulley, lowering him deeper and deeper. Malika stood silent and still as they drew first the inert body of her husband from the well and then her daughter. Fifteen people below Jaya would be pulled up in turn. But no others were alive. The blood on Jaya was her father's. Miraculously, the little girl was uninjured. Malika's comrades repeated this fact to her like a mantra.

"She is alive! She is alive!"

Malika held her child, tried to speak with her, comfort her. But Jaya, who had stopped crying, could no longer speak. A vacant look in Jaya's eyes told Malika she could not reach her daughter. Even with her children and comrades nearby, Malika felt utterly alone.

The new squad found the Reddy compound empty. Where were their comrades, the ones who should have been governing Korampally? A villager on the street said they had all left for Mahbub Nagar. The place was deserted. It was decided that ten men would guard the compound while the others slept.

The comrades distributed food and then found a place to sleep. Malika discovered a room with a bed, wardrobe, and water vessel, an unimaginable luxury for her and her children. She put the baby to sleep. Then she turned to Jaya. Jaya sat unmoving on the bed, except for her eyes, which darted around the room, as if she were searching for someone. Malika folded Jaya into her bosom and let her drink from her breasts. Then Malika spoke the words she hoped her daughter would understand.

"Jaya, you will see. You will have a place on this Earth, neither servant nor slave; you will have food in your belly and land beneath your feet. But more than riches, more than beauty, more than intelligence, you will have worth."

It was all she could hope for.

Malika found the vessel full of water and cleaned herself. She opened a small armoire and found a few saris and, in an old box, some infant's clothes. Aditi's room, she surmised. The young mistress must have given birth to a girl after Malika had fled. Malika could not remember if Surendra, Aditi, or their daughter were present when she drove the Reddys out of Korampally. Perhaps they had gotten away just in time. Malika tore apart a cotton sari, soaking one end in water. With that, she wiped the grime from her daughter's skin. She wrapped the other half of the sari around Jaya's torso and put her to sleep. She also found a plain cotton sari to change into. When the baby awoke, she fed him, washed him, and guided his tiny arms through the sleeves of an infant's yellow frock. Aditi's daughter's clothes. She smiled at her son. Vijay's mother could name him. A gift to temper the tragic news Malika would have to share. They would need to cross the river. Another challenge. But she had once lifted a suitcase high over her head as she traversed the river. She would find a way to carry her children. Feeding them and letting them rest took priority. Malika rocked the baby back to sleep. Then she lay down, spooned her little girl, and soon drifted off.

Malika wasn't sure whether it was her son crying or a koel cawing outside that woke her with a start. She propped herself up with her elbow and saw the baby was still asleep. Still there was an intermittent and muffled sound coming from her window. Perhaps it was the snore of a comrade, or an insistent dream trying to pull her back.

She sat up in the bed, the first mattress on which she had laid her body, the first pillow on which she had rested her head. Malika was in a palace bedroom made for a queen, not a servant who spent her days scrubbing and nights sleeping on the ground. Malika looked at her children, sleeping soundly. Then she remembered Vijay. A deep dread overcame her. She could not rest, so she got out of bed and stepped outside.

Clutching her rifle, Malika crept around the landlord's house, moving through the now deserted hall, which she had only entered the day Aditi had dressed her for her wedding. She roamed like a ghost, a widow who had not been properly wed, a mother still growing out of her own childhood, a daughter with no parents. She stepped into the familiar courtyard onto the tiles that she had swept, past the latrine that she had cleaned, and near the little room where Rayappa had taken advantage of her. It seemed a lifetime ago. She heard sobbing and looked to her comrades guarding the gate. Had they not heard it?

It was a woman's voice. Malika slowly parted the curtain of the little room. A form crouched at the foot of the cot in the pre-dawn darkness.

"Who are you?"

Malika made out that it was a woman wearing a burqa. Her face was hidden by her veil. Malika lifted it off with the butt of her rifle. The woman lurched at Malika's body, kneeling at her feet, begging for mercy. It was Linga Reddy's wife. Lalita.

"Please Amma, don't kill me."

"Get up off the floor and stand there. Who else is here? Where is he? Where is your husband?"

"No one. No one is here." Lalita rose slowly from the ground and stood against the wall.

"I don't believe you. Stay there!"

"Amma, don't kill me, please."

"Where did he go? Is he in the house?"

"No. I am alone. He left me."

"Why? Why would he leave you?" Malika watched Lalita while also guarding the door.

Lalita pulled her veil back over her face. "I am so ashamed. I have been ruined."

"Who did this to you? You are a Hindu woman. You are a Reddy."

"We came back here. The Indian Army promised to give our house back. They were soldiers, supposed to protect us. I simply wanted to draw water from the well." Lalita slid down to the ground sobbing.

Malika understood that the veiled Lalita had been violated, likely mistaken for what Malika herself had been, a poor Muslim servant girl. Malika, clutching her rifle, crouched down to Lalita's level. "How long have you been here?"

"Three days. After that happened, my husband deserted me. I am all alone."

"Come with us. You can travel with the squad."

"You are with the Communists?"

"Do you want protection or not? Come, get up."

"No, no." Lalita started pleading. "Please don't tell them I am here. Please don't take me to them."

"Lalita. You do not remember me. I am Malika. I swept your courtyard, cleaned the latrines."

Lalita backed away.

"Come with us. What else can you do?" Malika was angry now. She had to take her children across the river before dawn.

"Please don't leave me."

Lalita retreated in the corner as Malika returned to her room to gather her children.

*

In the darkness of early morning, Malika, with her children, walked across the arched bridge over the Vancha. She was surprised at how easy it was to cross. She simply put one foot in front of the other. Clutching Jaya's hand, Malika carried the baby in a sling on her back that helped camouflage her rifle. Malika decided to avoid the main road from the bridge and walk through the trees that lined the river's edge.

Malika heard a voice chanting and hid behind some mango trees. It was still dark, but as she drew closer, Malika saw Ashamma only six feet away, alone, praying, dropping flowers into the river. The baby gave out a wail. Ashamma, always attentive, turned. She followed the cry to the trees. She embraced Malika, feeling both the baby and the hard shape of her rifle.

Malika detached the sling on her back and passed the baby to Ashamma. "Vijay's baby. For you to name."

That was all Malika needed to say, to convey to Ashamma that Vijay had been alive, fathered a child, and was now dead. Ashamma simply rocked the baby, holding it close to her breast as tears streamed down her face. Then she handed the baby back to Malika and wiped her face with her palloo. She lifted Jaya up so she could pick a mango from the tree. While Malika nursed the baby, Ashamma peeled the skin from the fruit and fed Malika and Jaya the sweet and soft flesh. When they finished, Malika asked Ashamma to take her children.

"I have no shelter for them. I pull my mat here to sleep. The soldiers have taken over all the huts until they set up barracks. They wanted to relocate us, but where would I go? This is my home."

Malika, with her children, followed Ashamma through the forest, keeping hidden behind the trees. Ashamma directed Malika to peer out to look at her hut. Malika expected to find the thatched hut hidden in the mossy bank as it had been four years ago. Instead, the forest had been clear-cut; the hut was still standing but now army tents were set up nearby. A road had been carved out from where a footpath meandered, and military trucks and the tanks that Viswanathan had spoken of were visible. It was clear to Malika that this side of the river, once a hideout for Communists, had been appropriated by the Indian Army to launch its offensive against Korampally.

Malika knew she had to return to the Reddy compound. She had to warn the squad about the proximity of the army. They would have to move on immediately. Ashamma gave Malika her shawl so that she could better hide her rifle as she crossed back over the bridge.

Malika realized that Vijay had walked into a trap. The army had likely raised red flags, knowing the Communists would flock there. The other bodies in the well were likely Communists too. The ones who had occupied the headquarters at the Reddy compound. The squad with whom they had expected to meet.

Malika was numb as she left Ashamma and walked away from the sun that crept over the eastern horizon and illuminated her way across the bridge. She and her children were exposed to whomever might follow. When she neared the other side, a police car swerved in front of her. A policewoman jumped out and grabbed Malika's arm. A warm trickle of urine ran down her leg.

The policewoman shouted, "We need to get out of here!"

Malika folded her body over Jaya. The baby, still strapped to her back, started wailing.

Malika heard a familiar voice. "The army has seized the house. They've arrested the men."

It took a moment before Malika recognized the faces of the women in her squad. The woman in the police uniform unstrapped Malika's baby from the sling and passed him to Malika to quiet him. Then the woman helped Malika into the back seat, passing Malika's rifle to her, before getting into the front. There were five female squad members in the car, two in the front and three in back. One woman sat on another's lap to make room for Malika to climb in. The third woman pulled Jaya onto her lap. This woman explained that they had been in the back quarters of the Reddy compound when the army raided the house. The women hid in the latrines and escaped with this police vehicle and supplies, including the uniforms, left in the car.

Malika watched the blurred landscape pass by as they drove: the line of palm trees bending sympathetically towards them, the rushing river urging them to make haste, the grassy meadows that seemed to be waving good-bye, and the deep green forest that gave them cover. Malika was a girl again, revisiting the landscapes of her childhood. Or maybe she was dead.

"Where do we go now?" The woman who was driving turned her head to Malika.

Of course. Malika was their leader.

"Mahbub Nagar." Malika heard herself name the location without hesitation. She remembered the last instructions that Viswanathan had given her. "We must defend our strongholds."

The woman in the police uniform turned her head. "The new district collector is expected tomorrow at noon. They say he has ordered his men to shoot us on sight."

"Not if we shoot first." Malika felt the hard metal of her rifle against her knee.

*

They reached Mahbub Nagar at night and waited in the forest until the morning. Six women lay side by side; between them, two children slept. Malika woke to breathtaking beauty, birdsong, dew on the grass, and the perfume of hibiscus rising like mist. Her children were still asleep, exhaling warm breath on her back and arm. Malika was reassured that they were safe in the moment.

As she cleaned her rifle, she wondered how she had arrived here, if there could have been a different path. Perhaps she could have learned to read. Been given a title, a door, a desk, a paper, a pen, a purpose. She could have written a report about her experiences, listed the number of killings, the degree of suffering. She could have depicted the frenzied attacks by the Razakars, the strategic massacres by the Indian Army, the targeted executions by Hindu mobs, and even the violent tactics of the Communists themselves. If only she had a pen, what would she write about herself? That she targeted only the guilty? The tax collectors, police, the ruling class who raped sisters and starved children, enslaved fathers, and burned villages.

But Malika would never submit her report. No matter how much she wanted to divulge what she knew, she could never truly justify why she did what she did. She feared her story would be placed alongside the atrocities of the goondas, the Razakars, the Hindu mobs, the police, the landlords, the army. Her story was different. And she was not ready to recant or regret her choices. For what choices had she been given? She ran from the memory of her own violence, and from a future that was bent on repeating the past. She wanted life. If only to climb a tree, tumble down a hill. Feel the rush of the river and the urgency of her lover's touch. Respond to her son's cry and revel in her daughter's laughter. For all the death she saw, she still wanted life — the life she should have had. And even more than that, she wanted her children to have lives worth living.

Malika left Jaya and her newly named baby in the forest with her comrades, her new sisters. She would be back soon, she hoped with news of a successful mission, a cause for celebration after all their trials. Then she hid her rifle under the shawl Ashamma had given her and moved towards the town of Mahbub Nagar, where crowds were swelling in anticipation of the arrival of the new district collector.

1997 — The Prayer Wall

Parveen belongs to a global sisterhood whose members love and live for one another. It is where she finds belonging and support.

Committed to social justice, she volunteers for several women's organizations, but like everyone, Parveen must survive. So she earns her living by translating English into Telugu and back again. Many who work with Parveen call her a saint. Others accuse her of being a feminist.

Swami Antharyami is also referred to as a saint of sorts. But none call him a feminist. When Raghunandan Reddy decided to do right by the women he had wronged, the swami, rather than instructing Reddy to compensate for the harm he caused hundreds of women, encouraged him to make a symbolic redemptive gesture. "Choose one woman to represent your regret for sexual excess and grant her a wish." Swami insisted that in this way Reddy could fulfill dharma.

Raghunandan Reddy chose the first woman he had been with. A woman with whom he had fathered a child. A woman whom he saw as utterly and innocently beautiful. A woman who, at the time, was not a woman at all, but an eleven-year-old girl: Asha. He went through the proper channels and hired someone who presented as a saint, to do his begging. Through Parveen, he asked Ashamma, the aged village jogini, what she would accept from him.

Parveen agreed to the job but also vowed to look out for Ashamma's interests, refusing to enter any kind of agreement that might in any way compromise or harm Ashamma. Parveen hoped Ashamma would accept Reddy's offer of financial assistance, simply to assure Ashamma's comfort in old age. But Ashamma insisted that she had no need for comfort, and that all she wanted was to see her son by retrieving any trace of him that might be left on Earth.

Jaya seeks Parveen's help in returning the envelope of money to Linga Reddy. She doesn't want to hurt his feelings or to be disrespectful. She is

unsure of cultural norms and needs advice. Parveen suggested that they go
to a local tea shop and meet Linga there.

"It is neutral territory. It would be hard to return the gift on Reddy's turf.
You know he owns nearly sixty per cent of the village."

"That much?"

"From what I know. They may own even more land in other villages.
They were engaged in a legal case against the government. They've won
back much of what they owned and amassed even more. At one time they
controlled the entire district."

Jaya thinks about the bulging envelope in her purse, her own insecure
livelihood. She thinks about how easy it is for Anya to refuse the gift, even
as she has little income herself. Jaya agrees to meet Linga at the tea shop, and
Parveen promises to take her there.

Parveen arrives at the peach house on a light-blue moped. "Hop on!"

"You drive this? I expected you to come in an auto-rickshaw."

"The drivers complain when they go up steep roads. I want to take you
someplace special before we meet Linga."

Jaya thought she would not need to depend on Parveen after that first
meeting with Ashamma, but just like the convenience of the cook and dhobi,
Parveen is helpful and always there. Jaya, riding on the back of Parveen's
moped, does not know where they are going, nor does she care in this
moment. The wind, the heat, the speed give her the sensation that she is
free. They drive across the bridge, past the artisan stalls, the temple, and
the Reddy mansion. Parveen accelerates as they climb up a hill. They wind
through terraced lots on the hillside and come to an enclave of huts. Parveen
slows and pulls over.

Parveen leads Jaya on a footpath to a small clearing in which a nine-foot
stone wall stands. It is crumbling and there are gaps where stones have fallen
away. It appears that people have tried to fill these with rocks and pebbles.
There is a curved niche in the centre. A stone basin to the right of the wall,
with water vessels nearby for washing hands and feet.

"Why are we here?"

"You told me Malika was Muslim. This is likely where she would have
prayed in 1948. The community was quite small at the time and very poor.
They would have come here."

"Who told you this?

"I have been speaking with the local Muslims. My community."

"You are Muslim? Sorry, I assumed you were Hindu."

"You and most people. Parveen is both a Hindu and Muslim name. Like Malika."

Jaya reflects on this and moves towards the wall. "May I touch it?" She passes her hands over the stone.

"I'll teach you how to pray, if you wish." Parveen first goes to the basin and washes her feet and hands. Then she instructs Jaya to do the same. Parveen covers her head with her chunni, and kneels. Jaya stands and watches for a moment and then joins her.

She feels the hard ground at her knees, the coolness at her palms. And then she lowers herself so that her forehead touches the earth. Her head is lower than her heart. She feels humbled, she can no longer think, but she experiences a sense of calm as she imagines her mother in this place.

When they finish, Jaya thanks Parveen. "The last time I prayed was in 1975, at mass."

"You are Catholic?"

"No. I'm not much of anything, but I worked as a cook for the nuns. Sometimes we attended mass."

"Who is we?"

"Me and Anasuya."

"Anya's other mother."

Jaya nods. "She cleaned their toilets and I cooked their food. Together we kept an eye on what went in and came out of the nuns of Mount Saint Bernard."

Parveen laughed. "So you do have a sense of humour."

After walking around the terraced hills, Parveen drives Jaya back into the village and to the tea shop. There are few tables outside, where baskets filled with small disposable cups hang from poles. Jaya notes a few men drinking from these cups before throwing them in the garbage.

"The breeze is cool. Why don't we sit out here?"

Parveen hesitates. "It's probably more comfortable inside. Anyway, Reddy wouldn't like it; you don't get served outside."

"Why?"

"I'll explain later."

Inside the shop, a handful of customers are seated, drinking from glass or stainless-steel cups. As they move to a table, a waiter stops them. "Sorry, madame, we are closing. Please, you must leave immediately."

"What is the matter?" Parveen asks.

Jaya is aware of loud voices and turns to the street. There is a crowd out-side the shop, mostly men waving red flags. They pull down the baskets, spilling the disposable cups on the ground. "Same service for Dalits! Stop the two-tumbler system!" A small group of men enter the tea shop, shouting. "Shut down the tea stalls! Equality for Dalits!"

The waiter hurries Jaya and Parveen along with other patrons to the back door. They see Linga's car parked in the alley. The driver opens the door for the women. Linga is seated in the front seat and gestures to them to be quick. Jaya scrambles in. "Thank god you are here."

"I was just arriving when I saw the mob."

Parveen follows Jaya into the back and shuts the door. "They are hardly a mob."

"Maybe. But it will become one. Those Naxalites have a way of turning pacifists into militants. For years everyone happily accepted this two-glass tradition, and now they are dividing the poor. Turning one against the other."

"They are protesting an unfair practice." Parveen speaks evenly.

Parveen explains that these are small tea shops, owned not by rich land-owners but merchants. The Naxalites, who earlier focused their agitation around land redistribution, are now challenging the caste traditions. They demand that Mangali cut hair of Malas and that chakali wash the clothes of Madigas.

Linga signals the driver to move on. "It's all a waste of time. A hopeless cause. These backward castes have their fixed rules and will never let go. We'll take tea at the Krishna Lodge. It is close by." Jaya, once again, is grateful to Linga.

It is tea time, and the restaurant at the Krishna Lodge is full. Linga, Parveen, and Jaya are lucky to find a free table. Linga sits opposite the two women and listens to Jaya's heartfelt appreciation for rescuing them from the tea shop, then her profuse apology at not being able to accept the funds on behalf of her daughter.

"Don't worry about it. My father is convinced he must take care of Vijay Pullaya's family."

"Who?" Jaya asks.

"Ashamma's son. His descendants. You are Malika's daughter, are you not?"

Jaya is struck by her own ignorance. She thought Malika was the key to finding all her relations, including her father. But here is Linga, casually drop-ping names about her mother and others possibly connected to her.

Reddy picks up the envelope. "You may be correct in returning this. My father wants to rid himself of his property and money before he dies, but you never know, he may live another decade. Then what will he live off, especially with his declining health?"

Jaya regrets even entertaining the idea of keeping the money.

Linga withdraws the notes from the envelope and starts counting it. He slaps his hand on the table. Jaya is startled. "Three thousand rupees in small notes. Hardly worth returning." Linga leans back and folds his arms. "Let's stop the charade, shall we? What are you after?"

Jaya stumbles over her words. "The charade? We're ... we came to look for Malika. To learn about her."

"You're chasing a ghost. And you are trying to convince my father you are Kunti Vadu's daughter."

"Who? Who are you talk—"

"That some vague connection to that jogini will guarantee your name in my father's will?"

"Jogini?"

"But we all know that idiot could never father a child. He deserved his fate where he met it."

"Mr. Reddy, I don't know what you are talking about. Or why you are upset. If you know something about Malika, please tell me."

"She was a servant. She just worked for us. Very ungrateful. We all thought she went up in flames, but years later she and her Communist gang came back for revenge." Linga stares long and hard at Jaya. "We gave her a job, protection. And she turned vengeful and led a group of men, armed with Sten rifles, and broke into our house. She had all of us lined up in the courtyard, on our knees and pressed her rifle to my father's head while he begged for mercy. That same old man who governs this whole village. What a sight it was. And the whore was this big." Linga extends his arm from his belly. "She was pregnant. That was in 1948. How old are you?"

"I turned forty-nine this past September." Jaya speaks in a monotone, her hands tremble. Her eyes dart around the room, everywhere save Linga Reddy.

"Sometimes it's better not to go searching for your roots. My father is convinced you are Kunti Vadu's child, back to seek revenge and claim your inheritance."

"I need to go. There's been some mistake. The whole thing was a mistake."

"Never mind. My father is just playing with you. This proves it." Linga taps the envelope.

Parveen looks steadily at Linga. "But Malika didn't kill you."

"What?"

"You said she had a rifle. She could have killed you. Why didn't she? Even though she broke into your house, she chose to spare your lives. Perhaps she deserves some gratitude. After all, you are here to tell your story, but she is not."

Linga is already on his feet staring now at Parveen. "Don't forget who you work for." He empties the rupees from the envelope onto the table in front of Jaya. "Maybe this will buy you and your friend a bus ticket out of here."

Without a glance back, he heads for the door.

Jaya's whole body starts to tremble. Parveen takes Jaya's hand in hers.

9. Responsibility

After the fall of Hyderabad in 1948, the Nizam was given the title of Rajpramukh and permitted to retain millions of pounds as well as his private possessions. He continued to move through the streets of Hyderabad with a full entourage of carriages and courtiers. But no longer were the streets cleared for him, nor did his subjects line up to bow and place a gold coin in his palm. He could not collect the billions of rupees of tax revenues that once flowed from all parts of the Kingdom of Hyderabad. The Nizam was left with the appearance of glory and responsibility for his many wives and numerous children, who clawed desperately at their quickly disappearing inheritance. The Nizam lived elegantly as governor of Hyderabad, while the Republic of India expanded the scope and authority of its civil service.

In 1952, Nehru and the Congress Party won the first Indian general election. Narayan Reddy and his People's Democratic Front, the palatable name for the banned Communist Party, had, however, polled more votes than Nehru. This result made it clear that a sizable population still believed in the principles of communism.

Various groups agitated for the creation of language-based states across the country. Potti Sri Ramul, a freedom fighter in the Quit India movement, staged a fifty-six-day hunger strike and martyred himself for the cause. Overnight Nehru formed the Telugu State of Andhra Pradesh with the districts of Prakasam, Nellore, Guntur, West Godavari, East Godavari, Vizagapatam, and Srikakole. It also included the districts of Cuddapah, Kurnool, Anatapur, Bellary, and Chittor ceded by the Madras Presidency. Telangana was subsumed into Andhra Pradesh.

Irwin was much sought after for his skill in communicating in Andhra Telugu, the recognized lingua franca of the region. Telangana Telugu, the native dialect of Hyderabadis, was derided because speakers had fluidly incorporated Urdu words and phrases. It was deemed less pure, because it carried the taint of the Nizam's culture. Irwin was also fluent in Tamil and English, so he could easily communicate with new recruits in the civil service.

Irwin had gained respect and a place in the inner circle of the new Hyderabadi society while Dr. Benjamin was pushed out. As the former public health officer for the Nizam, Dr. Benjamin's objectivity was questioned by the new government, and he was released into the private sector. This proved too competitive for him. He had not practised medicine for years, and his qualifications were outdated compared to younger physicians who came from out of state. His stipend ended, his work faltered, and his mind wandered as he spent ample time doing nothing at home, a change Kanta resented deeply.

Governing positions from states to villages were being reorganized. Srikaram was appointed district collector of the town of Mahbub Nagar. Irwin, climbing each rung right behind his supervisor, became deputy collector. They would both have to move there for between five to ten years, depending on the success of their administration. Irwin was scheduled to travel to Mahbub Nagar early the next morning and was still in his office late in the day. He was sorting out documents for Srikaram, signaling issues worthy of his attention.

He read a recent report on Mahbub Nagar. "There has been an increase in rioting and unlawful assembly due to communal tension between Hindus and Muslims, the activities of the Communists, and the existence of local factions in some places. The police opened fire on twenty-four occasions to maintain law and order."

Irwin read the phrases *opened fire* and *twenty-four occasions* with indifference. Such reports had become commonplace. He was looking down at the page as the peon meekly entered with his trolley, delivering afternoon tea and mail to senior administrators. "Leave them there."

The peon placed the letters on the edge of Irwin's desk, and a large manila envelope landed on the floor. The worker did not bother to retrieve it, so Irwin picked it up. It was addressed to D.B. Srikaram, marked urgent and confidential.

"Wait, man."

But the peon had already gone. Irwin would have to deliver the envelope personally. He set it on his desk. Continuing his work of sorting documents, his eyes kept returning to the large manila envelope. He reread the address. Then curiosity swept in like a cool breeze. Irwin prided himself on his self-discipline and ability to resist temptation. He could squash curiosity like a fly, or he could flirt with curiosity before slapping it back. Curiosity made him feel alive. And his deputy collector title empowered him, allowing him to believe he was beyond reproach.

He discarded the report he had been reading and contemplated what was in this new envelope. If he didn't act, this exciting feeling would pass. The possibility of punishment fluttered by like the almost-invisible wings of a hummingbird. Irwin held the envelope over his steaming cup of tea to loosen the glue.

Irwin noted and was impressed by the names of the authors: Pandit Sundar Lal, Qazi Abdul Ghaffar, and Maulana Abdulla Misri. Sundar Lal was commissioned by Nehru himself to lead an investigation into the aftermath of Operation Polo in 1948, the military offensive of Hyderabad that overthrew a two-hundred-year-old dynasty in five days. It took only four army lines from the north, east, south, and west, acting on orders issued not by the Crown but by fellow countrymen. Reporters had minimized the invasion by calling it a "police action with a purpose of deposing the Nizam." Newspapers published descriptions of a bloodless victory and stated that the Telangana people welcomed the Indian Army to liberate them from the Nizam's autocratic rule. But this report, now in Irwin's possession, made it clear that the Indian Army did not stop there. It obliterated the Communist resistance and turned a blind eye to the atrocities committed against Muslims by Hindu mobs.

The Sunderlal Report detailed a massacre of up to forty thousand Muslims, committed by Hindus, seeking revenge on the Razakars. It was unbelievable. Forty thousand? Perhaps the Nizam's ruling paigahs, greedy jagirdars, the ruthless Razakars, were guilty of crimes that justified some form of punishment. But the others? The Muslim peasants, trade workers, and professionals, the women, their children? Malika? She was a Muslim peasant, an innocent. Where was she?

Irwin slipped the pages back into the manila envelope, knowing he was not finished with the report. What would he do with this knot of knowledge, obtained shamefully, pulled tight inside him? He prayed this anxiety was something the steam of tea could loosen, something that would dissipate with time, something that would not interrupt his career. Something that he would not lose sleep over.

He returned home to his wife, who was seated on the veranda. Normally he would have badgered Kanta, urging her to go for a walk to get some exercise. This evening, he would not demand anything from her. Inside his bag, pressed up against his consciousness, was the Sunderlal Report. *Urgent and Confidential.*

In the privacy of his room, Irwin opened the envelope and reread the cover letter. Nehru requested D.B. Srikaram's advice on the public release of the report, four years after its commission. Given the relative stability, Nehru hoped Srikaram, well-known for his diplomacy and management of communal tensions, might advise him on the current climate of the new Andhra Pradesh state. Srikaram was a known favourite of the Congress Party and had been courted to run for political office. Irwin would need to discreetly deliver this document to his supervisor without Srikaram detecting that it had been opened. Sliding the cover letter and the report back into the envelope, he fetched a suitcase from under his bed and began packing for Mahbub Nagar.

*

Kanta came to his room. Irwin was hopeful that she had come to lay with him, perhaps her way of saying goodbye. But this was not the case. She started chattering immediately. "I want to come with you. I need to get out of here. Papa will take care of Anasuya."

Kanta and Anasuya were intended to travel to Mahbub Nagar with Irwin, but Anasuya had a fever. Dr. Benjamin forbade Anasuya to travel. He also agreed to take care of her should Kanta still want to go. When Kanta entreated Irwin to take her with him, he glanced up from his suitcase and put his foot down. "The child cannot be without both father and mother. You must stay in Hyderabad. That is all."

Irwin surprised himself. In the old days, he would acquiesce and flatter people to win favour. But now, Irwin learned to command respect in a quiet and exacting way. Never abuse power, he thought, only use it when necessary.

He had come to realize marriage was a yoke for both women and men. The wife was expected to submit; the husband was expected to dominate. And this was no easy feat, especially with a more accomplished, wealthier man in the house. Living with Kanta and her father, Irwin often felt like a guest, a bystander, and, at times, an intruder. He had to work hard to carve out a space between a feisty daughter and a dominant father. The arrangement was wrong. He should have brought Kanta back to his home, where she could take care of him and his mother. Soon after his wedding, Alisamma had passed away. Her heart stopped as she curled over her sewing machine, straining to push thread through the eye of a needle. With the help of maternal relatives, Irwin's sisters were married off. He gave them his blessings and turned their futures over to their husbands. He was relieved, for he already had too many responsibilities. Now he didn't want the added stress of looking after and entertaining Kanta in Mahbub Nagar. He had important work to do there.

*

Srikaram had been assigned to Mahbub Nagar. He would replace the interim district collector who had been hastily removed for being ineffective in quelling progressive Communist gains in the area. A strong successor was needed to quash factions of rebels who refused to lay down their arms. Even though the CPI Marxist leadership had negotiated a truce with the Indian Republic in exchange for land redistribution, there were rogue dalams who fought fiercely against the odds, refusing to concede defeat. Some Communists did not learn about the ceasefire. Some did not read the newspaper. Some did not read at all.

After four years, those responsible for the assassination of the former district collector in Aminapally had not been found. This served as a message that rogue dalams were well-disguised and dangerous. It was planned that Irwin would travel the next day to Mahbub Nagar, preceding Srikaram's arrival. He was to act as a decoy, in case any violence should erupt. That he would take a bullet for Srikaram was a given. If no violence occurred Irwin would arrive at his destination. If this deception to the public were exposed, there was an easy explanation: Srikaram was called away, and the deputy district collector was sent in his place. The district collector's car would lead the motorcade into the region, an intentional display of power to demonstrate that the new district collector was in control and would not alter these important protocols, even if others had been targeted and killed in such events.

The day of his intended travel, Irwin woke early to Anasuya singing in her cot. Unlike the babblings of other toddlers, Anasuya seemed to pitch her voice exactly where she wanted it, jumping thirds then fifths and then cascading in a scale of microtones. Western and Eastern music already mingling in her vocalization. Her morning song filled him with relief that she might soon be feeling better.

"Naina," Anasuya called out.

Irwin went into Kanta's room, lifted Anasuya out of her cot, and held her close. She was flushed. Later, and for the rest of his life, Irwin would replay this scene. Anasuya had recognized him as father. "Naina." Was she identifying him or asking for help? Had he failed to understand the urgency of her call? Had she, in fact, asked him to stay?

Irwin put Anasuya back into her cot and set off on his assignment, the Sunderlal Report secure in his luggage.

*

Irwin was told that the district collector's bungalow in Mahbub Nagar was located on a hill and could be reached by a winding road. He pictured the hill thick with shrubs and vines and imagined that the greenery played a dual role, dissuading trespassers from entering its thorny and decussate web and hiding those who attempted to trespass.

The townspeople gathered to watch as the government vehicles passed through the town and up the serpentine road to the bungalow. Irwin sat in the back seat of the district collector's car. He scanned the faces of the villagers. As the car progressed slowly, Irwin felt that onlookers could see through him, that they recognized who he really was. An imposter. The car motored laboriously, then stalled, unable to pull its own weight up the hill. Luckily for Irwin, who was overheated in his wedding suit, the car stopped under the shade of a banyan tree.

"Press the gas."

The driver ground the gears. The car did not move.

Then Irwin felt it. Or perhaps he imagined it. The cold press of metal, the mouth of a rifle on the rise of his cheek. He turned quickly to look out the window. There, in the tree, was a woman. The driver revved the engine, and the car jolted forward. The woman dropped out of view. They drove by the waving crowd and reached the summit without incident.

The bungalow was surrounded by a cement wall and guarded by the reserve police. They were a unique regiment, distinguished from the local police by the hats they wore, the left side of the brim folded flat. They patrolled the perimeter day and night, shouting out periodically, "All is well!" Guards were also positioned within the grounds, shotguns in hand. A "take-no-prisoners" policy was firmly in place.

When the car reached the gate, Irwin uttered the password of the day. This was strict protocol. Even the district collector's six children needed to learn the daily password to access the premises. The password could be chess, bhootam, or any number of words, depending on the collector's preoccupations and sense of humour or lack thereof.

Some village children safely guarded their own passwords as they carried packages of food into the forest. These passwords would be whispered by strangers waiting for them. Sometimes the password was innocuous, the name of a fruit, but more often it carried meaning, an international code for insiders. Paul Robeson, for instance — the African American singer and actor, admired for his socialist views, familiar to children of Communists but unknown to most others. Upon hearing the password, the children would deposit their food packages into the hands of those they hoped would deliver their villages from bondage. The Communists disappeared into the forest, and the children remained to play games much like those that the district collector's children played within their walled compound.

The district collector's car safely reached its destination. There was a large garden with chiselled hedges and rose bushes, and in the centre stood a gazebo that overlooked a small pond. As instructed, the driver took Irwin behind the bungalow to the cottage reserved for Irwin and his family. A fifty-year-old servant, Chelamma, was there to greet him. Except for her, he had this whole cottage to himself. While Irwin was relieved to be separated from Kanta, he ached for Anasuya. As he unpacked his bag in the cottage, he recited a mantra to himself: *Responsibility. Morality. Tenacity. Duty.*

*

The Kalpana Cinema was located at the foot of the hill. It housed the only generator in the town. India had a burgeoning film industry. It advertised its latest films on billboards featuring pink-faced, voluptuous movie stars. The balcony seats were reserved for the district's royalty — middle- and upper-class residents — and the lower seats for the poor. Everyone gladly paid their hard-earned paisa to be transported by action, romance, and sexual innuendo. For three hours, the threat of police raids, the landlords' whips, the demands of work, and the cries of hungry children were forgotten.

On the same evening that Irwin arrived in Mahbub Nagar, the Kalpana Cinema was playing *Aan*, the first Technicolor film made in India. As the introductory music swelled and the film credits gave way to the opening scene, the crowd held its breath, anticipating Dilip Kumar's entrance. At this moment, the reel stopped, the hum of the projector died, and the cinema plunged into darkness. A collective groan resounded.

Ushers scurried down the aisles with torches reassuring the patrons. "Order, we need order please. The generator has had a mishap. We will resume the film shortly."

But the crowd had begun shouting. This was not the first time the generator had broken down. During a disruption, the proprietors enjoyed additional income from the sale of roasted peanuts and cool drinks. The anticipation would make the film experience even more satisfying. But today's wait was longer than usual. The lobby was stuffy, and those who kept to their seats threw balled-up paper at the screen. Others moved into the lobby, asking for the manager. A protest inside and outside the cinema ensued. The police swarmed and circled.

Safely ensconced in the cottage, Irwin had been reading the Sunderlal Report. It described the communal violence following the police action: thefts, rapes, and mass executions of Muslim peasants, nameless in the report. Again, he wondered about the peasants he knew. The one he couldn't forget. Was *she* dead?

Then the room went dark. Few in the village knew that the generator in the Kalpana Cinema provided electricity to the district collector's house. There was a bare bulb affixed to an eight-foot pole atop the roof of the bungalow. When lit, it indicated that the district collector was in residence, and the police were on alert. Now the cinema, the bungalow, and the cottage at the rear were in darkness. Irwin was startled by the sudden loss of light, as if he had been found out. He considered beckoning Chelamma, but he had observed that she was slow-moving. He might as well do everything himself. Feeling his way around the desk to the drawer, he retrieved some matches and lit the oil lamp. The room reappeared in pools of light and shadow. Irwin picked up the lamp and walked across the garden to the district collector's bungalow. He checked in with the guards on the premises and telephoned the chief of the local police, who informed him about a riot at the cinema.

Irwin tried to sound authoritative. "We may need additional enforcements here."

"Sir," the police chief responded, "our forces are quelling the riot. I will send what men I can spare."

"Fine."

After placing a call to Srikaram, apprising him of the situation, Irwin felt confident his duty was done. He told the guards, "I will retire now, and remember our take-no-prisoners policy."

Irwin opened the shutters of the cottage, allowing the night breeze to enter, and finally succumbed to sleep. Later he awoke to the yelping of a puppy. Irritated, he waited for Chelamma to respond. The yelping continued. It was coming from the porch. Irwin wondered whether its tail was caught in the door. One by one, Irwin unlocked the various bolts that secured him in the cottage. In his undershirt, pyjamas, and chappals, he stepped out into the warm night and almost tripped. At his feet was a bundle. "Chelamma!"

He crouched on the step to investigate when he noticed something move to his left. Two pairs of eyes, large and small. A mother and child in the bushes, crouching beside the wall of the cottage. The woman pressed a finger to her lips, full and red, out of place on a face so thin. "Please, don't shout."

He did not. But why shouldn't he shout? She was an intruder. She held close a little girl in a half sari. And before him in a makeshift bundle, was a restless infant wearing a yellow frock, her mouth gagged with a rag. Irwin looked at the mother with a sharp intake of breath.

"It is you? It was you in the tree?"

Malika nodded. "Theeskaundee. Take them." She pushed the girl towards Irwin. "*She* is yours."

Then Malika turned, and with her back bent low, sprinted away. A gazelle in a sari, she sped towards a nine-foot cement wall and leapt. The light from an electric torch flashed across Malika's body.

"Halt. Who's there?"

A shot rang out. Her body fell limp to the ground.

"Chess," Irwin had wanted to say. Perhaps he had. He tried to speak, but his voice was stuck in his throat. Chess. The password. He should have alerted her. He should have run after her. Another shot rang out, and another. There was silence, followed by footsteps as three guards rushed to the spot where Malika lay. From where he stood on his step, Irwin could see the mouths of the guards moving, but he heard only one voice.

"Please Lord God, no."

Someone was crying. The voice was pitched high; it was full of agony. Looking down, he saw her children. The older child looked at him with empathy. It was he, like a hysterical woman, letting out this wail.

Ashamed, he looked to the guards, still crouched over the body. He lifted both children into his arms, breathed in their rank smell, and pushed through the door of his cottage to deposit them onto his bed. Then he rushed to his beloved, who lay broken in the rose garden. Three guards stood at attention.

"We followed the policy."

"She is likely a Communist."

"Good we caught her."

The three stooges, Irwin thought. Then he looked into Malika's lifeless eyes. He felt for a pulse and gave orders to take the body away. The guards put Malika in a bag. With one effortless motion, a guard slung the bag over his shoulder. Irwin shuddered and followed the guards to a police vehicle. As they hoisted the body into the back seat, he was sure he saw it tremble. Did she move? Did she still have breath in her? Irwin did not say a word. Malika's body was taken to the police station to be identified or discarded.

From the gazebo, Irwin watched the police depart. The gazebo built on the edge of the pond was a place of beauty in the day, but eerie in the moonlight. Standing between the pillars of the gazebo, Irwin caught his reflection in the pond. His image imprisoned behind bars.

Malika had tried to scale the wall as she had done at the Reddy compound. This time, in this place, she had failed. And Irwin had failed her. Once again.

*

When Irwin returned to the cottage, he was faced with the feral children. The girl had retreated to the corner of his bed. Her amber eyes darted around the room. He could not tell whether they were wide with hunger, terror, or something else. Irwin removed the gag from around the baby's mouth, who then let out a wail. Irwin woke Chelamma and asked her to boil water for a bath. She responded with a snarl, likely for being wakened at this early hour with such a ridiculous request. Still, she managed to heave a bucket of water onto the grate at the back of the cottage. Irwin held her to secrecy and entreated her to bathe and feed the children. She scrunched her nose. "Where did they come from? Who are they belonging to?"

Irwin gave her no answer. She stubbornly refused to touch them unless he told her who they were. Irwin tried to bait her with the promise of newly minted Indian rupiyas, but she scoffed at the offer. These rupiyas meant nothing to her. It was only when Irwin placed some coins from the Nizam's currency in Chelamma's palm that she accepted her task.

The baby had fallen asleep, but the girl was alert. She had soiled herself. When Chelamma approached her, she scooted to the wall. She wouldn't let anyone get near her. They laid the sleeping baby on the bed and finally forced the girl to stand on a stoop behind Irwin's cottage. Lit by moonlight, Irwin held her arms behind her back, and cupped her mouth dare she shout out. But he needn't have. The girl was in shock. The only resistance she showed was her clenched left fist which she refused to open. Chelamma poured water over her and scrubbed her vigorously. By the time they finished washing her, the girl was exhausted, barely able to keep her eyes open. Chelamma led her inside, dried her off, and examined the girl's bruises, scabs, and scars. There was no recent injury on her. Chelamma dressed the girl in Irwin's undershirt. When Chelamma held out a chapati, the girl snatched it with one hand, the other still locked in a fist. She turned to the wall and ate it hastily. The baby woke up with a cry. Chelamma dipped a chapati in some water and put this near the baby's mouth. The baby sucked on it but continued crying.

"Quiet her down."

"She needs milk. She is still suckling."

"Well, think of something. Her cries will draw attention."

Chelamma glared at Irwin and went outside, leaving the baby on the cot. The cottage door swung shut behind her. Irwin anxiously waited for ten minutes then started after her, just as Chelamma re-entered pulling a nanny goat by a rope. It was kept, along with other animals, in a small barn on the property.

"The guards will think I am mad, milking the goat by moonlight." She tied the rope to the table leg and crouched in front of the animal. Then she manipulated its teats until two full cups of milk were drawn.

She held the baby close to her bosom and from a cup poured milk into the baby's mouth as it sought Chelamma's nipple through her blouse. Satisfied, the infant fell asleep on the kitchen mat, enclosed in Chelamma's embrace, and soothed by her snore. The older child sat crumpled in the corner of the room, her hollowed gaze set on Irwin. He reached for the child's hands, hoping to drag her away from the wall to the bedding Chelamma had prepared. But the girl's fist was still tightly clutching something. Her eyelids fluttered, and she finally gave way to sleep. Finger by finger he pried open her palm to find his gold watch, the hands still stuck at 5:05. Close to the actual time.

*

The next day, the power was restored, the lightbulb on the roof of the bungalow glowed, and the district collector and his family arrived. The riot was stifled, and a rumour circulated about how the district collector himself had discovered an intruder who was subsequently killed within the compound. This was proof that the newly assigned guards were doing their jobs. But Srikaram did not buy the story and asked many questions.

"Three guards could not restrain a woman?"

"She had a rifle," one guard said.

"Was she pointing it at you?" Srikaram was clearly annoyed.

"No sir."

"And the recovered rifle had no ammunition. Is that correct, Irwin?"

"It was on her back," another guard said.

"And you noted she was moving away rather than towards the house?"

"She was taking advantage of the power outage, no doubt."

Then Irwin interrupted. "It was dark, sir. The electricity had not been restored. It was difficult from where I stood on the porch to ascertain the direction in which she was headed. She might have been looking for a back door or window into the bungalow."

With Irwin's additional information, Srikaram, although not entirely satisfied, accepted the story.

"You do understand that while we have policies we also know that prisoners are useful. They can give us leads, be informants. And remember, they too are Indians and have a right to be tried for crimes."

"But sir, what about the take-no-prisoners policy? Are not the Communists trying to break the country apart?" Irwin was surprised that the guard dared question his superior but was glad he did. Irwin had the exact same thought.

Srikaram shook his head. "The policy is to frighten people into obeying the law. It is not a license to kill!"

Srikaram turned to Irwin and ordered a detailed report of the incident, including any identifiable features of the intruder and evidence to confirm her status as a Communist. Police could use this report to track other rebels.

While Srikaram's children explored their new playground, equipped with a gazebo, a pond, and tennis courts, the guards patted each other's backs, and Irwin returned to the cottage to write a report on Malika. Malika, the wall-climber, the child-abandoner, the rifle-carrier, the Communist rebel. But she had waved no red flag, uttered no political demands, fired no gun. Must he simply write she had the face of a Communist?

Or he could write the truth:

1. He knew her.
2. Most of her family was murdered.
3. She left him with her children.

Irwin pondered this last thought. What did she say to him? Her last words?

Irwin finished his report, documenting that a female Communist, identified by the type of rifle she carried, had breached the compound wall and was brought down by the skilled guards on the premises. He signed his name. Srikaram insisted that Irwin return to Hyderabad, to arrange for additional guards and fetch his family. After the event last night, they would be a comfort to him.

"Your child may be better now. And the publication of this case should deter any other rebels from trespassing."

As Irwin made his way back to the cottage, nausea and anxiety overtook him. These sensations had been kept at bay by the adrenaline rush in the aftermath of Malika's death. Irwin would have to find some way to manage this emotional turbulence. Not to mention the unexpected orphans.

*

Kanta stood on the veranda and watched as a Morris Minor passed through the gates. The driver was unloading suitcases from the trunk while Irwin reached for something from the back seat. He lifted an infant from a basket into the crook of one arm and managed to drag out what appeared to be a scrawny and unkempt three-year-old girl.

Kanta had been rereading *Wuthering Heights*. She related to Catherine, lulled by the comfort of her middle-class life but tugged by a violent passion. The story was reversed in Kanta's imagination. Kanta's Heathcliff had died, and she was left waiting for his reappearance at the window. After marriage and the birth of Anasuya, Kanta knew she would not play the role of the heroine after all, but the maid. The loyal servant who bore witness to the anguished lives around her, attending to all of them while remaining in the background.

"Fetch Lakshmi," Irwin called out to Kanta. And like a dutiful maid, she turned on her heel and reappeared with the real servant in tow.

"These children are casualties." Irwin passed the infant to Lakshmi. "They are our responsibility now." The casualties were not explained. The responsibility they entailed, unclear. "Take them inside and feed them."

The little girl had a gaunt face. Her large eyes looked as if they would tumble from their sockets with a firm pat on her back. Fifteen-year-old Lakshmi took the baby and the little girl into the house.

Irwin passed Kanta standing on the veranda, his driver following with the luggage.

"Are you not going to enquire about your sun and moon?" Kanta put her hand on his forearm. "Your daughter?"

"Of course. Where is she?"

"Osmania General Hospital. It's polio. Paralytic, the severest form. Did you not receive my telegram?"

Irwin's thoughts moved in reverse, tracking whether he had received the telegram or had put it aside. He had been so obsessed with the report, concerned about the riot, shocked by Malika's death and anxious about the children.

"Is your mind solely on the collector that you cannot respond?" Kanta's voice rose with each word. "Then you dare come back here with two urchins! What about your own daughter? You idiot! You idiot man."

Irwin slapped her. She froze. He slapped her again. And again.

Kanta's beautiful face flushed under the sting of Irwin's open palm. Her eyes watered, but she did not flinch. She stood stoic on the veranda. A perfect maid.

The driver interrupted. "Sir. Shall I take these bags inside?"

Irwin nodded. The driver walked into the house. Kanta turned to follow him, then stopped and addressed her husband, her back to him. "You take care of them."

Kanta had decided she would no longer play the role of maid.

*

The day Irwin set off for Mahbub Nagar, Anasuya's fever rose to a point of concern. Dr. Benjamin announced he would take the child to the hospital after breakfast. He ordered Kanta to get ready. She dressed for the hospital in an off-white kaasavu sari. She adjusted the fall to sit perfectly on the floor and then tucked some last strands of hair into her neat coconut-oiled plait. She took one last look at herself in the full-length mirror. Then she caught the reflection of her daughter staring at her. Anasuya was standing in her cot, extending her arm to Kanta.

"My poor girl is sick of this prison. How boring this must be for you." Kanta lifted Anasuya up.

While Dr. Benjamin was finishing breakfast, Kanta carried her restless child into the garden and set her down among the lilies, now opening orange and white.

"You are already looking better." Kanta was pleased that Anasuya had more colour in her face, a rosy blush. Then she sat on the wicker chair on the veranda and opened *Wuthering Heights* as she awaited her father. Anasuya was tottering nearby in the garden singing merrily when Kanta heard a thump. Anasuya's face was flat to the ground.

"Clumsy little girl."

But the child did not rise. Kanta rushed to her two-year old daughter, lifted her onto her feet. But Anasuya's legs buckled and she fell. The child seemed puzzled but did not cry out. Kanta did. "Papa!"

Anasuya looked frightened. Kanta felt her daughter's stiff neck.

In minutes, Kanta was in the back seat of her father's Ambassador, swabbing her daughter's burning forehead with a cool damp cloth. Her father, sitting in front with the driver, kept shouting.

"Why did you take her outside? Don't you know the danger of over-exertion? If you had studied medicine, you would know this."

Perhaps it was Kanta's fault. She should have studied medicine. She should have married the Thomas boy. She should have kept her daughter indoors. And if it were polio, there was nothing to be done. Kanta's thoughts kept going back to the image of happy Anasuya, playing in the garden. This was their secret, their moment of joy. It was a memory Kanta would hold on to as her fear gave way to resignation.

Soon they were pulling into the grounds of Osmania General Hospital. The pristine white domes and majestic facade now appeared sinister. Inside were dozens of iron lungs lined up like coffins.

*

After Irwin slapped Kanta on the veranda — one, two, three — she made up her mind to remain in her father's house, where she had been berated but never harmed. She promised herself never to move to Mahbub Nagar with a husband who was unpredictable and suddenly violent. Mahbub Nagar was a backwater. Let Irwin work, live, and ingratiate himself to the collector. Kanta would continue spending nights alone in her bed and days on the veranda.

The Nizam had provided Hyderabad with modern medical facilities, and Anasuya was admitted and put in an iron lung. Irwin asked Srikaram for leave in order to spend every day at the hospital. Kanta was left to oversee two urchins whose origins remained a mystery.

Kanta watched Irwin climb into the Morris Minor to drive to Osmania General Hospital. Sitting on the porch, watching overripe tamarind pods fall to the ground, Kanta saw her future. Her face drooping, her body sagging, her life expectancy shortening. Kanta was overcome with envy that her cousin Rebecca, less intelligent and less talented, had been admitted to a medical program in America. Disgusted with herself, Kanta stood and decided to unpack the newly arrived children and arrange them in the house.

She put her book down and went to the kitchen. There, Lakshmi sat on the floor rolling chapatis. The baby still dressed in the yellow frock was in the basket, crying, and the little girl sat folded into herself in the corner.

"What are you doing? I asked you to feed the baby."

"What, Amma? The baby will not take the bottle. I have tried everything."

Kanta lifted the baby into her arms and discovered she was feverish. Kanta stripped the child to bathe her and discovered that *she* was a *he*. "Why didn't you tell me this child is a boy?"

Lakshmi shrugged. "You are busy on the veranda." She pointed to the corner. That girl calls him Pilla." Pilla meant girl.

"And the little girl's name?" Kanta asked.

"She only talks to him. She won't answer me." Lakshmi continued rolling the dough.

Did it matter what the baby was called or how he was dressed? Kanta had her son.

There were limits to what a disappointed daughter, resentful wife, and reluctant mother could devote to her children. Kanta committed to one thing at a time. Keeping them alive was her priority. Even this proved difficult given that one child was hospitalized, another skinny and scab-covered, and the baby flushed with fever. The baby became her first concern. She hovered over him at night, swabbing him with a cool cloth. Kanta appealed once again to her father, suffering the humiliation of having to defer to him and then to submit again to his criticism. Dr. Benjamin examined the child and handed him back to Kanta.

"He needs nothing more than a mother." His tone was surprisingly empathetic.

Maybe he remembered that Kanta herself was a motherless child. Perhaps he looked back, past the moment of her wedding, to a time when he had unnecessarily pressured her. Perhaps he too began to feel affection for these urchin children, these casualties of war.

Kanta sang baby Pilla to sleep. He attached to her. His breath was rhythmic on her cheek, and his soft fingers pulled at her ear. Over time Pilla bloomed under Kanta's care. He became a happy, affectionate, and talkative child, free to explore, run, grow, and shine. All the things boys could do that girls couldn't. On the day Anasuya was born, Kanta had tried to communicate to Irwin that girls could never experience these things in the same way boys did without asking for permission, being constantly under someone's gaze, their freedoms curtailed.

Caring for Pilla reminded Kanta of her volunteering days as a medic. She had once again found purpose and pride, after having failed with Anasuya. It was hard to love a child in an iron lung, to make the trek to the hospital only to look upon Anasuya's head, emerging from a canister of steel. And the fact was, she could not outlove Irwin. Irwin planted himself at the hospital and played the role of perfect parent. When Anasuya stabilized and was transferred to a hospital bed, Irwin told stories that made her laugh. He sang her songs and brought her dolls, picture books, and colouring pencils. Doctors diagnosed Anasuya with asymmetrical paralysis that resulted in muscle weakness in her legs. After a six-month stay in hospital, Anasuya was discharged. Irwin returned to Mahbub Nagar. Back at home, Kanta was unable to get past the guilt and fear she started to embody that terrifying day when Anasuya fell to the ground in the garden. Kanta was timid, too precious with the child, and wouldn't let Anasuya get too close to her.

And Jaya?

Jaya was given a bed, but instead chose to sleep with Lakshmi on a mat in the kitchen. During the day, Jaya kept herself apart and refused to speak. Because Jaya did not scream or demand, Kanta assumed she was okay. When Kanta tried to smooth her hair, Jaya would shake her off, as if a mosquito had landed. If Kanta lifted Jaya onto her lap, the child would stiffen and slide off. Any attempt to embrace Jaya would be met with square-shouldered hardness. Kanta understood this behaviour as Jaya's nature and let her be.

Anasuya was moved into a room on the main floor of the house that opened out onto the veranda. This location would be convenient as she relearned how to walk. She would be able to access the outdoors easily and not have to negotiate the stairs. Jaya was finally coaxed away from her kitchen mat and given a cot next to Anasuya's, to keep her company. A nurse was hired to care for Anasuya. Jaya looked on curiously as the nurse removed Anasuya's steel braces and gently manipulated her little legs back to life. Anasuya sang herself to sleep. Jaya stayed awake, pushing away frightening images that would overwhelm her when she closed her eyes. Instead, she guarded the little patient by night and munched on the food she hoarded during the day. Eventually, Anasuya reached out her hand across the gap between their beds and rescued Jaya.

1997 — The Tea Room

Irwin sits in the tea room at the Krishna Lodge and remembers the moment when he was released from the hospital and Jaya asked him if he had known Malika.

Irwin thinks of a phrase from the new country to describe Malika's state the night her family perished in the fire. She had slipped between the tree and the wall of the Reddy's compound. Irwin had never seen Malika so helpless. When he hid her behind the curtain in his room, he had misread her trembling mouth, her longing eyes, her hand clutching his arm. Now he knows she had not sought his affection, only his protection. That night he acted on impulse, grasping at something poignant and raw, rushing forward on the adrenaline, believing he was saving her life.

The memory came back like a jolt. As did the image of Malika on the last night he saw her. She was running, hunched, across the grounds of the district collector's bungalow when she turned and their eyes met for a moment. Then the light from a torch exposed her. She was caught, once again, like a "deer in the headlights."

How could he *not* know Malika? The straight back, generous mouth, and luminous eyes. Malika was ever-present in Jaya. The daughter carried the mother in her stance, her skin, in the very shape of her. Jaya resembled Irwin not so much in features but in habit. His practicality. As a child, Jaya sorted and lined up her objects. One could hardly have called them toys. Stones, wooden sticks, Kanta's empty perfume bottles, little things that Jaya would collect and cherish. "We may need them someday." She was stockpiling rations. Preparing for a long battle. Chinnie Jaya. Little victory. Jaya, jaya. Jana-gana-mana-adhinayaka, jaya he.

*

When Linga Reddy walks past Irwin on his way out of the tea room in the Krishna Lodge, Irwin experiences a vague recollection. Like a flickering flame that arrests Irwin's attention. Momentarily, Irwin wonders, do I know him? He waves the question away, for he is distracted and distressed by someone else. He sees Jaya seated at a table with a woman. Could it be her, Anasuya? No. Someone else. A stranger.

But Jaya. *She* is here. Her elbow is on the table, and her hand props up her head. Her face has the shape of her mother's, but her amber eyes are like his. She is looking straight ahead. Then she covers her eyes with her hands. Her lovely long fingers, again, like her mother's. He watches her as she had watched him those twelve years in Toronto. Unseen.

She is weeping. A rare sight. An awkward and pitiful sight, he thinks. He wants her to stop. To help her stop. When she was young, had he ever comforted her? Did he ever tell her a story, feed her mithai, or sing a song to soothe her?

When he finally approaches the table, Jaya composes herself. She looks up briefly.

Irwin pulls out the chair that Linga Reddy occupied earlier. He sits opposite Jaya and is introduced to a woman named Parveen. He decides he must tell Jaya about Malika, but he doesn't know where to start. The first thing that comes to mind is "May I offer you some tea?"

Part Four
1965–1985

10. Childhood

In those years after he left Korampally, Irwin became a stranger to himself. His ambition kept growing as he sought purpose in each new chair, behind ever-grander desks, his titles growing in prestige. His rise in status from clerk to records manager, to civil administrator, and finally to deputy district collector should have given Irwin a sense of accomplishment and worth, but it made him uneasy. He felt the need to justify the promotions, which he considered a succession of mistakes. In each attempt to fit into more authoritative roles, he rehearsed lines, delivered believable performances, and erased his past.

In 1965, Irwin followed Srikaram back to Hyderabad and was assigned the role of Special Secretary in the Department of Minority Affairs. Dr. Benjamin had died of old age, and Irwin became the master of the Benjamin House. With the passing of the patriarch, Irwin had hoped that Kanta might seek his support if not his love. But she managed the household smoothly without his help and treated him as if he were a mosquito, constantly buzzing around, always in her way.

Thirteen years had passed since Irwin and Kanta had formally adopted Jaya and Pilla. Pilla grew up enveloped in the generous love of his adoptive mother. He planted soft kisses on her cheek and was duly rewarded with laddoos. He was given an allowance and spent it on films and concerts. He enjoyed life in a way that his biological parents could never have dreamed.

Pilla was eager to please everyone around him. His efforts in doing so brought out kindness in others. Most of his mates at school were gentle and affectionate with him. They walked hand in hand, rode together on scooters, and gossiped about the latest celebrities. Pilla was so attractive, affectionate, and popular that no one suspected his secret obsession.

As a toddler, his sisters dressed him up in frocks and ribbons, pushing him in their doll carriage around the courtyard, saying to visitors, "Look at our baby sister." Pilla happily played the role well into primary grades. He had a soft face and long lashes, and he would often part his hair and clip it to the side, just like the girls in his class. He imagined his to be a girl's face, and the rest of his body likewise feminine. He felt more comfortable dressing in his sisters' clothing and loved the feel of silky textures against his skin. He developed impeccable taste and helped his mother pick out beautiful saris.

Anasuya and Pilla attended private English-language schools, competing with each other for top grades. While Pilla excelled, Anasuya's grades went up and down in early childhood, mostly due to her absences. When she was twelve years old, she spent two months in hospital, much of the time wearing a full cast from neck to hips after undergoing an operation to correct her scoliosis, a complication of polio. This was in addition to numerous appointments and minor procedures to correct what Jaya affectionally called Anasuya's perfect parts—her shorter leg, her crooked back—that medical professionals deemed imperfect. Anasuya required both a heel pad and cane to walk longer distances down the road but abandoned these once inside the house. She moved relatively freely from room to room with a lopsided gait, leaning on strategically positioned furniture when feeling unbalanced.

When at five years old Anasuya regained control of her muscles and learned to walk, Dr. Benjamin credited the nurse who provided physiotherapy treatment for Anasuya's progress. No one knew that Jaya, who had been watching the nurse attentively, learned her techniques and gently massaged Anasuya's legs every evening before sleep. In return, Anasuya rallied Jaya to play games. Reaching across the gap between their beds, they would tap out songs on each other's hands until they slept. Sometimes they pushed their beds together, threw their arms around each other's shoulders, and stared at the ceiling fan while Anasuya chattered about everything and anything. It was through these playful interactions, only weeks after Anasuya was discharged from her first hospital stay, that Anasuya brought Jaya around to uttering her name, "Chinnie Jaya." Just as Jaya was unacknowledged for helping Anasuya walk, no one credited Anasuya for helping Jaya talk. Jaya's transformation was seamless and uneventful because no one was consciously aware that Jaya, upon first arriving at the Benjamin House, had refused to speak. Jaya hugged the walls or hid behind Lakshmi. Irwin and Kanta enticed Jaya to speak but didn't pressure her. When company visited, she curtseyed as she had been taught, and the adults thought she had spoken. They assumed that Jaya chatted easily with other children but was quiet and polite in their company.

Jaya was painfully shy, and as the beginning of the school year came closer, Jaya begged to remain at home. Kanta arranged that Jaya be home-schooled by tutors in the mornings. During her lessons her eyes wandered to the cracks in the walls or insects scurrying across the floor. She could not focus on the words in her storybooks nor hold a pencil correctly. In the afternoons, however, Lakshmi taught Jaya how to cook, and Jaya excelled at her lessons. Jaya could identify spices by their aromas; knew the medicinal properties of turmeric, ginger, and cumin; and could distinguish the appropriate ripeness for mangos to be pickled, blended into lassi, or simply bitten into. She began cooking at seven and was still called the Little Cook at sixteen.

When Anasuya turned fourteen years old, the fine physicians at Osmania General Hospital declared her cured of scoliosis, and Kanta enrolled her daughter in a boarding school for girls outside the city. Encouraged by her prose-loving mother and motivated to catch up to her classmates, Anasuya read tirelessly through the night. Articulate and energetic, Anasuya involved herself in as many academic and extra-curricular activities as possible. But she was lonely standing on the sidelines while other girls played field hockey and tennikoit. Anasuya yearned for school holidays when she would return to Afzal Gunj. There, she would sit on the veranda and regale Jaya with stories of her classes, and at night the two would resume the comforting game of patient and nurse. Each visit they explored yet more perilous illnesses and came up with more elaborate cures.

During the thirteen years that Irwin worked in Mahbub Nagar, he had come home periodically, and Kanta brought the children from time to time to visit him. But when he came back for good in 1965, he found a family he hardly knew. The children had grown more than halfway to adulthood with little guidance from him. Irwin often found himself alone at the dining table after Sunday lunch, quietly rubbing the dried rice and curry off his fingers, letting the flakes fall onto his empty plate. The children treated him like a ghost, looking straight through him as they plotted secret adventures.

*

On a January morning in 1966, Irwin took his family for a drive. The radio broadcast the election results. Indira Gandhi was voted the third prime minister of the Republic of India.

Motorcars joined throngs of rickshaws and bicycles on the large boulevards in Hyderabad. On Tank Bund Road, which wrapped around the heart-shaped Hussain Sagar, massive billboards featured paintings of pink Indian film stars in dramatic poses. Enlivening titles such as *Jab Phool Khile* and *Tarzan Comes to Dehli* stood out among advertisements for VAT 65 whiskey. Fountains, gardens, and sculptures sprouted on the perimeter of the boulevard. The country was racing towards the seventies with great optimism despite a weakened rupee.

Anasuya was showing off her newly acquired knowledge from boarding school. "Indira Gandhi will be a wonderful prime minister! She is intelligent, has vision, and is committed."

Anasuya, Jaya, Pilla, and their new friend Martin were crammed into the back seat of the mint-green Ambassador. Irwin was driving, and Kanta was in the front seat beside him. They were hoping to wander aimlessly through the gardens and have a picnic near the lake. A rare Sunday outing.

Martin Reynolds, their new British friend, rolled down the window. "And she is Nehru's daughter. That had to help."

Kanta's chiffon scarf blew towards the back seat and fluttered across the faces of the children. Pilla was delighted. "Mummy, I love that texture."

Anasuya reached across Pilla and slapped Martin on the arm. "What does being Nehru's daughter have to do with it?"

"No other woman would get the job."

"You are so chauvinistic. She beat her rival, Desai, fair and square."

"Kids! See there, see there!" Irwin pointed out the bronze figure erected in the middle of the roundabout. "Gold star if you can name that leader."

"Too easy, Papa. That is the late and great Dr. Bhimrao Ramji Ambedkar, the architect of India's constitution." Anasuya was confident.

"I know who he is."

Martin was the only child of missionaries mandated to set up schools for the tribals in east Andhra Pradesh. Irwin had met the missionaries when they requested permission to travel to some of the protected forests in the regions. As both parents were working in the field and there were no schools, let alone running water, Irwin recommended that they leave the boy behind. It was not safe. A rebellious group called the Naxalites had been agitating in the area. Irwin and Kanta agreed to take care of Martin until June, when he and his parents would return to Britain.

Anasuya challenged Martin. "Okay, so who is he?"

"Dad told me the British educated him."

"Not him in particular." Anasuya rolled her eyes. "Every Indian in the British Army received an education. Am I correct? Papa? Affirmation, please."

"Yes, Anu. But actually, it was Ambedkar's father that the British first educated. And after him, his son excelled, becoming an economist, a lawyer, and a politician."

"Still, he wouldn't be anything without the British. We brought education, the railway..."

"The only reason the British educated Indians was because they felt guilty about using slave labour to make them rich. Right, Papa? Papa told me it was blood money that financed missionary schools."

"Well Anu." Irwin tried to temper his daughter. "Even those who benefited from a missionary school education can be critical of British oppression and their motivation to convert the poor to Christianity. But some Indians found solace in Christ's teachings, and others even emulated the British."

"That's another thing I like about Indira Gandhi. She hated the British. At twelve she burned her British-made dolls to protest British rule." Anasuya emphasized *British,* driving home her point, and countering her father's more balanced view.

Then Pilla's softer voice joined the conversation. "Do you put cream on your legs? They are so shiny." Pilla touched Martin's hairless white thigh. Martin was too busy sparring with Anasuya to pay attention to the boy seated between them.

The four teenagers—Pilla, fourteen, Martin, fifteen, Anasuya, sixteen, and Jaya, seventeen—knocked knees in the back. The guest was given the window seat; Jaya, the other. She was silent, gazing at the blue, expansive lake.

Pilla, on the other hand, had constant questions. "What kind of a name is Martin?"

"I don't know. A normal one." Martin had little time for Pilla.

Anasuya came to the defense of her little brother. "Right. Like everything British is normal. How about we give you an Indian name. How about Nitram."

"That is not even a name, Anu," Pilla said.

"Agreed." Nitram shifted and removed Pilla's hand from his thigh. "It makes as much sense as giving a boy a girl's name."

"I like my name."

Martin rolled his eyes at Pilla. "That's not the point. Made-up names are not real names."

But the moniker stuck.

Nitram was fully accepted into the Peter family. He was moved into Pilla's room and made himself at home. After two weeks together, the teenagers were inseparable. As an only child, Martin had played audience to his parents' conversations on British history and Indian culture. In the Benjamin House, he took on a role of arrogant teacher or, as Anasuya put it, *know-it-all*. But no one wanted to hear his views on India, let alone British history. Jaya, Anasuya, and Pilla were more interested in what he had to offer in the way of British culture. He brought with him Beatles records, bell-bottoms, and new dance moves and spoke in his funny British accent. They learned the lyrics to all the songs on *Rubber Soul*, each taking on a Beatles persona. Anasuya was John Lennon because she was the critical thinker of the bunch; Nitram was Paul McCartney, claiming to be the best musician; sullen Jaya was deemed to be the reflective George Harrison; and happy-go-lucky Pilla, the likeable Ringo Starr. Mimicking Liverpudlian accents, the three siblings worked hard to undo the damage that British colonial education had wreaked on their dear Nitram.

Nitram told them about his own proud working-class roots and his hero, Harold Wilson, the Labour Party leader. Anasuya challenged the successes of Wilson, boasting how Indira Gandhi would do more than nationalize steel. "She will nationalize our banks. Ask Papa!"

Nitram was quick. "She's a new politician. They often make promises they can't keep."

Anasuya tried hard to think of a comeback. "Actually, it is more like England would be nowhere without India. You stole our labour and resources, while we financed and fought your war. You gave us trains. Big deal!"

Jaya turned her head to the window where the sun was pouring in. Closing her eyes tightly, she could see spots of red and gold dance on the insides of her eyelids. Pilla interjected with comments about the colourful checks on Nitram's Madras shorts, his ridiculously big hands, and his straight bangs, a fringed curtain above close-set green eyes.

Irwin bought them kulfi and candy floss, and Kanta found a bench in the shade where she sat and watched her children play.

*

It was a hot evening in April. The teens decided to take mats and sleep on the cement rooftop. A four-foot wall ran the width and length of the roof. The ledge of the wall was wide enough for a place setting, from which to have their meals, or to sit on. This was where the family flew kites during the Sankranti festival and slept during sweltering summer nights. They set up the portable turntable and played their records, and twisted and shouted to the Beatles and the Byrds. But it was Marianne Faithful's wistful voice that introduced them to a more intimate dance. Nitram took Anasuya's hand. They locked together in a slow sway, slower than the beat, slower than even their breath. Did their lips meet? It was hard to tell.

"Look at John and Paul kissing." Pilla giggled.

Jaya and Pilla sat on the ledge and looked on apprehensively. One worried about what she might lose, the other about what he might never have. The siblings had experienced immense loss, which they neither acknowledged to themselves nor to each other. They instinctively felt that their choices in love would be few and second chances impossible, so they had invested their affections early and never let go. Watching Nitram and Anasuya dancing cheek to cheek, Jaya and Pilla wrestled with fears of being invisible. While Pilla plotted to win the object of his desire, Jaya felt defeated. She realized that while she would be forever bound to Anasuya, Anasuya might not feel the same.

They were jolted out of their thoughts.

Irwin, who had come up to the roof to turn down the music, pulled the needle off the turntable. It screeched.

So did Nitram. "Uncle, you're scratching it!"

Nitram broke away from Anasuya. Irwin ordered the kids downstairs and back to their rooms. The party was over.

That night when Anasuya was sleeping, Jaya took her rolled-up mat and walked down the dark hall to the kitchen. She sensed she was no longer needed and made room for Anasuya to do whatever Anasuya wanted to do. Anasuya woke and saw Jaya's bed was empty. She panicked and felt trapped, restricted as if she were back in the iron lung. Even though her leg was aching from having danced, she got up and reached for her cane. Anasuya found Jaya sleeping on her mat on the kitchen floor, next to Lakshmi. Big cook and little cook.

"What are you doing here?"

Jaya opened her eyes but said nothing.

"Come back to our room."

Jaya didn't move. Anasuya could not tell whether Jaya's eyes were full of wonder or fear. But she knew Jaya wasn't going to listen. She backed herself against a wall, steadied herself with her cane until she slid down, and sat on the floor near Jaya. Jaya sat up but seemed to be retreating.

Anasuya smoothed Jaya's hair, and caressed her cheek. "Don't be jealous of Nitram, dear one."

Then Anasuya brought Jaya close and kissed her sister on the mouth.

The next morning Anasuya and Jaya woke in Anasuya's bed, their arms and legs entwined. The sun was bursting through the windows, illuminating their faces. They giggled as they heard Irwin singing in the hallway.

"Christians awake! Daughters, daughters. Come, get ready. You are almost as slow as the boys." Irwin rapped on their bedroom door.

Anasuya climbed out of bed, put on her housecoat, and threw open the door.

"Oh, Papa, I am so happy. You'll never guess what happened. I am in love."

She expected her father to grasp her hands and kiss them as he often did when she was elated about something. Instead, he firmly moved Anasuya aside and stepped into the doorway. Had Anasuya invited that boy to her room? Jaya brought her head up from under the covers.

Irwin shot a puzzled look at Anasuya, and looked at Jaya again. "Oh."

Then he turned on his heel. "Hurry up, then, church is in an hour."

*

That evening Martin and Pilla were told to go to bible study, while Anasuya and Jaya were given a talk. Irwin and Kanta sat directly opposite the girls. Irwin spoke loudly while Kanta rolled her eyes and sighed.

"You don't know where this slow dancing will lead. Next it will be kissing, then you will be pregnant, and our reputation as a family will be ruined. I will be cast out of the civil service, and we will all be destitute."

Irwin mustered the sternest voice he was capable of. His tone reminded Kanta of her father's the night of the tonga incident. How frightening Dr. Benjamin had sounded to her when he was angry, and how comical she found Irwin's voice. Anasuya thought the same and started to giggle. As he persisted, she became angry.

Destitute? Could they really become destitute because of her?

Irwin tried to read Anasuya's silence. Perhaps she had regretted disappointing him, or she was sad because Martin was scheduled to join his parents in less than a month and depart for Britain. Perhaps she really loved him.

But she did not. It bothered Anasuya that a meaningless dance with Nitram could make her father, who had never uttered a harsh word, humiliate her in this way. Her father needed only to ask her, and Anasuya would have promised never to dance with a boy again. She was distressed because the thing that Irwin feared happening was the thing she wanted most. To have a baby.

*

The dense forests surrounding Mahbub Nagar are dotted with large boulders, a distinctive feature of the landscape of Hyderabad Deccan. Jaya and Anasuya were on a picnic following an Easter concert in which their church choir had been invited to perform. Anasuya saw Jaya move away from the picnic site, and followed her. Jaya calmly and confidently pointed out the clusters of shrubs, the crooked-limbed neem tree, the forest canopy, and the rise of a particular boulder in the distance. She said repeatedly, "I know this place."

Jaya had known this place, or places like this. In the light and darkness. She became increasingly agitated as her mind was pulled back through the dense rough foliage and the crawl spaces between thorny shrubs and large rocks. She knew how to slither through the undergrowth without scraping herself. She recalled bird calls, sounds that could be sharp and terrifying. She remembered how to put her hand on her chest. "Be still," she told her rapid heartbeat. "Stop," she would tell her tears. "Shut up," she would tell her whimpering little brother, his mouth gagged with a piece of their mother's sari. The sari would be untied for him to nurse from the breast that was meant for Jaya, the milk that was rightfully hers. Her mother had explained that the baby had no teeth to chew bark, eat fruit, or chomp groundnuts, but that only made Jaya angry. After Pilla was finished suckling, her mother passed the baby to Jaya. Jaya would cradle his soft and sleepy body in her arms, forgetting that moments earlier she had hated him.

"Chinnie Amma, Chinnie Jaya." Her mother had smoothed Jaya's hair before creeping away with her rifle, leaving Jaya to hold the baby. Other women, strangers, kept watch over her and her brother.

*

Anasuya grasped Jaya's hand as she followed her, climbing higher and walking along the edge of a cliff. They hoped to get a view of their surroundings. The sun was beating down, their kurtas were damp and clinging to their backs.

"Get back." Jaya grabbed Anasuya before the sudden drop. Anasuya gasped but Jaya started hyperventilating.

Anasuya gently coached Jaya to take deep, slow breaths. "Have you been here before?"

Jaya nodded.

Anasuya balanced herself with her walking stick and reached her other
arm around Jaya's waist.

"You are shaking?"

"Am I?"

Anasuya pointed out Jaya's trembling hands. "Come. We will find our way
back."

They were lost and exhausted. After trying to make their way out of the
forest, they found themselves returning to a large flat boulder. Jaya sat on
the boulder ledge staring at the sun making its way towards the horizon. She
feared she would be trapped here forever. Her back was stiff, her fingers tense
from gripping the edge of the rock.

Anasuya approached Jaya. She massaged her shoulders, her arms, and her
back. With one hand, she lifted the front of Jaya's kurta and loosened the
string of her pyjama. Then she slipped her hand beneath the cotton, touching
Jaya gently at first, and then moving inside her with greater pressure. Anasuya
was aware of a profound sadness, a deep longing in Jaya that she couldn't
unlock. Still she tried to bring Jaya back, whispering that she loved her, would
always love her. She felt Jaya push hard against her hand and shudder. And
Anasuya, for the first time since she had known Jaya, witnessed her tears.
Anasuya had wakened Jaya to life and inexplicable grief.

Jaya slept on the hot smooth surface of the boulder, momentarily free from
her memories. Anasuya calculated that their best escape would be to walk
towards the dust cloud trailing a lorry. With the setting sun as her compass,
the shadows as her road map, Anasuya charted the way back to the picnic.

Jaya and Anasuya emerged from the forest, fatigued. Their choirmates were
relieved and full of questions. But neither Jaya nor Anasuya could respond.
Jaya was mute, overcome by a powerful memory. Anasuya, sensing this,
feared that lovely Jaya would be pulled back to her lonely place from which
Anasuya was shut out.

On returning from the picnic, Anasuya found Kanta alone on the veranda.
She rarely sought her mother's opinion but needed it today.

"Mummy, what keeps two people together?"

Kanta thought of Irwin, how he continued to irritate her. Then she looked
at her daughter. A dark shadow that Kanta had never observed before crossed
Anasuya's face. Then she answered.

"Their children."

*

Nitram teased Pilla mercilessly about how he was constantly "necking," flinging an arm around a pal's neck while walking. Soon Nitram was holding Pilla's hand as they walked to the cinemas along Tank Bund Road or while exploring the ruins of Golconda Fort. They were comfortable with each other. But as Nitram's departure day grew closer, a tension developed. Both boys expressed this differently: Nitram would fling Pilla's arm from his shoulder and Pilla would give Nitram the silent treatment, especially when Nitram spoke about all the things he was looking forward to in London. Nitram would tease and poke at Pilla until he responded, and then the cycle would begin again. The taut string that held them together was threatening to break.

On the night before his departure, Nitram walked into Anasuya's room, bent on kissing her goodbye. Instead, he caught Pilla standing in front of the full-length mirror, naked but for a delicate pair of panties. The boys stared at each other. Then came together quickly. It was urgent, exciting, and dangerous. But Nitram pulled away. In London, Nitram knew how people hated queers, and he despised himself for his own desire. The know-it-all realized he didn't know himself at all.

The next day, Nitram was gone. Pilla could not keep his heartbreak to himself and confessed to his sisters that he loved Nitram. That he had stood naked in front of Nitram and that something amazing had happened to his body. He told them how Nitram had fled the bedroom and refused to look at him when he left with his parents.

Nitram's dash away from Hyderabad marked the beginning of Pilla's chase. He aerogrammed love letters overseas. His words of devotion pursued Nitram to London, Manchester, Bombay, and finally caught up with him in Hyderabad in 1975. Then Pilla followed Nitram into the dense Andhra forest, where they hugged an ancient ash tree before embracing each other for the last time.

*

It was the start of monsoon season, 1966, when Nitram left Hyderabad. Pilla dove into his schoolwork, Jaya spent most of her time cooking, and Anasuya lazed around the house until she returned to boarding school in late June. Three months later, the school informed Irwin and Kanta that while excelling in all her subjects, Anasuya had been expelled.

*

The Peter family harboured little lies, unacknowledged, that travelled with them like stowaways. Some were lies of omission, some were lies of convenience, of embarrassment and of shame. Some were not lies at all but mistakes. Anasuya's lie of omission didn't seem to her like a lie at all because no one had asked her questions, and so she didn't tell. The family was not in the habit of telling. There was talking and laughing and arguing and tears, but no telling. The family would sit on the veranda and talk about the neighbours, Irwin would sometimes pontificate about current affairs, and Kanta would often chat about characters in her books. But telling? What happened to me, what happened to you? It was not something they did.

Irwin stood in the hallway and held the telephone receiver to his ear while the headmistress of the Stanley Girls' Boarding School did some telling.

"Although Anasuya is a brilliant student, there is nothing more I can do. We all thought she was just fatigued. She started coming late to classes, then missing them altogether. Finally, the nurse examined her."

Irwin was ashamed that a stranger knew personal details about his daughter, embarrassed that this stranger knew Anasuya's condition before he did. How could this have happened? He had watched over her; he had warned her. Perhaps he had been too liberal, too trusting. While Irwin was shocked to hear this news, Kanta seemed less surprised. She remembered that in the weeks after Martin left, Anasuya lay exhausted on the couch, refusing to dance when Pilla played his Beatles records, gifted from Martin. When Kanta tried rousing her daughter for choir, Anasuya, who never missed a practice, turned back to the soft depression in her pillow. At lunch time, Anasuya pushed away her plate of idli and sambar, and Lakshmi, sour-faced, had to send her ten-year-old son, Ravi, to buy pistachio kulfi. Anasuya need not have confessed. Subconsciously, Kanta knew it. Anasuya was pregnant.

*

Jaya and Anasuya knelt on Anasuya's cot, listening through the window that opened out to the veranda. Usually no one had to eavesdrop, as conversations moved fluidly between rooms and could be heard by all. But this was a rare, late-night, quiet conversation between a father and a mother who had stopped communicating with each other years ago. Jaya was pensive while Anasuya giggled from time to time, covering her mouth to stifle the sound that would give them away.

Kanta listened to Irwin, Dostoevsky's *Crime and Punishment* face down on her lap. Irwin's shirtsleeves were rolled up, his forearms pale compared to his tanned hands, his legs casually crossed, ready for a calm conversation. They were seated on two cane chairs, a teak table between them on which a silver vase was placed.

Kanta was practical. "She could terminate the pregnancy."

"What?"

"An abortion."

Irwin shook his head. "Impossible. She is four months already."

"It is her second term, but not impossible."

"That is out of the question. She would never agree, and she is overcome with joy. Have you seen the light in her eyes?"

"Light in her eyes. Overcome with joy." Kanta breathed. "Give her everything she wants. Make her believe she owns the world. Isn't that what you did? Stupid man."

Irwin raised his hand.

"What are you going to do, slap me?"

And still Anasuya giggled nervously, assuming her mother was telling some sort of joke. The idea of her father slapping her mother was preposterous. Anasuya did not realize her father had risen to his feet, was staring hard at her mother. She didn't know that all these years Irwin had blamed Anasuya's polio on Kanta's neglect.

Everyone could hear Irwin now. The night watchmen, the neighbours, even the dogs on the street. "She must get married."

"To Martin? It's too late for that. He's long gone. Should we send out a search warrant for him in London? And what makes you think he will marry her? He's just a boy."

"Somebody else then? There is the son of the deputy minister of agriculture, recently finished his engineering degree. He is Christian. They are just now looking for a bride."

"You think because you adore your daughter, that the son of a deputy minister no less, will equally love her and marry her? Ill-e-gi-ti-mate child and all!"

Anasuya stopped giggling.

Kanta was both buoyed and saddened by the fact that she was right.

"Even if we hid the pregnancy from a suitor, the complexion of the baby would betray her. The boy, his family, will treat her and even the child cruelly."

Irwin leaned towards Kanta, trying to reason with her. "If she does not marry, she will be ridiculed and shamed. We all will be."

Tears welled in Kanta's eyes, then disappeared with her sudden resolve. "No. She will not get married. My daughter will not be imprisoned by her condition."

A thunderous clatter on the veranda startled Anasuya. She grabbed her cane and hastened outside, Jaya followed close behind. A vase spun on the stone floor. Her mother clutched her book in her raised hand and threw it, hitting Irwin's head. He yelped.

"Idiot woman!" He lunged at Kanta, taking hold of her shoulders and pushing her against the wall.

"Mummy, Daddy, don't fight. Don't fight, please." Anasuya wedged herself in between them, and they pulled away from each other in horror.

Jaya watched from the shadows. A mother, a father, their child.

"It is my fault, all of this." Anasuya was now crying, "I will go to America. They have women's liberation there. There are lots of women who have children without husbands. It is okay. I'm sorry, Mummy."

Anasuya could not remember the last time she clung to her mother, but she held her tight. Kanta dried Anasuya's tears with the edge of her palloo. "Darling, you don't have to go. We can take care of you."

"No. The girl is right." Irwin was firm.

Kanta pulled away from Anasuya to confront her husband. "You think they are more liberated there? We have a female prime minister. You are only thinking of yourself. Your reputation. What Srikaram will think."

Then Kanta caught sight of Jaya, standing there, silently listening. An expression of fear and knowing. She looked like a stranger, now eighteen, legally an adult. How had Jaya suddenly become a woman? Kanta understood in that moment how her neglect failed more than just Anasuya. Jaya was a stranger to her, and she was losing Anasuya. She had not mothered her daughters well.

Kanta acquiesced to the possibility of them going to America, and Irwin found his escape.

In the month that followed, Irwin made his overseas applications. The only reply he received was a letter of invitation to fill a position as adjunct professor of international development at the Coady Institute at St. Francis Xavier University in Antigonish, Nova Scotia, Canada. Irwin composed his acceptance letter and located Antigonish on the map. Kanta was saddened to hear Irwin had actually found a job.

"I cannot go with you. We cannot interrupt Pilla's studies. He has worked so hard to gain acceptance to Osmania University. Do you want to throw that chance away?" What she really meant was *we cannot ruin the lives of all our children*.

So, Irwin valiantly committed to go to Canada alone with Anasuya.

"And who will help her through childbirth and take care of the baby?"

Irwin reflected on this and asked Jaya to come.

But it was Anasuya who answered. "I would never go anywhere without her."

1997 — The Peach House

Anya is puzzled. "What do you mean you are leaving?"

Anya and Jaya are in Jaya's bedroom in the peach house. A suitcase is open on Jaya's bed. She folds her chunnis and places them inside.

"It's time to go home."

"You can't just leave." Anya starts taking the clothes out of the suitcase. "There's so much more to do, to learn."

"Some things are better left unlearned."

"What things?"

"Perhaps you learn something you don't want to know."

"Like what?"

"Well." Jaya sits down. "Malika is dead. Irwin knows this, has known this. All these years."

"I'm sorry, Amma."

"So am I. I wish I had never come here."

"What? How can you say that? What about Ashamma?"

"I don't know. I don't even know if Ashamma is related to us. All that I know is that she was the lover or concubine or whatever of Linga's father."

"Oh. Okay. So what? Ashamma slept with the landlord."

"Never mind. It's complicated, and you don't understand the culture or speak..."

"And maybe you don't know the culture as well as you think. You obviously don't speak Telugu well enough to understand everything."

Jaya doesn't speak Telugu as well as she had in the past. Or maybe she never did. Anya's pointing this out triggers Jaya's abiding sense of worthlessness, a worthlessness that compelled her to grasp at almost anything to secure Anasuya's love.

Jaya hadn't thought of the consequences when, as a teenager, she had supported Anasuya's impulsive idea to conceive a baby. Anasuya wanted to create their own family, a lasting bond between them. All those years Jaya had suppressed her memories and never questioned her and Pilla's history. How they ended up in the Benjamin House. Why Irwin adopted them. Whether Irwin was related to her. Which of course would make her a blood relative of Anasuya. How could Jaya think it was okay to use her own brother to sire Anasuya's child? Now that very child is challenging her, doubting her, seeing her for what she is. Lost.

"I have to leave." Jaya repacks the clothes that Anya has removed.

"Great. Give up. You always give up."

"Meaning?" Jaya shuts the suitcase and thumps it heavily on the floor.

"You are giving up on Ashamma. The way you did with Thatha and Mum."

"Anasuya?"

"And now you are acting just like her. Running out the door when you can't face something."

Jaya considers this.

"I never gave up with Anasuya. How did I give up?"

"You could have stopped her. That's what. You *should* have stopped her. You could have fucking run after her, thrown yourself in front of the cab."

"You're right. I could have. And I would have if I had known the plane was going to explode. Believe me, I ..."

"You just let her go. I was the one who ran after her."

That June day in 1985. Jaya hears the click of the blinds closing, and feels the warmth of the sunlight fade. How many times has she relived that moment, wanting to take it back?

The scene from *Doctor Zhivago* suddenly comes to mind, when Omar Sharif runs up the stairs of his cottage in Siberia and breaks the window just to catch a glimpse of Julie Christie in the sleigh, moving away from him over the snowy fields. Jaya had a perfect view of Anasuya about to depart in the taxi. Anasuya looked up at Jaya, but Jaya turned away. Jaya claimed her small victory of rejecting Anasuya first.

"And then you let *me* go. Not once did you come after me when I was in the States. Did you ever think about coming to find me? I sent all those postcards hoping you would track me down. I was only eighteen, Amma. Mummy had just died."

Perhaps Jaya deserves this. Maybe Anya needs this too. A rite of passage. To blame and break away from Jaya. Such an outburst would be expected from an eighteen-year-old. But this is a thirty-year-old woman who has spent years away from home, has made her own decisions, supported herself. Now Anya is saying she had wanted an intervention.

Jaya has little faith that Anya will understand her inaction. Jaya simply could not have run down the stairs after Anasuya, could not have gotten on a Greyhound bus to search for Anya, could not have crossed the street to visit Irwin.

Anya lays the blame at Jaya's feet. But who does Jaya blame? She is still angry that Irwin showed up unannounced at their apartment in June 1985. But she knows he simply made a mistake. It wasn't Irwin's fault that a bomb was planted on the plane. Just as it wasn't the fault of others who put their loved ones on board. Jaya knew that there had been families like hers, who argued before takeoff, or cheated on their spouse the night before, or denied a farewell kiss to their child, a punishment for a pre-flight temper tantrum. Perhaps these people, like Jaya, were certain that they would have a sweeter reunion, a chance to make up, given distance, given time.

It was not Irwin that nagged at her. But Anasuya. After twelve years, the question still arises. Why did Anasuya go? Why did she listen to Irwin when he told her to get on that plane? Why didn't she fight him? Whatever her discomfort, whatever his argument, Anasuya could have said no. But she became the dutiful daughter she had never been and boarded the plane. Anasuya alone had made that choice. And Anya was right. Jaya didn't stop her. Yes, perhaps in that moment, she had made a feeble attempt. But all those years before, she hadn't tried to stop Anasuya, nor did she stop herself. Something short-circuited in Jaya, once she suspected a truth about who her father was. A truth she pushed down, not wanting to know. A truth, she believed, Anasuya came to know that June morning in 1985. The shame of it chased Anasuya from their apartment and onto the plane. Jaya hoped to escape this shame by seeking a different truth. She travelled halfway across the world to meet and question an old woman who might provide an alternate beginning to Jaya's life. So that Jaya could once more cherish the memory of her and Anasuya's relationship. Jaya realizes she will go back to Canada unchanged. Her life unredeemed. Her shame intact.

11. Separation

On their flight across the Atlantic, Irwin turned his attention away from the icy ocean to the two creatures beside him. His daughters, asleep, oblivious. How had they come to this? How would they survive? And a baby on the way.

Pulling the pamphlet from the pocket of the seat in front of him, Irwin read. "In case of emergency, fix oxygen mask on face before assisting children, the elderly, anyone in need." He reread the words, knowing that he alone was in a position to help, and he would likely be called on to help, again and again.

They arrived in Halifax in January 1967. Irwin, Jaya, and Anasuya stared with dismay onto the slick, black tarmac. It was only 5 p.m., but the sky was already dark. A severe ice storm prevented the university administrator from driving to the airport to meet them. Exhausted yet relieved that they were on solid ground, Irwin purchased the last available bus tickets to Antigonish. The freezing rain was relentless, and the bus had to terminate its journey in Truro, the hub of Nova Scotia. Passengers were given motel vouchers. Irwin, slipping the chit into the sleeve of his wallet, felt like a child with a special prize.

They checked into the Rainbow Motel and ordered a pizza. Irwin was appalled that they had spent so much money for something that tasted like cardboard. Anasuya and Jaya twisted the knob on the television from channel three to five, curiously settling on a program where men in black trousers slid a large stone down a sheet of indoor ice while others swept a path in front of it.

Irwin found a bookmark, laid it horizontally on the open Colchester County phonebook, and pushed it down the S column until he found a name he could recognize. He had been looking for a Singh. He knew many Sikhs had settled in Canada, though they tended to gravitate to the West Coast rather than the East. Unsuccessful, he kept descending until he landed on Sodhi. First name, Samardeep. He dialed Sodhi's number and became acquainted with the only Indian in town, an East Coast Sikh. They arranged to meet for breakfast the next morning, before the afternoon bus departed to Antigonish.

His teenaged daughters fell asleep despite the piercing tone from the television that signalled the end of network programming. Jaya slept with her arm around Anasuya in the double bed as she had done when they were children. Irwin looked out the window at ice pellets that smacked violently on the pavement then bounced off it. Irwin memorized Mr. Sodhi's number, 895-3814, and sent up a prayer of thanksgiving for having found one of his countrymen in this cold and desolate place.

*

Irwin was in shock over the bifurcation of their family, unprepared for the onslaught of the maritime winter, and desperate to establish some kind of security for his daughters. The rupee was weak, the dollar strong, and Irwin had several months before he would start work and collect a paycheque. He invested all his savings to secure a mortgage for the cheapest house in the area.

The old farmhouse stood alone on a hill and overlooked a snow-covered meadow and pewter sea. It had a view across Cape George and the jagged coast. It was situated far enough from the town of Antigonish to leave the little family to itself, but not far enough away to escape curious stares and whispers, particularly about the unwed pregnant teenager.

Irwin tried his best to ignore gossip and realized the West was not as emancipated as he once believed. So he did what many immigrants do. He told their story, embellished the facts, making it palatable to others, in order to get through to the other side of a conversation. This was survival. To answer prying questions about Anasuya's pregnancy, Irwin concocted a believable but tragic story that her husband, the son of British missionaries, was killed in a train collision in Hyderabad. It was the first thing that popped into his mind. He had provided too much information to backtrack. Irwin instructed Anasuya and Jaya to learn the details of the story, to adopt this narrative or maintain silence on the subject. The Nova Scotians were none the wiser. Anya was born from this myth and grew up in a mix of social isolation, familial affection, and genetic ambiguity. When Anya was five and started school, Anasuya took a job at Mount Saint Bernard College, where Jaya had worked upon arrival in Antigonish. Jaya cooked and Anasuya cleaned for the nuns. By that time, Irwin was already a reputable Canadian working as an adjunct professor of international development at the Coady Institute, St. Francis Xavier University.

The vast meadows, open sky, and expansive sea gave the Peter family a feeling of space and a sense of distance from their personal histories. They were disconnected from the chaos and conflict that Irwin associated with his homeland. The necessary tasks involved in settling kept them busy. Even so, Irwin could not help but be curious about the history of this new land, and the political tensions that stirred under the surface. He found Canada had unexpected similarities to India. No matter how far he travelled, he could not escape the colonial presence of Britain, nor the devastating impacts its legacy continued to have on the original inhabitants. Canada's relationship with the Mi'kmaq reminded Irwin of the struggle for land and dignity in Korampally and the failure of the nation state. Irwin had wanted to divorce himself from India, but India would not accept divorce. She re-entered his life by way of Kanta's frequent letters. From them he learned:

1. The Nizam died and thousands of people lined the streets of Hyderabad in mourning.
2. Indira Gandhi had declared a state of emergency after being accused of election fraud.
3. Pilla, his sweet son, had been killed by Indian police in defence of an ash tree.

*

Multinational corporations appropriated land, water, trees, and other natural resources from India, occupying the role that the British had once played. This motivated Nitram, an environmental activist, to join the Chipko movement to protest the clear-cutting of trees by corporations in the East Godavari Forest. The forest where his parents had taught tribal people. Pilla followed Nitram to East Godavari. Together they learned effective acts of resistance from the Indigenous peoples of the area. Tribal women tied red Rakhi threads around the trunks of ash trees, relying on shared spiritual beliefs to provide protection. The tribal workers operating the heavy machinery recognized the power of the sacred thread, stopped their engines, and walked away.

As environmentalists around the world threw their support behind these acts of resistance, the Chipko movement gained international attention. The multinational companies responded by hiring atheists to begin the felling of trees. Pilla and Nitram were among the protestors when the machines started up again and the Indian Army was sent in to manage the protests. The British Embassy swooped in, rescuing Nitram.

As part of the Emergency Act, Indira Gandhi granted the army sweeping powers to plough down the people. The families of the protestors, the local villagers and tribals whose unceded land was now decimated, mourned those who died. Pilla, twenty-three, fell along with many others. Most of the dead were women, Pilla's familiar source of strength and protection.

*

Anya was born the colour of wheat. She grew amidst children of long-rooted Mi'kmaw, African, Celtic, and Anglo-Saxon stock. In Cape George, five-year-old Anya followed her grandfather around the house, mimicking his voice and humming the deep resonance of her Thatha's snore. She explored the land around the farmhouse, crunching out rhythms in knee-deep snow and on straw, brittle with August heat. She sang to herself, gazing across the ocean or all alone in the schoolyard. She tapped her pencils on her desk like a drum when she became bored, and on the window of the school bus following the curves of the northeastern byway.

Anya had a natural ear for music and, in particular, rhythm. Irwin bought her a bodhran that she played constantly, even in the wee hours of the night. She would often wake up, spooked by a bird call or an unfamiliar image in her dreams, and create rhythmic patterns to soothe herself. When Pilla died, eight-year-old Anya watched Jaya stare blankly into the bathroom mirror, and chop off her long hair. Anya wrapped her arms around a weeping Anasuya and tried to tickle her out of her grief. Anya did not understand why her mothers were suddenly sad, and she acted out. She refused to eat at the table, she threw her lunch box across the room, and wet her bed. Anasuya and Jaya had to take notice of their child in a way they hadn't before. It was time to tell Anya the truth.

Anasuya gently explained the love between her and her adopted siblings. How they needed to create something beautiful to bind them together forever. A blood connection. The recipe was simple really. Pilla had the sperm and Anasuya the egg. These were the main ingredients. They just had to find a way to put them together. Dr. Benjamin, Anya's great grandfather, had lots of medical books that came in handy. Pilla privately released his sperm into a cup, and Jaya drew it up in the syringe that they took from Peda Thatha's medical bag. Anasuya carefully put it into her vagina, the tunnel that led to her egg. The sperm swam in Anasuya's body to meet the egg, and Anya started to grow. Because Pilla and Jaya had the same blood, Anya would be a little bit like Jaya, Anasuya, and Pilla. Jaya said that recipes take two or three tries before successful. But making Anya they were first-time lucky.

This was how Anya came to be. Not fathered by the son of British missionaries, or by accident. She was desired and intentional. All this was too magical for Thatha to understand. It was to remain their secret. Anya was fascinated by her own conception and embraced the memory of Pilla, even if she had never known him.

Anasuya could not bring herself to tell Irwin. He was invested in his own story and Anasuya realized there was some part of her that feared some part of him. She and Jaya didn't want Anya to grow up ashamed, and they needed a community of like-minded women to help raise their child. It was 1975, International Women's Year, and Anasuya and Jaya saw that they could be a part of this quest for liberation. They wrapped Anya in her favourite red cape and boarded a train to Toronto in an attempt to live their lives authentically. Irwin, certain that his daughters would not succeed in the city, offered them a home should they wish to return. He expected them back in a month.

In the ten years that followed, Irwin immersed himself in his work, monitoring the political situation in India from afar. With Pilla's death, Irwin became angry, dismayed, and cynical about Indira Gandhi's leadership. And the Republic continued to turn on itself. He reflected on the continued conflict in Kashmir, the rise of the Naxalites in Bengal, and most prominently, the growing demand for a separate Sikh state called Khalistan. But when colleagues sought his views on these matters, Irwin would offer no comment. Instead, he methodically filled his time with academia and maintained relations with his daughters and granddaughter through friendly phone conversations and periodic visits. Then, in 1985, an administrator at the university laid a newspaper on his desk.

"Your daughters have made the front page and people are talking."

1997 — The Bridge

Ashamma does not measure time in the conventional way but tracks her history with the images that foreshadow each disappearance of a loved one: her mother, coughing up blood on a mud floor; her son, one horrid night in the castrator's shed; her grandson, the day the Indian Army occupied this side of the river.

She cannot reveal her age because she does not know it. She counts the harvests, her miscarriages, the peasants that dropped dead from illness or violence. Her suffering stretches beyond what she believes anyone should endure and accept. The upper castes think suffering makes women like her stronger. They say, "Their bodies are made for such work." Ashamma knows suffering is useless. At times, her strength is a badge of honour and at other times, a burden. But what of it? She and others like her have no choice.

Urged by Anya to stay a little longer in Korampally, Jaya leaves Anya to finish reading the notebook and finds Ashamma by the river.

Ashamma leads Jaya along the footpath. "This path has always been here, but in those days, there were trees all around. You could not see my hut. See those rocks? That is the way your mother would cross the river in the early days. When the bridge was built, she simply walked over it and brought you to me."

"What was I like?"

"This high." Ashamma, a small woman herself, gestures to her mid-thigh. "Your Amma was desperate, with you at her side and the baby on her back. By that time, I and anyone who lived near here were in service to the Indian Army. They cleared the trees and set up camp."

Ashamma stoops and breaks a yellow calendula flower from its stem. "See this. We use this for medicine and to honour our gods. I was offering these to the river to remember my son. I heard a baby cry, looked to the trees just up there, and saw Malika's face. Your mother was like a ghost. We both wanted to wail upon seeing each other, but we kept it all in here." Ashamma beats her breast so hard that Jaya instinctively grabs the old woman's forearm to stop her. Jaya's grip startles Ashamma who looks attentively at Jaya. Jaya wonders what Ashamma sees.

"She was alone with you children. She thought I could keep you. But we heard men coming. The army. I told her it was not safe to stay. She, with a rifle on her back." Then Ashamma pauses, purses her lips. "I held the baby boy. Dressed in a yellow frock, like this flower, so bright. Your brother."

"Why didn't you tell me earlier?"

"I am telling you now. Your mother said she would find some villagers to keep you. Someone nearby. I wanted you, all of you, with me. But I couldn't...I...there, I told you."

Jaya tries to soothe Ashamma. "It was dangerous. You couldn't keep us."

"Better to be together in danger than safe and apart. No?"

Jaya has no response to this. Her thoughts fly to Anasuya. Thousands of miles above the earth, suspended in fear. In danger. Alone.

Ashamma looks out to the river. "Tell me again. Are you sure Malika died?"

"My father Irwin told me. Only yesterday at the Krishna Lodge. He said Malika was killed on the night he found me and my brother."

"You are like your Amma, Malika. Teasing, always teasing, bringing good news, bringing bad news."

"Kshaminchaali. Forgive me."

"I was hoping when you came, you would—all of you—come. Even the boy."

"He died not too far from here. In the forests of East Godavari."

Jaya reaches into her purse and takes out a photograph. A close-up of Pilla's face, aged twenty-three. She passes it to Ashamma. Ashamma handles the photograph tenderly, cupping it in her rough palm. She stares at it for a long time.

"I can see Vijay's eyes now. My manamadu, my grandson."

Jaya wonders if it is joy that spreads across Ashamma's face.

Ashamma points towards the bridge. "Malika crossed back to the other side. The sky was still not morning. She clutched you with one hand, and carried the baby on her back. I saw his head bump against the rifle. I wanted to cry out. I could not." Ashamma stretches her neck upwards and grasps her throat, rubbing it roughly. "There was nothing here. All gone." She stares at the photo. "Malika asked me to name Vijay's son."

"Vijay's son. Vijay was Pilla's father?" Jaya speaks out loud to confirm it. This wonderful truth.

"Yes. Malika told me my Vijay had been alive for years but died, before she came to see me. She gave me the gift of my grandchild."

"And me, was Vijay my father?"

"You have a father, isn't it?"

Jaya nods.

Ashamma pats Jaya's arm. "I named the baby Jashuva."

"Jashuva?" Jaya smiles. "It's a lovely name, but I like Pilla better."

"Pilla is a silly name for a boy." Ashamma laughs. She hands the photo back to Jaya.

"Keep this. It is yours."

Ashamma slips the small photo into the heart-side of her blouse then walks, hunchbacked, up the path to her home.

*

Anya was growing more uncomfortable with all that she had learned from the notebook. At first it was curious anthropological observations and charts, which she couldn't get her head around. But then she stumbled on something else. The scribbled fears and feelings of the author, Rayappa. She had broken the code of decency, trespassed on private property, and witnessed intimate confessions. She recognized both her grandfather's handwriting and his voice.

Anya opens the gate of the peach house and finds Ashamma sitting outside her hut, peeling garlic, depositing the husks like insect carcasses into an old straw basket, a basket made by her son. Anya shows Ashamma the notebook. No reaction. Then Anya asks in her patchwork Telugu, "Do you know Rayappa?"

"He is not good." This is the rough translation of Ashamma's reply that Anya understands. Ashamma's expression is easier to decipher. It is disdain.

Anya sits beside Ashamma and lays open the notebook in her lap. With her finger, she underlines the cursive writing that flows across the yellowed page. Anya watches Ashamma examine it and wonders what fascination this scrawl holds for her. Why Ashamma held on to the notebook when she cannot read.

Ashamma turns to Anya speaking words she knows Anya will not understand. "Malika, your grandmother, carried this inside a suitcase across the river." Ashamma wipes her hands on her palloo, reaches under her sari and unties the rope from around her waist. She sets the rope on her lap. She pats the rope and then pats her chest. She pats the notebook and then she pats Anya's chest. She touches Anya's face gently, worried that her fingertips feel dry and coarse on Anya's nose, forehead, and cheeks. "You have your grandfather Vijay's nose and thick eyebrows."

Ashamma cannot suppress her toothless and radiant smile. She repeatedly touches Anya's face as if to affirm she exists. The mere fact of Anya being on the Earth tells Ashamma that her son Vijay persisted in two lives. And one of those lives is with her now.

*

Anya walks the bridge from Ashamma's hut towards the village. She pauses at the halfway point and leans against the protective barrier, gazing out to where the water meets the horizon. Their blues almost match. It is that time in the day, just after sunset, when earth and sky seem to bleed into each other. In the four weeks that she has been in Korampally, she has crossed the bridge by foot, but never in the evening. Anya looks up at the sky for reassurance as she did when she lived in New York City and had to navigate unfamiliar streets. She would think, "I can't be lost since the sky is still above me." From the windows of a stranger's room, having risen from a stranger's bed, Anya would seek reassurance from the sky. It had become her habit over the years to play a set, make a pass at a musician, and find a bed for the night. She had convinced herself this was part of the "scene." In the morning, she would send up a prayer of thanks to the sky for watching over her. The same sky that watched over Jaya in Toronto and Irwin in Antigonish, where she thought he was at the time. It was the same sky that took her mother up and out of their lives, only to release her into the water below.

Anya pulls away from the railing. This fragile notebook that she clutches to her chest has led her into a story that so far has no ending. She feels she will forever be wandering inside the story, like *Alice in Wonderland*, each chapter more bizarre than the last. Under the protection of the sky, in daytime or night, Anya keeps walking towards the village and towards her grandfather, to quell her fear of knowing the end.

*

Not since Anasuya's death has Irwin cried so hard. But the sight of the yellowed pages, his own handwriting, his name, Rayappa, in Telugu script, reminds him of the young man he had left behind and never mourned. Perhaps it is Anya's quiet presence that allows him to express himself, or perhaps there is simply no controlling it. Irwin weeps beside the window of his spartan room, while across from the Krishna Lodge a chainsaw slices into the peepal tree.

Anya knows the notebook is Irwin's. He doesn't have to tell her that he was ashamed of his name, that he witnessed the horrific violence in Korampally, or that he had been in love with Malika, Jaya's mother. He doesn't even have to tell her that quite possibly he is Jaya's biological father. Just as one suddenly makes connections between astrological predictions or recognizes coincidences as fate, there is no investigation required, no proof needed. Anya simply feels it in her gut.

While Irwin prides himself on his reasoning mind, he admits to Anya he has behaved irrationally. He overreacted that June day in 1985. Anasuya, in turn, likely did the same. Irwin remembers the instructions in the airplane emergency pamphlet, but realizes he only followed the first step. He secured the oxygen mask to his face but forgot to protect Jaya, Anasuya, Pilla, and Anya. Irwin never considered the consequences of his actions on his children throughout his life, or when he paid that surprise visit to Anasuya in Toronto. And so, he weeps.

12. Reckoning

At 6 a.m. Anasuya knocked on Anya's bedroom door. "Anya, get up. Thatha is here."

Irwin was sitting on the couch, clutching a rolled-up newspaper. He had brought with him a cardboard box that sat at his feet.

"It's early, but Anya will be excited to see you."

Irwin hoped his granddaughter would not wake up and hear what he had to say. Anasuya went to prepare tea and called out from the kitchen. "As children, we were always up before six, eager to start the day."

It was early, even for her. But not for Jaya. She was already in Kensington Market, shopping for fresh produce and cuts of meat. Anasuya set a stainless-steel cup of chai on the table. She sat across from her father and gestured to the cup. "Please, have some. Strong and sweet, the way you like it."

"Did you make it?"

"Jaya did. She prepares chai every Saturday morning. Her ritual."

Irwin did not look at her but stirred the tea, around and around, clinking the spoon several times on the edge of the cup. A habit of his that irritated Anasuya this morning.

"What's in the box?"

"A present. For Jaya... and you."

"That's nice."

"Mostly for Jaya. An idli steamer. I bought it especially."

Irwin stared at the box. Upon arriving in Toronto the night before, he had tried to get in touch with his daughters. He even waited outside their apartment. Finally, he gave up and caught the streetcar east to Little India on Gerrard Street. Irwin would get something to eat and buy a gift for Jaya. He hoped the gift would soften the blow after he had revealed the truth of her paternity. But he felt uneasy about the gift. Angry about the experience he had to endure when buying it. The store was owned by a

Brahmin-turned-merchant, an oxymoron, he had thought. After what started as a friendly exchange, sharing immigration stories and discovering that they both hailed from Andhra Pradesh, the Brahmin insisted on knowing Irwin's community name.

"Rayappa." Irwin thought he had made a friend.

"Scavengers." The shopkeeper scowled. Irwin hadn't been called this since he was a child. He was appalled that this derision persisted beyond India. What did it matter?

"My family were Madigas. We are Christian now. Casteless."

"Oh well, money is now the name of the game. Yours is as good as anyone else's."

The shopkeeper took Irwin's money.

Looking at the box on the floor beside him, Irwin nudged it with his foot. Something about the gift now seemed tainted. Cursed.

"We're happy you are here, Papa, of course, but we were expecting your visit next week for Anya's graduation. Do you know she has three scholarships to study music? University of Toronto, York University, and Humber. Humber is just a college, but that's her first choice. And we can't argue with her. She has straight A's, could choose any profession. But she wants what she wants. Maybe you can talk some sense into her. She will listen to you. She takes after you. Thank goodness she doesn't take after me. School dropout, can't keep a job."

Anasuya rattled on. Desperate for Irwin to interrupt her and state the reason for his sudden arrival. But he remained silent.

"Jaya would have prepared biriyani. She is at the market. If she knew you were coming, she could have bought the mutton. Maybe tomorrow. How long are you staying?" Anasuya exhausted herself and took a seat opposite Irwin. She observed how he kept unravelling and then tightly rolling up the newspaper in his grip as if preparing to hit something, a fly or a dog. "Papa, what is it?"

Irwin had come early, specifically hoping to speak with Jaya. Jaya was pragmatic like him, would receive his words calmly and do what was necessary. Irwin tucked the rolled-up newspaper under his arm and reached into his lapel pocket. He retrieved two airline tickets and slid them across the table to Anasuya.

"What is this?" She opened and scanned them and then smiled. "Are these for me and Anya? Papa?"

"Yes." Irwin tapped the roll of newspaper on the table. "They cost me a lot of money at short notice. I hope you won't disappoint me."

"To India?"

"For a little while. Go see your mother."

"Is she ill? Did she ask for me?" Anasuya was now completely puzzled. "Papa, answer me. How is Mummy?"

"Yes. She is ill. Nothing serious. It is best you go."

"Papa, you are scaring me. Tell me."

"Just go."

"How can you expect me to go on such short notice?"

"It is an evening flight. With a change in Montreal. You have plenty of time to get ready, pack, travel to the airport and be there three hours before the flight. I have thought of everything."

"It doesn't make sense. What's going on?"

Irwin was on his feet. "Everything is going on, and nothing is okay. You must go back. Now. That is all."

The time for persuasion had passed. He was commanding his daughter with all the authority he could muster.

Lines knitted together on Anasuya's smooth forehead. She was more puzzled than annoyed. "What about Jaya? And Anya has a week of school to finish."

Irwin stared at his daughter, his lips pursed. Was she daft? He began hitting the rolled-up newspaper against his thigh. Anasuya reached over.

"Let me take that." She rescued the newspaper from his grasp and unrolled it to the photograph on the cover. She and Jaya kissing at last year's Pride Parade. They had been caught off guard among the jubilant crowd. Happy to be part of it. *Xtra!,* the Lesbian and Gay biweekly had used their photograph to publicize this year's upcoming celebration.

Anasuya now understood Irwin's upset. "You saw this?"

Irwin sat back down but could not meet her gaze. He tapped his spoon on the side of the teacup again and again.

"But Papa, you knew. Don't tell me you are shocked? We were together years ago, in Hyderabad. It's only here in Canada we can be out, it is more acceptable. Not completely, but..."

She laid the newspaper open on the coffee table, speaking calmly. She had nothing to hide.

Irwin put his head in his hands. How could he have known? They had shared a bedroom, like many sisters do. There was nothing suspect about it.

Many Indian women did this, right into adulthood. If he had been aware, could he have prevented it? Irwin tried to suppress the image of his daughters in bed together, naked. But it kept coming up. It gave him the creeps. Now that it was publicly known, anyone could conjure up this image. Irwin felt vulnerable, convinced that the photo in the newspaper had condemned the whole family, exposing them for what they were. Deviants. Throughout his life, he had battled against the irrational and denigrating belief that his caste made him lesser. That he was not deserving of dignity. Here was proof.

Irwin raised his head. Anasuya had her mother's face. Doe eyes, with a slight downward slant that sometimes made her look sad. A look that could warm any cold-hearted soul. Anyone would call her a beauty, but sitting there in her housecoat, hair uncombed, confirmed lesbian, she appeared ugly to him. Or was it the resemblance to her mother that irked him? Kanta, who had mocked him, belittling both his masculinity and intellect.

"I think it's best that you and Jaya separate. Stop this at once." He was trying to contain his anger, as he would with a disobedient child.

"I understand this may be a shock, but we're adults, Papa."

"Don't call me that." Suddenly the word seemed childish.

"Okay, but honestly, what does it matter?"

"It doesn't matter that *I* know. There is gossip, talk in town."

Anasuya stifled a laugh. "So Antigonish reads *Xtra!* Okay, I understand your embarrassment. Look, we can talk this through, go for family counselling."

"You are sisters!"

"Not really." Anasuya was so confident.

Irwin slammed his hand down on the newspaper, smacking the faces of both his daughters.

"Yes, really. Genetically, biologically."

The room was quiet for a moment. Then came the sound of footsteps from down the hall.

"Thatha, Thatha, Thatha!" Anya, her eyes widening in surprise, was dressed in a sweatshirt and pyjama bottoms. "What are you doing here?"

Relieved by the distraction, Irwin embraced her. He wondered for a moment if he had overreacted. Long ago, he had learned to compartmentalize his concerns. File them in some part of his brain for later. Maybe he could...

Anasuya commanded Anya briskly. "Go, wash up. Brush your teeth and have a shower."

"Sorry, do I have bad breath?" Anya blew onto her palm and sniffed. "No." She moved towards the stainless-steel cup to pick it up. "Can I?"

"It's Thatha's."

Anya ignored her mother and sipped the tea. "We thought you were coming next week for my graduation?"

"Anya, go get ready. Thatha has given us a present. Tickets to India, you need to pack. Get ready quickly."

"What? Today?"

Irwin smiled at Anya. "Everything is taken care of." Irwin was calmed by her presence. His chinnie sitaphal.

"That's crazy. Amazing, but crazy. Is Amma coming?"

Anasuya started moving Anya towards the bathroom.

"We'll talk later. Now go on. We have lots to do."

Anya went into the bathroom, then popped out again to grab a clean towel. Anasuya felt she could have thrown a book at her daughter. She wanted her out of the room. When the bathroom door finally closed and the shower turned on, Anasuya exhaled. She hugged her housecoat tightly around her body.

"Anu." Irwin addressed her quietly now. "In 1947, I worked for some time in the village of Korampally. While I was there, I met a woman. Malika. We had a tryst, I suppose. When she died, she left me her children."

"You never told us."

"How could I have? Your mother wouldn't have accepted it, or them. I couldn't just leave Jaya and the boy."

"Pilla?"

"Of course. You knew they were siblings."

"You have to go." Anasuya shook her head and moved towards the door.

"Take the tickets. You and Jaya must be separated. It's for the best." Irwin was pleading now. Sensing Anasuya's sorrow, he was filled with love and pity. How could he have hated her a moment ago. "Try not to be upset."

"I'm not upset. Go now. Please."

Anasuya's mind reeled with the implications. If Pilla was Irwin's child, Anya was a child of incest. Or something like that. She couldn't work it out.

Irwin looked at the cardboard box. "Don't forget to give Jaya..."

"Get out!"

Irwin was struck by the frightened face of his beloved daughter, the one who woke the morning with her sweet singing, who hobbled into his arms as she bravely relearned to walk, who proudly gave birth to his granddaughter, who cleaned toilets for the nuns, who kissed her sister on the mouth in public. With a heavy heart, he left the apartment and descended the staircase to the street. There, he hailed a cab and exited her life.

*

Returning from the market with two bags of produce, Jaya was feeling content. She was drawing up menus for the week in her mind when she spotted the cab in front of their apartment building. The elderly cab driver was trying, with difficulty, to lift a soft faux-leather suitcase. Jaya set her grocery bags down on the step and offered to help.

"Don't worry," she said to him. "I am very strong." And with that, Jaya squatted and lifted the bulging suitcase and deposited it into the trunk. Then she looked more closely at the luggage.

"Is this from the upstairs apartment?"

"Yes. It was very heavy carrying it down three flights of stairs." The driver slid back into his seat. Jaya picked up her grocery bags and hurried up to the apartment.

"Anasuya. What's going on?"

Anya was stuffing clothes into another suitcase open on the couch.

"Amma! Mum and I are going to India. Thatha dropped off some tickets. He couldn't get one for you, though. Maybe you can meet us there?"

Anya was not making any sense.

"India? What are you talking about? Where's Mum?"

Anya gestured towards Anasuya and Jaya's bedroom.

"She's in her mood again, sulking."

"Anasuya, are you okay? What is going on?" Jaya called down the hall.

Anya ducked back into her room as Anasuya emerged from her and Jaya's room, her tote bag open and slung over her shoulder.

"Jaya, where is Anya's passport?"

"Anu, stop. Tell me what is happening?"

"We need to go home."

"Home? Hyderabad? Did Irwin win the lottery?"

"Can you find me Anya's passport, then I will tell you."

Jaya exhaled and carried the grocery bags to the kitchen. She found and laid the passport on the coffee table.

"There. Now please explain."

"Papa gave us these tickets and..."

"He was here? In Toronto? What is the matter?"

"I don't know, I told you. We just have to go."

"Is it Mummy?"

Anasuya could not bring herself to lie. "Kind of."

Anya came out of her room, with her toiletries case.

"Anya, you tell me what's going on."

"Thatha was here. He dropped off these tickets and left. He didn't even wait to say goodbye. He was a bit weird."

It had finally happened. The penny had dropped. Their relationship was too much for him.

"You're not going anywhere." Jaya picked up the passport.

"Of course she is." Anasuya reached for the passport in Jaya's hand.

"Neither of you are going. This is ridiculous. Anya has her graduation." Jaya raised her voice. A strange, unfamiliar voice. Anasuya tried to grab the passport. Jaya lifted the passport well above Anasuya's head. Anasuya jumped to grab it. She clenched Jaya's arm, who in turn pushed Anasuya away.

"Amma, stop it!" Anya shouted. "What has gotten into you?"

Anasuya stumbled back and fell.

Jaya reached out. "Anu, sorry. I would never..."

Anasuya held out her palm like a stop sign. "Don't touch me."

Anya moved toward her mother, but Anasuya shook her head. "Nobody touch me."

There was a sharpness to Anasuya's voice. Jaya and Anya watched each excruciating move as Anasuya pushed herself into a sitting position. She grasped the table leg with one hand and with the other, the chair. Her breathing was heavy as she bent her left leg and heaved herself up, pulling her weaker right leg under herself to stand.

Jaya reached out her hand. "Anu, I don't know why I..."

"She is coming with me. You have no rights over her."

Anasuya had said it. Words she could use as a weapon but was certain she never would. Words that Jaya feared but hoped she would never hear.

Jaya flung the passport at Anasuya. "You can go to hell."

Anya sobbed, "Mum, I'm not going. I can't. I don't want to go."

Anasuya flipped through Anya's passport. She studied it for a moment. Then she set it on the table.

"Fine. Stay if you want. You don't have a visa anyway."

Irwin hadn't thought of everything, Anasuya realized. She and Jaya had sentimentally kept their Indian passports, but Anya was a Canadian.

Jaya looked from Anya to Anasuya. "Kanta is not sick, is she?"

"No. But I need to see her." Anasuya remembered when Kanta told her that couples stay together for the sake of their children. Anasuya felt sick to her stomach.

"Look." Anya took her mother's hand. "I can finish school, just one more week, then we can meet you in India. Right, Amma? We can both come. Just call us when you arrive, Mum. It will be okay."

The sound of the horn reminded Anasuya that the cab had been waiting. She reached for her cane with one hand and adjusted her totebag with the other. Then she glanced at the newspaper on the coffee table.

"Papa brought that for us. You may want to take a look." Anasuya left the apartment. Anya followed Anasuya to see her off.

Jaya waited for the door to close before she looked at the photograph of her and Anasuya. Jaya saw what Irwin had seen. She moved to the window and watched Anasuya open the cab door, pause, and glance up at the window. Jaya closed the blind and turned away. Then she unpacked the idli steamer.

*

That evening, or early morning, or noon, depending on where you were in the world, telephone numbers were dialed. Receivers were picked up, and voices began to deliver the news that would irreparably alter, if not ruin lives. "There were no survivors." The conversation began with sorry and ended with anguish in English, French, Hindi, Punjabi, Tamil, Telugu, Bengali, Finnish, Russian, Portuguese, and Spanish. Later, the prime minister of Canada would send condolences to the prime minister of India, even though the greater percentage of passengers on board the disappeared flight were Canadians. With these words, he denied that this was Canada's tragedy. The bodies on board were reassigned a different citizenship or left to fall weightless and stateless from the black sky to sea.

Irwin never received the call, because he was not home. He was in Toronto, in a motel room. He ordered takeout, and fell asleep listening to the radio. Awakened by the breaking news, he wanted to hit playback, rewind the announcement, but he could not. Instead, he sat stunned, waiting for each hourly update until the irreversible reality sank in. Air India Flight 182 had disappeared with his daughter and granddaughter aboard.

The next morning, Irwin folded and re-folded the newspaper into a square, framing the name of his daughter. Then he carefully placed the newspaper in his canvas bag. He stared at his uneaten steak, and picked up the knife. It was a stubborn piece of meat. Reaching for his glass left him breathless. Trying to drink, he could not swallow. Alone, in a rundown motel room, Irwin Peter was found unconscious.

*

Irwin was admitted to the Queen Street Mental Health Centre. Recovering from the botched carving of his wrist, he lay in bed and pieced together his actions over the previous forty-eight hours, as if preparing for an interrogation and inevitable indictment. He had acted from a sense of decency, and had made a conscious decision. The result: *he* was alive, and *they* were not.

Irwin could not deny what he had done. He tried to remember the term that defined the act of a parent murdering a child. *Infanticide* came to mind. But then at thirty-five, Anasuya was hardly an infant. Was there a word for the murder of a grandchild?

Perhaps his responses to the psychiatrist's questions would lead to a diagnosis: severe depression, suicide ideation, psychosis. But he was not ill and his mind was not turning soft. Irwin read everything he could find, searching for an explanation for why this had happened. A list formed in his mind.

1. The plane exploded off the Irish coast.
2. A bomb was planted on board by militants.
3. They were seeking revenge for the horrific pogroms targeting Sikhs in India.
4. These pogroms were the acts of vengeance by Hindus after a Sikh bodyguard assassinated Indira Gandhi.
5. This killing was in a response to Indira Gandhi's invasion of the Golden Temple in Amritsar and on and on.

Their anger was understandable, their revenge misplaced, their actions incomprehensible. The politics of dissent and the growth of secessionist movements were the repercussions of a "united" republic. Indians were trying to break free of India. But India wouldn't let them go. This fight was staged thousands of miles away from the mother country, not on land but in the sky. This ridiculous dream of nationhood, forced down the throats of so many, had soured and turned on him and others who had left India,

hunting them down as if *they* were responsible. After all, hadn't these cow-
ardly immigrants run away, refusing to stay and fight for their long-won
democracy? Irwin could accept the blame. But why should Anasuya have
paid the price? His daughter, born three years after India's birthday? And his
daughter's daughter, born twenty years after? All these lives lost for some idea
of homeland, nation, state. His family, and others, pulled apart in another
ridiculous quest.

Nothing could shift Irwin's urge to die. There were endless tests, talks, and
tablets prescribed, but he could not emerge from the despair that enveloped
him. A curious outsider, he witnessed his own body on a metal-framed bed.
He admired the tucked-in linen and queried the four-point restraints on his
arms and legs. He was cold but refused a blanket. He was hungry but would
not eat. He was lonely but insisted on isolation. How could he take comfort
when there was none to be had on the bleak ocean floor?

*

Approximately five hours into the flight and one hour before the detonation,
Anasuya asked the man in the aisle seat beside her to kindly trade places.
Her leg hurt, restricted in the small space between her middle seat and the
one in front. Apologizing, she explained that the trip was unexpected, and
she would have requested a different seat. Anasuya looked earnestly at him.
"We hadn't planned very well. This is only the second time I am travelling
by plane."

The sardarji had the distinguished features of a statesman, the strong bones
of a warrior, the gentle gaze of a grandfather. He was the only turbaned
Sikh on board. How many generations had wrapped and layered this proud
headdress, still banned in various institutions in Canada. In that moment, so
many questions passed between them. Why did we leave our country? Was
it ever ours? What is "country" anyway? A field to seed, a tree to climb, a
river to swim, a wall to scale, a city to conquer, a coastline to trace from a
window in a plane. The sardarji moved aside and helped Anasuya up. Then
he slid his bulk into the middle seat and waited until Anasuya settled before
he asked. "What is the reason for your travel?"

"Well, this trip is sudden. My father insisted I visit my mother. But my
daughter couldn't come." Anasuya shrugged sadly.

"Ah. A mother separated from her child. You are naturally worried."

"But she'll be all right. She is with her other mother, my partner, Jaya."

The sardarji smiled. "Ah. You are Lesbian Gay? My grandson also. You needn't worry then. Your daughter is looked after. You are free to do your duty."

"I suppose so. Thank you. And thank you for the seat."

Anasuya stretched her leg into the aisle. Perhaps she was mistaken in thinking that her relationship with Jaya, given her new knowledge, was somehow wrong. If it was against the law of nature, would there be such love? And Anya? Did Anya's blood flow around itself, two rivers from the same sea? But without that circling blood, there would be no Anya. And Anya was perfect. They would all learn how Anya came to be. It would be difficult and take longer for her family to come to terms with it.

But Anasuya hadn't the luxury of time. She was hurtling towards the future. She would soon be reunited not with her distant mother but with her departed brother. Her daughter's father and her father's son. At least that was the conclusion Anasuya had made. Closing her eyes, she settled in for the inevitable journey ahead.

Part Five
1997

13. The River

At Anya's insistence, Irwin finally agrees to visit Ashamma.

His notebook confirms that Malika's mother's name was Fariza. Many names were written down, fading now on yellowed paper, but he had lifted Malika's family out of obscurity. The notebook holds no trace of Ashamma. This confirms to Irwin that she is not only a fraud but a thief. For how did his notes come into her possession? Had she read them and concocted a narrative to hook Jaya and extort money? This woman is intelligent, it seems, if not cunning. He will meet Ashamma and get to the bottom of this. It will have to be a careful manipulation or Ashamma will sense she is being found out. Irwin will maintain his manners. He will buy her a shawl or a sari, something to win her trust and manage her expectations. Then he will expose her deception to Jaya and Anya, and they can finally go home.

In Raja's Cloth Emporium the merchant sits cross-legged on the store's platform and lays out simple, inexpensive saris in muted colours.

"No husband? Elderly? Then this is what you need."

Irwin chooses a pale-yellow sari with a green border. His gift purchased, he turns and sees a familiar face. The man initiates the introduction.

"Hello. I am Sivraj, from the Reddys' house."

It is Irwin's partner-soldier, with whom he had exchanged bows like the guards at Buckingham Palace, December mornings in 1947. Ah, Sivraj, the loyal groundskeeper of the Reddy compound.

Sivraj, who was aware that Irwin had returned to Kormapally, easily recognized the aged man who once occupied his room. Rayappa, the assistant to the Angrezi anthropologist. They exchange a few memories about the past, but neither is really interested in dwelling on those turbulent times. Sivraj is more interested in the future.

He purchases a sherwani for his grandnephew, a frilly frock for his grand-niece, as well as saris for his niece and sister-in-law. He beams as he describes his brother's grandchildren to Irwin. The brother who had remained in the fields while Sivraj entered the service of the Reddy family over fifty years ago. Sivraj's dedication to the Reddys had not allowed time for a personal life, so his brother's family became his.

"But there must be some occasion?" Irwin queries.

"No occasion."

Sivraj's buoyant spirits betray that he harbours a secret. A belief that Reddy has willed a portion of his wealth to those who have cared for him. The swami, of course, and other devoted servants who have kept the master company in his old age.

Last night Raghunandan Reddy had specifically called Sivraj to his bedside and ordered all others, including his nurse, to leave.

"Sivraj, you will keep me company tonight."

Sivraj remained awake all night at his master's bedside.

At sunrise, Reddy woke up. "Go, turn down the dial."

The doctor had taped the tube to Reddy's nose to deter the patient from removing it.

Sivraj hesitated. "Are you sure, sir? Will it be okay?"

"It is okay. This humming bothers me so. I cannot sleep."

But Sivraj was unsure.

"Please. It will be fine. And there, on the table is a token of appreciation for the small task you performed."

Sivraj picked up the envelope and peered inside.

Reddy grinned. "There will be more of that if you remain obedient. Now turn the dial. All the way down to the red spot. You see?"

Sivraj did what he was told, unwittingly granting his master's last wish. After weeks of incessant humming, the room went silent.

"Ah, quiet. Now I may rest. You may leave."

Sivraj took the envelope and left. Three seconds later, Raghunandan Reddy's heart stopped.

Later, Sivraj would discover what the villagers already had heard. Instead of being able to claim his reward in Reddy's will, Sivraj would be cloaked with suspicion and sent out of the house by Linga Reddy.

*

With a pale-yellow sari wrapped in paper, Irwin walks up the footpath with Anya, towards Ashamma's hut. He doesn't realize that Ashamma, who never officially married, has this morning become a widow of sorts.

A koel picks up a shiny object in its beak near Irwin's feet. Gold-threaded black beads, like the eyes of his feathered companion. A thali, thin and worn, perhaps discarded after a broken wedding vow, washed up by the river after a cremation or snatched and thrown violently away by an angry husband.

The beads, traditionally worn by married women, were used for a different type of nuptial. Decades earlier, Asha's mother tied black beads around her daughter's neck, marrying her to the goddess Pochamma. She believed the goddess would protect her daughter from evil and the cruelty of men. Villagers celebrated Asha's initiation into puberty and her role as a jogini. They brought her new clothes, applauded her when she danced, and flattered her burgeoning ego. That evening, decked in flowers, and filled with an awareness that she was special, Asha returned to her hut to be raped by landlords and Brahmin priests. Over and over and over again. No laws were broken, and nobody's reputation was destroyed. She was called idi, "it," and woke up the next day to more of the same.

Ashamma wore these beads from the age of eleven and discarded them when she was fifty. By that time, her face was lined, her body wrecked, and she was not much use to anyone. And now, in her eighties, her skin is dry as leather, her breasts sag to her belly, and her back is so hunched that she cannot lift her face high enough to look someone directly in the eye. The first man who raped her when she was a child has died peacefully in his bed. Ashamma knows it is a blessing that Raghunandan Reddy looks his ninety-seven years. Ashamma, at least a decade his junior, appears much older than he.

It is no wonder that Irwin doesn't recognize her when Anya ushers him into her hut. Ashamma, who sits cross-legged on the floor with Jaya, gestures for him to sit on the stool.

She asks Jaya, "Is this your father?"

"Yes. This is Irwin."

Ashamma frowns. "Rayappa. You have come back."

Hearing his name spoken with familiarity, Irwin sees layers of time and abuse fall from Ashamma's face. He retrieves her image, recalling the only place he ever saw her. East of the village, near the river, held down on the ground in the castrator's shed. He even remembers the castrator's name, Ramulu. But this woman? She had no name. They had only referred to her as jogini. Whore.

The muscle in Irwin's cheek flexes involuntarily, making his knowing evident to Ashamma. She dismisses him with a snort.

Ashamma is telling Jaya about her son. She recalls how villagers called him names to denigrate him, because he was blind, because he was clubfooted.

"Guddi Kuntodu, Kunti Vadu, was your son?" Irwin unintentionally speaks aloud his thoughts.

The intensity and volume of his voice startles Ashamma.

"Vijay. I named him Vijay. And I also named his son Jashuva."

"He had a son? That means he survived the river." Irwin is astonished.

"Of course. What do you think?"

Now Ashamma speaks as if Irwin is still the young man that visited their village. Reprimanding him for not being clever enough. As if he sat at her table every day, a useless husband or hopeless servant.

"Do you think you were the only one to escape this place?" She says this without looking at him, the way someone tosses a remark over a shoulder.

"People said he walked into the river. Took his own life. I searched for him over and over."

"How could you search? Do you know these forests, these banks, this river?" There is hostility in her voice. And something else. An edge of pride in being rooted to this place, belonging here and knowing much more than this learned man from the West.

Irwin sees Ashamma now and imagines her then. A jogini. The mother of the young man who was cruelly and hideously forced upon her. She had been an outcast, even among outcastes. Realizing what she must have endured, Irwin turns his eyes away, not wanting to shame her.

After the assault in Ramulu's shed, and finally free from the goonda's clutches, Ashamma had summoned the strength to search for Vijay. She appealed to the Madiga elder who soon had a team of fishermen and Communists searching.

"Do you think we are completely friendless? That our community is as uncaring as yours?"

Ashamma puts Irwin outside her circle and into the Reddys'. He senses this exclusion, his self-created exile and now wishes to be recognized as one of her clan, a Dalit.

Ashamma explains how Vijay had been pulled from the river onto a boat and joined the revolution with Malika. Ashamma smiles at Jaya. "Your mother told me that."

Irwin is dumbfounded. "You knew Malika? But what happened to *you*?"

Ashamma has no more to offer. She does not want Irwin to linger on that memory. She knows men are titillated by such details and she has retired from these obligations.

Ashamma traces Anya's face with her fingers, kisses her own palms, and cracks her knuckles on the side of her own head.

"My son, Vijay, was your grandfather."

"Grandfather?" Irwin feels heat rising in his body, but contains himself. "How is Vijay Anya's grandfather?"

"Here, I will show you." From her blouse, Ashamma retrieves the picture of Pilla that Jaya gave her. "See. Jashuva is just like my Vijay. And Anya is just like Jashuva."

How could Irwin not have seen Pilla in Anya? Irwin realizes he is not the only one who has kept secrets. He looks to Jaya.

"Just yesterday I learned that Vijay was Pilla's father. But I have known for thirty years that Pilla was Anya's father by insemination. I am sorry I did not tell you, Naina."

"Not the British boy? And Pilla's father... Malika finally married Vijay, Kunti Vadu, the blind and lame?" Irwin repeats this again, incredulously.

Ashamma snarls at Irwin.

"He was much more than that. Look here."

Ashamma goes to the suitcase.

Irwin follows her. "That suitcase. Where did you get it?"

"Malika brought it across the river, the night she was to be wed to my son."

Irwin kneels and touches the brass buckles. A photograph is on the suitcase propped against the wall. Irwin recognizes Connelly's documentation of the peasants in the field.

Irwin searches the photograph for Malika. Where is she? She is not there. While Connelly was photographing the peasants, Malika and her mother had waited by the cart for the extra food that he had promised them.

Ashamma points out Vijay. "He is the only one on a mule. The others had to stand in the sun."

Jaya gently takes the photograph from Irwin and recognizes Vijay's gentle face, the person she loved and knew as her father.

*

Four-year-old Jaya felt the strength of her father's legs. She held his hand and was his eyes as they walked through the forest. The heat of him, the edge of his dhoti brushing her face, the uneven rhythm of his footsteps. She drew him, sightless, out of the forest to a moonlit path. The same path where her mother, Malika, had once walked with her own mother, Fariza, on a riotous night in 1947. This path led to the well. The well where the Razakars had dumped their rifles, fleeing the Indian Army. The well where the Hindu mobs fished for and found the abandoned rifles, then turned them on their neighbours. The well where the squad was to meet and use whatever rifles remained against the Indian Army. Vijay came with Jaya to the well not for rifles but to await the arrival of Malika and their infant son. This was Communist territory. Their well.

"Is anyone there, chinnie?" Vijay asked Jaya.

Fixed on the moon and the silhouette of trees, Jaya said no. She led her father closer to the well. When she reached its stony wall, she drew her father's hand to rest upon it.

Standing near its periphery, he whispered to her. "Listen to the well. It says summer is coming. The level is low."

Vijay touched her ears.

"What do you see?"

"An ugly old well and a beautiful moon."

"Then you get to fly to the moon."

Lifted up by her father, Jaya rose like a kite into the sky. She looked upon the shadowed square. Then west to the hills with their terraced plots cast silvery blue by the moonlight. Then she looked in the other direction, down the road, at the shape of a large peepal tree. Chinnie Jaya saw what her mother had seen, in her youth. The beauty of the place left Jaya breathless. She knew her father could sense her wonder, as he smiled proudly and brought her close in his embrace.

The shot rang out. Jaya dropped with such speed into darkness. Her world flattened as she landed on the bodies of others. And her father's body fell heavily upon hers.

*

The ancient rite continues even after rivers are polluted and purity exists merely as metaphor. The funeral of Raghunandan Reddy is meant to cast the notorious deshmukh as a saint and a superstar. The village comes to pay respect to the man who survived ninety-seven years, just three years short of the end of the twentieth century. His followers will remember him as a benevolent patriarch who contributed money, men, and arms to Europe's war and who fed the nation by ensuring his forty thousand acres remained fertile and productive. Reddy was a friend to Muslims and other minorities and was

a loyal servant and benefactor of the Nizam, Hyderabad's last reigning monarch. He supported the Razakar Army, who fought the radical Communists.
And when his land was taken from him, he wrested it back, forging a tacit
understanding with, and loyalty to, the newly formed Republic of India. He
died a father of two legitimate sons, a grandfather of four, a great-grandfather
to seven. His progeny are politicians, landowners, agriculturalists, doctors,
lawyers, engineers, administrators, teachers, scientists, businesswomen, art-
ists, musicians, feminists, academics, labourers, peasants, capitalists, Marxists,
and Dalits. He gave to charity and was said to be kind to his servants. He is
predeceased by his devoted wife, Veena. He is survived by his son Surendra
and widowed son Linga, who shot an intruder at the village well on a moonlit
night in 1952. Technically, an act of fratricide.

It is said that Raghunandan Reddy was a good man. Whether this is true
depends on how one defines goodness.

*

Ashamma follows Rayappa as he leaves the hut and wanders off down the
footpath to the river's edge. Irwin inches his way closer to the water, peering
into his future.

Ashamma recalls standing by the riverside years ago, just after her son disappeared following the assault in the castrator's shed. She couldn't remember
whether she was trying to comfort him or convey who she was, when she
sang a familiar lullaby in his ear. For years, Ashamma questioned herself. If
she had concealed her identity, could she have endured the assault and borne
the burden of shame alone, sparing her son his suffering? But she knew Linga
and his men would never have maintained this secret. Ashamma believed that
her revelation pushed Vijay towards the river, towards death. But he simply
went underground.

Ashamma approaches Rayappa who stares into the water.

"I meant to protect my daughter, Anasuya. Instead I drove her away. No
one was there to pull her up."

Ashamma rests her hand on Rayappa's arm as if to say, I know what you
are doing, but don't. Or, you made a mistake, now say sorry. Or perhaps she
means, come now, supper is ready. There are too many people to mourn,
and Ashamma is not ready to have another disappear. Rayappa is now connected to her. Vijay has re-emerged in the form of her granddaughter, Anya.
Anasuya is also a part of Anya. And Anya is theirs. Both hers and Rayappa's.

Whatever Rayappa hears from Ashamma is acknowledged. He reaches into his pocket and passes Ashamma a small basket that fits into the centre of her palm. It has passed from Vijay to Malika, from Malika to Rayappa. From Rayappa to Ashamma, full circle. Something to have. Number eighteen on his list of possessions. He feels lighter as they walk back to the hut.

*

Jaya and Anya can no longer accept anything from Linga Reddy and decide to move back to the Krishna Lodge the next morning. Exhausted, they skip supper and retire to their separate rooms in the peach house. But Jaya cannot sleep. She sits up in bed, realizing it is not the moonlight but lamplight from the outer porch streaming into her window. Someone is there.

She rises quietly and creeps through the kitchen. She picks up a frying pan, praying she won't have to use it. Approaching the porch, she wonders why the groundskeeper hasn't roused her to warn of this intruder. When she peers around the doorway, she sees the reason. Anya sits in a wicker chair, hugging her knees to her chest.

"What are you doing?"

Anya holds out the notebook to Jaya. "Thatha gifted this to me. Read it."

"I can't."

"You mean you won't."

"No. I can't read."

Anya leans forward.

"I relied on Anasuya. For everything. Those postcards you sent me..."

Anya rises and reaches out to Jaya. Jaya drops the frying pan, letting it clatter. There is no food to cook and no mouths to feed. Nothing to do with her hands but pull her daughter close.

*

Irwin wakes at 4 a.m. in the Krishna Lodge, haunted by a dream. Ashamma is leading him down a dark well, half-flying, half-falling towards a face, smiling and mocking him. The face of an evil man.

He reaches for his medication. The bottle is empty. Irwin has doubled his dose over the past four weeks, so naturally the pills have run out. He puts on yesterday's short-sleeved shirt and trousers and goes to the washroom for a glass of water. There he finds the bucket. Perhaps he can soak his feet. Then he realizes there is no water service until five. He carries the bucket down the flight of stairs, out the door, past the butchered peepal tree. Sharp stones on the dirt road slice tiny cuts into the dry soles of his bare feet. In the pre-dawn he stumbles against the flank of a cow. Disoriented, he rights himself and walks with intention in search of the well.

The sun behind him casts its first light over the river and across the valley. Irwin recognizes the hills in the distance where he once saw a crop burning at night. These were the same fiery hills that Malika escaped, that night she turned to him for help and he stupidly mistook her desperation for desire. He recognizes the landlord's mansion up ahead, as he arrives at the village well. He is fortunate a rope hangs from the pulley. Irwin ties the rope to the bucket and lowers it.

Out of sight but not far away, the chakalis are cleaning and dressing Raghunandan Reddy's body. They would never have been allowed to touch his body when alive. The Malas lay it upon a bamboo bier as the professional village mourners begin their lament. Women beat their breasts. The lowliest people and least connected to Reddy raise a chorus of grief.

> *Na nayina…*
> *Ee badhalu anni evvarito cheppudu, o nayino…*
> *Mammalni badhallo petti pothivi, o nayino…*
> *(Oh father/dora/man*
> *Who can we tell our sorrows to, o nayino…*
> *You have left us in much sorrow, nayino…)*

The cremation grounds are on the other side of the village, past the Krishna Lodge, near the river. The procession begins at the Reddy compound, with Linga and the servants carrying the body. The power brokers of the village and wealthy landowners have come to witness the procession. Traders, craftsmen, farmers, peasants, and beggars try to catch a glimpse of Raghunandan Reddy and join the march to the funeral pyre. Most of the participants are indebted in some way to Reddy. Leading the procession are the Madigas, playing dappus, creating the rhythm to deliver Raghunandan Reddy to his next life.

Irwin swings his bucket full of water, lightening his load with each splash. He is intent on bringing the bucket back to the Krishna Lodge, but these people are blocking him. A wedding, he thinks, so many guests. But where is the shehnai, the bridegroom riding on the horse? Irwin soon falls in step, shoulder to shoulder with six men carrying a bier, covered with a cloth, laden with flowers. They head towards a large stone slab. Here, he hopes, there might be a clearing, an opening in the crowd where he can sit and find relief for his blistered and bleeding feet. The men who carry the bier start circling the stone slab on which a wood pile has been built. From the strain of the men's shoulders, Irwin can see that the bier is heavy, sagging in the middle. Then the bier slides out of the men's grip and thuds on the woodpile. A head flops off the side of the bier. A man hastily pushes the head back and hides it under the cloth.

Irwin elbows his way closer. It all comes back. He recognizes this man from his dream. It was not far from here, in the castrator's shed, where a woman lay. And this evil man pushed her own son upon her. Faces change both in life and in memory, but names stay with Irwin. Linga Reddy.

Now that same man, Linga Reddy, clutches a clay pot and circles the wood pile, around and around. The rhythm from the drums grow louder and more frantic. Irwin watches intensely as Linga lifts the pot above his head and smashes it down on the skull he just covered up. Using the bucket as a shield, Irwin breaks out in front of the crowd to see the evil man strike a match setting the wood pile on fire. Irwin swings the bucket and hurls the water towards the flames.

*

The number of people in the procession has grown by the time Jaya and Anya arrive at the Krishna Lodge in search of Irwin. Not finding him in his room, they go back out. The street is full of chanting and the rhythm of the dappu. It gives the impression of a parade. Anya knows nothing of these rituals. Christian funerals, from what she sees in movies, seem in comparison dry and dull. Everyone in black, silent and downcast. Perhaps it is the drumming, the smell of incense burning and the colourful flowers that entice Jaya and Anya to follow along. They are carried by a wave of mourners to the cremation grounds near the river's edge. The crowd is dense and the two women feel the weight of men's bodies pressing against them. Jaya hears a high-pitched yelp and grabs Anya's hand. People rush towards the sound, up ahead near the funeral pyre. Bodies gather in a circle, and fists and canes are seen rising and coming down upon something.

"What's happening?" Jaya asks a man nearby.

"They're beating a dog."

"Come on, let's get out of here." Jaya leads Anya away, moving against the crowd that pushes them back towards the scuffle. The poor dog must be cowering. Why this senseless abuse?

"But we have to find Thatha."

Jaya stops, tightens her grip on Anya, and leads her back towards the fight.

*

After many attempts, Raghunandan Reddy's body will not burn. His soul cannot be released. But no one cares. Instead the crowd turns to focus on a lynching. For what is a dead body compared to a beating fuelled by indignant rage? Rage aimed at one who dares disrupt the sacrosanct ritual owed to the dead. And not just any dead: Raghunandan Reddy.

Linga tries unsuccessfully to set his father aflame. He summons Antharyami, Ragaviah, the Pandits, but it starts to rain. The unseasonal downpour makes them question Raghunandan Reddy's readiness to fulfill dharma. Linga finally gives up and abandons the body. When mourners see that Raghunandan Reddy's body refuses to burn, they think of him as less virtuous. As days pass, vultures circle and the corpse begins to stink. Linga forfeits his rights as eldest son. Later he takes the body to a crematorium in a nearby city where the homeless and other unclaimed bodies are incinerated.

As villagers return to their work, their crops, and their children, a messenger comes to Ashamma's hut, bearing a letter regarding the last will and testament of Raghunandan Reddy. Anya is sitting outside playing a dappu, a drum created and played by Madigas that she took notice of during the funeral procession. She puts her dappu aside and accepts a letter addressed to her. She learns that Linga Reddy has been cut out of the will as his inheritance was contingent on performing the funeral rites as eldest son. Debts have been forgiven, and most of Raghunandan Reddy's land is given in trust to Antharyami. There are four acres by the river, on which the peach house and Ashamma's hut stand. This is willed to Anya Peter, granddaughter of Vijay Pullaya Reddy.

Anya will need Parveen to translate the news, as Ashamma will need Parveen to tell Anya about her great-grandfather, Raghunandan Reddy. And her great-great-grandfather, the British Dora. If indeed it matters.

For now, Anya folds the letter, and she and Ashamma visit the pond where Malika and Vijay first met.

*

The day of Raghunandan Reddy's funeral, Jaya cradles her lover's father, her daughter's grandfather. Her mother's ... what was Irwin to Malika? Regardless, and inescapably, Rayappa Irwin Peter is surely Jaya's father.

Jaya hopes to hide his beaten-up body from Anya, who is sobbing at her side. He has suffered many blows. His nose is broken and bleeding. There are red welts on his forearms. His watch has been snatched off his left wrist, exposing a thin jagged scar from his suicide attempt. Jaya is grateful she cannot see his broken ribs, the punctured lung, or the internal hemorrhaging.

She wants to block out Irwin's suffering. To retreat to her place at the window, behind the blind, where she could watch Irwin from a distance. How she blamed him, using her anger against him, to stoke her own grief. How different had she been from this angry mob? The mob now dispersed, with one command from Linga Reddy.

"*Po!*"

Get away!

The crowd hushed and backed off. Leaving Irwin on the ground and allowing space for Jaya and Anya. Affording them a view of the river.

Irwin's eyelids flutter. "The Vancha."

"Naina?" Father.

Irwin struggles to breathe and grasps his heart as if to pull it from his chest. Jaya puts her hand on his and feels something inside his breast pocket. She retrieves the gold pocket watch. The same one she had held when Irwin first found her. The time arrested at 5:05. Jaya aches to know everything. Even what Irwin doesn't want her to know.

*

In 1952, Malika lay astride the branch of a banyan tree. As her mother did, Jaya recognizes Rayappa and lets him pass.

Epilogue, 2010

Toronto

On June 23, Anya stands in front of the old apartment on Queen Street West, waiting for the streetcar. With her suitcase beside her, she will head to the airport to catch a flight to Hyderabad. She opens a newspaper. An article covers yesterday's twenty-fifth commemoration for the victims of the Air India disaster. The prime minister made a public apology, recognizing the event as the greatest national tragedy targeting Canadian civilians. A public inquiry deemed the Canadian government culpable for bungling the investigation into the bombing. Some reporters assert that the Indian government had knowledge of the plot and did nothing to stop it. In the end, only one person was convicted for his part in the tragedy. Yet Anya knows that so many more, through history, are complicit.

Anya folds the newspaper and glances up at the apartment window where she lived with Jaya and Anasuya many years ago. The apartment was Anya's home for the past thirteen years, time spent learning the mridangam from Canada's Karnatak music master and performing in Toronto and beyond. She fell in love with South Indian music after picking up the dappu in 1997. Now the apartment is empty of all their possessions, the keys dropped in the lockbox.

Over the next month, Anya will decide whether to accept a teaching position at St. Francis Xavier University. She could move back to the farmhouse at Cape George, and continue to learn from the Mi'kmaq on whose land she was born and raised. Or she could settle in Korampally, the land of her ancestors. Perhaps she will grow a family.

Jaya has been living with Parveen in Korampally. They are caring for Ashamma, whose health is failing. Somehow, they figured out that Ashamma is ninety-eight years old, which means she has surpassed Raghunandan Reddy's ninety-seven years. Not that it's a competition, but Anya knows these little wins make Ashamma smile.

The streetcar stops. Anya gets on and rides west, past the Centre for Addiction and Mental Health, the new name for 999. With plenty of time before her flight, Anya will break her journey at the Air India Memorial on the shore of Lake Ontario. She chose to visit today, to avoid the political speeches of yesterday's ceremony.

When she arrives, Anya reflects on the sundial and reads the inscription. She moves to the polished black wall on which the names of the deceased are engraved. She traces her fingers over her mother's name and pauses. Anya gradually accepts what has happened to her family here and in India. She can still hear the koel's call, the calf's moan, and the rumbling wheels. But they no longer scare her, for she can place them. They are part of her.

Anya walks along a footpath to the edge of the lake and picks bluebells, yellow cowslips, and orange flowers for which she has no name. So she gives them names: Vijay Pullaya, Malika Hajam, Pilla Jashuva, Anasuya Peter, Kanta Benjamin, Rayappa Irwin. She performs a ritual learned from her great-grandmother, acknowledging the ever-present sky and the land on which she stands. Then she looks eastward across the lake, as she has done across an ocean and a river. With one bold gesture, Anya casts the wild flowers towards the water. The breeze blows a few petals back, catching in her hair. Some drift to the ground, but many of them fall to the surface and float away. She knows her ritual is imperfect, clumsy even. Not the way Ashamma would have released the flowers. But still, it feels good to have let them all go. Together.

*

Conscious of the time, Anya shakes out her hair and gathers it into a green scrunchy. She hauls her suitcase back to the road and hails a cab to catch her flight.

Acknowledgements

I am grateful to the many people who generously contributed to the creation of this book. They are:

Gita Ramaswamy, whose lived experience, knowledge, critical feedback, and friendship simply made this book possible.

Dionne Brand for her inspiration over the years and mentorship at the Banff Centre.

Seemi Ghazi for reading my words back to me and offering her valuable perspective.

Rachel Kalpana James, for kind and constant support throughout my writing process and connecting me with GLE.

Bethany Gibson for her exacting editorial eye and for keeping me on story and everyone at Goose Lane Editions.

The late V.K. Bawa, Chinnaiah Jangam and the late Narendra Luther for their writings and conversations.

Dona Gazale, Rosemary MacPhee, Paul Pasmore, Alex Richmond, and Shuni Tsou for feedback on early versions of the manuscript.

Shauna Singh Baldwin, Denise Bukowski, Elizabeth Eve, Aida Jordao, and Karen Tisch for providing editing support to various versions.

Poroma Deb, who gifted me *The Remembered Village* and other books.

Chataala Surender who guided me on visits to Telangana villages.

Melina Young and Neesha Meminger for support along the way.

I offer my deepest love and appreciation to my parents and entire family for sharing their stories throughout my childhood and adult life.

And, as always, to my Jugal, Nalin, and Dinesh, thanks for being you and for being there!

I am grateful for the Hyderabad Book Trust and the Deccan Studies Archives.

This book was developed through the support of the Banff Centre for Arts and Creativity, Writer's Studio, 2014, and with funding support from the City of Ottawa.

Author's Note

When I was twelve, my history teacher, Mrs. Zann, asked our class to write about our ancestors. I was living in Nova Scotia with my family, who had emigrated from India. I had only been to India once and knew very little about my extended family, so I asked my father to tell me their story. He started by drawing a map of India circa 1947 and outlined a large area in the heart of the subcontinent that he called the "Princely State of Hyderabad."

Then he went on to tell me the story of "How My Grandfather Won the War!" by describing my Thatha opening the gates of the city of Hyderabad and welcoming the Indian Army to quell a rebellion.

It went something like that, at least in my memory.

My father explained how my ancestors on his side were perceived as "untouchables" and how Dalits, the respectful term for those deemed sub-castes, were oppressed. As an example, he said historically they were forced to walk backwards and sweep their footprints so as not to pollute caste Hindus who might follow in their wake. He said my great grandparents were amongst some of the lower castes and sub-castes who converted to Christianity, with a possible hope to shed the stigma of untouchability. He also said that while caste oppression still continued after conversion, there were some benefits such as education, employment, and dignity.

I was curious and horrified at the very concept of untouchability that deprives a person of their humanness.

For another assignment, I again turned to my father, who read aloud "Elegy Written in a Country Churchyard" by Thomas Gray. He came to the verse "Full many a gem of purest ray serene, The dark unfathom'd caves of ocean bear; Full many a flow'r is born to blush unseen, and waste its sweetness on the desert air." He said many poor people, just like the gems in the ocean caves or the flowers blooming in the desert, have beauty and potential that may never be valued or realized.

Twenty years later I spent half a year in India trying to learn Telugu and studying Karnatak music but mostly collaborating with feminists in the group called Anveshi. Anveshi members recommended the book '*We Were Making History.*' The photo on the cover featured women. They were Communists, held rifles, and were fighting against oppressive landlords and a feudal social system during the rule of Mir Osman Ali Khan. Reading this book, I realized that the rebellion, referenced in my grade seven essay, was actually the Telangana People's Struggle (1946-1951). My immediate thought was that my grandfather was on the wrong side. I later came to know my grandfather moved from Nellore to Hyderabad after the the police action in 1948 and therefore could not have "opened the gates."

I had to learn more about both this history and my family's part in it. I researched the histories of the Telangana People's Rebellion, the Nizam's rule of Hyderabad, and the lived experience of Dalits. I visited villages and attended conferences in India. At one conference, a Dalit woman, in her presentation, spoke about a horrific incident where caste Hindus forced a Dalit man to rape his mother. That stayed with me.

The more I learned, the more disturbed I was to realize how this oppression still persists, even in Canada. My father had experienced caste prejudice after revealing his family name when asked by an ex-pat Indian. Our name is Pilli, meaning *cat* in Telugu, commonly derived from the Mala caste.

While family lore may have inspired this book, it is not our story.

I am trying to make meaning from these complex histories and oppressive social structures. It is an attempt to recognize the inherent value of the lives of those, like many of us, who search for a sense of worth and justice.

*

This book is a work of fiction. I use a mix of historical facts and imagined places and scenes, including some involving public figures. I take liberty with some dates and locations. Characters are created and have no resemblance to real people. All inaccuracies cultural and historical are mine.

I am grateful to storytellers who lived through the Telangana People's Struggle (1946–1951), the police action in Hyderabad in 1948, and were impacted by the Air India bombing in 1985. I relied on articles, books, and videos on all related subjects. While too numerous to name every source, I have listed some below. In particular, I drew inspiration from and relied heavily on the following three sources.

For Malika's story, I looked to the lived experiences of women involved in the Telangana People's Struggle who were interviewed by, and whose stories were compiled by, members of Stree Shakti Sanghatana: Lalita K., Vasantha Kannabiran, Rama Melkote, Uma Maheshwari, Susie Tharu, Veena Shatrugna, *'We Were Making History': Life Stories of Women in the Telangana People's Struggle* (New Delhi: Kali for Women, 1989). The story of the district collector in Aminapally was inspired by the chapter on Mallu Swarajyam, specifically page 228. The story of Sujana and the women in Aminapally was inspired by Vajramma's story on page 56.

For the description of customs in Korampally and the landlord's house, I relied heavily on M.N. Srinivas, *The Remembered Village* (New Delhi: Oxford University Press, 1976). The methodology for castration and inspiration for the scene was based on page 50.

For Kanta's experience of the 1948 police action, I relied on events described by Narendra Luther, *Hyderabad: A Biography* (New Delhi: Oxford University Press, 2006). I quoted the following, attributed to Zafar, "We were independent. We are independent. We will remain independent," from page 282.

*

Other references include:

Bawa, Vasant K. *The Last Nizam: The Life and Times of Mir Osman Ali Khan.* Hyderabad: Centre for Deccan Studies, 2010. First published 1992 by Penguin India.

Bawa, Vasant K. and A. Satyanarayana, eds. *Special Issue on States Reorganization in the Deccan.* Hyderabad: Centre for Deccan Studies, 2011.

Black, Maggie. *Women in Ritual Slavery: Devadasi, Jogini and Mathamma in Karnataka and Andhra Pradesh, Southern India.* Anti-Slavery International, July 2007, antislavery.org.

Desai, V.H. *Vande Mataram to Jana Gana Mana: Saga of Hyderabad Freedom Struggle.* Bombay: Bharatiya Vidya Bhavan, 1990.

Franco, Fernando, Jyotsna Macwan, and Suguna Ramanathan, eds. *The Silken Swing: The Cultural Universe of Dalit Women.* Calcutta: STREE, 2000.

Ilaiah, Kancha. *Why I Am Not a Hindu: A Sudra Critique of Hindutva Philosophy, Culture and Political Economy.* Calcutta: Samya, 1996.

Jangam, Chinnaiah. *Dalits and the Making of Modern India.* New Delhi: Oxford University Press, 2017.

Lal, Pundit Sundar, Qazi Abdul Ghaffar, and Maulana Adbulla Misri. *Detailed Report on the Aftermath of the Police Action (Military Invasion) by the Indian Army of the Hyderabad State in September, 1948*. New Delhi: Government of India, 1948.

Mahendra, K.L. *Events and Movements*. Hyderabad: Prachee Publications, 2005.

Noorani, A.G. *The Destruction of Hyderabad*. London: C. Hurst & Co., 2014.

Pavier, Barry. *The Telangana Movement, 1944-51*. New Delhi: Vikas Publishing House, 1981.

Ramaswamy, Gita. *India Stinking: Manual Scavengers in Andhra Pradesh and Their Work*. Chennai: Navayana Publishing, 2005.

Ramesan, N., ed. *The Freedom Struggle in Hyderabad, Vol. IV (1921-1947)*. Hyderabad: Andhra Pradesh State Committee Appointed for the Compilation of a History of the Freedom Struggle in Andhra Pradesh, 1966.

Ranga Reddy, K.V. *The Struggle and the Betrayal: The Telangana Story*. Hyderabad: Vignyana Sarovara Prachuranalu, 2010.

Rao, B. Narsing, ed., with Ravi Narayan Reddy Felicitation Committee. *Telangana: The Era of Mass Politics: A Felicitation of Ravi Narayan Reddy*. Hyderabad: Dawn Press, 1983.

Sherman, Taylor C. *Muslim Belonging in Secular India: Negotiating Citizenship in Postcolonial Hyderabad*. Cambridge: Cambridge University Press, 2015.

Teltumbde, Anand. *The Persistence of Caste: The Khairlanji Murders and India's Hidden Apartheid*. New Delhi: Navayana Publishing, 2008.

Thirumali, Inukonda. *Against Dora and Nizam, People's Movement in Telangana (1939-1948)*. New Delhi: Kanishka Publishers, 2003.

Velchala, Kondal Rao, J.V. Raghavendra Rao, and B. Narsing Rao. *The Telangana Struggle for Identity*. Hyderabad: Telangana Cultural Forum Publication, 2010.

*

I'd like to acknowledge a number of quotes, films, and song titles that made their way into the world of this story.

In the scene at the Queen Street Mental Health Hospital (999), Anya taps out a rhythm for Irwin. I use "Dum Maro Dam," the song from the film with the same name (1971), lyrics by Anand Bakshi, composed by Rahul Dev Burman. When Rayappa teaches Malika in the Reddy compound, I quote from Thomas Gray, "Elegy Written in a Country Churchyard." After the tonga incident, when Kanta seeks comfort in her room, I quote from Jane Austen, *Persuasion*. In the scene at the Benjamin House at the time of the police action, I quote Saqib Lakhnavi. At the Kalpana Cinema in Mahbub Nagar, the film *Aan* is playing, written by S. Ali Raza, story by R.S. Choudhury, and directed and produced by Mehboob Khan. When Irwin courts Kanta, I quote from Robbie Burns, "My Love is Like a Red, Red Rose," Percy Bysshe Shelley, "To the Moon," and William Shakespeare's Sonnet 18. In the scene describing Tank Bund Road in Hyderabad, I reference the films *Jab Phool Khile* (1965), written by Brij Katyal and directed by Suraj Prakash, and *Tarzan Comes to Delhi* (1965), directed by Kedar Kapoor. In the peach house, in the scene between Jaya and Anya, I reference a scene from the film *Doctor Zhivago*, directed by David Lean, screenplay by Robert Bolt, based on the 1957 novel by Boris Pasternak. During Raghunandan Reddy's funeral procession I quote a Telugu folk song, "Na nayia..."

Glossary

Languages are indicated with the following abbreviations:
Arabic (A), Hindi (H), Sanskrit (S), Telegu (T), Urdu (U)

aaru (T) six
abbu (U) father
Adivasis (H) Indigenous peoples in India
aidu (T) five
alletodu (T) basket weaver
amma (T) mother
ammi (U) mother
Angrezi (U) relating to England, its people, or its language
arrack (A/U) fermented palm wine
arrey (T) hey
arthum aiyindha (T) do you understand
As Salam u Alaikum (A/Persian) may peace be upon you
aunandi (T) yes sir
Ayya (T) sir
azaan (A) Muslim call to prayer
baaggannaaru (T) greeting equivalent to hello/how are you but literally
   meaning "are you good?"
babu (T) a respectful way to address a man, usually educated, dominant
   class/caste
badkhao (U) motherfucker
baghara baingan (U) eggplant dish, a Hyderabadi specialty
bhajan (S) Hindu genre of devotional songs or hymns
bania (H) caste of merchants, traders, moneylenders
bhai (H/U) brother
beedi (H) a thin cigarette made of unprocessed tobacco rolled in a tendu
   leaf and tied with a string

bendakai (T) okra

beti (H/U) daughter

bhaji (H) deep-fried, battered, vegetable fritter, usually onion

bhootam (T) ghost

biriyani (U) a rice dish originating from the Mughals in India, cooked with
  meat or vegetables, nuts, spices, and saffron

bismillah (A) I /we start with Allah

Brahmin (H) dominant caste of priests

chai (H) tea

chakali (T) washerman/washerwoman

channa (H) chickpeas

chapati (H) Indian flatbread made with wheat flour

chappals (H) sandals, usually leather with a small or no heel

chascha (U) uncle, father's brother

chembu (T) small brass cup or vessel

chinni, chinnie (T) small

chunni (H) scarf used to drape over breasts, shoulders, or head

dal (H) a stew made with lentils and spices

dalam (T) armed squad of the Communist Party

Dalit (H) from Sanskrit term dalita (oppressed); adopted by people once
  deemed "untouchable" as a more respectful term of self-identification

dappu (T) a folk drum played at all occasions by Madigas

deepam (T) oil lamp, usually lit in ceremonies or when there was no
  electricity

deshmukh (U) feudal landlord controlling many villages and owning
  thousands of acres

dharma (H) eternal and inherent nature of truth and reality in Hinduism;
  cosmic law that outlines good behaviour and social order

dhobi (H) washerman/washerwoman

dhoti (T) a long piece of unstitched cloth worn by men; can be tied up
  between legs like a loin cloth or left to fall to the ankles

dora (U) wealthy landowner

dorasani (U) wife of the landlord

Dunnevaanniki Bhoomi (T) land to the tiller

ghazals (U) Persian lyric poetry with fixed verses and repeated rhymes,
  often set to music; originating from romantic Arabic poetry, ghazals are
  constructed with couplets set to rhyme

ghunghat (H) a part of the sari, scarf, or covering draped over the head and face

golla (T) subcaste of shepherds

goondas (H) thugs

Gudi Eluguvallu (T) Muslim caste in Telangana

guddi kuntodu (T) blind and crippled

gouds (T) caste of toddy tappers, men who scale palm trees to tap flower sap and make palm wine

Harijan (Gujarati/H) children of god; term created by the Gujarati poet Narsinh Mehta and adopted by Gandhi to refer to subcastes or "untouchables." Now unacceptable to them.

hareem (A/U) living quarters for female members of a household in Muslim families

imam (A/U) spiritual leader who leads Muslims in worship

jaggery (H) coarse, non-processed sugar made from evaporated cane/palm sap

jagirdar (U) owner of jagir, land gifted to be used in service of the ruler

Jai Ram (H) victory to Ram

Jana-gana-mana-adhinayaka, jaya he (H) thou are the ruler of the minds of all people (from the Indian national anthem)

Jatara (T) temple festival in Telangana and Andhra regions

jeetagadus (T) farmhands, literally bonded labourers

jogini (T) traditional sex slave in Telangana region, married to god/goddess or given to the temple as a child, expected to be in sexual service to priests, landlords, and other gentry

kaasavu (Malayalam) gold-threaded handloom technique from Kerala used to make saris

Kapu (T) landowning agricultural caste, traditionally commanders and warriors in ancient kingdoms, living in the Telangana and Andhra districts

karma (H) associated with rebirth based on actions in this life and consequences or rewards in the next

Karnatak (S) South Indian classical music

khadi (H) homespun cotton cloth, the production of which was promoted by Gandhi

Khammam city and district in Telangana

koduku (T) son

kshaminchaali (T) forgive me

kulfi (U) frozen dairy sweet originating in Delhi during the Mughal era

kunti vadu (T) pejorative term for the physically disabled

kurta (H) a long, loose collarless shirt worn by men and women

laddoos (H) spherical sweet made of sugar or jaggery syrup, chickpea powder, spices, and nuts

lassi (H) curd whipped up and sweetened with sugar

lungi (H) a men's sarong tied below the waist

Madigas (T) group of people deemed subcaste ("untouchable") in Telangana and Andhra Pradesh

Mahasabha (H) congress or group to discuss ideas or politics

Mala (T) group of people deemed subcaste ("untouchable") in Telangana and Andhra Pradesh

manamadu (T) grandson

mandir (H) Hindu temple

Mangali (T) caste of barbers

masala (H) combination of spices for Indian cooking

masjid (U) mosque

mithai (H) sweets

mridangam (S/T) a drum from ancient tradition played in Karnatak or South Indian classical music

Mulki (U) colloquial term for natives of Telangana

musaldi (T) pejorative for old woman

naina (T) father

Nakkala (T) scheduled caste, traditionally nomadic fox hunters

namaaz (A) Islamic worship or prayer

namascaram (S) a respectful greeting or parting; "I bow to you"

nashincali (T) to end, put a stop to

nawab (A/U) a governor or nobleman in the Mogul Empire

paisa (H) small monetary unit, equal to one hundredth of a rupee

paigahs (U) noblemen of the Nizam's court, usually of Shia origin

palloo (T) the part of the sari that drapes over the shoulder; can be worn above the head

pedda metaru (T) head farmhand

pilla (T) girl

po (T) get away

Pochamma (T) village goddess worshipped in Telangana; has aspects of goddess Kali; protector but also punishes those who do not worship her as they should

picchivaadu (T) madman (pejorative)

purdah (A/U) a practice of women living in separate quarters away from men, sometimes in seclusion, and wearing garments to cover body and face

puja (H) ceremonial worship or ritual consisting of offerings of flowers, fruits, chanting prayers, incense to image of god/goddess

pujari (T) priest

pyjama (H) loose trousers with a drawstring at waist

Rakhi (H) short for Raksha Bandhan festival, which celebrates a brother's love for his sisters; thread tied on a brother's wrist

rangoli (H) floor decoration or folk art signifying prosperity, made with coloured flour, sand, or soft stone

Reddy (T) landowner caste

rupiya (H) basic monetary unit

sadhu (H) religious ascetic, or holy man, in Hinduism

Samrajyavadam Nashinchaali (T) down with imperialism

Sangham (T) an organization often defined by the type of members — e.g. Mahila Sangham is a women's organization

Sankranti (S) festival to celebrate the transition of the sun from Sagittarius to Capricorn (Makara Rashi)

sardarji (H/Punjabi) Sikh men who wear a turban

satyagraha (H) holding to truth; a form of non-violent or passive resistance

shah (U) king

shehnai (U) a double-reeded instrument with a long horn and flared bell

sherwani (U) a long-sleeved, close-fitting, knee-length coat with a stand-up collar

sitaphal (H/U) custard apple

Subhana Rabbi al A'la (U) glory be to my sustainer most high

swami (H) male Hindu religious teacher

taqiyah (U) a short, rounded cap worn by Muslim men

tennikoit (H) game played by tossing a circular ring on a court over a net

termeh (U) handwoven Persian cloth

thali (T) chain worn by women when married; usually the groom ties three
   knots in the chain

thatha (T) grandfather

thathagaru (T) grandfather, addressed respectfully

thati kallu (T) palm wine

theesko (T) take

tonga (T) light horse-drawn, two-wheeled vehicle

vetti (T) forced or bonded labour, reducing peasants to serfdom

voddu (T) don't want

vodla purugu (T) paddy insect with harsh sting

Wa Alaikumus Salaam (A) may peace be upon you

yaar (U) friend

zindabad (U) cheer for a leader; shah zindabad = long live the king

Sheila James (she/elle) is a writer and multi-disciplinary artist, born in the UK and raised in Nova Scotia, Canada, by parents who hail from Telangana and Andhra Pradesh, India. She is the author of *Outcaste*, her first novel, and the short story collection *In the Wake of Loss*, a finalist for the Ottawa Book Awards.

James's media works have been screened and broadcast internationally to acclaim, including *Unmapping Desire*, a joint winner of the Akua Award for Best Lesbian Short Film at Toronto's Inside Out Festival.

In addition to her film and video work, James has also authored several stage plays including *Canadian Monsoon*, one of the first plays in Toronto to be written and directed by a South Asian woman, and recorded *Radio K.I.D.S.*, a children's album of ten original songs. Over the past twenty years, James has led innovative equity, diversity, and inclusion initiatives through her company DEVI and in institutions including the Canada Council for the Arts. A holder of an MFA and LLM, Sheila James lives in Ottawa and is grateful to the Algonquin Anishnaabeg People whose unceded land she calls home.

Photo: Dinesh Shah